The Dragon Chronicles

WINDRIFT BOOKS

Subscribe to *The Future Chronicles* newsletter for news of upcoming titles in this series, and to be eligible for draws for paperbacks, e-books and more – *http://smarturl.it/chronicles-news*

THE DRAGON CHRONICLES

The Dragon Chronicles

STORY SYNOPSES

Ten Things You Should Know About Dragons (*Elle Casey*)
If you're going to train to be a Dragon Rider, you need to know the basics, and Ishmail Windwalker is the guy to teach them to you. In fact, he's the only one left to teach anything to anyone about Dragons, being the last of a dying breed. Join him as he gives a seminar about Dragons and their partners and keepers, the Dragon Riders.

Of Sand and Starlight (*Daniel Arenson*)
Erry is a dock rat, an orphan, living on the boardwalk of a crumbling town, rummaging through trash for food. She's hurt, haunted, and the sea keeps calling her to sleep forever in its depths. Erry can also turn into a dragon. Her magic is ancient, the magic that lets her people grow scales, breathe fire, and rise as dragons. Yet her power is outlawed. A cruel emperor rules her land, and only his soldiers may use the magic. Erry must choose: her freedom on the boardwalk, hungry and hurt…or servitude with a tyrant, as a dragon.

Tasty Dragon Meat (*K.J. Colt*)
Dragon meat. It's for dinner. In the town of Bolopsy lives a humble butcher, Nogdo, who's quietly making a fortune selling dragon meat. But when the town's children start growing

black dragon scales, Nogdo is horrified. The source of his new fortune is cursed. He wipes dragon meat off the menu and hopes the problem goes away on its own. It doesn't. Now his youngest son is growing scales. Poor Nogdo seeks guidance from the Dark Magician. But the quest involves retrieving two dragon eggs...from a very angry dragon mother, and father, and a horde of barbarians.

Transparency (*Alex Albrinck*)

Damir, a fire dragon, must protect the underworld from invasion by the ice dragons. He's worked to dismantle a growing complacency among his kind, and counter growing movements claiming that the ice dragon threat and the surface are both outdated myths. Damir's dream: to lead his people to the surface and reclaim the land that's rightfully theirs. But when a personal scandal erupts, Damir must confront the unthinkable: that the greatest threat to his invasion plans comes not from the mortal enemies flying above, but from those he trusts above all others.

Sacrifice (*David Adams*)

Before the Godsdeath we had power. Dragons commanded the arcane and the divine equally. We could have raised our still-born eggs to life. Such things were not unusual for our kind, especially not those who had magic or motivation. I had both.

It's Time to Change (*Terah Edun*)

Since he was little, Vedaris knew that to be a dragon he needed to be able to shape shift. But what happens when you're born a freak? Without the ability to turn and the natural magic of his dragon race, Vedaris is more than just a desperate outcast…he's in mortal danger.

Dragon Play (*Ted Cross*)
All their lives the group of young Vikings had heard of their clan's past glories, but all they have known is the terror of being relegated to living within the shadow of a dragon's mountain. When the chieftain's daughter finds an ancient scroll showing a hidden back entrance to the dragon's lair, she and her three friends decide to sneak in and retrieve the lost talisman that held the luck of their clan.

A Diversion in Time (*Nina Croft*)
At last there is peace in the Universe. But some people just aren't interested in peace, so once the dust has settled, the crew of the Blood Hunter set off in search of a little excitement. They are heading back to Earth and going back in time. Along for the ride are a couple of stowaways: Angel, a young werewolf in search of adventure, and Kronus, an ancient dragon, seeking to regain the power his people once wielded. But when things don't go entirely as planned, can the two overcome their differences and help each other find what they are looking for?

The Book of Safkhet (*Kim Wells*)
The nature of history, of the origins of civilization, and our own human story, may be changed forever by the discovery of an ancient scroll that tells the story of a doomsday device that threatens civilization as we know it. The Dragons, empathic interstellar navigators of uncertain origin, may be able to save some. But where will the survivors go?

Grey (*Chris Pourteau*)

When Amanda stumbles into a cave, she discovers it's the lair of an old dragon, the last of his kind. Not yet old enough to know she should fear the creature, Amanda is quickly won over by his kindness toward her. Over time, the human and the dragon—whose respective races are age-old enemies, prey and predator—become fast friends. When an army of savages known as The Bane threatens her village, Amanda's people decide to flee. She seeks help from her old friend, but the dragon refuses her. When The Bane attack, what will become of Amanda and the friendship she feels has been betrayed by her ancient, erstwhile friend?

The Storymaster (*Vincent Trigili*)

The era of dragons has passed but is not forgotten. There will be at least this one last ride, one last battle, before the masters of the domain of air fade into history and become legend.

Judgment (*Monica Enderle Pierce*)

Consequences are dire when vigilantes falsely accuse Peregrine Long of murder and horse theft. But guns and hanging aren't the scariest things a cowboy can face in the town of Bonesteel. A dragon's opinion and appetite are even harder to reckon with, especially for men who have trouble telling the truth.

CONTENTS

FOREWORD
by Samuel Peralta

*"I do not care what comes after; I have seen
the dragons on the wind of morning."*
– Ursula K. Le Guin

THE STONE MY FATHER put in my hand was small and round, like a pebble, perhaps a centimeter in diameter. I was nine or ten, and my father was an archeologist with the National Museum.

He'd come back from one of his many expeditions through the mountains and jungles of the Philippine islands, and while my mother boiled water for some coffee, he'd lay out on the kitchen table some of the finds from his recent journey.

They ranged from bird skulls to blow-guns, flint stone tools to flutes – discoveries, mementos, personal gifts from tribesmen so sequestered in their mountainous habitats that they didn't have a word for *ocean*.

My father would spin stories about every object – how he'd found the fragile skull outside his tent flap one morning, how the tribesmen would hunt with blow-gun darts tipped with poison from the same plant used in the arrows that felled Ferdinand Magellan in the Battle of Mactan, how he'd made the flake tool himself by hammering a rock against a carefully chosen slab of cryptocrystalline quartz.

And this stone –

Tektite, my father said, a new word for me. The stone was dark, a deep and glassy black that was unlike anything I had ever seen, textured with what looked like trapped air that had somehow bubbled to the surface of the mineral, then frozen.

It had been formed tens of millions ago – he said, as my mother brought the coffee – thrown up from the impact of a meteorite as it crashed into the surface of the earth, droplets of the earth melted like glass from the intense heat and flung from the impact crater. I couldn't imagine the heat, the kind of heat that could melt stone. What was it like?

Like the center of a volcano. My father leaned forward, blowing the steam from his cup. *Like the fire of dragons.*

That last image stuck with me as I went to bed that night. My two younger brothers had gone to sleep before my father had come home; under the mosquito net, I was still awake. I could feel the tektite pulse with warmth in my clenched hand, a stone that had been touched by dragon-fire.

When I did close my eyes, in my dreams I flew with dragons, spiralling up from the jungles of Palawan. The wind that blew through my hair was infused with music, with the notes of the flute that my father played for my mother in the kitchen outside our room. Meteors streaked across the sky, against the smoke of volcanos. The night was obsidian, ranged with stars;

and as I rode, the great beast paused its wings, breathed in, and roared a mighty breath of white-hot dragon-fire.

From then on dragons surrounded me, the dragons of Ursula K. Le Guin and Anne McCaffrey, of J.R.R. Tolkien and J.K. Rowling and George R.R. Martin, in tapestries and on canvas, on paper and in film, stories filled with improbable magic.

Indeed, we live in a time of magic – a time where electronic ink forms words across handheld screens that respond to touch, a time when moving pictures stream wirelessly to phones. We live in a time when holographic headsets and force-sensors allow you to experience dragon-flight. But the essence of that magic remains the same as that which made an ordinary black stone breathe fire – the magic of storytelling.

As I write this, I have on my bedside table that stone my father put in my hand, that night decades ago. It has travelled with me from the island of Luzon to the vineyards of California, through the summers of South Wales to the winters of Ontario. My hair is streaked with grey now, and when I look into the mirror, those are my father's eyes.

I take that stone in hand, and I swear I still feel the heat of that dragon-fire within. It speaks to me still of that wonder, that magic, this gift that my father gave to me.

www.amazon.com/author/samuelperalta

Ten Things You Should Know About Dragons
by Elle Casey

THE VERY FIRST THING you should know about Dragons is they are my life. Now, that might not seem like such a momentous thing, because you're only just now making my acquaintance, but it's a very important piece of information, trust me. Right now I'm the only one left in our world who knows anything worth knowing about these mystical and misunderstood beasts. We are a dying breed.

Not the Dragons, of course; they're fine—plentiful in number and species, size, and color. It's the Riders who are almost extinct. We do tend to meet the most untimely ends. With this training program, however, I hope to change that. We can't have a world full of Dragons without Riders. The entire balance of the universe would shift, and then I wouldn't want to be around to find out what would happen next. It wouldn't be good, that's for certain.

And so, since I am so attached to my continued existence, here we are—at the first annual Dragon Rider Training Seminar, hosted by yours truly. Please save all questions for the end, and feel free to take notes. If you find yourself unprepared for note-taking, not to worry. I call your attention to the fact that my good friend and second cousin, Dalys, whom I had to pay to be here because he's deathly afraid of Dragons, is sitting over here to my right transcribing my every word so that this training manual can be copied and made available to you for a small but reasonable sum. Dalys will keep the original in the village down in that valley just over there to your left, in his blue-shuttered cottage, under his bed where he hides anytime he hears Othello, my Dragon-partner calling out.

Ouch! Okay, stop with the rocks, already, Dalys. And don't put that part in the manual.

A-hem. So. As I was saying. My name is Ishmail Windwalker, but my friends call me Ish. Unfortunately, this nickname makes it easier for my detractors to seem clever when they mock me. They say I'm normal-Ish. Funny-Ish. Nice-Ish. It doesn't matter, though. I let them say what they will. I know it's just jealousy moving their tongues. Not everyone can be a Dragon Rider, least of all those prone to feelings of inadequacy and less-ness. Dragons can spot a pretender from ten leagues away, and they like to set them on fire.

I see some of you eyeing me skeptically. Believe me, I understand. I've seen the same expressions of doubt on people's faces all my life. I'm nineteen years old, pretty young to be doing what I do, of course, but old compared to many in my village. As you know, war has taken its toll, like a scythe cutting down the healthy wheat, the able-bodied and strong, leaving behind the softer materials: the women, the frail, and the very young. Not that you're softer materials, of course. You must be able-bodied and strong to be here in the first place. But you're probably much like I am; I've managed to survive this long without dying in a battle because I'm strong-Ish, able to withstand the siren song that is the promise of wealth and land that the overlords are always slinging around. 'Come join us and earn your place at the foot of the mountain!' they cry.

Bah, I say to that. I live *in* the mountain, and I find that it suits me much better than merely toiling at the foot of it. You know what the foot of a mountain is to a dragon? Its toilet. Everything runs downhill in our world, and no amount of wartime pseudo-magic is going to change that.

I took my first ride on a dragon when I was but five years old. Yes, I know that sounds unbelievable, but it's true. It was more an accident than a purposeful venture, but it did happen and I have witnesses. My poor mother, may her earthly soul rest in peace while her eternal soul continues to soar the heavenly skies, took her eyes from me for just a moment — this is her story, somewhat hotly disputed by my father's mother — and I was gone, one minute at her heels asking her 'Why? Why? Why?' and the next with my belt hooked onto the claw of a mighty flying beast. I soared over the village, laughing the entire way. No one knew then why I wasn't killed and eaten by the Great Mortan that day, but I do. And that leads me to my second point about dragons that you must know before we take another step in this training program.

* * *

Dragons are very tricky beasts. I mean that in the practical sense and the enchanted sense. Their existence is an integral part of the magical fabric that makes up our universe and all the worlds within it. They also get bored easily. Add these things together and you come up with the Dragon: an oversized, gargoyle-like, fire-breathing creature with the wingspan of a trading ship and the mischievous nature of a three-year-old. You don't want to be on the wrong side of a Dragon's mood ever, unless of course you have the right armor on hand. I will discuss the official uniform of the Dragon Rider in the latter part of this seminar.

My Dragon Partner is Othello. I chose neither him nor his name. He chose his Rider and his moniker for himself, as is their nature. Every Rider will need to determine his Dragon's chosen name in the way that works for them. Again, I remind you that the Dragon is tricky.

In my case, I was forced to tell stories for weeks on end, about wanderers, warriors, sorcerers, and village folk until Othello heard the word that pleased him most. He let me know what that word was by setting my eyebrows on fire. I'm sure you're familiar with the Tale of Othello and Spartacus. As soon as I got to the part where Othello leaped from the top of the tower to prove his love for the fair maiden Lilyput, out came the fire and off went my facial hair. He has been known as Othello ever since. Dragons choose a name for life, just as they choose their Rider.

For those of you who thought you would train with me

and then walk out into a field of Dragons and choose one for yourself, let me disabuse you of that notion now. It is a fact of Dragon Rider life that we do not choose our partner; our partner chooses us. One might never get chosen, and that is okay. If you are not selected as a Rider-partner, all is not lost; you can of course move back to the village or join the merry bands of warriors wreaking havoc all over the countryside. Your life can still have meaning and consequence, even though you will never fly through clouds and slide down rainbows.

As I said, I have lost some facial hair as a consequence of my occupation. The good news is, it usually grows back. The bad news is, well, most people do not look good without eyebrows or with portions of their scalp singed. If you choose to be a Dragon Rider, you must know to the depths of your heart one truth about these beasts, and that leads me to my third point.

* * *

Dragons are the most dangerous creatures you will ever come into contact with in your entire life. Do not kid yourself that they aren't, and never become complacent. Compared to a Dragon, lions are day-old kittens, poisonous serpents are the crenn under a Dragon's talon, and angry mothers-in-marriage are innocent babes squalling in their box-beds. You absolutely must respect the Dragon and his capabilities, proclivities, and natural conditions if you have any hope of surviving even a single day as a Dragon Rider.

Dragons breathe fire. Yes, it's true; it's not just a scary story your mother told you to get to you come home when the sun went low in the sky. They like to snack on the sulfuric rock that lines the mouths of the active volcanoes in our world, and it gives them gas. Their intestinal fortitude is without equal in the animal kingdom, but it does have its weaknesses and drawbacks.

Dragons have two and sometimes three rows of razor-sharp teeth that need to be brushed weekly. A leafy tree branch is a good tool to keep on hand for this chore. If you can find spruce, even better as it gives them slightly less offensive breath odor for a few minutes after. Most Dragons can be trained to keep their mouths open and their sulfurous belches on hold as you climb around in there and do your business as a Dragon Keeper, but as I've already mentioned, they are tricky beasts. It behooves you to keep safety measures in place in the event you are inside the Dragon's mouth when he decides he's fin-ished with the brushing of the teeth. My preferred method is a quick poke on the tongue with my hand-spear. Dragon-Riders should holster a hand-spear at all times. I recommend sleeping and bathing with it as well.

Dragons have talons capable of spearing anything from a baby to a wooled mammoth. They can lift any living creature and most conveyances high into the air and release them at will. They may look bulky and clumsy, yet they are anything but. Othello can curl his talon around a small fruit and bring it to his mouth without a thought. He can catch the edge of my clothing and halt my movement with nary a scratch to my skin ... or he can decide to take a little skin to prove a point. This leads me to the fourth item on my training list, one that most people have difficulty believing.

* * *

Dragons love practical jokes. They have a wicked sense of humor. And when I say *wicked* I mean it both literally and figuratively. Nothing makes a Dragon happier than to be laughing at a good prank; and if he's laughing, he's spurting either fire or copious amounts of smoke. You must be prepared for both the tricks he plays and the aftereffects of his good humor.

Dragons have been known to sneak up on their Riders from behind and blast them with a sulfurous odor so strong as to cause unconsciousness. Of course in this case, the Rider cannot escape the aftereffects of his partner's humor and often ends up not just with a headache but also a singed rear end.

You might think this would earn a Rider a day off to mend his affairs, but you would be wrong about that; a Rider never gets vacation — not without his partner in attendance, that is. And a vacation with a Dragon isn't what you'd expect. It's not soaring above the clouds of Antiguan and diving into the depths of its turquoise sea from a Dragon's back. It's keeping him out of trouble and out of sight. Dragons of our land tend to scare people when viewed in close proximity. Believe it or not, the majority of the world believes Dragons to be extinct, so when they show their faces, their claws, their brilliant opalescent-fire scales, people most often fly off in a panic.

Othello is especially fond of practical jokes. Just last week he had a merry old time at my expense. I'm not the kiss-and-tell type, so I'll just say I was with a person of the female persuasion, trying to enjoy a moment of solitude and privacy as Othello napped. I could have sworn I heard his even breathing and occasional snores, a sure sign he's indisposed; I'm still not sure what went wrong there — it's possible he was working in consort with his brother. Just as an aside, Dragons have been known to collude when it strikes them as advantageous. In any case, I was enjoying a few moments with the softer and gentler of our kind when out of nowhere the bloody carcass of a chicken dropped from the sky and landed on my head. My lady-love took one look at my new head-wear, screamed in fright, and ran from the mountain, never to be seen again.

You might believe as a Rider you'll have many occasions to enjoy the fame that comes with the badge and the attentions it brings, it would be unfair and unwise of me to allow you to continue under that illusion; this life is one of solitude. It is you and your partner-Dragon mostly alone, nearly all the time. And if it isn't ... if you do find yourself without your Dragon, I suggest you look *up*. He is most likely flying above you very silently, waiting for the best moment to scare you into losing your bladder.

Speaking of losing control of one's bodily functions, that reminds me of a very unpleasant part of this job. I'm sure that you're already aware of a Dragon's odors since we are close enough to Othello's lair and downwind, but until you actually live with one, and have to clean up after one, you can never truly appreciate the fact that Dragons have a very, shall we say, *distinct* odor.

* * *

Dragons stink more than the worst thing you could imagine.

Five-day-old socks worn in the boots of a warrior? I consider them equal to roses now.

An outhouse left full too long in the middle of summer? Candy pops flavored of fruits and berries. The dead body of an ox left in a molten puddle of pig slime? I'll take a second portion, please.

No, none of these odors bother me anymore, because I have lived with Othello, the smelliest beast that ever flew the skies, for going on ten years now. He farts, he burps, his digestion disagrees with him on a five-times-daily basis, and he's not potty trained. Yes, you heard that right. His cave is a nightmare, and I am the only man with a shovel who will go near him.

You can ask your Dragon to be more solicitous of your human presence. No one will stop you from trying. Some of them might even agree to be tidier, once in a while. But find me a single Dragon who always does what you ask him to do for your own good health and I'll sleep on a pile of Othello's dung for a month.

Dragons are not nice people, which makes perfect sense, because they are not human. Do not fall into the trap of anthropomorphism. It's tempting, especially when your Dragon's tail wraps around your leg and keeps you warm in winter and when he reads your mind and does the one thing you need done in order to be happy again. But it's a dangerous trap. Don't do it.

You're not a Dragon, you're a person. Your Dragon's not a person, he's a Dragon. A person will shower and shave the beard from his face and find nice things to scent his body and clothing with. A Dragon will grow talons that fill with his own rotten dung and he will eat live animals and sleep on their rotting remains and he will bathe in the blood of his enemies.

If it makes you feel any better, Othello thinks I smell horrible too. His kind believes that to be truly one with the Universe, you must *be* the odor of its most basic parts: earth, wind, fire, and water. I've suggested that he assimilate the water scent a bit more, but he never takes me seriously. Dragons think we joke all the time, so it's difficult to convince them we're ever serious.

Dragons *will* bathe, however, so if you're lucky enough to find a Dragon with an affinity for that element, bully for you. It's a true rarity. Of course, you'll find yourself sopping wet more often than dry, because the water is an excellent way for Dragons to cool down, but at least you won't smell of rotten polecat.

Speaking of Dragons cooling off, I cannot neglect my next point, that being the temperature ranges you will find within the species.

* * *

Most Dragons tend to run on the hotter side. I'm sure that's no mystery to you. Othello's miles away and yet here at the base of his cave, you find it quite warm, don't you? I see a few of you looking skyward. Not to worry. He's not due back for at least another four hours. He's left to search for his mate, a She-Dragon he has not yet met. More on that later. In any case, you're safe here now at this training program, I promise.

As I was saying, Dragons can run hot and then not so hot. They have a natural internal temperature that will be somewhat steady when they are underground, resting inside their chosen dwelling, but when they emerge, anything can happen.

I haven't yet figured it out, to be honest. In the winter, when you'd expect Othello to be cold to the touch, you'll often find snow melting several arms-length away from him. Other times, the condensation will cling to his scales as a frost. I've observed him eating and determined it's not his diet causing the fluctuations. It's not, as I've mentioned, the external temperatures either. Perhaps it's the magic that surrounds him and all Dragons, something I'm sure I will never understand.

More study in this area is needed obviously, however, for our purposes, it's important to know, in simple terms, that Dragons can be hot—hot enough to melt things you don't want melted. For that reason, you should not keep things with a propensity to liquefy anywhere near the Dragon's dwelling. That includes candles, of course, but also any non-natural fibers you may have acquired from someone who practices the dark arts or things held together with tree sap or hair of any kind. Your uniform and the relationship you have with your Dragon will keep most of your own hair safe, but anything made with animal hair or fibers is not destined to last long in the presence of a Dragon.

This means you must use torches to see in the dark and when inside your Dragon's dwelling, with your rags dipped in pitch or — in a pinch — the mucus from inside a Dragon's nostrils. Disgusting, yes, I agree, even though I'll admit to having used it many times over the past ten years. It's quite handy, clean-burning, and not as smelly as you'd imagine, although it does tend to smoke quite a bit.

Some of you might be tempted to use a crystal lamp for

seeing at night and in the darkened halls and corridors of whatever mountain you're living inside, especially one of those new-fangled hand-held versions, but I must warn you that it's probably not a good idea. Crystals look like jewels and jewels are shiny, and these kinds of things are one of the many that you must sacrifice when you become a Rider. All of your worldly possessions will be winnowed down to the clothing on your back, your heat-resistant boots, your unadorned weapons, and a blanket to keep you warm when not at home. This is not because you are a monk or a priest and must give everything to the needy. Not at all. It's because of the Dragon. They might stink and eschew regular bathing, but they do love their jewelry. And Dragons are very greedy creatures.

* * *

Dragons are greedy. There's no point in trying to beat around the bush; we'll just tell it like it is.

My mother gave me an emerald necklace that was to be my future wife's marriage bounty. I haven't seen it since the day I met Othello. He has it hidden somewhere in his den, but I'm not going to go look for it. I like all my body parts attached in their proper spots.

Have you heard that crows seek out sparkling things and carry them to their nests? Dragons are like crows only much bigger, much hotter, and much more determined. Shine, sparkle, brilliance — they crave all these things, be they found in jewels, coins, or even crystals sewn onto a wedding dress. We have one of those, by the way. An actual wedding dress. Othello wears it over his right eye when he's in a certain mood. I believe he fancies himself quite dapper with it hanging there. It's brown with age and misuse, but the crystals still catch the light. When they become too dirty, Othello mopes until I cannot stand it any longer and offer to clean them off for him. That always earns me a decent meal and long lie-in the next day. Othello may be a beast, but he can be grateful when the spirit moves.

But I must warn you: never, *ever* touch a Dragon's personal treasure without his consent. His eyesight is without equal in the animal or human world. He knows exactly what he has and where he has put it. He knows the size of every ruby and the cut of every diamond, even when they are only big enough to fit in the crack of my fingernail. And joking around with his possessions, moving things here and there just to see if he'll notice, is not a practical joke I recommend playing on your partner. You'll notice the scar here on my left arm? I speak from experience.

Dragons also don't like sharing food. I'm not sure how they are about sharing with their mates, as Othello hasn't yet found his one true love, but I know for a fact that Othello hunts for himself and he hunts for me, but he does not hunt for *us*.

Usually, it's not a problem; I'm handy with a bow and arrow and the food around here is plentiful. But we have traveled afar where a bow does me no good and the hares are less abundant, and in those cases, I've had to wait for Othello to find me something suitable before I could eat.

I suppose food-greed is a good personality trait for a Dragon to have, considering his favorite meal is a musk ox. Have you ever tried a meal of musk ox? Suffice to say, it's not my favorite. If Othello got it into his thick head that we were to start sharing, I'd have to accustom my stomach to such things, and for that reason I'm grateful he's not a good sharer.

Not that this has anything to do with his greed, but I have a theory about Dragons. I believe that a property found in the musk ox's meat is the reason Dragons can fly so fast, but I've no scientific evidence to back me up on that. All I know is that after he's eaten a particularly stout meal of this smelly beast, we fly like the wind, which leads me to a point I know you've all been waiting to hear about: a Dragon's speed.

* * *

Believe me or not, I don't care, but I'm going to tell you this amazing fact about Dragons: they can break the barrier of time, they fly so fast. Don't frown at me! It's true! I've experienced it for myself, literally on Dragonback.

They can soar through the sky, from altitudes of air so thin you can hardly take a breath to a spot just inches from the ground, plummeting to the earth with wings tucked into their sides. And just at the very last moment, when you're certain you will die being pulverized into the stones near your toes, they will arch their necks and backs, and pull up and rise into the sky so fast you lose your sight and everything goes black and you must hold onto your leather rigging straps or you will surely fall and die.

Somewhere along this harrowing trip you reach a point in your flight that something incredible happens. Time folds or refuses to go forward for just a moment. You are going too fast for the world to keep up with you. And then you'll hear it. A loud *BOOM*. The sign that you've left behind the regular world and all its people for a half of a half of a second. It's nothing short of exhilarating.

The loud explosion is not so evident when on the Dragon, but people on the ground will hear it and they will tell you about it later. They'll also probably tell you that they thought the entire village was about to be turned to burnt and crispy bits, so it's generally not mentioned in an admiring tone of voice. But still, it's an amazing, wonderful thing that only a Dragon can do. No horse, no ox, no donkey, no large cat, no camel, no four- or two-legged beast can even dream of achieving this height, this skill, this talent, this utter *magical* state of being.

But even so, I don't recommend you accompany your Dragon on these speed-trips nor do I think it's a good idea to encourage it. Simply put, it's not good public relations for either the Dragon or you. Villagers tend to frown on fire-breathing, beastly activity happening above their heads, even when it is magnificent. A mere hint of an unhappy dragon has them running about with torches and incendiary devices and threats of blowing up mountains, and a speedy Dragon does tend to look a bit cranky. It's better that they live in ignorance of the Dragon's true greatness. Try it once if you must, if possible over an unpopulated area, and then never do it again. That is my sound advice.

Also, just so you know, you will most likely lose your water and any stomach contents you may be in possession of during this type of flight, because there is no way to protect oneself from the forces that press into a Rider as the Dragon takes his inside turns. I call them D-Forces for lack of a better word.

I can see some of you are a little nervous about my mention of angry villagers. Let me put your mind to rest about that once and for all. Yes, it's true that some Dragons have garnered bad reputations with the ignorant of our species. But you need not fear for your partner's life. It's a known fact that while we might be quite vulnerable as Riders, Dragons, on the other hand, are very hard to kill.

* * *

Dragons are nearly impossible to kill. Their scales are immune to fire, burning pitch, spears, arrows, knives, rain, snow, hail, and anything else I've ever seen in their presence. They lie atop one another in alternating rows, two layers thick, and they cannot be broken or even cracked by anything I've ever held in my hand. Believe me, I've tried. Not because I wanted to harm my Dragon, of course, but to test his strength. Plus, it amuses him and helps pass the time.

The Dragon's hide underneath his scales is also quite tough, although I do know it's penetrable by a very sharp spear. This is how Othello's mother was killed — by a very misguided and spear-wielding so-called hero who was hired by a village that feared her nightly raids on their cattle. To be fair, she really shouldn't have been picking from their herds, but still... A conversation between the parties could have fixed the problem. There was no need for sharp weapons to be involved.

Scales that slough off the Dragon once yearly, usually in spring, make handy shields for your own use. Leather straps attached to metal bands fastened around them make them easy to carry and load onto your Dragon-saddle or your own back.

As you can see, my personal body armor has several scales incorporated. Quite lovely when they catch the light, aren't they? They maintain their properties on the Dragon and while on a Rider's body. You could shoot a flaming arrow at my chest right now and it would merely bounce off, leaving nothing but a spark behind. Not only is this convenient in the event an angry individual decides to start a fight, it's also quite helpful when a dragon is in a foul humor or has an upset stomach wherein fire-belches are a possibility. Being fire-proof is a real asset to the relationship.

Dragons have two eyelids for each eye, one that comes from the top, and one that comes from the bottom, and part of one or both are always drawing towards the center. The entire eyeball itself is never exposed. This is for their protection, as the organ itself is quite sensitive to sharp objects. Their half-lidded gaze is what makes them seem so angry all the time, but it's really not the thing to be looking at when trying to determine a Dragon's mood. You're more apt to see the general state of his humor in his nostrils than anywhere else.

Dragon nostrils are one of the magical mysteries of our world. They contain passages that can manage both fire and pitch-like mucus, yet they can also spout water after a swim with fire immediately after, creating steam. They flare when the Dragon is angry, wobble when he is sad, wiggle when he's happy, droop when he is tired, and flatten when he's about to let a large ball of flame shoot out and destroy something. If you want to know how your Dragon-partner feels, don't look him in the eyes; look him in the nostrils.

I do encourage all Riders to spend the time it takes to get to this level of personal connection with their Dragon-partners. Othello and I have had ten years of nostril reading behind us, which has allowed us to communicate on a level not possible between humans. There is a certain magic involved in the relationship between a Dragon and his Rider, a Rider and his Dragon.

Othello knows what I'm thinking and feeling the moment I'm thinking and feeling it. He's a master at reading my body language and moods. He's not uncaring or unfeeling, either. His practical jokes are often designed to cheer me up. I've fallen I don't know how many times from his back, but to date, he's always retrieved me before I've crashed to the earth. I will admit that he does like to wait until the very last second sometimes, but as I said, he does enjoy a good joke and he has that wicked sense of humor common to his species. I can hardly blame him for being who he is, living the life of a Dragon honestly and fully.

So, my friends, it's almost time for us to part ways so that you can take the time you need to decide if this is the life for you, but before we do that, I just want to mention one more thing you must know about Dragons, in the event that what I've said so far has scared you away from the idea of becoming a Rider.

The life of a Dragon Rider is not all doom and gloom and last-minute rescues from body-splattering falls, or singed facial hair, or the disgusting odor of dragon mess. There is something very special about Dragons that most people will never find in the human world, no matter how long and dutifully they might seek it. I'm going to tell you what that is before we leave one another, because I want to be sure you get a very clear picture of this beast: the good, the bad, and the ugly. You've seen the bad, you've heard of the ugly, and now it's time you learn the good, the very best thing a Dragon has to offer his Rider.

* * *

Dragons are the most loyal creatures you will ever know. Yes, they might get a little argy bargy when they can't find a mate after five years of looking; and yes, they might like to play jokes on you that end up with you missing some body hair or covered in grime. But when push comes to shove, and someone other than him is threatening your life or good health, all games are over. Your Dragon will be there, standing between you and whoever threatens you, fighting until the death to ensure you remain safe and alive.

I'm going to share a personal story, something I've never even told my cousin Dalys before, so you can truly appreciate what I mean when I say a Dragon is loyal.

One year ago, when I was coming home from a visit to my aunt's village, I encountered a band of men who had come from a distant land for the purpose of raiding whatever villages they came across and taking what wasn't theirs without compensation. Yes. I'm talking about thieves. War mongers. Men who have very bad things on their minds and darkness in their hearts.

I knew they were headed to my family's village, and if they

arrived there, all would be lost. There were twelve of them and one of me. Othello had not accompanied me to the village, because of course people flee when they see him coming and I prefer to visit my aunt and cousins in their homes and not running through the countryside at break-neck speed while they scream in fear. My Dragon-partner had agreed to remain at our mountain home while I spent the day with my family.

And so I found myself without my Dragon armor and without my Dragon-partner, facing down the points of twelve angry men's spears and arrows. I had only a small knife I keep in my belt, which was no match for the weapons I saw that night. I admit to being more afraid than I'd ever been in my entire life, and that includes the times I'd flown upside-down over active volcanoes.

As they advanced, I began counting all the things I hadn't yet had time to accomplish, frustrated that my life would end at the age of fifteen. I didn't realize it, but I was saying those things aloud, yelling them out into the night.

"I haven't learned to do a back flip yet!" I'd been trying for months, but always ended up on my rear end. It can get boring hanging around while a Dragon sleeps sometimes.

"I'm only an amateur swordsman!" Dragons are horrible teachers. A flick of a claw and you're bowled over backwards in the dust.

"My last meal was a squirrel! I can't have squirrel as my last meal!" I'd always pictured a nice, juicy steak or a fresh trout with pickled beets on the side.

And then I thought of my partner. The Dragon who I spent my formative years with, the creature I thought I'd grow old with, soaring the skies of our world as I grew gray hair and he singed it off my head.

"Othello hasn't yet found his mate! Neither have I!"

"Who's Othello?" one of the savages said. It was the first and last word uttered by those men.

Othello appeared out of the night sky above me and swooped down, letting out a stream of blue fire that obliterated them, turning them into dust. And not a single hair on my head was harmed.

Othello had used the one weapon I'd never seen him use before and had never known existed before that night: Blue Fire. It touches only the things he wants it to touch and leaves the rest alone. It was magic. Dark and dangerous, yes, but magic nonetheless.

I climbed onto Othello's back that night without harness, without ropes, without any safety equipment of any kind. I knew then that he'd protect me for as long as I needed protecting and that I had nothing to fear from him.

And with that, I will leave you to your thoughts and decisions ... unless there are any questions?

A WORD FROM ELLE CASEY

In the 3-book continuation of the *War of the Fae* series (currently a 7-book Urban Fantasy series, which will soon be a 10 book series with these new releases), you will find reference to this short-story "Ten Things You Should Know About Dragons" that you just read. If you enjoyed it, and you like reading Contemporary Urban Fantasy, I recommend you give this series a try. *War of the Fae, Book 1 (The Changelings)* is free at most online retailers.

Want to get an email when my next book is released? Sign up here: http://eepurl.com/h3aYM

If you enjoyed this book, please take a moment to leave a review on the site where you bought this book, Amazon, Goodreads, or any book blogs you participate in, and tell your friends! I love interacting with my readers, so if you feel like shooting the breeze or talking about books or your family or pets, please visit me. You can find me at...

www.ElleCasey.com
www.Facebook.com/ellecaseytheauthor
www.Twitter.com/ellecasey

Elle Casey is a prolific American writer who lives in Southern France with her husband, three kids, and several furry friends. She writes in several genres and publishes an average of one full-length novel per month.

Of Sand and Starlight
by Daniel Arenson

"YOU SHITE-GUZZLING, pig-shagging stains of codpiece juice!" Erry swung her stick, eyes burning with tears. "Get the Abyss off my beach, or I'll slice off your lying heads and shove 'em up your fat, flea-infested arses!"

The women stared at her for a moment, then burst out laughing. A cruel laughter. A taunting laughter. The laughter Erry had been hearing all her life.

"Get outta here!" she shouted. The tears were now flowing down her cheeks, and she snarled like a wild animal. Perhaps that's all she was now. A wild animal roaming the beaches, feral and hungry. "I'm gonna crack open your skulls and piss in 'em!"

Clouds hid the moon. Only the candles burning inside the rotting houses on the boardwalk lit the beach. Driftwood littered the sand, and when Erry took a step forward, a dead fish squished beneath her bare foot. This whole city was a corpse washed onto the shore. This whole damn place was a maggoty hive of filth, a wart on the backside of a wretched empire.

The women laughed again, surrounding Erry. All but one. This one stood a couple paces back, eyes simmering with hatred. This one's teeth were bared, and her hand clutched a rusty knife. A heavyset, dark-haired woman with scabby knuckles. Getya. The baker's wife.

"Move aside." Getya stepped forward between her companions, raising her blade. "I'm going to gut this whore myself."

Erry growled, spinning from side to side, brandishing her branch. They said she looked like a boy, her body small, her dark hair cropped short, but Erry was an adult already, if you counted the years. For eighteen winters, she had scavenged upon this beach, rummaging in the trash, eating dead fish, fighting off her enemies with sticks and stones. An adult, yes, yet still so small, standing five feet only on tiptoes, her limbs no thicker than the stick she wielded. Years of hunger had left her small, but they had given her strength, kept the fire inside her burning.

These women around her—jackals, all of them—were a dozen years older, a dozen inches taller. But Erry knew she could face them, kill them if she had to. And if they beat her bloody? Well, she had been beaten bloody too many times to count and survived. And if they killed her? Well, perhaps that would be even sweeter than cracking their skulls.

"I'm no whore." She spat on Getya's feet. "Take that back or the next time I spit, it'll be onto your maggoty corpse."

Getya pointed her blade. "You are one! You are! You... you

bedded him. My husband. For money. You're nothing but a dock rat whore! Just like your mother."

Erry sucked in breath through clenched teeth.

Dock rat.

Whore.

The rage, the pain, the nightmares flared through her. Whore? No. Her mother had been a whore. Her mother had been a goddamn whore who slit her goddamn wrists, leaving Erry alone on this beach.

I'll bed men for food. For shelter in a storm. For companionship on a dark, moonless night when the nightmares fill me. But never for money. Never.

She stepped even closer to Getya, arms shaking, branch raised, teeth grinding. She stood only an inch away from the taller, older woman. Erry barely reached Getya's shoulders, and her branch was no match for the woman's blade, but she refused to back down. She tilted back her head and glared into Getya's eyes.

"Yes," Erry hissed. "Yes, Getya. Your husband took me into his bed. He took off my clothes. And I bedded him. But not for money. You know what he gave me?" A chaotic smile twisted her lips. "Honey cakes. The same honey cakes you baked him. And oh... they were delicious, Getya." Erry licked her lips. "Nice and warm and puffy. You baked them for him, and I ate them all up while he thrust into me."

Getya's eyes flooded, and for a moment Erry thought the woman would collapse into sobs. But then Getya roared and lashed her knife.

Erry leaped back, swinging her stick.

The blade blazed across Erry's arm, ripping through her stained rags, cutting her skin. Blood sprayed. Before Erry could even register the pain, her branch slammed into Getya's head with a *crack*.

The branch shattered.

Getya howled, blood gushing from her head.

The other women leaped forward.

And Erry fought them. Her branch was shattered, and she weighed barely ninety pounds soaking wet, but she fought them. With teeth. With nails. With the desperation inside her, the pain of a dock rat, her sailor father gone across the sea, her whore of a mother dead, her belly aching with hunger, her heart burning with her rage. As the fists slammed into her head, she kept standing. Kept fighting. As the kicks drove into her belly, she refused to fall. She kicked them back. She roared with her pain as they beat her. Roared for her father leaving them, leaving Erry's mother to slit her wrists in the alley, leaving Erry to a slow death of starvation and beatings and sand and blood in a rotten carcass of a town.

"I'm no whore!" she shouted, hoarse, blood in her mouth. She kept shouting as they knocked her onto the sand, as they kicked her, spat on her, then turned to leave. They walked away, still laughing, blood on their knuckles.

The beach spun around her.

The clouds wept, the rain stinging Erry, washing her blood away.

She lay in the darkness, trembling, wheezing, coughing out blood.

Another fight lost, she thought, and a smile rose on her

bruised lips. She tasted fresh blood. *Another pack of jackals I survived.*

She could not walk, not even after eating the cakes last night—not after so many days of hunger, with these bruises and cuts across her, with her head that would not stop spinning. But she could crawl.

I should crawl into the sea, she thought. She turned and stared at the black waves, and again they called to her, beckoning, their whisper a siren's song.

Come rest in our depths. Come join our darkness.

A black demon. A dark mother. Always waiting. Always there for a last, cold embrace.

She crawled away.

Not yet. Maybe some night I will join you. But not this night.

She dragged herself through the sand and onto the cobblestones of the boardwalk, her home. She pulled herself to her feet, then doubled over and gagged, losing whatever honey cakes that still filled her belly. Her head reeled. Her blood dripped. She thought one of her ribs might be broken. She stumbled forward, limping, falling, crawling, pulling herself back up.

She made her way across the wretched boardwalk. This place had once been called the Jewel of the South, they said. But that had been a long time ago. Back before the Cadigus family had slaughtered the old king, taking over this land called Requiem. Back when magic had still filled these people. Back when dragons had flown.

A land of magic crushed. Of dragons lost.

Perhaps once this boardwalk had been a place of plenty,

but no longer. The old shops had mostly closed. Their wooden beams now rotted away, and holes filled their tiled roofs. A handful of buildings still housed a few last tradesmen—a baker, a roper, a potter—but they too were hungry. After the long wars, trade had died, and now even the living rotted away, withering, fading... all fading to nothing, to bones, then ash. Like her.

"Dock rat, get away!" cried a portly man from the window of a chandlery. "Go! Shoo! Shoo!"

He tilted a slop bucket over the window, and the filth rained down, staining Erry's feet, splashing against her rags, filling her wounds. She coughed. She gagged again. She limped on.

Finally she reached the place. The closest thing she had to a house. The abandoned windmill rose in the shadows, weeds growing around it. Its wooden sails had rotted and fallen years ago, long before Erry had been born. Now it was just an empty shell, a skeleton of stone, like the rest of this city.

Erry fell onto the cobblestones, bloodying her knees. She crawled into the windmill.

A few stray cats greeted her with hisses, bristling. The place stank. The cats shit and pissed over the rags Erry had placed on the floor, and the carcass of a kitten rotted in the corner. Just another piece of filth. Just like the rest of Cadport. Just like her.

Erry stumbled to the corner. She lay on the soiled rags. She had no food. Nothing unless she wanted to eat the dead mice the cats sometimes brought in. But she had a bottle. She reached for it now, lifting it with a shaky, sandy hand. Moonshine. Real booze. She had let a man bed her for three nights for this bottle. She drank, letting the spirits wash away the pain, letting herself drown in the warm, stinging embrace of the bottle.

She slept.

Dawn rose, and she woke, eyes sticky. She coughed and trembled. It was winter, and rain still fell outside, but she was so hot. Sweaty. Shaking. She drank some more, emptying the bottle. She slept again.

She did not know how long she slept for. Dawn and dusk had lost all meaning to her. She woke several times, slept again, hovering between wakefulness and slumber and nightmares. Dreams of that night she had found her mother in the alley, her wrists slit. Dreams of who her father might have been, of the distant deserts he had sailed from, lands of gold and splendor where there was no hunger, no blood, no rot, no loneliness. When Erry finally woke and shuffled outside, it was night again. She had always been a creature of shadows, slinking, hiding.

I need food. I need water.

She walked along the silent boardwalk. Once more clouds hid the stars and moon. She reached the trash bin behind the cobbler's house, and she leaned inside, rummaging with her shaky hands, picking out potato peels, apple cores, a few chicken bones.

"Dock rat! Get out of here!" Lamplight kindled in the window. "Go!"

The door slammed open, and the cobbler emerged, waving a mallet. Erry ran, clutching her cache to her chest, and took her meal to the beach.

She sat on the sand, and she ate—picking bits of skin and

fat off the chicken bones, nibbling the potato peels, eating the apple cores and spitting out the seeds. She was so thirsty but she had no water—no water but the salty waves that still whispered ahead, beckoning to her.

Join us. Let the hunger and thirst end. Drown with us. Rule as a queen in our kingdom in the depths.

"One night, perhaps," Erry whispered. "Not yet. Not this night."

Her belly gave a twist. Rotten. Erry doubled over and vomited it out.

She lay on her back in the sand, too weak to rise, and tears flowed down her cheeks.

I want to die, she thought. *I can't do this anymore. I can't be this dock rat, some loving me for a night, others beating me. I want to join the waves. Please, whatever gods are up there… give me the strength I need to walk into the water. To sink.*

Above her, the clouds parted.

Erry gazed up through the veil of tears, and her breath trembled.

Between the clouds shone stars. The Draco constellation. The stars that looked like a dragon. They said that long ago, before the Cadigus family had seized the throne, that these stars had been a goddess to Requiem. A kingdom where the old magic had been welcomed, not forbidden. Where dragons had soared in the open, covering the sky. Today, the emperor forbade worshipping those stars, forbade using their magic.

But this night, it seemed like those old stars were watching Erry, comforting her, warming her in the cold.

You are not alone, child. You are a daughter of Requiem.

Erry rose to her feet, almost too weak to stand. She stared up at those distant lights.

"I'm a half-breed," she whispered. "My father was a sailor from a foreign desert land. My mother was nothing but a whore. The magic is forbidden. If I use the magic, and the soldiers of the city catch me, they will break me upon the wheel, they... "

She let her words die off. What did she fear of soldiers? Let them catch her. Let them break her bones. Let them raise her on a wagon wheel, displaying her mutilated body to the crowds. So what? She would scream for a day and then welcome death.

"But first I will welcome magic," she whispered.

She had not used her magic for a year now. Not since the last person had been caught shifting, had been broken with hammers. But tonight Erry was starving, dying, brave or perhaps foolish. Tonight the stars blessed her.

Tonight she would fly.

As the boardwalk crumbled behind her, as the waves called to her, Erry stood in the sand, raised her chin, and summoned her magic.

Scales grew across her skin, coppery and chinking. Leathern wings stretched out from her shoulder blades, unfurling, creaking. Her teeth lengthened into fangs, her fingernails into claws. Her scrawny, famished body ballooned.

In the darkness, she beat her wings.

She rose into the air, a dragon with fire in her jaws.

And Erry flew.

She flew off the beach and over the black sea. She flew

until the lights of Cadport faded behind her. She flew through the wind, over the clouds and rain. The stars shone brilliantly above, the Draco constellation brightest among them. She did not feel the cold as a dragon. She did not feel the hunger, the thirst, the pain of her wounds. She was no longer a weak dock rat, scrambling to survive, but a powerful beast of legend. A dragon roaring fire.

She breathed her fire, sending forth a great, crackling pillar of heat and light.

All those back in the city had this magic. The women who beat her. The men who bedded her. All those who pelted her with refuse, who mocked her, who called her a dock rat, a harlot. But they did not dare use it. Not with the old kingdom of Requiem dead, with the Cadigus family now grinding them under its heel.

But Erry dared.

She flew, roaring out her pain.

I'm not a dock rat. I'm not a whore. I am a dragon.

* * *

Dawn rose and she wandered the beach, only a human again. Barefoot. Her dark hair cropped short, full of sand and flecks of blood. Her thin, bruised limbs sticking out from her rags. She found a dead fish on the beach and ate. It didn't seem more than a day old, good enough to stave off the hunger. She nibbled seaweed. She scoured the boardwalk for puddles, knelt, and drank. She survived.

The sunlight broke between the clouds. It was getting too

bright. The first sunrays hit the castle on the hill, the crumbly old fort that had once been a bastion of Requiem, the kingdom of dragons. Now it was a lair of Cadigus's troops, of brutes far crueler than any vengeful wives. Erry stood on the boardwalk, staring past the rotting roofs of a city that had once been great. Soldiers were emerging from the fortress, armor shining in the dawn. On the hillside they became dragons and soared, wings wide, not bothering to hide their magic.

Imperial thugs. Hatred rumbled in Erry's belly like her hunger. *They summon their magic openly. They fly as dragons, patrolling our sky, grinding us into the ground. Yet if we shift, they tie us to a wagon wheel, shatter our bones with hammers, and leave us to die outside the city courthouse.*

As Erry stared up at the dragons, all her hatred and rage flowed toward them. If not for the Emperor Cadigus's wars overseas, Erry's father might have been able to sail back here, tend to her, raise her in a real house. If not for Cadigus crushing the merchants of the city, perhaps her mother could have found real work, not bedded sailors for coins. If not for Cadigus, the kingdom of Requiem would still be full of magic and wonder and wealth—not this despair, this poverty that left an orphan dock rat to slowly starve on the water, here in a town that had once been a jewel.

If Erry could, she would smash that castle on the hill. She would slay every soldier inside. And then she would fly north over forests, fields, and rivers, reach the capital, and burn down the emperor himself.

Yet she only crawled back into her windmill. She nestled among the cats on the piss-soaked rags. And she slept again.

When darkness fell, her hunger became a terrible thing. A living demon inside her, begging, clawing at her, screaming for sustenance. It was time to hunt.

Lanterns kindled along the boardwalk. Shops that had once sold jewelry, silk, exotic pets, and spices from across the world had closed long ago; they were now hives of mold, stray cats, and vagrants that would kill Erry if she encroached upon their territory. Once, merchants, tradesmen, priests, and travelers from distant lands would wander the boardwalk. Jugglers and puppeteers would perform, families would laugh, and her father would sail here on a great brigantine. Now only a few urchins, beggars, and drunkards roamed the boardwalk, searching for food, for booze, for spice, for a warm pair of breasts to fondle. Erry had no breasts to speak of, not as scrawny as she was, but she still knew how to please a man, still knew how to find a warm meal.

It didn't take long. Not even an hour of wandering the boardwalk, and he approached. She knew this one. Yoram. A soldier of the city, stationed in that fort on the hill. He was twice Erry's age, three times her size, an unshaven brute, but a woman could not live off trash and washed up fish forever.

"Erry!" he said to her. "Erry Docker!"

She approached him. She stood on the cobblestones, chin raised. She was barefoot; he wore fine leather boots. She wore rags; he donned fine steel armor. She was an urchin; he was a soldier. But they both needed something tonight. Meat for meat. Some warmth in the darkness. A brief moment of respite from the fear, from the crushing loneliness.

"Yoram," she said. "I'm god-damn famished. I'm just about ready to gnaw on your own flesh."

His eyes softened. Some of the other soldiers would beat Erry, bruise her, thrust into her only to mock her, hurt her, toss her a few wafers for her services. Yoram was different. Sometimes Erry could swear that the fool truly loved her.

He caressed her cheek with sausage fingers. "Come with me. Let's get something to eat."

He shifted into a dragon before her. As a soldier wearing the Red Spiral sigil of the emperor, he could become a dragon without suffering the wheel. His red scales gleamed in the lamplight, and he beat creaking wings. Gently, like a mother lifting her cub, he wrapped his claws around her.

He soared, taking her with him. They flew over the city. From up here, the boardwalk seemed so small, a mere vein along the southern sea. North of the boardwalk coiled the streets of Cadport, and countless homes rose in a hive. So many roofs. So many hearths. So many lives in warmth, in safety, even under the heel of the empire. As the dragon carried her, Erry imagined that she lived in one of those houses. That she had a mother and father who loved her. Or perhaps that she was married to a man, someone who tended to her, who saw her as more than a dock rat, more than flesh for hire.

But that's not my lot. It was never meant to be mine. I'm just Erry Docker. A dock rat. A half breed. The daughter of a whore. That's all.

The red dragon flew toward the hill, his claws wrapped around her. Yoram descended outside the fortress, put her down, and released his magic. He returned to human form again, a scruffy soldier, his breastplate squeezing his girth, his face unshaven, his helmet too large. He reached out and took her hand. His palm was pink, sweaty, drowning her tiny hand.

"Let's go eat," he said, not unkindly, but she saw the lust in his eyes, saw how his gaze trailed across her body, even as she stood covered in rags and bruises.

He took her into the fortress. The main hall was a place of smoke, sweat, and firelight. Embers burned in iron braziers. Soldiers bustled about, armor clanking. A few prostitutes from the docks lurked in the shadows between limestone columns, smoking pipes of forbidden spice.

"Dock rat!" one man called, reaching toward her. She knew this one—a soldier named Gorm, a brute she had bedded once for a fistful of walnuts. "Ditch that tub of lard. Join me in my bed tonight, if you want to feel real loving."

Erry shoved his hand away. "Piss off! Your manhood is more shriveled up than a dead shrimp. Stinks as bad too. Try to grab me again, and I'll cut off that shrimp and toss it into the stew."

The other soldiers roared with laughter. Gorm's face reddened, and he made to leap toward Erry again. She growled and raised her fists.

"Enough!" Yoram barked, placing his stocky form between them. "Gorm, go spear one of the women in the shadows. Erry ain't one of your cheap whores."

More laugher filled the hall. "Dock rat's got a name, does she? Erry? Only thing 'erry here is my arse." Gorm pulled down his pants to demonstrate.

Erry groaned and rolled her eyes. Cheeks flushing, Yoram pulled her away, and they left the main hall. They walked up a craggy, spiraling staircase, moving up a tower. Through arrow-slits, Erry could see the city below. A maze of alleyways and homes, lanterns shining in their windows, pockets of warmth and safety. Another few steps, and she saw the boardwalk, the beach, her windmill. A few more steps, and the staircase revealed the sea, the black waves like a blanket, calling her.

Come to us, Erry. Fall asleep in our arms. You will awake a great queen of Waterdepths, a mistress of sea and shadows and light.

"Not tonight," she whispered, letting Yoram lead her onward.

They stepped into his chamber, an unadorned room with rough brick walls, barely better than a prison cell, a palace compared to Erry's haunts on the boardwalk. Several bunks filled the place. A drunkard snored in one.

And on the table it awaited her: a meal.

A feast.

"Oh stars," Erry whispered.

Food. Real food. Bread rolls. Dates. A jug of wine. Smoked sausages.

A miracle.

"Eat." Yoram smiled.

Erry pounced and ate.

She stuffed the bread, the dates, and the sausages into her mouth faster than she could chew. Her cheeks puffed up. She gulped down wine like it was water. She wanted to save some, to stuff a bread roll and sausage into her pocket. But she could not resist. She devoured the meal within moments, so fast her belly ached and she worried she'd lose the food.

Stars. Oh stars, it's wonderful.

It was amazing, she thought. Even with the pain and loneliness in her belly. Even standing in this place, the halls of the empire. Even here, food became a thing more blessed than a mother's love, than a warm embrace. A thing of wonder. Of beauty. The most primal need of a person—to eat. Wonderful, wonderful eating.

Yoram stroked her short dark hair. "You're beautiful."

She snorted. "I look like a starved rat."

He shook his head. "You're the most beautiful woman in Requiem."

She rolled her eyes. She knew what to do. She pulled off her rags and tossed them into the corner. Standing naked before Yoram, she saw the desire in his eyes. He leaned down and tried to kiss her, but she turned her head aside.

"No," she whispered.

She would let him claim her body for a night, but only her body. Never her love. Never her soul. That soul was buried deep, wrapped in chains, too fragile to ever give.

She climbed onto his cot, lay on her belly, and closed her eyes. He tried to embrace her, to kiss her again, but she wriggled away from him, burying her face in a pillow, only relaxing when he finally mounted her. Then he became a wild thing, grunting above her, his body sticky with sweat. This was good. This Erry could understand. To be an animal, feral, just living on instincts, just craving food, water, sex. This was her life. Never to feel. Never to love. Never to hope. Humans felt pain; things could not feel.

He groaned when he was done and rolled off her. She grabbed her rags, pulled them over her body, and walked toward the door.

He reached toward her from the bed, naked.

"Stay." The same loneliness and pain Erry knew from her

own heart showed in his eyes. "Erry, stay with me. Sleep here tonight. I have leave tomorrow, and we can fly to the cliffs, or walk along the beach, or—"

"I don't stay anywhere." She stared at him, this large, soft, weak, powerful soldier. This man who could become a dragon, who was everything she was not, could never be. "I don't stay with anyone."

She left.

As she left so many.

All those men who had wanted to save her, to use her, to feed her, to take her body, her love, to give her comfort, to take comfort from her on a dark night. Some who beat her. Some who saw her as a delicate rose, struggling to bloom from the muck, a thing to cherish, to save, to foster and watch bloom. She left them all. She left him too. She walked downhill, reached the boardwalk, and slept on the sand, and again she watched the waves, listening to them calling.

* * *

She sat on the beach, staring at the waves as the dawn rose around her. Normally she hid from the light. Normally as the sun rose, she would crawl into an alleyway, into her windmill, or into a cave in the cliffs, sleep and hide until the darkness. But this morning Erry sat and watched the sun rise, beads of light gleaming on the water. The tide rose, kissing her feet.

"Are you out there, Father?" she whispered.

She reached into her pocket and pulled out the amulet. The silver sunburst amulet from a distant land. Her father's amulet.

"You paid for my mother with this amulet," she whispered.

"You made me for a silver sun."

She wanted to toss the talisman into the sea. She wanted to drown with it. Yet she kept this memento, had kept it since her mother had died. A thing from a distant kingdom, a place without cold, without soldiers, without waves that called one to drown. A land called Tiranor, a land whence ships had once sailed, bringing silk, spices, hope. A land Erry would never reach, a land so far she could not fly there, could not hope to ever see. A dream, that was all. A dream beyond a sea that beckoned.

Maybe I should try to fly there, she thought. *I can fly for a day until my strength wanes, until I fall into the water, until I sink... and then the pain would be over. I would be nothing. Forgotten. At peace.*

She rose to her feet, staring at the water, clutching the amulet so hard her palm ached. The magic tingled inside her, as real as her hunger.

"Erry?"

She turned and saw him standing there.

"Rune Brewer." She rubbed her eyes. "Get the Abyss off my beach. You ain't no urchin. Go back to your cozy, prissy home."

He scoffed. "I'm as much a boardwalker as you are, Docker."

Rune was a young man, seventeen years old, a soft-cheeked boy who sometimes brought her food at the beach. He worked back at the Old Wheel Tavern, the only inn that still operated on the boardwalk. His hair was dark and just long enough to cover his brow and ears—like hers—but his eyes were softer. Not as pained. Not as haunted as she was. What did he know of life on the docks?

"You ain't no boardwalker." She snorted. "Next time you eat a pigeon, maybe you'll be like me. Rich boy. What you doing on my beach anyway?"

He came to stand beside her. He gazed into the sea with her, silent, staring. "They're leaving tomorrow." His voice was soft. "Five hundred of them. Recruitment day. And… Tilla will be among them."

Erry raised an eyebrow. "Ropemaker's daughter? Tall girl? One that walks like she got a stick up her arse?"

Rune winced. "She's my friend."

"You just like her teats." Erry snickered. "Got your own stick burning in your breeches, I reckon. Let 'em recruit her. Army would be better for her. Better than being stuck in this piss-pot of a town."

"Not when they're shipped off to war. Not when they'll face the Resistance in battle. Not when I'll lose my friend, when—"

Erry reeled toward him. "Soldiers get beds to sleep on. Soldiers get food to eat. Soldiers get to become dragons, Rune. Real dragons who can fly, blow fire, be strong." She grabbed the boy's shoulders, sneering at him. "That's better than this life we live, crawling here on the boardwalk like cockroaches, the emperor grinding us to sand. I don't feel sorry for Tilla. I envy her." She shoved him. "So stop your whining, kid. Go shove your stick into a loaf of bread and forget about the girl. Soon enough they'll draft you too, and you can both die together in battle. Better than slow death here. Better than this. Than eating shite. Than shivering in the cold. Than being weak."

She expected to see Rune rage, but his eyes remained soft. He looked down at the bruises on her limbs.

"I heard you fought Getya and her gang." He sighed. "Erry,

you can't keep fighting them. They're bigger than you. There's more of them. I can't keep seeing more bruises on you."

She snorted. "Rich boy in his rich home. I don't look for fights, but I ain't gonna run from 'em either."

"Come into my 'rich home' then." He looked up at the clouds. "Hard rain's gonna fall. Come into the Old Wheel. Let me give you some breakfast. We got eggs and sausages. Real eggs! And cheese too."

Erry tilted her head. "Where you get cheese and eggs from? You're rich, but not that rich. Only soldiers get cheese and eggs."

"We had a soldier stay last night. Paid for his ale and bed with a basket of cheese and eggs. I'll share them."

She grabbed his arm and bared her teeth at him. "This ain't charity. I don't take no charity."

He shook his head. "A meal between friends."

"I don't got no friends."

"Erry!" Rune groaned. "Just come and eat the damn eggs, or I'll have to drag you into my tavern, tie you down, and force feed you."

They left the beach together and stepped back onto the boardwalk. Erry glanced around nervously. She rarely walked here during the day. The other urchins were gone, as were the beggars and whores. A scrawny dog ran into an alleyway. A few children played with a barrel hoop. An old priest tapped his cane. Erry followed Rune past empty buildings, once shops selling wool and porcelain, until they reached the Old Wheel Tavern.

The building rose three stories tall, built of wattle and daub. The timber foundation was rotting like everything else in this town, and the roof was missing several tiles. But the chimney still pumped out smoke, and life still filled this place, guttering like a candle but still casting light.

They stepped into the common room. Several empty tables stood on a scratched wooden floor. A wagon wheel hung from the ceiling, holding unlit candles—a makeshift chandelier. Casks of ale stood along a wall behind the bar, and a staircase led to an upper floor.

A black dog lay on a rug by the hearth, lazily flicking his tail. When he noticed them, he leaped up and ran toward them. Erry patted his head.

"Hello, Scraggles."

The mutt leaped up, tail wagging, and licked her. He was as tall as she was when he stood up like this, and he probably weighed more. She laughed, gently pushing him down.

"Don't knock me over, Scraggles!"

He licked her again, his entire body wagging. Erry couldn't help but laugh. Humans hurt her. Humans beat her, desired her, scorned her. But animals were still Erry's friends.

While she patted Scraggles, Rune stepped into the kitchen, then returned with a tray of food. As promised, he brought hardboiled eggs—real chicken eggs!—and cheese. They sat at a table and ate. Unlike the meal last night in the castle, Erry tried to savor every bite, to let the tangy cheese roll across her tongue, to let the rich yolk fill her mouth.

Rune ate too, only picking at his food. Silent. Hesitating.

"What the Abyss is wrong with you?" Erry glared at him. "Why are you moping?"

He put down his fork and stared at her. "I told you, Docker. Tomorrow. Five hundred youths drafted, all those who turned eighteen. Tilla among them. My best friend. It's hard to lose somebody."

Erry let out a groan so loud Scraggles started. She rose to her feet, pulled off her rags, and tossed them down. She walked toward the hearth, naked, and lay on the rug.

"Well, come on. Just pull out your stick and put it here. You'll soon forget about Tilla."

Rune stared at her, eyes wide, mouth hanging open. As if he had never seen a naked woman before. Perhaps he hadn't. Perhaps the boy was just a green virgin who knew nothing about hunger, about sex, about loss.

He rose from his seat, walked toward her, and knelt, awkwardly looking away from her nakedness.

"You don't have to do this. I didn't bring you here for that."

She raised an eyebrow. "You know what they say about me in the town. You know what they call me. You know what Getya called me, why she cut me. You gave me food. You offered me shelter in a storm. Here's my payment. Here's what I always pay."

Such sadness seemed to fill Rune that Erry herself wanted to cry. He walked toward a wall, took a coat off a peg, and draped it across her skinny, battered frame.

"You don't have to be this person." He touched her hair. "You can be somebody else, Erry Docker. You can stay here with us, with me and Scraggles. You can work in the kitchen. You can—"

"I can't do those things!" Now her tears did fall, and she rose to her feet, shaking. "I can't be that person! I can't... I can't stay anywhere. I can't love anyone. I can't have a home. I can't have people in my life."

"Why?" he whispered.

"Because it hurts! It hurts too much when they leave you. When they sail away. When they spit on you, beat you, kick you out into the cold. Do you know how many men offered this to me?" She laughed bitterly, tears on her lips. "How many offered me a home, a life with them, safety? How many then hurt me? My own father, Rune! My own father left us. My own mother, Rune! She took the coward's way out. Cut up her damn wrists and left me too." She was sobbing now, hating herself for showing this weakness. "You'd just hurt me too. I'd be here for a few days. Maybe a month. Only to get kicked out again. I can't love people. I'll just hurt you too. I'll lash out. I'll drink too much or scream or cry, and—"

She bit down on her words. He was staring at her with so much pity that Erry couldn't take it. She shoved past him, still wearing his coat. She burst out of the tavern. And she ran. She ran along the boardwalk, and she ran along the beach, and she ran until she finally fell to her knees in the sand.

I can't do this. I can't. I can't.

She crawled along the sand into the water, and she swam.

Welcome, Erry, whispered the waves. *We've been waiting.*

She let the water claim her. She sank.

She opened her eyes in the stinging saltwater, and she saw swaying seaweed, a fish, beads of light. It was peaceful down here. Her own kingdom. A place where she could be a queen, free of the pain, of the loss. The kingdom that had awaited her all her life, calling to her.

She took the coward's way out! Erry's own voice echoed in her mind. *Coward. Coward.*

Erry trembled, sinking in the water. Her mother had sunk

into her own sea of despair, had fled too to death. Her mother had left her here.

Erry's voice echoed again.

I don't look for fights, but I ain't gonna run from 'em either.

Her lungs ached for breath. She felt herself weakening, the water tugging her, the waves welcoming her. She swam. She fought them.

She would not run. She would win this fight, too.

She kicked, swung her arms, rose higher... and her head burst out from the water. She gulped down air.

The sun shone above her—the full daylight, golden, beautiful, the sunlight she had hidden from for so many years. She had always been a child of shadows.

You don't have to be this person, Rune had said. *You can be somebody else, Erry Docker.*

That goddamn boy.

She swam and crawled back onto the beach, shuddering. Just a weak girl. Just a dock rat. Just the half-breed daughter of a dead whore.

A girl who could become a dragon.

She knelt in the sand, and she stared up at that fortress on the hill. The fort where soldiers lived, where they could become dragons. Where she herself could serve.

She rose to her feet, and her hands balled into fists.

They came the next day, the soldiers from the north.

They flew in as dragons, and they herded the youths of the city into the square. They stood clad in steel, swords at their sides, shouting out names. Between them, five hundred youths shuffled forward, glancing around nervously, some weeping. Cannon fodder. Recruits for the northern war.

Youths who were escaping this place.

Erry knelt on a rooftop, staring down at them. They would be sent to a northern fortress, trained in grueling conditions. They would be shipped off to battle, maybe to death. They would see blood, war, fire on the front lines.

They would fly as dragons.

"And I will fly among them," Erry whispered.

She leaped off the roof. She ran barefoot along the cobbled streets. She had never run from a fight. Never. She would not run from this one either.

You don't have to be this person.

I will be a dragon.

In the square, the soldiers of the city turned toward her, gripping their swords. The recruits stared with wide, frightened eyes. Erry skidded to a halt, smirked, and raised her chin.

"My name is Erry Docker," she said. "I believe that you forgot me."

In the cold morning, wagons rolled out of the city, holding five hundred whispering, shivering youths… and one dock rat fleeing the sea.

A WORD FROM
DANIEL ARENSON

A few years ago, I began writing fantasy novels set in Requiem, an ancient kingdom whose people can turn into dragons. Requiem slowly grew, with five trilogies currently released and two more (at least) planned.

One of the Requiem trilogies is titled *The Dragon War*. In it, a tyrant has taken over Requiem, allowing only himself and his soldiers to become dragons. For all others, the magic is outlawed.

The trilogy tells of two childhood friends—Rune and Tilla—who find themselves fighting on opposite sides of a civil war. Rune joins a rebellion, while Tilla serves the emperor as a soldier.

One of the secondary characters in *The Dragon War* is named Erry. She's an orphan girl who lives on a boardwalk of a crumbling town, struggling to survive. Her role slowly grows throughout the trilogy, and while her past is hinted at, it's never fully explored.

I wrote "Of Sand and Starlight" as a prequel to *The Dragon War*, focusing on Erry and where she came from. If you haven't yet read Requiem, this story can give you a taste of that world.

If you're already familiar with the series, this will fill out a little blank.

You can learn more about Requiem at:

www.DanielArenson.com/Requiem

Tasty Dragon Meat
by K.J. Colt

NO ONE EVER THOUGHT that dragon meat could be tasty. Oh no, not those ugly lizard things with blood-red eyes, fiery breath, and demonic tempers. And perhaps the secret of their delicious flesh would have remained undiscovered if Nogdo, a butcher from the quaint town of Bolopsy, hadn't been brave enough—or desperate enough—to taste some.

One day, Nogdo fractured a beloved meat cleaver while carving prime rump off a prized cow. The butcher decided to take six days off work and make the long journey south to Krowtogor—a small hamlet just outside of Ashos, the capital of the Kingdom—to get the knife fixed by a renowned blacksmith. He set off at noon the following day with Pumpkin, a good-for-nothing draught horse with a lazy eye, and a carefully crafted buggy—his pride and joy—that Nogdo had built himself.

Spring's newly hatched birds, butterflies, and blooming blossoms made for a delightful journey. While Nogdo happily hummed a tune of tulips, a dragon the size of a house tumbled out of the sky and smashed the rear end of his buggy. Nogdo was catapulted into the air, and landed with a hard thump.

Stunned for a moment, he gathered his wits and, terrified of being eaten, scampered across the dirt to hide behind the nearest tree. Pumpkin whinnied and thrashed against the restraints keeping her tied to the useless cart. The straps broke, and she galloped away, dragging bits of the broken buggy behind her.

Afraid the dragon was still alive, Nogdo sat trembling behind the trunk, trying to mimic the stillness of a rock. Heartbeats later, when not a sound was heard, he slowly edged around the tree to peek at the dragon.

Only a youngling, Nogdo thought, examining the mass of glossy, triangular scales and stunted horns. Its jaw, strong and square, was fit to grate bones to powder. Dragons were known for eating slowly and ageing even slower. He guessed the beast's age at three hundred years, give or take fifty years.

The butcher shifted his foot, the toe of his boot snapping a twig. The dragon's eyes flicked open and fixed Nogdo with a murderous glare. *I'm dead,* Nogdo thought, a lump swelling in his throat. As the dragon rolled onto its feet, the butcher said a silent farewell to his current life and prayed for a pleasant journey to the next one.

Nogdo jumped when fifty or so dragon hunters burst out of the woodlands, brandishing swords and maces. The injured dragon hobbled back, one wing drooping lifelessly at its side.

The warriors cast a net, which missed its target, so they flung themselves onto the lizard's back from their horses.

Seeing bows being drawn and arrows nocked, the dragon made an effort to fly away with some hunters still on its back. But the wounded wing prevented the beast from gaining height, and the arrows pierced its chest. The dragon spluttered and fell lifelessly to the earth, causing the ground to shudder.

Satisfied with their kill, the hunters put away their weapons and pulled out hatchets and skinning knives. They hacked off the horns, yanked out teeth, pried off scales, and stripped the wing-flesh. The hunters would use these parts for oils and other salves. The horns were used to decorate the hunters' shields. After filling large sacks with their bounty, they turned their attention to ransacking Nogdo's cart. Once every item was plundered, the hunters departed in a cloud of dust.

The butcher allowed several minutes to pass before venturing out from his hiding place. With no food or horse, Nogdo despaired. He was three days' walk from Bolopsy *and* Krowtogor, and he had no tools for hunting. As the sun fell, Nogdo's stomach quivered with hunger, and the dry air cooled his skin. A chunk of flint lay near a broken cartwheel, and he was thankful the hunters had overlooked it. Gathering twigs and dead leaves into a mound, he set fire to them using flint and stone. As he added on branches and logs, the flames grew higher and the warmth soothed his misery.

Nogdo was not a man used to being hungry, so when the bubbling emptiness turned to sharp pangs of pain, he cried out with self-pity. Rubbing his belly, he glanced curiously at the heap of dragon flesh the hunters had left behind. Out of all the meats—white, black, pink, grey—listed in his butcher's book, the terrifying and legendary dragons were not among them. Nogdo grasped his sharp rock and wandered over to the fresh carcass. After hacking off a sample of thigh, wing, and breast, he twisted off a metal hinge from his buggy to create a make-shift cooking pan.

He placed the samples side-by-side on the hot tray and licked his lips with desire as the moist meat popped and sizzled. When the flesh was cooked brown and crispy, Nogdo inhaled the aromatic, savoury fragrance until his mouth watered. Using two twigs, he transferred the sinewy meat to cool on a piece of broken wood and waited. Minutes passed. Unable to wait another moment, he surrendered to his instincts and tipped his head back a little, shovelling the meat into his mouth.

The warm juices from the cooked meat dribbled over his tongue and down his throat. Elation and joy consumed him in a flurry of spice, tang, and sweetness. His eyes closed involun-tarily, and he drifted along the blissful journey of taste. After stoking the fire and reheating the crude pan, the butcher ran back to the dead dragon to procure more of the delicious flesh.

Moments passed in a blur of bliss and tears. Nogdo real-ised he'd found the secret to a fortune. The land he could buy with his riches would bring him titles and prestige. When his stomach had stretched to bursting and his eyes drooped with overwhelming exhaustion, Nogdo drifted into imaginings of his wondrous new world where, for once, his dreams would come true.

* * *

Dragons and humans usually avoided each other, but in recent years, the increasing numbers of dragons had seen a staunch competition for food. Fortunately, dragons didn't like the taste of men.

The lord of Bolopsy, a generally fair master, employed barbarian dragon hunters to kill the beasts. Up to three dragons were killed each day, and their foul corpses were left for the local Poop Scoopers—those that disposed of unwanted waste—to clean up.

After a couple of days being stranded by the side of the road, a passing merchant found Nogdo and delivered him home. The butcher thanked the trader and immediately sought out the Poop Scoopers, offering them two hundred silver coins—all his hard-earned savings—if they discreetly supplied him with dragon flesh for two weeks. The men were gobsmacked. Divided between the four men, fifty silvers apiece equalled two months' wages for a Poop Scooper. Poor sods. They struck their secret deal, and for a time, Nogdo had a constant supply of dragon meat.

Of course, it wouldn't be right to promote 'Dragon Meat' on his shop's menu, and so the butcher renamed it 'Mountain Ox', and priced it according to its rarity. Only two days were needed for news of the delicious meat to spread across the lands. Its popularity soared, as did Nogdo's prices and his hunger for the flesh. The butcher found himself thinking more about eating the meat than loving his wife or taking care of himself. Frightened he would soon lose control over his hunger, he stopped eating it altogether—but with no such concerns for his patrons, he continued selling.

A pound of breast fetched a silver coin, then two, then three, and before long, by raising his prices, Nogdo became the richest man in Bolopsy—second only to the lord—and the most famous merchant in the southern half of the kingdom.

People travelled for days to Cut-Less, his quaint butcher shop. At dawn, the doors would bulge inwards under the strain of hundreds of people pushing and shoving, each one desperate to be served first. They waved their purses and shouted out orders. An hour saw all the dragon meat bought, so many went without.

One day, a disgruntled customer attacked an old woman who'd been first in line to make a purchase. When the elderly woman reported the assault to the local citadel, guards arrived to manage Nogdo's crowds. Relieved and grateful, the butcher gave the soldiers free tail cuts—the juiciest part of the dragon.

Another two weeks passed, and the butcher bought the deed to an exquisite marble mansion with an attached two-level shop that was five times the size of his old one. To commemorate the time when he'd first tasted dragon meat, Nogdo hung up the broken wheel from the buggy that the dragon had destroyed. Sadly, he never found his mare, Pumpkin. The corners of his lips twitched upward at a beautiful thought.

Perhaps, like him, she had found greener pastures.

* * *

Nogdo chuckled a lot these days, both in public and in private. At the market, the people fawned over him. His wife and children constantly praised him. Nogdo stood tall and took long, confident strides. He was rich. Rich, rich, rich! And then his good fortune took an unexpected turn. The children of Bolopsy were struck down by a horrible affliction where ebony, triangular scales grew in place of their tender, human flesh.

The children were deemed tainted and infectious. Snatched from their families, they were isolated at Fort Greystone, a run-down ruin-turned-infirmary. The parents of the children were treated like pariahs and accused of cavorting with devils. Nogdo's soldier friends reported rumours of soothsayers and witches being employed to cure the outbreak of Blackscale, so called after a nocturnal flesh-eating fish that lived in the waterways. So far, the diseased children had been fed horrible potions and suffered through torturous experiments, to no avail.

A lingering sorrow befell the town of Bolopsy, erasing smiles and eliminating all good cheer. Many who lost their children slept outside Nogdo's butchery, hoping to find one last cheerful moment by eating his Mountain Ox. Nogdo saw madness in their eyes, and he recognised the same dependence on the meat as he'd observed in drunks outside a tavern.

Over time, Blackscale consumed the skin of the Fort Greystone children, and wings sprouted from their backs, or so he'd heard. Regardless, Nogdo suspected his dragon meat was responsible; after all, a common folktale warned children against going near dragons, lest they be turned into one.

With a heavy heart, he removed Mountain Ox from the menu.

Tribulation struck his house when Kibsigy, the youngest of his three sons, developed the horrible scaling of the Blackscale affliction. Gut-wrenching dread almost debilitated Nogdo.

He'd never allowed his family to touch the stuff, and a week had passed since he'd sold any Mountain Ox.

'You had any of my Mountain Ox, lad?' Nogdo asked as he inspected his son's naked body at bath time. Those nasty scales—black and leathery on the underside of the boy's arms—infuriated the butcher.

Kibsigy stared at his father with eyes as round as moons, making it difficult for Nogdo to stay angry.

'No, sir,' his son said.

'Don't lie, boy. You been in Papa's shop eating cuts!'

Kibsigy should have known better than to disobey him. Though the boy's scales hardly covered a hand-sized patch, rumours told that the passing of weeks would see the skin of his chest and neck consumed. The frightened child stared at the bathwater, whispering, 'A month ago. Only a little.'

Nogdo struck his son's temple. The child flinched, and water splashed over the side of the tub and onto the floor.

'And *who* said you could do that? Stupid boy.'

'Oi!' bellowed Marella, turning sharply into the bathing room. 'He doesn't know what he's done.' His wife passed the boy a towel, and once he was covered, took his hand, and helped him from the tub. 'Besides, it ain't his fault you sold cursed meat to our neighbours. What if they find out?'

Nogdo threw his hands into the air. 'Well done! Blather it a bit louder, why don't you? Now Kibsigy will chinwag to his friends, and I'll be hung for sorcery.'

'I won't say a word, Papa.' The boy had used his towel to swaddle himself in a sort of cocoon. The butcher felt an overwhelming and paternal need to cradle his frightened son and hug away his fears. The boy didn't deserve this burden, and Nogdo would die before he'd let the child be taken to the awful torture camp.

'You got that look,' said Marella.

The butcher glanced up to meet his beloved's eyes. 'What look?'

'The one you get before you do somethin' stupid.'

'Can't just do nothin', can I? Look at him.'

Marella *did* look at her son, and her eyes greyed and glistened, reminding him of winter's frosted grass. 'He'll grow wings before long.'

'My love, we got enough coin to live without workin' another day. The shop can close forever.'

'What do you mean?'

'There must be a cure,' Nogdo insisted, 'and I intend to find it.'

'You're goin' to leave me here with him while you go off? What if Kibsigy dies while you're gone, eh?'

The boy bowed his head.

'He lives, woman, as do the other boys. I'll be back before the leaves turn orange.'

'That's two months!'

Nogdo ignored her and set about packing a knapsack while she badgered him to stay. The butcher had always been stubborn and narrow of mind, and Marella knew she wasted her efforts. If there was a cure for the scaling, then Nogdo would discover it.

Even if he paid with his life.

* * *

Everybody in Bolopsy knew that when magic caused chaos, there was only one place to go: the Dark Magician's lair. It was so named to frighten away impetuous children and discourage troublemakers whose nosiness undermined their better sense.

Nogdo travelled for days across rivers and mountains on his newly bought horse, Fleabag. Eventually, he reached the magician's crumbling, brick-and-mortar fort. Vines strangled an assortment of skulls, animal bones, and rusty tools that were nailed to the walls.

The butcher slid from the saddle and his boots crunched against the rocky ground. He led Fleabag to the nearest tree and tied her up. Nogdo pushed aside the thick clump of cocksfoot grass that clogged the entryway to reveal a scowling gargoyle knocker. He reached out to the heavy, brass ring, pulled it back with a squeak, and rapped three times.

'Who is it?' came a disgruntled, wobbly voice.

'Name's Nogdo, sir. We've never met. I'd like to speak with you.'

'Nogdo. Nogdo. I've a freshly brewed cup of claw and blood to curse you with if you've brought mischief to my home.'

'No, no, it ain't like that. I got a question about dragons.'

'Too bad. I'm busy. Be off with you.'

The butcher glanced around the neglected courtyard and scratched his head. 'I'll pay you.'

'Coin? Hah! I've no need of coin when I have magic.'

'A favour, then. I'll do you a favour in return.'

Silence.

'Anything you want,' Nogdo added with instant regret.

The magician appeared in the shadows of the nearest broken window. 'Anything, you say?'

Fear brewed in Nogdo's belly. 'Anything.'

The figure moved back into the dark. Nogdo counted thirty of his unsettled heartbeats and glanced around helplessly. If anyone learned that he'd caused the Blackscale disease, he'd be put in the stocks and stoned—or worse, end up in the capital's Steel King Prison.

'It's about'—Nogdo closed his eyes and inhaled—'dragon meat.'

There was a bang, a clang, and a screech of rusty hinges as the front door opened. Nogdo steeled his expression as a wrinkly, twisted face peered out from the crack in the door.

'Dragon meat, you say?' said the ugly magician, whose face bore a bent nose and sagging lips.

'Yes.'

He flung the door open with a flourish. 'In with you, then. Sit, stand, dance, I don't care.' The old, dwarfish man shuffled into his drawing room. He tripped over his long, grey beard, grumbled, and then wound it about his arm. Nogdo hadn't moved yet from the doorway.

'Well? Are you coming in or not?' he asked impatiently.

Nogdo took a cautious step inside. An icy wind slipped between the shifted bricks, stirring up dank, rotten smells. Next to a smoking hearth was a rickety table covered in chopped bits of frog, bird, candle wax, and other unidentifiable objects, the very sight of which made him feel ill.

There were several chairs, but each one contained a sleeping cat. One licked its paws while another just stared with in-different superiority. Nogdo hated cats.

'Just shove them off, they think they own the place,' the magician said, pointing feebly in the felines' direction.

'I'll stand.' Nogdo didn't think the magician seemed very dark, and he wondered how he'd acquired such a reputation.

The elderly sorcerer shrugged and plonked himself down into a tattered rocking chair. Two cats immediately claimed his lap. The magician inspected Nogdo's clothes and smacked his lips together. 'So you ate dragon meat? Want more?'

'No.'

'Then no harm done.'

'Not me, sir. My son.'

The magician's green eyes snapped up to Nogdo's. 'You gave meat from the fiery ones to a child? Stupid, stupid man. Haven't you heard the stories?'

Nogdo's stomach did a little flip. 'I'm just a poor butcher from a small town.'

'Even the stupidest of men would think twice before snack-ing on dragon hide. It's outlawed for a reason. You must be extraordinarily brainless.' The old magician grumbled under his breath as he got up from his chair. He hobbled over to a mortar and pestle, added herbs and spices into the bowl, and started pounding. Nogdo's spirits lifted at seeing the magician working on a cure, but the hope faded when the old man took the powder and massaged it into the long, raw strips of freshly skinned rabbit laid out on the table.

'What's it look like?' the magician asked.

'What?'

'Wooo! You really are dumb.'

Nogdo scowled at the magician, who returned his contempt with a sigh of exasperation.

'What are your son's symptoms?'

'Black scales under the arms.'

The magician paused with narrowed eyes. 'I see. Huh. Three months. He'll be a dragon in three months.'

'It's not just my son.'

'There are more?' the magician said in a raised voice, and the corners of his mouth twisted into a sneer. 'Oh dear, oh dear, you made a pretty penny, didn't you? Greedy man. Greedy butcher.' The magician wiped his hands on his tunic and pointed a sharp fingernail at Nogdo. 'Bolopsy, isn't it? Everyone's heard about that Blackscale plague. They're at Fort Greystone now, ain't they? I'll be able to trade something rare for this tale.' The magician tapped his chin and then clicked his fingers. 'Aha! The butcher who butchered his family! Hrmm, no…not the right ring…' The magician hit his head. 'Think, you old codger.'

Nogdo stared at the floor, accepting the old man's ridicule. 'I'll do anything.'

'Dragon eggs.'

Nogdo blinked several times. 'What?'

'Two of them. Fetch the eggs and I'll help you.'

Dragons were known for their acute senses and fiery nature. He was no thief, and if he were discovered taking an egg, he'd be turned to charcoal in seconds. 'How?' Nogdo asked hopelessly.

The old man hobbled to his bookcase and selected a long

scroll. He stretched the parchment across a wax-stained table. 'See that?' He pointed to a spot on the map. 'Seven days' ride to the Dragon Cliffs. A female lives near the summit, she laid a fresh clutch of eggs three weeks ago.'

'How do you know?'

The magician held Nogdo's gaze. 'I know.'

'She'll be guardin' them, won't she?'

The magician hit Nogdo on the forehead with ring-covered fingers. 'Stop saying dumb things. Of course she'll be there. She's a mother. Mothers protect their young. Fathers are the stupid ones.'

Nogdo rubbed his sore forehead. He didn't like being hit, and he hated being spoken to as if he were scum. 'What will you do with the eggs?' he asked as he imagined ways to teach the old man a lesson.

'When I have them in my hands, we'll talk more. Hurry! Just as time devours the daylight, the dragons' curse takes your son's body.'

Nogdo didn't trust the magician, but there was no other choice to be had. 'You best be telling me the truth. If not, I'll—'

'What?' The old man shuffled right up to Nogdo's face and huffed a pungent breath of garlic and blood.

The butcher's stomach churned, and he clamped a hand over his nose. 'Nothin'.'

'That's right, nothing. There's nothing you can do to me, young man. Stop wasting time and get those eggs.'

Nogdo snorted and snatched the map from the table. He slammed the rickety door behind him as he left, startling Flea-bag. He cussed. The tale of the dragons' curse was a story told to keep people from being eaten by dragons, not the other way around. The story needed to be spread with more truth, and by soldiers and town criers, not by lying bards and mad sooth-sayers. When all the children were cured, Nogdo vowed to visit King Geldon of Enslain and reveal the truth about dragon meat.

* * *

The seven days' ride saw the lands become hot and dry and the grounds grow sparse of greenery. The changes to the landscape shocked and frightened him as he pondered where the nearest water source might be. By the time Nogdo arrived at the desolate base of the Dragon Cliffs, only three days' worth of food remained in his knapsack. He'd have to buy more soon.

The cliffs reminded him of dragon spines; the tallest mountain leaned on a severe slant, and Nogdo guessed it would take him half a day to surmount.

Before long, the hot dirt and giant boulders made the upward ascent wearisome. Fleabag panted as she attempted to gain traction in the dry, rocky clay. Nogdo dismounted, gathered her reins, and led her to a stump surrounded by a meagre patch of brown grass. There he tied her up. Nogdo unhooked his water skin and butcher's belt from Fleabag's saddle. The belt held four different kinds of knives. In a confrontation with a dragon, they'd be the only thing standing between him and a horrible, agonising death.

Scaling more crags on his hands and feet, Nogdo's muscles began to fatigue. Flies swarmed him, and he grew weary of their hum as the hours passed. Sweat soaked his clothes. At one point, his legs refused to lift far enough to reach the next ledge. He rested until his heart stopped pounding, then he made one last effort to catch the ledge with his wobbly legs. When his boot caught, he used all his might to haul himself onto the plateau. Panting hard, he lay still and closed his eyes. The moaning wind caressed his forehead, its touch soothing to his clammy skin. The climb up with the unsteady sand was difficult, but the descent would be even worse. Nogdo groaned.

Quicker I do it, the quicker I can go home, he thought. His eyes snapped open, and as he sat upright, they absorbed the scenery. The Kingdom of Enslain was vast indeed, and Nogdo marvelled as he took all the landscape in at once. The eastern horizon was unending; the clouds seemed so close that he wished he were a dragon so he could discover what lay beyond them.

Smoke from wood fires hovered in the direction of Bolopsy, beyond the woodlands. The thought of Marella and Kibsigy and his other two boys warmed his heart, and so, with a sense of renewed strength, he struggled to his feet. When he turned around, he faced a cavern entrance.

That must be it!

He counted each short step as he moved toward the cave. His heart thumped so hard he feared it would rouse the sleeping dragons within.

Piles of bones and dung lay in heaps at the base of the walls. He found a man-sized hollow in the rock and hid there for a moment. As his eyes adjusted to the dark, he noticed that his hiding hole was actually a dimly lit tunnel. Slowly, he fumbled his way down the narrow space. A light flickered in the distance, and the tunnel merged once more with the main cavern.

Blood surged through his veins, and the dank, stale air made breathing unpleasant. With shaking hands, he peered toward the back of the cave and froze at what he saw.

Smoking animal corpses. Stacks of burning wood and debris kept the suffocating darkness at bay. Nogdo gulped and snuck forward, expecting a searing ball of fire to melt his skin at any moment.

The butcher's throat dried and tightened. Every time a rock crunched or shifted underfoot, he winced and prayed his presence remained unnoticed.

Rounding yet another corner, he saw them: eggs cradled in a square nest constructed of expertly woven sticks. The nest lining was an assortment of fur, skin, and carcasses from unidentifiable animals. Nogdo pinched his nose at the pungent stench of corruption and decay.

Several more steps and he could accurately identify each of the exquisite, black-dotted ruby eggs. Six in total. After sizing them up, he was certain he could carry one and fit at least one other in his knapsack. He darted to the nest now and placed his ear against a warm egg, listening for life inside.

Nothing.

Dragon eggs took months to mature and hatch, and since these eggs were only three weeks old, the life inside was still developing. Nogdo rubbed his hands together, slid his arms around one of the toasty eggs, and lifted with a strain. It weighed as much as a boulder. He tried again, lifting from his legs and straining his back, but the egg shifted only slightly. The exertion of the effort made him collapse to the ground, panting. He leaned back against the nest to rest.

After catching his breath, he turned around in determination and clawed at the nest, throwing handfuls of twigs, feather, skin, and bone over his shoulder. Halfway through, a foul, yellow paste coated his hands, and he gagged.

The beating of wings echoed down the tunnel, making Nogdo's heart leap with alarm. His mind froze. His bones turned to mush. Unable to stand on his wobbling legs, he crawled around the nest to cower.

Thump! A cloud of dust settled on Nogdo and the eggs. When the dragon went quiet, the butcher was even more terrified. After a while, he couldn't stand the silence and he carefully peered over the nest. The sudden thump of a foot made him drop back down into a shaking mess.

A long, scaly snout with two large nostrils appeared above him. Nogdo slammed a silencing hand over his mouth as the nostrils rippled and snorted. The dragon lurched forward and curled its long neck so it could fix its black, menacing eyes on poor, defenceless Nogdo.

Urine soaked the butcher's pants, and he hoped the bitter smell didn't upset the beast. He scooted across the floor, keeping one eye on the dragon as he put distance between himself and the eggs. The dragon perched itself protectively over the nest and snarled at him, exposing a mouth full of piercing teeth. Nogdo crossed his arms over his face, bracing himself for the blistering heat. Instead, the beast shut its mouth.

'Please! Please! Don't kill me!' Nogdo cried. Tears stung his eyes as he huddled against the cavern wall.

The dragon stepped forward until its sulphurous breath warmed his face. 'I might say the same to you.'

Her gentle voice surprised Nogdo. For some reason, he'd always seen dragons as male, though he remembered the magician telling him different. For a moment, he wondered if he was dreaming, or if he had gone mad. He allowed one hand to drop from his face, and the mother dragon raised her head, allowing him a fresh breath.

'H-how are you—?' he stammered foolishly.

'You've eaten dragon meat, haven't you?' Those bleak, death-filled eyes changed to a leafy green.

'Yes,' he replied, realising a little too late that he'd just admitted to eating one of her kind. 'How do you know?'

She narrowed her eyes, and he couldn't help marvel at how the scales moved and stretched to express her feelings. 'Because you understand me. Only those who've eaten the flesh of dragons may hear our growls as words. You reek of deception,' she hissed. 'You want one of my eggs.'

Nogdo bit the inside of his cheek. 'My son—'

The dragon interrupted him with an evil, throaty laugh. 'He sprouts a tail and wings.' The dragon nuzzled her eggs, checking them for damage.

'Yes,' Nogdo said helplessly.

'They're mine!' she snarled. 'I should teach you a lesson. Thirty days and my babies will be hatched and hungry. What a pleasing first meal you would make for them.'

'I-I'll leave. Now. I won't come back. Please, just let me go.' Nogdo knew he had no tricks up his sleeve.

'Can you fight?' asked the dragon.

Nogdo widened his eyes. 'I can't fight you!'

'*Can you fight?*' she boomed.

'I can use a carvin' knife.' With a shaky hand, the butcher drew a slender blade and showed it to the dragon. 'See?'

She snorted. 'Dragon hunters captured my mate, the father

of my beloved brood.' Her scaly eyes closed mournfully. When they opened again, they blistered with hate. 'Their mobile contraptions fire spears into the sky.' She lifted her wing, exposing a red scar. 'I can't get close!'

The tales of hunters battling dragons kept bards fed and old women gossiping. Though they were handsomely paid for their work, hunters were savages that despised normal folk. And normal folk, although accepting of their necessity, despised them just as equally.

'Let me help,' Nogdo offered in vain. He could think of no other way to escape with his life.

The dragon shook its long, scaly neck, the red of it gleaming under firelight. 'If you rescue my beloved, you may have one of my eggs. A life for a life.' Sharp teeth peeked between thin lips as the dragon attempted to smile or sneer; Nogdo couldn't tell the difference.

'How do I cure my son with the egg?' the butcher asked, knowing the magician wouldn't help him if he only had one egg.

She spread her bat-like wings. 'The antidote requires magic and fire. Only a magician can conjure the spell.'

Darn it! The butcher pondered his options. At Fort Greystone, magicians were already trying to cure the scaling children. Why didn't *they* know about the dragon egg remedy? Maybe they did—or maybe they didn't realise that Blackscale was caused by eating dragon flesh. Would one egg heal Kibsigy, as well as the rest?

'So be it,' Nogdo said despondently. 'I'll find your mate.'

'Tolcan is his name.'

'And 'cause I've eaten dragon meat, I'll be able to under-stand him as well.'

'Yes,' she replied. 'I can take you now. Your horse is too tired anyway.'

How did she know about Fleabag?

The dragon hunched down and flattened her neck against the ground. 'Climb on, butcher.'

Nogdo's mouth fell open. He knew of no accounts of a dragon ever being ridden by a man. Would he be the first? Eye-ing the sharp spines on her back, he hesitated.

'At the base of my neck,' she said. 'You're not afraid of heights, are you?'

Nogdo didn't know, but climbing the mountain hadn't bothered him. He stepped forward and swung his leg over the scaly muscles of her neck.

Slowly, she raised her head, and Nogdo slid down into the groove above her shoulders. As she rose further, he hugged her neck.

'Not so tight,' she complained, and then strode purposeful-ly to the cavern opening. She perched on the cliff's edge, and Nogdo stared past his boot to the tiny features of the landscape below. His moist hands slipped on her oily scales, so he gripped harder with his knees.

'Prepare yourself,' she said as she spread her wings, extend-ed her neck like a swan, and leaped from the ledge. Nogdo's stomach rose into his chest and stayed there until, with two jolting beats of the dragon's wings, they soared evenly across the sky.

Nogdo's exhilaration made him cry out. He laughed and

glanced back over his shoulder to view the Dragon Cliffs. Below, a herd of wildebeest crossed a river, and to his right, a flock of migrating ducks formed a V in the distance.

The butcher considered that Kibsigy, if the disease claimed him completely, might fly through the skies. He could ride on his son's back—no, that would be cruel. Kibsigy deserved to be a normal boy.

'We're nearly there,' the mother dragon said.

Nogdo was amazed at the speed with which they'd crossed the lands. The sun moved down the sky, giving the mountains a golden halo that produced long, sweeping shadows. As they began their descent, Nogdo spotted smoke rising from a ravine. *The hunters must be there,* he thought.

'Why didn't they just kill Tolcan?' Nogdo asked.

'They are using him. They want my eggs as well.'

'Why?' he asked.

Upon landing, his joints jolted painfully. Nogdo turned his head and massaged the base of his skull.

'Tell him Venussa sent you,' she said. 'Tell him to return you to me once you have freed him.' Her voice cracked with sadness. 'I cannot stay here.' She spread her wings and turned abruptly, her tail sweeping above him.

Nogdo ducked and stretched a hand. 'Wait!' But she was already rising into the air. As she flew back to her nest, her crimson scales blended with the fiery sunset.

The butcher lost count of the different tendrils of smoke rising in the distance. *How many hunters live here?* The dragon hunters were rumoured to enjoy the taste of man flesh. Nogdo didn't particularly want to become someone's evening meal, and so, with a heavy heart, he began his journey home.

As he trudged, he could only think of Kibsigy in pain and crying out as the dragon scales enveloped his body. Nogdo wasn't a religious man, but he felt as if the universe had aligned to punish him for some misdeed. He angled his face upwards and cried, 'Why me?'

When no one replied, he felt more alone than ever and angrily kicked a stump. Would Marella still love him if he returned home empty-handed? Would the lord of Bolopsy have Kibsigy killed upon his complete transformation into a dragon? If he didn't do the right thing, then he and his family would experience great suffering, and it would be his fault.

Again, Nogdo arrived at the conclusion that his life didn't matter. And so after having walked for an hour in the opposite direction, he turned around and ran back to the valley which housed the dragon hunters' camp.

The rolling mountains and sparsely decorated countryside were easily navigated, unlike his growing fear. Using the love for his son, he managed to drown out his cowardly impulses by remembering memories of precious times. Nogdo especially adored the memory of when he'd taken Kibsigy fishing for the first time.

'I want to be a fishmonger!' his very proud five-year-old son had declared after reeling in his first fish: a flapping gobbler.

'Fisherman,' Nogdo had corrected him. "A fishmonger sells fish at markets.'

'Ewl, I don't want to do that, Papa,' Kibsigy had said.

Nogdo chuckled at the memory.

Boisterous voices from the valley below interrupted his reminiscing. Following the barbaric shouts were the roars of a distraught dragon. The sound echoed across the valley and bounced off the mountains. The sadness of it plucked Nogdo's heartstrings.

The butcher peered down at the hundreds of tents erected across the sprawling gorge, the whole encampment surrounded by segments of shoddy stockades. Fifteen or so campfires and a lot more torches provided light against the looming darkness. When Tolcan roared again, Nogdo spotted the dragon's tail poking out from behind a tent.

Nogdo took a deep breath and then started down the hillside.

* * *

The illumination caused by the fiery sunlight had long since become a grey twilight as Nogdo waited patiently.

The butcher—hiding at the southern end of the camp—crawled from behind a bush to the nearest tent. The rattling of chains and heavy panting of the captured dragon grew louder as the world quietened. Nogdo reached the tent unseen, and he braved a peek around the side to see the blue-scaled dragon—easily twice the size of Venussa—restrained by eight steel chains, each as thick as Nogdo's thighs.

To the butcher's dismay, the hairy, burly hunters sat at ring of campfires spaced evenly around the dragon. They tended to rotating spits of rabbit, goat, and boar. The smells and sounds of sizzling meat made Nogdo's stomach rumble, and he wondered if Tolcan had been fed or watered.

Nogdo had no choice but to wait while the men sung scores of off-pitch ballads that began and ended with the loud clunks of their ale flagons slamming together.

The painful hours of inane ruffian chatter made Nogdo grow restless, so he lifted the back flap of the tent and carefully peeled back the lining. Between the gaps of fabric, he saw the empty space and stepped inside. Dragon teeth and horns sat between rows of cowhide-covered cots. Solid wooden chests spewed gems, trinkets, and coins onto the ground. Archaic lamps painted the leather walls with patterned light.

The butcher paused, listening for crunching boots or approaching voices from outside. As his bravery grew, a scroll of fine vellum wrapped in glimmering gold thread drew his attention (dragon hunters weren't known for being literate). After a cautious glance at the tent entrance, he crept to the scroll. He slipped off the scroll's thread and unrolled the crinkled parchment pages. Nogdo expected to find script; instead, there were dimly lit charcoal strokes. Bringing an oil lamp closer, he gasped as the lines resolved into a clear image: A soldier clutching a crossbow, riding a dragon.

He quickly folded the parchment and shoved it in his pocket. To talk well of dragons—to mention peace between beast and men—was punishable by beheading under the laws of the land. He might use it against them later.

A sudden noise startled Nogdo. He darted to the back of the tent and slipped into the night. Crouching outside, he snatched a carving knife from his butcher's belt, held it with trembling hands, and braced himself for attack.

An hour later, his presence remained unnoticed. His eyelids drooped, but the chilled air stung his nostrils and made his teeth ache. This kept him awake. The last of the revellers had finally succumbed to their inebriation, their snores drowning out his thoughts. As he stepped out into the open, he remembered a traumatic memory of a bully yanking down his pants in the fountain square on Ashos' market day. That same terrifying feeling of exposure haunted him now.

His boot hit something soft and sloshy: a bloated water skin. He unplugged the cork and sniffed the stale contents, expecting his nose to tingle with bitterness, but it never came. *Just water.* He doused the nearest fire, the coals hissing loudly. Nogdo cursed his stupidity and winced; fortunately, the nasally chorus of snores continued. The butcher had been so preoccupied with not getting caught that he'd forgotten the dragon. As he met Tolcan's eyes, he sensed the dragon's astuteness. *The beast knows what I'm up to.* The fine hairs on Nogdo's arms stood on end as he doused the five other fires.

Having snuffed all fires on the western side, the dragon's hefty figure cast an eastern shadow. Nogdo moved more confidently in the dim light, inspecting the dragon's glossy form. But the hide of the beast did not glisten because of sleekness, or perspiration, but rather blood. It seeped between the scales pried up from the cutting chains.

'Your female sent me,' Nogdo whispered, and the dragon blinked once, his head raising slightly, softly rattling the manacles. 'Venussa, she flew me here to save you,' he added.

'Lies, dragon eater!' The dragon said with a crackling, throaty growl. 'You are human. And humans always lie. Especially ones that eat dragon meat.' He snarled, and the hunters' snores grew erratic.

'Hush, please,' Nogdo pleaded. 'I'm here to help you.'

'Then remove my steel bonds, dragon eater.'

Nogdo was filled with fear when the dragon called him

a dragon eater for the second time. And it made him second guess letting the dragon go free. He observed the beast's bonds. Gigantic metal spikes secured the beast's chains to rock, clay, and tree. Trying to pry them out would wake the hunters.

'Well?' Tolcan asked, his eyes becoming slits.

'I'll wake 'em up. We'll wait until they leave.'

'That may never happen.' The dragon revealed a single, long canine. 'How do you know my mate's name?'

'I told you, she brought me here. You gotta trust me if you want help.'

The dragon gave a smoky snort. 'There can be no trust between dragon and man.'

'Your den is amongst the Dragon Cliffs, to the east,' Nogdo said, folding his arms.

The dragon showed every single tooth now, and its eyes blazed. 'I might live somewhere else.'

Nogdo took a step back, raising his hands. 'Be that way, but I was there not half a day ago. I want a dragon egg and'—he remembered how angry Venussa had been when he'd told her about Kibsigy and decided to omit it—'Venussa promised me one in exchange for saving you.'

The deadly gleam in Tolcan's eyes dulled slightly. 'Why did you not ask the dragon you killed?'

Nogdo stepped forward. 'I swear I never killed one.'

'Never?' Tolcan said, his eyes gleaming with hostility. 'Then how did *you* come to eat dragon meat?'

'It was hunters. Maybe even these ones.' He nodded in the direction of the sleeping barbarians. The hunters might have had the king's protection, but everyone knew them to be savages. 'They shot down one of your kind while it was flyin'. It crushed my buggy. I was stranded with nothin' to eat. Didn't have no choice.' Nogdo shrugged.

The dragon's lips turned upwards. 'We taste good.'

'Too good,' Nogdo added sadly, and the strong cravings returned with such force that he considered munching on the dragon's thick, juicy tail.

A string of drool seeped from a crack of the dragon's mouth. 'But not good for children.'

Clever, Nogdo thought. 'So you know…'

The dragon's lip curled upwards. 'There are only two reasons why you would want our eggs: To raise a dragon like a dog, or to stop a child from turning into one of us.' Nogdo froze at the smell of sulphur on the dragon's breath. 'How did your child come to eat our meat?' Tolcan asked. 'Were you not travelling alone?'

'I took some home with me.'

The dragon let out a surprisingly loud roar of laughter, and the butcher froze.

'Shuddup!' yelled one of the barbarians, who flung his shoe at Tolcan's head and missed. The brute immediately went back to sleep.

'Somehow,' the dragon said, quieter this time, 'these hunters found a scroll from your Dark Times, when men and dragons turned on each other. I cannot let these savages spread the secrets of our dragon meat.'

The Dark Times had passed five hundred years ago. No one knew why, but the history and knowledge of that era had never been recorded.

'Dragons and men lived in peace?' Nogdo asked.

'For a time. The king who governed the lands, King Samire, favoured dragons, and did not fear us as had his forefathers. After uncovering the nearby lair of a ten thousand-year-old dragon named Ashella, King Samire sent a hundred cows to the base of her mountain, as an offering of affection. Over time, the king won Ashella's trust, and their unity inspired other dragons to live closer to humans and help them tend to farms, build structures, and clear forests.'

'That doesn't sound so bad to me,' Nogdo said as he touched his pocket, considering the picture drawn on the parchment. 'Did men ever ride dragons?'

'Only the king, and only Ashella. One day he tried to saddle her, and she burned his hand. He never rode her again.' Tolcan's cracked lips twisted into a sneer.

'Did King Samire eat dragon meat?'

'No.'

'So Ashella and the king didn't talk.'

'That is right,' Tolcan said. 'But when Ashella died, the king's heart cracked in two. He cooked and ate a piece of her flesh so she could live within him. Ashella was an old dragon, and that meant her flesh, when eaten by a man, caused obsession. That one bite consumed King Samire. Neither food nor sleep could eliminate his hunger for dragon flesh. Madness claimed him, and under the guise of peace, he used Ashella's name to call a meeting with the dragons across the Kingdom of Enslain. That day, King Samire used great spear machines to slaughter thirty of my kind.'

Even though Nogdo wasn't to blame for what had happened, he couldn't help feeling shame for what the past king had done. The continued rivalry between men and dragons had taken thousands of lives since. Nogdo daydreamed of what might have happened if the truce had continued. The Kingdom of Enslain sat at the base of the southern Frozen Mountains.

'The week of that slaughter,' Tolcan continued, 'the citizens ceased work. Instead of farming and trading, the king forced them to slice, strip, and preserve with salt the meat from the thirty dragon corpses.'

The dragon sighed. 'Summer neared, and King Samire feared his dragon meat would spoil in the hot, corrupting temperatures. Roads leading up to the Jagged Mountains were built so the meat could be frozen and thus preserved. Tens of thousands of men died creating those treacherous roads, but the king's madness deepened. He sent a vast army to the northern mountains, far away, in pursuit of the remaining dragons.

'Fie! No wonder your kind hate us.'

Tolcan's nostrils flared. 'The king's son, but eleven years of age, happened upon our leftover meat on his father's plate, and ate it. The king discovered him, and like your son, the boy scaled and sprouted wings. He locked his son away in a cave. The king saw the curse on his son as punishment for what he'd done to the dragons. But he couldn't stop. Through torturing another of my kind, King Samire learned how to cure his son's affliction, and took up a quest to search out a dragon egg. The army had killed so many dragons that there were no eggs to be found.'

Nogdo hung on the dragon's every word.

'In becoming one of us,' Tolcan said smugly, 'the prince

had our memories, and learned the truth about his father. He desired revenge. While the king was away on his quest for a dragon egg, the prince, now a dragon, escaped the cave in which he had been imprisoned. He lured a little boy back to his cave, bit off the top of his tail, and cooked the meat. The little boy, captivated by the young dragon, happily ate the Dragon Prince's flesh. They conspired together and gathered a hundred children to the cave to eat more dragon flesh stolen from the Jagged Mountain stores. The Dragon Prince taught his new kin hatred for the race of men, and together, they destroyed the city of Ashos with fire.'

Nogdo couldn't believe his ears. What a horrible tale of the past. Now he knew why the Dark Times were so named. Ashos must have been rebuilt since then. Surely the current monarch, King Geldon, knew these truths. 'So what then?'

'Over time, The Dragon Prince became so powerful that he was made Dragon King. Over time, he regretted destroying Ashos, and has since worked hard to convince dragons to leave towns and farmlands be. The Dragon King can force dragons to obey him, but he desires that dragons *choose* to be peaceful. Now, times are harder. Men have multiplied, as have dragons, and so we are thrown into each other's paths.'

The dragon breathed out heavily, dust and leaves whipped across the ground. 'Your son is innocent, dragon eater, but I cannot feel any sympathy for you.'

Nogdo scratched his beard. 'Are there dragons that would give me their eggs? Do you know the ingredients for the cure? How many eggs would it take to cure a hundred children?'

Tolcan's eyes narrowed. 'So you're the one who sold our

meat to all those innocent children.' The dragon snarled at Nogdo, and this time, the noise woke one of the sleeping men.

'Oi! What are you doing 'ere?' came a deep voice, and Nogdo turned in time to see a burly dragon hunter with a short neck, swinging a bludgeon at his head.

Thunk. The butcher slipped into darkness.

* * *

Dirty faces, sneering lips with ale-tainted breath, peered down at Nogdo as he stirred. A searing pain started at the back of his skull and stopped as an ache behind his left eye. Two men hauled him to his feet, and Nogdo met the crinkled eyes of a black-bearded man with muscular arms clad in golden cuffs.

'Talk, butcher,' he said with deadly calm. He held his sword to Nogdo's throat.

'How do you know I'm a butcher?'

The stoic man's bicep flexed as he tightened his grip on the hilt of his short sword. 'The dragon told me.'

The butcher regarded Tolcan several metres away, tail shaking, smoke pouring from his nostrils.

'Are you in charge?' Nogdo asked, surprised by his courage in the face of a blade's tip.

'My name is Orgvand, master of dragon hunters. And yours?'

'Nogdo.'

'Are you here for a dragon egg?' asked the master.

That earned a round of snickers from the onlookers.

'Quiet,' yelled Orgvand, silencing the camp so that only the gentle rustling of leaves was heard.

'Why do *you* need an egg?' Nogdo inquired.

'I'm asking the questions.' Beneath the hairs of his moustache, Orgvand pursed his lips. 'Why is it that a butcher wants a dragon egg?'

Why did the dragon hunter care? Nogdo remembered the picture on the parchment hidden in his pocket, and smiled. 'I want to ride a dragon.'

Orgvand revealed a row of half-rotten teeth. 'And why would you, a half-wit butcher, be interested in something like that?'

Everyone knew that dragons couldn't be tamed, even those captured at birth. If King Samire couldn't convince Ashella to bear a saddle, then the dragon hunters had even less chance. Maybe they had seen the picture and thought it possible. It was probably a fanciful drawing produced by a long-dead artist. If it had been hidden among other Dark Times treasures, maybe they thought it some replica of truth. 'My son is turning into a dragon and I need the egg—'

One of Orgvand's men punched Nogdo in the face. 'Think you're amusin', do ya?'

Nogdo rubbed his jaw. 'Ask the dragon if you don't believe me, then, you dog.'

All heads turned to look at Orgvand, and while they were distracted, Nogdo tried to think up a foolproof plan. Disappointingly, none of his ideas brought him any closer to freeing Tolcan.

Orgvand took Nogdo by the neck and dragged him within inches of Tolcan's face.

'Dragon,' Orgvand said. 'How can a child turn into one of you?'

Tolcan raised his head, and as he opened his mouth, blistering hot air rushed out to dry Nogdo's eyes. They felt like shrivelling prunes in the summer sun. He moaned and tried wriggle out of the hunter's grasp. Seeing the butcher's discomfort, Tolcan turned his face away.

'Thank you,' said Nogdo, and someone punched him in the lower back.

'If a child, not yet developed into a man or woman, eats our flesh,' said Tolcan, 'he or she becomes one of us.'

When Orgvand conveyed the dragon's words to his followers, murmurs erupted from the crowd of hunters. 'Is this child dragon like you, or is it faulty in some way?' asked Master Orgvand.

Tolcan exhaled with a sigh. 'The child dragon is exactly like us, except he retains his human memories.'

Orgvand's mouth curled into a hideous smugness. 'What luck!' Then he turned to Nogdo. 'You may live, butcher, for you have given me more than you know.' Then he raised his hands to the sky. 'Kill the dragon, cook his flesh, and salt it. Tonight, we capture children and create our dragon army!'

Hundreds of men punched the night sky, cheering. Orgvand pushed Nogdo aside and raised his sword to the side of Tolcan's neck. The dragon roared and thrashed about, desperate to free himself. More scales were uprooted now; blood dripped to the ground.

'Wait!' Nogdo shouted.

Orgvand's eyes snapped to the butcher's. 'Speak!' he barked.

If he didn't save Tolcan, then Venussa wouldn't give him her egg and Kibsigy's life would be ruined. The butcher filled with hateful, awful regret at the next words he spoke. 'There's a hundred more children, like my son, already kept at an isolated encampment. They're becoming dragons as we speak!'

The hunters shuffled forward, their faces lit with sickening curiosity.

Orgvand lowered his sword from Tolcan's neck. 'Why so many?'

'Haven't you heard of the famous Mountain Ox meat?' Nogdo asked.

Recognition filled Orgvand's eyes as his eyebrows rose. 'Aye. So that's what the plague is.' He stared at his sword for a moment. 'It'll be easier if we just capture the cursed dragon children.'

'Grant me my life,' Tolcan said to Orgvand, 'and I will persuade those fledglings to follow and obey you.'

Orgvand let out a short laugh. 'Hah! Don't mistake me for a fool.'

'The Dark Times,' Nogdo said ominously.

The master took a swig from a pitcher of ale. 'What of them?'

'I know you got artefacts.'

'And?'

'The king of that time, his son turned into a dragon and burned Ashos to the ground. Can't you see the danger?'

The hunter shrugged. 'I care not.'

'We're tired of horses,' came a drunken voice. 'We want to soar through the skies!'

Orgvand grinned while raising his sword. 'Well said.'

'Dim-witted rats!' Tolcan roared. 'You cannot tame a dragon. Our respect must be earned. We cannot be saddled!'

When the hunters broke down with laughter, Tolcan widened his mouth a crack, revealing a blazing light within.

'Fire!'

Everyone dove out of the way, including Nogdo. A thin and harmless fire stream singed a plate-sized patch of grass. The hunters rolled around on the ground with uncontrollable laughter. Humiliated and defeated, Tolcan lowered his head.

'Let the dragon go,' Nogdo pleaded, 'you have no use for him.'

Orgvand tapped the flat of his blade against the dragon's nose. 'Seems you made a friend.' He turned to Nogdo, eyes flashing. 'Tomorrow, you'll show us where the children are kept. For now'—the master clicked his fingers, and made some gesture over Nogdo's shoulder—'you can wait here with your pet.'

The barbarians took rope, wound it around Nogdo's arms and ankles, and tied him to Tolcan's front leg. The ropes were tightened to the point of chafing. From the corner of his eye, the butcher watched the dragon arch his neck to look at him. The beast's steamy breath caressed the butcher's hair. A splash of drool landed on his shoulder.

'I saved your life,' Nogdo said quickly, trying to rid the dragon of any idea of eating him.

'I am not going to harm you, even though you deserve it.'

A tear trickled down the butcher's cheek. 'I'm a wretched

soul. I know. But can't you see I'm tryin' to make it right?' Then his despair with the situation—his guilt, shame, all of it—turned into a kind of self-hatred. 'If you won't give me an egg, kill me. Kill me now.' Nogdo balled his hands into fists, concentrating on the moistness of his palms and the beating of his heart. The time had come to die.

Tolcan howled like a wolf. 'I cannot slay you without cause.' It seemed as if the dragon was sad.

'Losing my son will be like death itself! It's nothin' to you, nothin'! So why not do it?'

The beast's bowels rippled. The dragon could scorch his skin and crunch his bones, for Nogdo no longer valued his life. 'Coward. Fix this mess you have created and redeem yourself.'

'Will you give me an egg, then?' Nogdo asked.

'I will not.'

Then there was nothing left to be said. Tomorrow, Nogdo would try to stop the barbarians, and *they* would kill him. The thought of eternal peace calmed the butcher's mind, and he drifted into a pleasurable slumber.

* * *

The dawn light, bright and offensive, made Nogdo scowl. *Still alive,* he thought miserably. It didn't make sense that Orgvand hadn't killed him yet. The butcher could only guess that the leader of the dragon hunters had some other use for him. The barbarians seemed capable of finding Fort Greystone all on their own. His arms and legs were numb, and what little he *could* feel ached.

Tolcan shook his head, waking from his slumber. He

yawned, revealing spider web saliva strings strung between sharp canines. A forked tongue flicked rhythmically. The dragon rolled his eye around to inspect the butcher, but said nothing.

I got nothin' to say to you anyways, Nogdo thought.

The hunters had almost finished packing up the camp; their speed and efficiency annoyed him.

Orgvand approached, his golden cuffs gleaming in the morning light. This time, he came wearing polished armour crafted from fine leather. In the centre of his plackart was a dragon sigil. Orgvand met Tolcan's eyes and raised one arm high into the air. Twenty men rushed over.

'I will set you free, dragon,' Orgvand said. 'But if I so much as hear the flap of your wings, or feel the cold brush of your shadow, I will slit this butcher's throat. Understand?'

Nogdo frowned. Why did Orgvand think his threat would work? Tolcan didn't care about him one bit. Nogdo assumed the dragon would be disgusted by him. It was the beast's pity that kept him alive. As soon as he was free, Tolcan would fly back to his cosy mountain home to nurture his offspring and continue to hate men.

Every resident of the barbarian camp had taken up weapons, and they pointed them at Tolcan while he was being set free of his bonds. Metal spikes were removed from the ground, metal braces unclasped, and chains were thrown into a heap. Tolcan stayed very still. As the last tail brace fell, the barbarians cautiously stepped back. The dragon turned his head to lick his wounds before he stretched and experimentally flapped his wings a few times.

He leaped from the ground, almost severing heads with his sharp wings as he rose. The men ducked and growled, but they didn't attack. Tolcan soared through the valley...but then he circled back.

Orgvand brought a dagger to Nogdo's neck, yelling, 'Leave, dragon! Or he dies.'

Tolcan growled at the master of dragon hunters, sprayed a few carts with fire, then flew west in the direction of Dragon Cliffs. As his winged form disappeared over the valley bluffs, Nogdo's heart sank. A part of him had hoped that the dragon might save him after all.

'All right, we're moving on. To Bolopsy!'

'Bolopsy...' Nogdo echoed, bewildered. 'Why are we...?'

The men laughed as they surrounded the butcher. They tied him up with rope and threw him onto the back of a horse.

'Let's go!' Orgvand commanded.

Nogdo spent that day trying to discover why they travelled to Bolopsy when Fort Greystone was situated further north. Maybe they didn't know where the camp was after all.

Five days of uncomfortable night-time travel saw them arrive at Bolopsy. Instead of riding straight into the town, they took cover in nearby woodlands. Soldiers regularly patrolled the roads leading in and out of the town, and seeing so many dragon hunters would raise a lot of questions as they typically travelled in groups of thirty to forty, rather than hundreds.

'Looks pretty quiet to me,' Orgvand said, and then he glanced at Nogdo. 'Where do you live?'

'I'll not say,' Nogdo declared.

Orgvand cut the rope from Nogdo's wrists and shoved his

face against the muddy ground. 'Bring us *your* child and we'll give you a dragon egg.'

Nogdo was flabbergasted. 'I-I don't understand. You don't have an egg, that's why you had Tolcan chained—'

The master of dragon hunters clicked his fingers and two men dragged the butcher to one of the carts. Orgvand ripped back a tarp, revealing two red dragon eggs identical to the ones in Venussa's nest.

Nogdo's mouth fell open. 'How did you…?'

'Choose, butcher. Bring me your son, and he lives, or we kill your wife.'

'Why?' Nogdo shouted in dismay. 'Why do you want him?'

Orgvand cocked his head. 'I wish to see his scaling. He will come to no harm.'

'Swear it!' Nogdo shouted.

The master of dragon hunters covered his left breast with his hand. 'By my sword, I swear.'

'It'll take me a half hour at least, and then I'll come back.' Nogdo glanced at the eggs again and felt his optimism renew. He desperately wanted to alert the soldiers to the dragon hunters' presence, but they'd committed no crime. Besides, the hunters, though not considered civilised, had risked their lives to protect Bolopsy's farms. Without them, the people would have starved. Nogdo's crime was far worse, and if the people knew what he had done, they'd hang him.

* * *

'You're back!' Marella said, as Nogdo entered into his wife's private parlour. 'I thought you'd be wolf food by now!' She put her arms around her husband and nuzzled into his neck, sighing with relief.

Nogdo stroked his wife's long brown hair. 'Where's Kibsigy?' he asked.

Marella leaned back, a frown on her face, and accusation formed in her sudden, rigid stance. 'I can see it.' She pointed at his face. 'Trouble, right there in your eyes. Spit it out, what you done now?'

Nogdo averted his gaze to stare at the floor. 'Dragon hunters. They're waitin' for me.'

'Dragon hunters! Has the madness taken you?' Marella puckered her lips and puffed a lock of hair from her eyes.

'It's too hard to explain,' Nogdo said. 'I need Kibsigy.'

The butcher turned to the doorway with the intention of visiting his son's room, but Marella threw herself in the middle of the doorframe, blocking his exit. 'If anyone sees him, they'll take him to that cursed fort! Tell me what you know, Nogdo, before I slit your throat!'

'The hunters know about the dragon meat curse,' he hissed. 'They only want to look at his scales, then they'll give us an egg and leave us alone.'

Marella's forehead crinkled, as did the skin at the corner of her aging eyes. 'And you need a dragon egg because...?'

'That's what cures the curse.'

'Oh, good,' her eyes brimmed with tears. 'There is a cure for the curse.' But then her eyes dimmed a little. 'What do they want with the children, then? They ain't gonna kill them, are they?'

'No. They're gonna fly 'em, once they turn into proper dragons. They want to mount 'em and use 'em like horses.'

Marella's mouth was wide open now. 'They're children!' she shrieked. 'We gots to alert the soldiers. They'll deal—'

'Papa?' Kibsigy appeared shirtless under Marella's arms, still raised to block the exit. A thin fold of skin now connected his ribs to his arm, like a bat-wing. His fingernails had lengthened into claws.

Nogdo felt his innards being crushed with the grief of his son's grotesque transformation. Unbearable, heart-wrenching guilt held his breath prisoner in his lungs. He scooped his son into his arms and gazed intensely into his wife's eyes. 'I met a magician,' he told her. 'He can heal him with the egg.' Nogdo patted the boy's head and smiled at him warmly. 'We're going to fix you right up.'

Kibsigy gasped gleefully. 'Really? Thank you, Papa.'

Without another word, Nogdo picked up a cream-coloured shawl from a nearby armchair and wrapped it about his son's naked torso. He pushed past Marella, ignored her shouting, and left his home.

'What's wrong with Mama?' Kibsigy asked, his eyes wide with fear.

'We're gonna meet some warriors, they want to see your scales,' Nogdo replied, lifting his son up. 'Be brave, we'll be back home soon.'

'I trust you, Papa.'

As they made their way into the forest, Nogdo focused on the chirps of chit-chit birds and the squeaks of squirrels. As they approached the hundred or so barbarians, Kibsigy leaned in closer to his father.

Orgvand inclined his head and said, 'I didn't think you'd come back.'

Nogdo froze, his arms tightening around his son.

'Put him down,' the master ordered.

'Yeah? And what'll you do with him, eh?'

'We've decided he's to come with us to Fort Greystone. I will keep my word, no harm will come to either of you.'

Nogdo curled his upper lip. 'My wife, she'll worry. She'll come looking for us.'

'Put him down,' Orgvand ordered coldly.

Several barbarian hands went to the hilts and handles of weapons.

'Papa,' Kibsigy said with a trembling voice.

Nogdo put him down. 'It'll be well, lad.'

'Come here, boy,' said Orgvand. 'I only wish to see your beautiful new markings.'

Kibsigy hugged himself and cautiously stepped forward. The barbarian towered over Nogdo, and he must have seemed a giant to Kibsigy.

'Are you pained?' Orgvand asked the child.

'Sometimes,' he squeaked. 'It itches, mostly.'

Orgvand met Nogdo's eyes. 'We will take control of Fort Greystone tonight. Only when we succeed may you return home.'

'With the egg,' Nogdo said, challenging the master with a stern expression.

'Of course.'

'None of this makes any sense. Why do you need me to go to Fort Greystone? How do you even know where the children are being kept?' the butcher asked.

The dragon hunter sneered at him. 'You will see. King Geldon of Enslain wants all dragons dead. But not I, no, not me. We will have a dragon army, and the king will see their use, once and for all.'

Orgvand clicked his fingers. Nogdo and Kibsigy were seized, tied up, blindfolded, and thrown into the back of a cart.

Nogdo felt warm breath in his ear. 'And if you say anything, butcher,' Orgvand whispered menacingly, 'I will teach you the true meaning of pain.'

* * *

When their blindfolds were removed, twilight had descended. Nogdo manoeuvred his legs about so he could sit up and peer over the side of the rickety cart. In the distance, across grassy lands, was a stockade erected around an old fort. Signs pierced the ground like spines on a porcupine. The writing on the signs gave Nogdo chills.

Go Back
Unclean
Blackscale Plague

In the opposite direction of the Fort Greystone stockade, further down the way, a campfire sparked and flickered in the grey darkness. From the clang of steel and gruff voices he heard, Nogdo guessed they were soldiers posted to further enforce the warnings.

He stole a quick look at Kibsigy, who buried his face into his drawn legs.

'Be brave, boy, all will be well,' Nogdo said.

Kibsigy glanced up briefly from beneath his lashes, but he looked no more reassured.

Nogdo looked back at the soldiers, then again inspected the walls of the stockade. Was that it? Five guards? Maybe there were more inside.

The butcher worried that the dragon hunters would start a war with the dragons, who would swarm together to scorch the lands of Enslain.

If Kibsigy weren't sitting across from him, he'd have been plotting Orgvand's death. As it was, such things were impossible. If he failed, his son would see him die, and if he succeeded and lived—however unlikely that was—his son would see him commit murder. He sighed hopelessly.

A cry rang out, sad and forlorn. As if the sun would never rise, and the flowers never bloom. The soulful sound lingered in the air long enough for Nogdo's heart to weep with the sufferer. It was a young dragon's cry. He imagined that would be Kibsigy in a month's time, and his stomach sunk with despair.

'Did you hear that, Papa?' Kibsigy asked, his face raised above his knees, his fingers spread on the ground beside him.

Nogdo inclined his head.

'That sound, it seems familiar.' Kibsigy clutched his neck. 'I can feel them in my throat. Dry. In pain.' The boy reached out to Nogdo. 'Can we help them?'

Orgvand whispered orders to his men, distracting the butcher from his son's questions. 'Take out the guards,' the master of dragons said.

Ten warriors slunk through the bushes in such a stealthy, crafty manner that it took the butcher by surprise.

Soon, a shout came, then two more. The soldiers' campfire died. The creeping warriors returned.

'Bring the boy!' Orgvand ordered with a raised hand, keeping his eyes fixed on Fort Greystone.

'Papa!' Kibsigy cried as men seized him.

'Courage, my son!' Nogdo watched helplessly. Orgvand mounted his horse, pulling Kibsigy up by one arm and positioning him over the front of the saddle.

The dragon hunters started moving forward, breaking free of the trees and exposing themselves under the large moon. The butcher's gaze flicked anxiously between his son and the stockade.

The whooshing chorus of beating wings made the hairs stand up on Nogdo's arms. The blurred outlines of hundreds of dragons appeared against the grey sky. An ominous, terrifying sight, they even *looked* like giant bats. Kibsigy started crying. Nogdo wanted to shush him out of fear he'd upset Orgvand or the dragons.

Orgvand dismounted, pulling Kibsigy off with him, and they stood two metres in front of the group. He drew a large dagger and glanced over his shoulder. 'Bring the butcher.'

The ropes on Nogdo's wrists were severed, as were the ties about his ankles. He quickly ran to the master, collapsing on his knees and embracing his son. Kibsigy hugged him tighter than he ever had.

'I can't be brave, Papa. They're going to feed me to the dragons.' He burst into sobs and wailed loudly in Nogdo's ear. 'What did I do, Papa? I'm sorry for whatever it is.'

'Quiet!' ordered Orgvand. 'Light your torches, men!'

Nogdo hadn't noticed that every hunter now clutched a blade and a lamp of some kind. The darkness retreated as the soft, yellow light flooded the field, making it more difficult to see the dragons in the sky. Nogdo released Kibsigy and put a finger to his lips. The boy clamped a hand over his mouth, but continued whimpering.

The dragon swarm circled the fort in a wide, sweeping curl. After their threatening display of roaring, swooping, and fire-breathing, the dragons landed out of reach of the light emanating from the hunters' lamps. As the beasts hit the ground, Nogdo felt the vibrations in his legs and boots. About forty must have landed at once, for the ground rumbled beneath them. The butcher gathered up his son's hand, squeezing it tight to comfort not the boy, but himself.

Tolcan and Venussa stepped forward into the light. Nogdo's eyes widened. Wedged between their teeth were dragon eggs. They carefully placed them on the ground and rolled them forward a little.

A figure slid from Venussa's back; whoever it was held up a staff, or a torch. Venussa let out a small bolt of fire and hit the shaft, and the torch sparked to life. Fire illuminated the figure's face. The magician!

What is he doing here?

As more dragons stepped forward, Nogdo inspected their faces. All carried eggs. They were here to save the children!

Orgvand sneered at the magician. 'Old fool. Should have killed you the last time we met, eh?'

The magician crossed his arms. 'Magic versus steel? You didn't have a chance then, and you've less of a chance now.'

The magician cackled and tugged at his beard. 'Leave now, and you'll live. Smelly barbarian.'

Tolcan roared in support of the magician's words.

'What...?' Nogdo gaped at Tolcan. 'Why are you here?'

The beast glanced at him. 'I am the Dragon King.'

The butcher glanced at Orgvand, who showed no surprise at this news. The master of dragon hunters already knew!

'Huh? So you're—'

'King Samire's son, yes. With me now are the children I turned into dragons. The shame—'

'He's so ashamed'—Orgvand shouted loud so that both man and beast could hear—'that I knew he would come here this night to stop us, to save the children.'

'You set a trap!' Nogdo blurted, then realised he'd pointed out the obvious.

A cheer rang out from the dragon hunters.

Orgvand's face crinkled into a joyous and triumphant smile. Quicker than the blink of an eye, his hand clutched a handful of Kibsigy's hair. Nogdo stepped forward, but he was quickly restrained.

Smoke poured out of Tolcan's nostrils as he watched. A warning growl bubbled in his throat.

'Stop!' Nogdo cried, never taking his eyes off his son. 'You swore him no harm.'

Kibsigy's arms were raised to his side defensively. His hands trembled as Orgvand pushed him closer to Tolcan.

'You promised!' Nogdo shouted at the master.

Orgvand stopped just short of Tolcan's towering head and glanced over his shoulder. 'Provided the Dragon King grants me leadership over all dragons, the boy will live.'

Every beast raised its head to shriek at the moon. Nogdo's ears rang. Younger, more innocent growls returned the dragons' call from behind the stockade. How many *were* there?

Tolcan snarled so ferociously, the butcher feared he might accidentally bite off Kibsigy's head. The Dragon King's eyes flashed like lightning strikes. 'Never.'

Orgvand choked Kibsigy a little and exposed his neck. He put the tip of his dagger to the boy's throat and nicked the soft, fleshy skin. 'I *will* kill him.'

Beside him, Orgvand's men shuffled uneasily. The men knew they were outnumbered by dragons and if the master was bluffing, they would all die this night.

'Only a dragon can be a Dragon King,' replied Tolcan.

Orgvand clicked his tongue impatiently. 'Come now, dragon. We both know that isn't true.'

'Master Orgvand,' Nogdo said.

The hunter turned, a scowling, murderous gaze locked on the butcher. 'What?'

'Let me convince Tolcan.'

He considered the butcher's words for a moment. 'Very well.'

Nogdo was freed, and he moved closer to Tolcan. When he was two feet away from the master, he pretended to trip. He dived on top of his son and flattened him against the ground, shielding him with his body.

Cold, sharp pain made him gasp as Orgvand's dagger sunk into the left side of his back, at the edge of his shoulder blade. He raised himself a little, afraid the blade might go through to Kibsigy underneath him. Nogdo squashed his face into the dirt to keep from screaming.

He felt a horrible, suffocating pressure grip his chest; he tried to breathe, but painful, bubbling fluid crawled into his throat. The blade must have punctured one of his lungs.

Tolcan roared overhead, and the butcher turned just in time to see the dragon rend Orgvand's head from his body. The other dragons surged forward, and the barbarians roared as they charged forward to meet them.

After seeing several barbarians dismembered by giant dragon claws, Nogdo put his cheek against Kibsigy's face and said, 'Keep your eyes closed, my son.' As he spoke, his voice cracked a little.

'Retreat! Back to the forests!' cried a barbarian, but Nogdo knew they would never get away. The dragons were too numerous, and far too powerful.

When the horrible, nightmarish sounds of the slaughter faded, Kibsigy whispered, 'Papa.' And opened his eyes.

Nogdo rolled off his son and gazed at the battlefield. There were few corpses, but many discarded weapons and torches. Horses galloped away, whinnying with fear. A dragon half flew, half galloped after one of them, and as it sunk its jaws into the mount's hide, Nogdo covered his son's eyes.

The magician touched the butcher's shoulder. 'Get up, butcher. Silly butcher, half-wit butcher.'

Nogdo tried to get to his feet, but he felt dizzy, and weakness sapped his strength. A horrible series of coughs followed, and bloody froth dribbled down his chin. The pain in his chest was unlike anything he'd ever felt. His forehead broke out in a sweat.

'Papa!' Kibsigy said in dismay.

The butcher turned his head, trying to fixate clearly on his son's face. 'I'm well. See? I can talk. I'm well.'

The magician knocked the boy out of the way and started administering vials of awful liquid that he'd stowed away in the deep pockets of his robes. When Nogdo spluttered, he grasped the butcher's jaw and forced it down his throat. The pain dissipated, and a peaceful hum replaced the jarring, searing agony. He breathed easier, and his left lung felt freer.

A sudden flash of icy cold jolted through his body, as if he lay in snow, not against grass warmed by the day's blazing sun.

Tolcan and Venussa peered down at him. 'It is good to see you again, butcher.'

'Good?' Nogdo echoed doubtfully, then he smiled and his lungs crackled as he laughed. He gasped for a proper breath but failed.

Kibsigy clutched his father's hand so desperately that he thought his fingers might break. The boy's eyes were swollen; his tears had washed away all dirt from his rosy, delicate cheeks. 'Oh, Papa.'

'I love you, son. And I'm proud of you.'

'Can you save him?' Tolcan asked the magician.

The magician glared at the dragon. 'No, but you can, can't you? A silly, stupid question to ask in front of his child anyway. This man deserves to live. Why not grant him your—?'

'No!' Tolcan growled. 'To give him power over all dragons would be foolish!'

'Dragons and men need to stop their squabbling,' the magician shouted. 'Save his life.'

Nogdo coughed, and as his throat closed a little, he took a sharp, raspy breath. 'Stop talkin' in riddles, you two.'

The magician leaned over the butcher, his beard sticking

to some blood on the man's shirt. 'If the dragon names you Dragon King, you will heal and live on for many thousands of years.'

Nogdo laughed—and then coughed, hard. This time, gooey clumps of blood filled his mouth, and he spat them out. *Not long now*, he thought. He raised a limp hand and squeezed the magician's shoulder. 'No. Not me. No.' He slid his eyes to his grieving son. 'Kibsigy?'

'Yes, Papa.' The boy leaned in close, nuzzling his father's face.

'Promise your Papa you will be a friend to all dragons.'

'I will,' he squeaked.

'Tolcan,' Nogdo said.

'Yes?'

'Teach Kibsigy…of your'—he inhaled sharply, almost drowning—'history. Bring men and dragons together. That is my dying wish.'

'In your name, brave Nogdo, the most foolish of butchers to ever live, I will try one final time to bring beast and man together.' A single tear escaped the dragon's sullen eyes. '…and more. I will do so much more.'

And Nogdo's life slipped away.

* * *

Ten years later.

The sun sat halfway down the western horizon. The clouds were thick pillows spaced separately from one another. Tolcan soared over the capital city of Ashos. Spears from thirty ballistic towers flew at him from every direction. He tipped one way, then another, and when one nearly caught his head, he ducked and lowered himself to avoid five more. He'd spent years training for this moment.

'Did you see that one? So close!' Kibsigy shouted. He gripped Tolcan's saddle and sat up in his seat, the toes of his boots secured against pegs. Now a young man, skilled as both a flyer and a hunter, Kibsigy had spent his life as his father had wished with his dying breath—learning the ways of dragons. He'd made no progress in securing a peace treaty with the King of Enslain.

Hundreds of dragons emerged from the underside of the cloudbank, and their sudden appearance confused the soldiers firing the spears.

Riding those hundreds of dragons were more men and women like Kibsigy, who strived for peace between dragons and men.

Most of the dragons distracted the towers by doing a strange, elliptical dance in the sky while thirty others strategically destroyed the functional ballistic mechanisms with fireballs. They'd hit their marks perfectly, sparing the towers' integrity, and thus killing no one. Kibsigy had spent his years preaching about the kind nature of dragons. Thousands supported his quest now, and in some towns, where the dragons helped the people with hauling rock, clearing forests, and other difficult tasks, the people worshipped the beasts.

In the face of growing support for the dragons, the king raised the dragon hunters' commissions. The gold was irresistible to young men from starving families. They dreamed of better lives, and so the king had been successful in recruiting many new warriors to his crusade. Ashos had become a military centre, spending all its resources on producing soldiers, and the surrounding lands suffered from raised taxes so the king could fund the massive expense of the men's training.

The towns seen conspiring with dragons were punished the most severely. When those people could no longer afford food, Kibsigy had strung four corners of a giant net to four dragons and taken them to the great lakes. They had dragged the nets through the water and dumped house-high piles of fish in the middle of starving settlements. But the people needed more than fish to survive, so he'd been forced to see the king at the castle several times.

Each time, the king had grown angry and thrown him out. When Kibsigy was banned from Ashos altogether, he decided to turn the people against the king.

Today was the great summer feast. Overnight, Kibsigy and his followers had snuck into the city and replaced two thirds of the meat intended to be served at the city banquet with cooked dragon flesh obtained from fresh dragon corpses left behind by hunters.

Lunch time had passed. Many would have consumed the dragon meat, so they could now hear Tolcan speak for himself. And Kibsigy would continue coming to the city until the people took the side of the dragons and forced their king to call off all soldiers, and cease his dragon-slaying quest.

'Are you ready?' Kibsigy asked his scaly friend, staring at the back of Tolcan's giant head.

'Today, we make a new history, son of Nogdo!'

Kibsigy felt a thrill shoot up his body and he said to himself, 'This one's for you, Father.'

A WORD FROM K.J. COLT

Whimsical is a type of narrative I quite enjoy, and whenever I read a whimsical narrative, I often imagine Stephen Fry's voice in my head. Isn't that odd? Maybe I've just been overindulging in Harry Potter audiobooks, or playing too much Little Big Planet for PS3. So I braved a whimsical piece of fiction this time. Whimsical, sweet and simple.

Even though I write fantasy fiction, I hadn't yet dared write a dragon novel because their mythology is vast, their subject is well explored, and to think I might have anything new to contribute seemed borderline arrogant.

So I thought I'd revise a short piece I started three years ago, which I only wrote because my partner said, quite tritely, "You're writing fantasy, eh? You should write a dragon story."

I felt like saying, "Of course, I'll write this long and complex 100,000-word novel while you finish up the dishes and we can celebrate with Chinese takeout tonight." Despite my short-lived sarcasm, I decided to humour my partner (now fiancé)—and myself—by writing "Tasty Dragon Meat". In general, when writing fiction, I prefer my protagonist to be an ordinary person thrown into extraordinary circumstances (cue drama and conflict). In "Tasty Dragon Meat", a simple butcher becomes filthy rich, and then goes on to become one of the most important figures in that kingdom's history (nothing to do with his being rich, though—that would be sending the wrong message).

But no one will remember the butcher's name. No one will remember the sacrifices he made. In our modern world, on planet Earth, people sacrifice, work hard, and do extraordinary things to make our world a better place. Sadly, most of us will never know who these people are or why they make the choices they do. People are continually, silently, humbly participating in the endeavour to enrich the human race. Or so I like to believe.

It's a lofty goal for anyone to set: to enrich the human race. But I think it's one with immeasurable value and that is beautifully complex. Nogdo, the main character in my story, didn't venture to become notable. I'd argue his initial acts were self-serving, but in the end, it was love and compassion that atoned for his mistakes. And it's love and compassion that I believe motivates so many of us to make planet Earth a better place.

www.kjcolt.com

Transparency
by Alex Albrinck

NATARIA FLEW ABOVE THE CLOUDS. The droplets in the puffy sky ornaments hid the form of the water creature from the eyes of any creature below able to see the wavelengths generated by her body. Ice dragons argued among themselves as to whether theirs were bodies of air held together by water, or bodies of water held together by air. Those core elements gave the ice dragons a shimmering, silvery, translucent appearance, save for the golden eyes. Though she measured some fifteen feet in length, excluding her tail, Nataria usually weighed less than an average-sized dog.

Not today, though. The three eggs she carried weighed her down, straining her wings. She looked through the clouds to the surface below, looking for the welcome relief of a lake. The land, comprised of earth, was a poison to her pearly skin; she'd land there only in an emergency, and only after ensuring hideous fire dragons had kindly absented themselves from the area. They'd take no sympathy on a pregnant ice dragon suffering the first pangs of dehydration. It wasn't in their genetic makeup. The two dragon species had warred since time immemorial, and though her ancestors had driven the land dragons belowground, they still existed, lurking in hidden caves, lying in wait for the foolish ice dragon who dared approach the land alone.

They'd make sure she didn't return.

She finally spotted what she wanted. Her natural affinity with the element told her the water was fresh and cool, exactly what she needed. She circled down, settling her feet into the shallowest water to mitigate the damage from contact with the land, dipped her head below the water, and drank deeply. As her water stores refilled, her senses came alive. She felt the warmth of the sun; the sun's warmth and light were the only exceptions to her kind's aversion to heat and fire. A gentle breeze rippled the water's surface and ran over her smooth skin. She spread her wings and dipped them below the surface, the water a natural tonic to injury or fatigue for her kind. Her wings felt renewed, and she was now certain she'd have little difficulty staying aloft for the remainder of her gestation period.

She moved before becoming consciously aware of the threat, springing into the air just above the blasts of flame aimed at her from three sides. She heard the sizzle as the water fell from her body and diffused the flames. She kept flying, dodging, avoiding the repeated volleys fired her way, until she found herself three hundred feet above the ground. She looped around and hovered, assessing the situation.

They were there, three of those demons from Hell, glaring

up at their mortal enemy, denied the kill they'd desired. She sneered back at them. Like all her kind, she found the very appearance of the fire breathers repulsive. Thick scales covered their hides. Horns grew from the heads of the males, including two of her three would-be murderers. They had six legs, rather than four, a necessity for creatures twice her size and fifty times her mass. And the colors! All manner of earthy, fiery colors: red, orange, green, brown and black. Each of the fire dragons possessed its own unique hue of one of those primary colors. Their affinity with the land meant a natural camouflaging effect took place, much as air and cloud camouflaged her in flight. She'd heard them and felt the warmth before she'd seen them.

She saw them now, though. Disgusting, evil, ugly creatures.

They'd stationed themselves as near the lake as they could; the water that gave her life was poison to them. Now that they'd been spotted, they backed farther away from that poison.

If she thought rationally, Nataria would take advantage of the situation and fly away, living to fight another day… and, more importantly, living to deliver her clutch into one of her kind's life-giving pools of water before they hatched a few weeks later. But instinct, borne of thousands of years of warfare, overrode even the basic instincts of self-preservation and maternal protectiveness. You did not leave fire dragons alive; you fought them until they were dead. If you did not kill them, you could be certain that they'd one day kill you.

One of the dragons roared, blasting a stream of flame in her direction. It was a challenge, daring her to resume the fight. It was the fire dragon's way of calling the ice dragon above a coward.

She'd spill their blood over that insult. Ice dragons weren't cowards. And she'd prove it.

Nataria flew higher, ignoring the telepathic taunts flowing her way as she did, and glided toward the far side of the lake. The clouds called to her, begging her to return home, but she'd not do so until she'd honored the ice dragons with a triple kill of the insult-laden fire breathers below. She angled herself downward and tucked her wings in, feeling the glorious wind on her skin as she accelerated toward the lake's surface and shore with the waiting fire breathers, still bellowing their challenges. She reached her peak velocity as her body ripped through the surface of the lake, the speed alone generating a huge splash. Nataria altered her angle under the water and shot back above the surface, spreading her wings. The upward explosion generated a second wave of water, and as she rose above the surface, she relished the sounds of agony as the water found its mark. The fire breathers screamed; water droplets ate through their scales like acid and bored into their skin. The pathetic creatures rolled upon the earth, using the loose soil as a sponge that would suction the poisonous water from their bodies, writhing in pain, oblivious to the very real threat of a very angry ice breather hovering above.

Though she enjoyed their suffering, Nataria knew it was time to end them. She flapped her wings to gain a bit more height and then dove once more, a killing machine en route to her victims, prepared to unleash her icy breath upon them. Their bodies, consumed with expelling the poison inside, would suffer a severe drop in temperature. Cold affected the fire breathers like dehydration affected her. With additional passes, she could literally freeze them to death, encasing them in ice and then shattering their ugly bodies across the land they so loved.

She heard the grunt and saw the flash of brown in her peripheral vision as searing pain ripped through her. She crashed to the ground seconds after hearing a thunderous boom from the ground nearby.

She looked down. Something had ripped her abdomen open. Vital organs and fluid leaked out. The shuddering pains brought on by her contact with the ground shut down her capacity to feel. She knew only one thing with certainty: she'd die here. She'd not return to the air. She'd never lay her eggs, never watch her children hatch, never again know the joy of flight.

The brown male fire dragon who'd hidden nearest to the lake, the fourth dragon she'd never seen until he'd ripped through her hide, stomped over, a sneer upon his face. *Suffer, you creature of evil. Suffer in agony until you breathe your last.*

She felt the end coming on. Death brought with it a clarity she'd never before known. That clarity told her that her death came from a fire dragon *jumping* into the air. But fire dragons didn't jump. They *couldn't* jump. Leaving the ground for even a few seconds had deleterious effects upon their health. But there was no other explanation. She'd been too high for him to otherwise reach her.

She'd heard the rumors. She'd found the concept impossible, disgusting, unnatural. And yet here was tangible proof. She fixed her golden eyes upon him. *There is something unnatural about you, dragon.*

Her world went dark as he blasted her with the searing heat of his flaming breath, and she passed into oblivion.

* * *

Eirene, a fire dragon with scales colored a deep blood red, watched the fight unfold from the safety of the tunnel entrance. The cave, large enough to hold several massive dragons, was camouflaged, a mixture of earth and stone and vegetation maintained by the Guard, a subset of their kind dedicated to preventing a second desolation like the one that drove them from their rightful place on the surface into the bowels of the earth. She'd grown up doubting the existence of the ice dragons; generations of dragons grew up without ever seeing the surface. When a dragon never saw the surface, she might reasonably assume the sky did not exist, and if the sky did not exist, why should one believe in the existence of the puny, ugly, flying dragons formed of air and water?

Many also believed that with the existence of ice dragons reasonably questioned, it called also into question the necessity of the Guard. Why maintain a defense force against a non-existent threat? Those dragons, whether the younger volunteers or the older dragons taking a mandatory shift at the direction of Cato, their leader, could better spend time seeking raw meat to feed their slowly growing numbers, rather than dallying in fanciful rituals from times gone by, from eras when older dragons believed in the mythical flying creatures.

She'd met Damir years earlier, and had come to believe in the Guard, though she maintained the skepticism over the existence, numbers, and existential threat posed by ice dragons. That skepticism had vanished as she saw the creature land, watched it douse her friends and mate with poison, had watched Damir leap from the ground and drown the evil being with one swipe of his powerful claw.

She sensed the mood and telepathic thoughts of those, like her, claw-picked to watch the Guard in action. Like her, the others had never been to the surface; seeing the clear blue sky, the puffy white clouds, the green grass and trees and vegetation, the rocky mountains surrounding them, and even the poisonous stream-fed lake had proved to all of them, beyond a reasonable doubt, that the surface was real.

The dead icer proved that their enemies, likewise, were no mere figment of overactive imaginations. They'd been chosen for this trip for their demonstrated courage, for their fearlessness in defending their ideals, and for their youth. Damir would gain recruits for his Guard through this program, but he'd more critically gain vocal advocates to help reverse the tide of doubt and preparations that settled among a species so long untested and unchallenged.

With the single icer dead, Damir signaled to the visitors that all was clear, that it was now safe for them to venture from the cave. Eirene was the only one who moved. She relished the feel of the sun-drenched earth against the padding on her feet, and gripped chunks of fresh soil with each of her six claws as she moved. The tall grasses, swaying in the wind, brushed against her scales, soothing aches she'd not known she'd had. It was part of their construction, their magic. As creatures of fire and earth, her kind drew strength and healing from contact with those elements; pitch a fire dragon into a deep lake or hold them off the ground, and they'd deteriorate quickly to the point of death. Icers killed members of the Guard, driving them toward cliffs or large bodies of water with relentless barrages of their icy breath, overwhelming the large land dwellers with superior numbers. Woe to the fire dragon caught in such an ambush; Damir reported that they'd find shattered scales matching the description of Guard dragons gone missing on a regular basis.

The three who'd baited the icer were still burrowing themselves into the soil, their physical agitation clearly abating as the earth pulled the moisture from their bodies. Though soil naturally contained *some* fluid, the earth element overpowered water given the relative composition ratio. Swamp-like soil, more water than earth, wouldn't help them.

Eirene moved to her mate. Damir gave off an air of power, and possessed a powerful personality that commanded respect despite his relatively small size. She loved the deep brown coloring of his scales. She gasped out, spotting a scale on his tale still sizzling from the geyser the icer had unleashed.

Damir glanced at his tail, laughing at the lone damaged scale he'd sustained in the battle. *Relax, Eirene. It's just a scale wound. Just one scale. I'll be fine. Look.* He rutted his spiky tail into the soil, building a furrow of earth, and burrowed the damaged section of his tail inside. *See? I'm fine.*

She watched his face, reveling in his smile. *That was impressive. They really are a threat, aren't they?*

That wasn't too challenging; they're rarely stupid enough to make a hydration run alone. We think the female was pregnant and couldn't wait for others prepared to hit the lake. So we've effectively got four kills today. A good day. He glanced at his team, watching the female and the two males relax as their water-based injuries healed, and his face turned grim. *We don't always emerge from battles without sustaining losses of our own. Today was a good day.*

Eirene had always thought his talk about the danger inherent in his work was made for dramatic purposes, the bravado of a young male looking to impress a potential mate. She knew better now. *I can see why. You outnumbered her, out-massed her, and yet she still inflicted serious injuries on three of ours.* She paused. *The surface, Damir. It's... it's... it's better and more beautiful than I ever dreamed or dared hope.*

I know, he replied. *It's wonderful, isn't it? Fresh soil. Meat available in larger quantities than we harvest below ground. And though the air today is tainted with the scent of one of those damned icers, it's still far sweeter than the air we breathe on a regular basis.* He stomped one foreclaw upon the ground. *This land, the surface, this is rightfully ours, Eirene. We are the rulers of earth. The icers can have their sky and clouds and lakes full of poison. But they will not deprive us and our children of our land. We must fight, Eirene. We must!*

She felt the deep stirring of passion and pride. Damir wasn't the largest of their kind, and yet the strength and conviction of his words motivated even their most powerful brethren to action. Many already spoke of him as the obvious heir-apparent to Cato. *You're right, Damir. You're absolutely right. We must reclaim our rightful heritage.*

His grin, contagious as always, revealed his rows of sharp teeth. *And you'll help me and support me in that effort?*

She nodded, digging a claw into the earth and spreading the dirt upon a scale damaged by the spray of poisonous water kicked up by the dead icer. *I've pledged to be your lifelong mate, Damir, and proudly so. I will always support you. Always.*

* * *

Two months later.

Eirene yawned, the minor roar rumbling through the main tunnel used by fire dragons as they traveled between major living and social areas. She'd slept fitfully during the past two months, and the lack of sleep had taken its toll. Damir, ever thoughtful, did his best to comfort her, but his words did little to help. He'd correctly assessed that it was the memory of the trip to the surface that haunted her dreams.

But he didn't know what it was about those memories that so disturbed her.

Eirene nodded at the familiar faces she passed, exchanged friendly greetings with friends, stopping occasionally to relight the torches providing the only lighting in their underground domain. Each flickering torch and each shadow dancing along the rocky walls reminded her that their light was a pathetic replica of the glorious, brightly lit world above. The dull colors of the earth and rock seemed pale and lifeless now that she'd seen the radiant colors of the surface foliage and witnessed the sky when lit by the brilliant sun. She'd never noticed the stale, lifeless air she'd breathed her entire life, not until she'd tasted the sweet scent flowing freely all around in the world above. She'd mentioned this to Damir, the recognition that her senses were dulled here below. He'd frowned handsomely and told her it was common with new members of his Guard. They'd see the world above and, for a time, they'd hate their home, unable to avoid the comparisons and the realization that they lived in an inferior space. But after the first few water scars and frozen limbs in a battle with icers, they'd happily return to the dull off-duty safety of their homes. Eirene had nodded and admitted that it made sense. He'd repeated those statements that morning, following them up with the all-too-familiar question. They'd been pledged mates for nearly a year, now, and the fact that they'd yet to produce a clutch of eggs worried him. She'd told him again today that nothing had changed on that front, but that she expected that she'd soon be nesting and warming their burgundy red eggs—her color—with the deep brown spots—his color—and they'd need to start thinking of names for their children. He'd smiled at the idea and murmured a few name ideas, but apprehension remained on his face.

She wondered what his depths of worry might be if he learned of her current course of action. Their minor delays in producing a clutch of eggs would likely pale in comparison.

She'd left the common educational area after finishing her teaching shift. She'd taught young dragons how to produce fire, how to vary the levels of heat, and how to replenish fire they'd burned through their breathing. Fire wasn't inexhaustible, and it was important that they not waste flame on trivial matters to ensure they had it available in critical situations and emergences. When one of the young dragons mockingly asked if that meant ice dragon invasions, she'd answered in the affirmative, describing an icer attack in such graphic detail that two of the youngest dragons left her class shaking with fear, convinced they'd be encased in ice before reaching home.

She'd probably hear from parents about her response. But she felt it critical that young dragons know about and prepare for the greatest threats they'd face in lives that might stretch centuries. Those threats weren't formed of childhood pranks, but serious threats they might not yet understand. Ice dragons, whether they thought them real or imaginary, were a perfect metaphor for a lesson on the importance of preparedness and alertness over complacency and idleness.

And yes, she'd tell them, ice dragons *were* real.

She slid unnoticed into a side tunnel filled with the webs of spiders likely long dead, a tunnel so long unused that it lacked the familiar torches mounted on the walls of every other tunnel and cave within their underground domain. She'd passed the unused spur a week earlier and had found herself intoxicated by the faint scent emanating forth. It was the scent of fresh surface air, a scent she'd longed to revisit somewhere other than her dreams. The allure of the surface, and what she'd hoped to find on her return, forced her into action.

She used her flame sparingly, breathing thin wisps of fire that consumed the sticky webs decorating the walls, using the burning strands as light to guide her passage upward. She didn't fear any living creature she might find here—fire breathing dragons coated with thick scales didn't fear anything living at these depths—but she did need to avoid any missteps and the resulting torn muscles or chipped scales, injuries she'd find difficult to explain to a mate wondering exactly what and how she'd taught her students that she'd come home injured.

Perhaps her honest answer about icers earlier would be the truth he'd need to hear to derive an answer that suited both of them.

The pull of the surface had its own gravity, a force that grew with each step and each change in elevation. She'd move her foreclaws first, stabilize her position with her midclaws, and then push her body forward with her hind legs, claws clamped to clumps of dirt and rock when not in motion. The six limbs were an efficient means of movement. Damir told her he'd once seen a sentient surface creature with only four legs; more curiously, the creature moved about balanced upon only its hind legs. She'd scoffed at the idea, a notion foolish beyond compare, before remembering she'd once scoffed at the idea of the icers' existence.

After a careful hour of claw-straining movement, she reached the cave marking the end of the tunnel. The interior glowed faintly, lit by trace phosphorescence in the walls illuminated by the sunlight piercing the hidden interior. She'd one day attempt an understanding of how a fire dragon remained so high above the land and yet still kept a fire burning brightly for half of each day. Her more immediate interest was something else entirely.

She'd been deeply enthralled with all things about the surface since that first visit—the fresh air, the foliage, even the sound of the poisonous water rippling on the surface of the lake. But there was one thing she longed to see more than anything else.

She'd watched the ice dragon sweeping up out of the water and soaring through the air, spraying water upon her mate and his team, and had then watched her work to finish the execution of the much larger fire dragons. She'd failed, of course; Damir's cleverness and curious jumping ability had seen to that. But it also left Eirene realizing a terrible truth.

She found ice dragons beautiful.

The smooth, translucent skin, so bright a silver that it

seemed nearly transparent. The brilliant golden eyes. The powerful wings. And the courage displayed against overwhelming odds. It was that image, the admired image of the bitterest enemy of her kind that called to her from her dreams, and lured her once more to the surface. She wanted to see that beauty again, to fix the image firmly in her mind for all time. She did not care if the source of that image was male or female, young or old. She would seek out an ice dragon so as to witness that pure beauty one last time.

And then she'd return belowground and help her mate plot the destruction of a species that she alone among her kind found so beautiful, and wonder why neither the sense of wonder toward the icers, nor the desire for their complete destruction, seemed foreign.

She peered out upon the glorious coloring of the surface world. She saw the familiar lake, but from the opposite side. She squinted, spying the telltale markings of the official tunnel she'd used on her previous journey, an eternal journey away across a death trap. She stepped out of the cave, eyes and ears alert for signs of icers. She crept low along the ground as best a creature twenty-five feet long and massing several tons could. She felt the natural, pleasant warmth of the fire in the sky along with the frightening chill of the breeze brushing over her scales. She moved closer to the lake, trembling as she went. She'd subtly asked why the deceased icer spent time in the water, and learned they generated their horrible, frosty breath only through continual absorption of pure water. Their bodies chilled the raw material of water into that icy breath, much as her own body turned raw material into flame. The icer had used up its moisture and had risked landing in the shallowest regions of the lake to drink and refuel the depleted moisture stores in her body. That knowledge provided the information she needed. The lake was both her greatest personal risk here—outside an ambush by a dozen angry icers—and also acted as the beacon calling icers to her. She accepted the risk inherent in her plan as it provided her best chance to see the beautiful dragons one last time, before she emerged in a more official capacity as a member of Damir's fighting force emerging to reclaim the surface world at some future date.

She moved as close to the lake as she dared before sinking into the comforting embrace of the soil and the silky grasses swaying in the breeze. Then she waited. She knew word of the dead icer had reached the clouds by now. They'd know the fire breathers were here, and thus they'd land elsewhere, at least in Damir's experience. Only a desperate, dehydrated icer would risk landing here now. Damir's Guard knew that; they'd not bother posting sentries here. She gambled that it also meant she'd only deal with one enemy dragon at a time. The odds were high she'd see nothing and return to her home unfulfilled.

She waited. Her eyes flitted about, left and right, looking at the small, furry creatures skittering to and fro. They seemed not to notice her, as though the massive carnivore crouching in the grass were invisible. She longed to snap up a few of the foolish creatures, enjoying a small snack of the freshest and tastiest meat she'd eat for quite some time, until Damir's future surface invasion completed and she had free reign of this land. For now, though, she avoided that temptation.

A sound to her left caught her attention, and she snapped her head to the side.

The sight took her breath away.

It was a male this time, one slightly larger than the female executed by the Guard a few weeks earlier. The image was a near perfect match for the dead icer she'd seen before. Silvery, smooth, nearly transparent skin, an undulating and graceful body, and radiant, golden eyes. The magnificent wings bloomed around the creature's body as it settled into a hovering pattern just off the ground, not daring to touch the soil. Eirene watched as he looked around, visibly sniffing the air for threats, the golden eyes scouring the surface for the fire dragons it suspected were hidden nearby.

Like her.

Eirene dropped lower toward the ground but didn't take her eyes off him, etching her mind with every line and color variation in a desperate effort to brand the image forever inside her. A small furry creature brushed by her mouth, and she instinctively snapped it up, adding the savory taste of meat and blood to the blissful image before her.

That joy didn't last.

The icer heard the rustling grass and her snapping jaws. It bounced backward, something she'd thought impossible for an airborne creature, and craned its magnificent head in the direction of the noise. The wing muscles tensed and flexed as the creature prepared to burst high above the ground at the discovery of the threat. The golden eyes turned fierce, and it showed its mouthful of sharp teeth, trying to frighten the would-be threat.

She sucked in her breath. He was magnificent, the perfect image of pure beauty.

The golden eyes snapped toward her as he rose a bit higher,

hovering a dozen feet off the ground. She stood up, rising to her own full height, never taking her eyes from him.

As an afterthought she bared her teeth in his direction, trying to preemptively prevent any insulting accusations of fear he might lob her way.

The handsome face frowned and he dropped closer to the surface. *You are not one of them. Why are you here?*

Them? I am not one of whom?

Them. The killers. The murderers who slaughtered my sister and smashed the eggs she carried. You are not one of them.

I am a dragon of the fire, ice breather! Eirene snapped her words at him with force, and he bounced back, startled. *It is the nature of my kind to kill those from the air, for failure to do so—*

Will one day result in our own deaths at the claws of those left alive. He blinked at her, twice, and she realized that the ice dragons feared for their safety while in the proximity of her kind as fire dragons feared for their survival around icers. Both species preached similar phrases relating to personal safety and longevity. *None of this excuses the wanton slaughter of a single pregnant female. I will have my revenge!*

She let out a small puff of flame. *Any whom you might target in your thirst for revenge are my kin and brethren, icer. I will not allow it.*

He snorted, and she watched the mesmerizing frost engulf his head, watched as the golden eyes and handsome head reappeared as the smoky mist dissipated. Why did she find these images so beautiful, when the very sight of him ought to drive her mad with blood lust and rage?

He dove at her, launching a torrent of icy breath toward

her. Instinct took over. Eirene rolled to the side, whipping her long tail behind her so that she returned to her feet facing toward the water. He'd climbed high into the sky, and she briefly thought he'd decided that attacking her was pointless, that he'd chosen survival over his stated goal of revenge.

His ascent halted, and as he plunged back toward the lake she recognized his intent. She ran, turning away from the lake as she moved, and then sprinted at her top speed away from the water and toward the tunnel entrance. She thought better of that plan and veered right, heading away from the mouth of the cave and the tunnel leading to her home. She'd not give away an entrance to the underworld to him.

She winced as the water droplets hit the last few feet of her tail. She'd moved far enough away that the major wave he'd unleashed fell harmlessly upon the soil, but even the minor contact with moisture hurt. She whirled again, simultaneously roaring flame at his ascending form and dredging her tail into the soothing earth.

Her flames missed. He flew higher, then returned toward the surface. She crouched lower, fangs bared. Their dueling instincts demanded a fight to the death. She felt that internal compulsion, a genetic demand that she charge and belch forth the flame that would destroy him.

She held still, waiting for him to soar once more into the air before launching another high speed aerial assault.

But he remained still, staring at her instead.

She puffed out another wafting bit of smoke, taunting him, trying to get him to move first. Cool mist formed around his head; he, too, wanted to react.

Eirene found herself confused. Was he resisting instinct as well?

The ice dragon cocked his head. *Why do you not attack me?*

She snorted a small bit of flame. *I wondered the same of you.*

I... I did not attack because... he paused. *I did not want to.*

She blinked several times. *I did not wish to attack you, either. I had always been taught that icers are horrible, ugly creatures, the epitome of evil and deserving of death.*

He nodded slowly. *But... you do not think I am a horrible creature?*

I do not know, she admitted.

You do not think I deserve death?

Not today, Eirene responded. *But I reserve the right to change my mind if you attack me.*

His wings twitched and he floated closer. *You... do not think me ugly?*

She hesitated before opting for honesty. *No, I do not.*

He moved closer once more, hesitant, eyes blinking rapidly. She wondered if he just now recognized the size differential, that her fire would easily reach and cook him should she elect an attack. He was larger than most icers and she was smaller than most fire dragons, but she still outmassed him by a considerable margin. *I have been taught the same, that the demons of the underworld are the source of all evil and ugliness in the world, deserving of death for the crime of existence. When I learned of my sister's death, I found those statements confirmed. And yet...*

Eirene found herself smiling. *And yet you do not find me evil or ugly or deserving of death.*

No, he replied. *I do not find you any of those things. In fact...*

He paused. *In fact, I find you… oddly beautiful. How is it that I, one of the mighty Jokul, would find the spawn of Misae an object of beauty?*

This is impossible, she thought in reply. *Our kind have been at war, driven to kill by instinct bred by millennia of hostilities. Why is it that neither of us feels that compulsion to kill the other?*

Perhaps, he replied, *it is because we each see the beauty in the other, rather than the ugliness.*

He moved closer to her, until they were nearly touching.

Eirene smiled at the contact.

* * *

Two months later.

Damir stirred from his sleep and stretched, noting the pleasant sensation of Eirene nestled next to him. She remained asleep, a contented smile upon her face, the look of one experiencing a pleasant dream. The mating pledge had come over a year earlier, the oath a lifetime commitment of fidelity, and thus one not undertaken lightly given the potential lifespans of dragonkind. Eirene was intelligent, courageous, and possessed of a wicked sense of humor, all qualities he found admirable. She understood his work, recognized the importance of what he did, and offered her support through her teaching and public statements to friends and colleagues.

She was his ideal mate in every way.

He felt her awaken and begin stirring next to him. *Good morning, my love.*

A good morning to you as well. She paused. *Why do we call it morning when we do not see the sun of the day or the stars of night?*

You will see the sun again soon, he replied. *We shall reclaim the surface land which is rightfully ours.*

I look forward to that day, she replied, fixing him with a blissful gaze.

He cocked his head. *What makes you smile like that?*

Her mouth broadened into a toothy smile. *I have good news, Damir. It is the news you have longed to hear since the day of our mating pledge.*

He sprang to his feet. *Truly? You feel the eggs of our first clutch growing inside you?*

She nodded her head. *I do.*

Damir's smile nearly lit the darkened cave, and Eirene wondered if that glow meant they'd never use the torches in their nest ever again.

* * *

One year later.

Damir's claws clutched the soil of the tunnel more tightly than usual, helping him move along at a faster pace than generally accepted. Friends and colleagues smiled, understanding the likely cause of the urgency, while strangers and foes scowled at the impolite behavior. He'd completed his latest shift with the Guard, gleefully slaying another pair of icers. But his thoughts remained with Eirene. Her primary gestation period should end this day, meaning that she'd deliver from her body the eggs with their future children inside. Within two weeks, those young dragons would crack open the deep red shells mottled with brown spots, and friends would comment about how their coloring more closely matched one parent or the other. The thought spurred him to an even greater, more reckless speed as he moved through one spur after another in the pursuit of their shared nest.

He wanted to touch the shells, to put his physical imprint there, to let his children sense his presence. He heard and felt the small rumbles behind him, generated by two close friends and members of the Guard, who'd insisted upon joining him to offer their congratulations to Eirene as she prepared for two weeks of nest-sitting with her eggs.

Damir reached the isolated nest he shared with Eirene, a small, cozy cave above the major nesting and communal areas. Wait here, he told his friends. *I'll first ensure that visitors are welcome.*

Damir moved through the mouth into the darkened cave. *Eirene?*

He heard her scurrying. *Stay away, Damir. It's… it's best you stay away.*

Why are the torches extinguished, Eirene? He felt a small sliver of panic. *Why did you not relight them?*

Go away, Damir. Her tone was fearful, pleading. *Please. You must trust me on this.*

His panic grew. *No, Eirene. You are my pledged mate. Whatever troubles you is my burden to share.*

He blew a small bit of flame, helping him locate the torches lining the walls in the nest they called home. He caught sight of the first torch with the brief burst of light, but also saw Eirene's panicked face. He blew forth his flame, lighting the torch, and used the growing light to bring flame to each additional torch.

He finally turned toward Eirene. Her face remained taut with fear, with worry, with apprehension. Had something gone wrong? Had the eggs not yet arrived? He had heard horror stories of delivered eggs that were misshapen and deformed, the young dragons inside dead before ever breathing their first bit of air. Had such an evil befallen them? Were Eirene's words of warning her effort to spare him a grief she'd already felt?

He caught a glimpse of a shell sheltered and warmed by her body. He saw just the top, and saw in that sliver of egg shell Eirene's deep red coloring. He could not see the rest, though. *Eirene? What's wrong? I want to see the eggs. I want to see our children.*

Please leave, Damir.

He felt the anger rise. *Move, Eirene. What are you hiding from me?*

Her eyes rested upon him, somber, sad, as if she'd rather not answer that question. But at long last, resigned to the inevitable, she rose to her feet and stepped aside, revealing what she'd rested upon.

Damir glanced at the sight, and felt the color drain from his scales. The sight horrified him to his core. He stared at his mate, horrified. *No. Eirene. How can this be?*

I'm so sorry, Damir. I… I don't know what happened. I…

But Damir knew, knew exactly the meaning of the sight before him. He moved to the mouth of the cave and spoke to his long-time friend, Cort. *Go and fetch Cato immediately. Makoto, remain here until Cato arrives. We will need his advice and judgment here.*

Cort stared at his leader. He'd expected a jubilant emergence and an invitation inside to offer his congratulations to the mother-to-be. Instead, Damir looked traumatized. *Damir? What's wrong? Why do we need Cato's assistance? Why do you send me away, rather than inviting me inside? I have not come to run errands, but to see the eggs of your first clutch!*

Damir shook his head. *You do not want to see, Cort. Please. Trust me on this. I only wish I could un-see what has already scarred my eyes.*

* * *

The ancient dragon arrived, preceded by the messenger Cort. The younger dragon stepped aside, and Cato moved into the nesting area. His eyes took in everything in an instant, and it took a mere moment before he expressed his reaction and initial thoughts through his eyes. He gazed upon Damir with sympathy and frowned at Eirene. He turned his attention to the Guard leader. *Bring Cort and Makoto in, Damir. They know something has happened. We must... educate them.*

Educate them? There is no education required here, Cato. The evidence is plain.

Cato turned his gaze upon the younger dragon. *Is that evidence what you'd like explained to the rest of our kind?*

Damir paused. *You're right, Cato. I understand. This... this is not something I'd like publicized.*

Cato nodded, his eyes once more sympathetic.

Cort and Makoto joined them. Their telepathic gasps filled the nesting area as they looked upon the egg there before turning withering gazes upon Eirene.

Cato spoke, projecting his thoughts to all present in the nest. *The mating bond is our strongest, deepest tradition. It must be an oath inviolable by anyone. Infidelity cannot be tolerated. Our offspring, through the coloring of the eggs in which they grow before final hatching, provide us with irrefutable evidence of such violations.* His eyes filled with sadness. *That is the unfortunate case here.*

He glanced at the egg, the egg colored with the deep red of Eirene the mother. But Damir's deep brown color, which one expected to find in the spots mottling the egg's surface, was nowhere to be found.

Instead, thin streaks of a nearly transparent silver marred the shell.

I urge you, Cort, and you, Makoto, to avoid any public recounting of the evidence and conversation here. I have brought you into the nesting area so that the two of you, and only the two of you, may understand the true nature of the grief Damir will endure for some time to come. Let me repeat and implore you: do not speak to others of what you've witnessed here today. Is that clear?

The younger dragons nodded, delivering looks of deepest sympathy to the leader once more.

Cato nodded before continuing. *The punishment for this heinous crime will effectively hide for all eternity the evidence of that crime, but our memories are eternal. You must each listen carefully, and that includes you, Damir.*

The brown dragon blinked before recognizing Cato's words and nodding his assent.

Cato resumed. *Our story is this. In the final days before laying the eggs of her first clutch, Eirene, fearful for the safety of her future children after hearing about the horrors on the surface and the threat posed by the ice dragons, decided to take action into her own claws. She decided that she must fight, just like her mate Damir. She found a hidden tunnel near her nest, one unused for centuries, and followed that tunnel to the surface. She emerged and looked for ice dragons, feeling a deep need to spill their blood as a means of protecting those future children. Sadly, she got her wish. She found icers, a dozen of them, and though she fought gallantly, they killed her and crushed the eggs she carried. Damir, puzzled at finding his nest empty rather than finding a nesting Eirene, searched for her. He found her trail and arrived at the surface just as the fatal blow fell upon his beloved. Enraged, he destroyed those who'd murdered his mate.*

Cato paused. *This story will strengthen your position among our kind, Damir. The loss of your mate and her clutch of eggs represent the deepest and most personal of all potential losses. The fact that those came at the claws of the icers will further fuel your rage at our eternal enemies, and will hasten your desire to wage direct warfare for control of the surface. Your ability to destroy a dozen icers without assistance will prove you an even greater leader than previously believed, and provide hope that we can overcome any odds or obstacles in our fight. Cato faced Cort and Makoto. The story of Eirene's demise makes her a martyr to that cause, rather than one caught in violation of our most sacred oath, and thus precludes any shame others may direct at her mate.*

Damir's face made clear he'd listened to little of Cato's speech. Instead, her turned and faced Eirene. *Why? Who? When?*

Eirene said nothing.

Damir moved closer. *I must know, Eirene. Infidelity is not an individual act. One of my brethren, one who knew of our mating bond, has dishonored me. I will have his name, Eirene. And then I will have my vengeance.*

But she remained silent, meeting his fiery gaze with cool determination.

Cato moved between them. *We will uncover the identity of the father in due course, Damir. For now, though, we must carry out Eirene's sentence. Makoto, if you will, fetch and carry the egg in question. Follow me, all of you. Damir, I suggest you follow Eirene to ensure that she moves to our destination and makes no effort to escape her punishment.*

Eirene's eyes flicked toward Cato, as if she wanted to ask the nature of the punishment. Instead, she remained silent.

They emerged from the nest, with somber faces and awkward telepathic silence. Cato led the way, followed by Eirene, Makoto, Damir, and Cort. The ancient dragon proved portions of his story true, clawing through a thin wall hiding an old tunnel long abandoned. He lit torches as they moved, slowly, silently, and obviously upward. It took an hour, but the caravan finally reached the cave at the tunnel's termination point. The bright sunlight of the surface lit the cave, and the silvery streaks marring the otherwise perfect egg glowed, taunting all of them, making clear the crime committed here. A lake, one of similar size and coloring and surrounding vegetation as the one Eirene had visited with group just over a year before, rippled in the light breeze outside. The poison water shimmered in the sunlight, frightening each of them in turn. The nearest edge of the lake stood a mere dozen yards from where they gathered. Eirene's eyes surveyed the surface—the water, the blue sky, the greenery—with something approaching reverence.

Makoto set the egg before Cato.

Eirene! Cato's projected thought gathered the attention of the assembled fire dragons. *I find you guilty of violating the sacred oath of the mating ceremony, producing from an illicit and unauthorized union an egg bearing the mark of your fellow conspirator. That egg, the evidence and memory of your crime, is evil. It must therefore suffer its own ultimate punishment.*

With a speed that seemed impossible, the ancient dragon brushed the back side of his foreclaw against the egg, sending it hurtling out of the cave and through the air. The egg landed in the lake full of rippling, poisonous water.

The egg slowly began sinking below the water's surface.

No! Eirene's mental scream of anguish cut through all of them, her grief at the loss of her only surviving egg a staggering emotional blow. She burst from the cave and raced to the edge of the lake, stopping as near the water as she dared, trying, in vain, to stretch one claw out far enough to scoop her egg, her child, from its slow death.

Cato moved to the mouth of the cave. *Our kind cannot tolerate those who violate their oaths. Your punishment for this crime, Eirene, is banishment. You are hereby forbidden to return to the underground world of the fire dragons. Your survival will depend solely upon your wit, your cunning, and your resourcefulness... and, perhaps, your ability to integrate into the world of the icers. Let me be quite clear. Should word reach me that you have returned—after your reported death, mind you—then I will personally carry out the death sentence.*

Eirene seemed not to hear, so deep was her grief. The top of the egg, the last part visible, slipped beneath the surface of the lake. Eirene lay down in the long grass surrounding the shore, her despair so deep it seemed she'd never move from the spot, waiting until death in some form claimed her.

The dragons in the cave stood there for a moment before Cato spoke. *Cort, Makoto, you are dismissed. I have matters of importance to discuss with Damir.*

Still stunned at the events of the day, the Guard dragons turned and moved down the tunnel. Cort glanced over his shoulder, as if trying to read Damir's emotion, but the leader of the Guard betrayed nothing.

Cato and Damir stood in silence for several minutes.

Damir finally spoke. *She didn't violate her mating oath, Cato. Did she?*

She did not, Damir. The old dragon sighed. *If she'd succeeded in keeping you away until after the hatching, we might never have found ourselves trying to deal with the obvious merging of her blood with one carrying the blood of the icers.*

Damir paused. *She tried to send me away, Cato. But I refused to heed her wishes. This, including my mate's banishment, is my fault.*

It is not your fault, Damir. You had no idea that this would happen, and acted as any dragon would act in your apparent circumstances. Alas, once you'd viewed the evidence, prudence required action on both your part and mine. I could not expose you, Damir. You are far too important to the future of our kind. Nor would I expose Eirene to the mobs who'd seek her out and attempt to inflict upon her whatever punishment they might consider appropriate. That is why I had to choose banishment.

The old dragon paused. *There is another reason. You had two witnesses who knew you were distressed by the sight of the egg, and they would, without any malicious intent, allow that news to reach the masses. In bringing them in as your inner circle on this matter, we've helped mitigate their potential desire to speak to those outside that inner circle. With Eirene vanished, they will soon forget or never realize that the egg's coloring was impossible in the mating of two purebred fire dragons.* Cato paused. *Your secret, though, would remain better hidden if you avoided leaping in an effort to catch your prey. Fire dragons are creatures of the land. We do not jump.*

Damir nodded once. He and Cato alone knew that his mother had been an ice dragon. Cato had rescued the discarded egg, left as a meal for the wild predators of the surface, and ensured that the newborn Damir had a home in an area set aside for the children of dragons killed before those children reached adulthood. He knew Cato manipulated events so his actual father had "adopted" the "orphan" Damir.

When the child reached physical maturity, Cato took him aside and revealed the truth of his origins. Damir learned through the story the importance of hiding his mixed parentage, while at the same time developing a raging hatred toward the species that rendered his mother unfit, who left an unhatched egg behind as a sacrifice to the larger predators of the surface.

Damir thought his secret permanently hidden. His own egg bore the marks of his paternal grandparents, both fire breathers, and thus masked the identity of his mother. He grew like any other fire child, eventually moving into the ranks of the Guard. He'd almost forgotten his unfortunate beginnings over the long intervening years until he'd seen the transparent coloring of icer blood in the egg. He knew he had to act, and brought in the ancient dragon for advice to ensure they enacted the best decision.

It meant he'd risked an unfortunate decision, and unfortunately the odds weren't working in his favor. He'd made peace with Cato's judgment, whatever it might be. He puffed a fiery sigh. *I will miss her, Cato. She was… perfect.*

Cato smiled faintly. *She will live, Damir. Let me remind of something critical: you know how to get here, and there's nothing to prevent you from establishing meeting dates and times. You may eventually feel pressure to take a mate not banished from our world for the sake of appearance, but I will publicly encourage a patient decision on that point.* He nodded. *She remains in possession of her personality, appearance, and, memories. She has always remained loyal to both the letter and spirit of the mating oath. There is no reason to consider that oath broken now. I suggest you go spend quality time with your mate.*

Cato turned and left, leaving a stunned, trembling Damir behind at the mouth of the cave, trying to understand the gift given him. A moment later, the projected words reached the old dragon. *Thank you, Cato.*

Cato shuffled down the tunnel toward his own nest. Damir and Eirene were by no means the first half-breeds—a mix of fire and icer blood—living among them. But they'd produced a problem he'd not yet experienced: a half-breed with egg coloring suggesting the eventual outward appearance of an icer. He'd no way of knowing if there were half-breeds living among the icers. But this child? This child, once hatched from the natural icer hatching zone in the water, would live among those who appeared to be his kind. Cato could use him, teaching the child leadership and persuasive projection techniques that would move him up the ranks like his father Damir.

He thought of the others, and he thought of the half-breed he'd only discovered this day.

Eirene.

She'd recognized the message of the egg's coloring and sought Cato out for guidance. He'd advised her to keep Damir away; if only Eirene and Cato knew, this dragon might pass through a similar upbringing as his father Damir. But she'd failed, unable to keep the truth from her mate when a lie would serve both far better. Eirene confessed to Cato the story of her second trip to the surface, of her meeting and long conversation with the ice dragon, a meeting in which they'd done nothing but talk in violation of all rules of nature. Her resistance levels toward attacking all icers, her overpowering attraction to the ice dragon form, meant that she, too, was a half-breed, one Cato himself hadn't previously identified. When he'd made that connection, he realized that Eirene's nesting efforts were preventing a very icer child from full growth. The egg needed hydration. In batting the egg into the lake, he'd enacted in the eyes of Cort and Makoto a harsh penalty, one they'd recognized as in their future if they talked.

The old dragon reached his own nest and ducked inside. He moved to the far wall, and, after looking over his shoulder to ensure no one had followed, he scratched away a loose pile of earth near the ground. He stared at the deep red egg, mottled with dark brown spots, and wondered when Eirene would confess to Damir that she'd laid two eggs, one with the coloring they'd long expected, one she'd given over to Cato's care in anticipation of an assumed harsh punishment. He'd let her choose the time of those revelations. In the interim, though, he bore responsibility for this child's hatching and upbringing. Cato knew the path.

It was the same as the one his father had lived through over the past few decades.

Cato recovered the egg. He would have powerful half-breeds ready to fight in a few decades more, half-breeds ready and eager to fight, half-breeds who'd struggle to kill those who looked like a parent.

He smiled. That's when he'd reveal the true enemy, the one all dragons must unite against, the one all dragons must fear.

Humans.

A WORD FROM ALEX ALBRINCK

As a child, I read voraciously, focusing on tomes in the realms of science fiction, fantasy, and mystery, eventually expanding my scope into the thriller genre. I enjoyed the fantasy realm for the ability to use magic systems and fantastic creatures as a means of exploring the human condition, and while I started my writing career more deeply focused in the science fiction realm, I knew I'd write pure fantasy stories. Over time, my interest in the fantasy realm evolved, my preference moving away from magic-wielding humans to magical creatures.

My favorite magical creatures, as you might guess, were dragons.

Dragons seem to represent the epitome of natural existence, creatures typically depicted as possessors of great wisdom, lifespan, and power. Conflict in dragon stories often came in the form of dragons finding their place in a modern, human-dominated world, or perhaps engaging in territorial wars. Creatures of such immense power—*They can fly! They can breathe fire!*—are a natural fit for stories of huge wars and massive conflicts.

I chose to use those common themes as a backdrop for what amounted to a love story, an effort for two dragons to learn their own truths of existence. "Transparency", the title, most directly referred to their efforts to speak and find truth when faced with difficult choices. Eirene knew life would be far simpler if she pushed her mate aside for just a short time, until the physical evidence of her apparent infidelity to Damir no longer existed. And yet her love kept her from engaging in a lie, even one meant to spare him deep pain. Instead, his secret, encoded in the form of the clear, transparent coloring of the eggshell stripes, was laid bare for all who knew where to look.

Cato, the wise old dragon, is ironically the one least capable of transparency. He sets the young couple up to live hidden lives, doesn't tell Damir that Eirene, too, is a half-breed, and doesn't tell *her* that either. He doesn't tell Damir that his mate laid two eggs, and he certainly hasn't told another dragon soul of his true target in the impending war for the surface.

The writing experience was both enjoyable and challenging, giving me the chance to write on a topic—dragons—I've always loved, but also requiring that I invent from scratch an entire mythology. Two sub-species of dragons, the nature and cause of the eternal conflict between them, and the impending battle that will unite the dragons in a war for planetary supremacy against humans. At the moment, for purposes of full transparency, it's the only story I've written in this universe.

But I suspect that will change in the not-too-distant future.

www.alexalbrinck.com

Sacrifice
by David Adams

Fifty years before the destruction of Atikala
and the events of Ren of Atikala

"I'M HERE," I REASSURED my mate, Ophiliana the Gold-heart, my voice the gentle thunder in the distance; it echoed around the vast, underground limestone cavern that was our shared home. The sound bounced off water and stone, reverberating and distorting, as though a thousand voices spoke with me, punctuating their whispers with drips of water from the ceiling. "The egg has nearly emerged. Be ready to push again."

The pain of the laying was etched on her face. Rarely did males see such things; this was female's work, the labour squarely planted on her back. All I could do was give food, water, a reassuring touch.

Despite tradition and both our instincts urging me away, I stayed. We had tried so many times, and this time could be the time; I had to be here for her.

Pain should be shared.

"I am right here," I said again. Her foreclaw squeezed mine with a grip that was iron. I squeezed back. "With you, beside you, always. We shall endure this together."

The cave was dark, darker than it had to be. Dim magical lights floated all around but they were barely as bright as candles; rainbow hues reflected off the water, bouncing all around the cave in a coalescence of light that was as subtle as it was deceptive.

Light would reveal the truth. Neither of us truly wanted to see.

Ophiliana's face contorted and she whined like stressed metal. Her hindquarters twitched and undulated, ripples running across her scales. She gave a tortured groan, shimmering eyes half lidded, her claws tearing lines out of the stone beneath her. There must be a thousand such gouges by now, carved out over the centuries, new ones created every birthing.

And then it ended. Just as it always had. She rested, breathing through her nose, the product of her labours cupped by her tail. A thin shelled egg, the size of a dog, slick with golden blood. It lay on a pile of coins we had set aside for it. All dragons needed a hoard, even hatchlings.

Her eyes, full of worry and pain—the pain that hurt the heart, not the flesh—sought mine. I struggled to avoid them, staring at the egg, imagining its insides. A golden dragon, scales purest metal, a daughter or a son for us both; joy from pain, life from a score of failures, the first success in centuries of trying. It had to be.

"Contremulus," she said, the words a gentle croak. "Please. Check it for me."

Hope and hopelessness. This egg seemed like the others; an opalescent sheen over semi-translucent metal, a dragon's egg to be sure. But was it viable? Time would reveal all.

"Can't we wait?" I said, finally looking at her. "Do we have to find out right away?"

"I could not bear it," she said, in a tone that cracked my heart. "I must know."

The flickers of magical light soared throughout the cave, my mental command stoking them and bringing illumination. The rainbow pattern became a flood, a barrage of light into our home that exalted the creation of this new life. I threw everything into it, forcing the glow to be as fiery white as Drathari's sun itself, penetrating the shell of the egg from all sides.

I cupped it in both of my foreclaws, Ophiliana doing the same. We watched the tiny thing within—and it was such a tiny creature, barely a foot long, suspended in a floating golden fluid—and we waited for signs of movement within.

And we waited.

"I am sorry," I said, the words strained with the effort of their telling. "It is my fault."

"It is *nobody's* fault," said Ophiliana, leaning against me. I draped my wing across her body, drawing her close. "Not yours, not mine. None save the Gods, choosing to abandon us in our moments of need."

Before the Godsdeath we had the power. Dragons commanded the arcane and the divine equally. We could have raised the eggs to life. Such things were not unusual for our kind, especially not those who had magic and motivation. I had both.

Ophiliana was the better fighter. I was the better spellcaster. We were, however, both dragons; magic and muscle in one package, wings that could block out the sun, flame that could burn a horse to the bone, eyes as sharp as eagle's.

Eyes that cried tears the size of a man's head.

To me, this was the greatest evidence of all that the Gods were not missing, not absent, but truly dead. Always had our deities been kind to mortals—and dragons, although nearly timeless and mightier than whole armies, were mortal too— but now tragedies piled up on us, too many to count. Crops wilted and died. Men died of treatable wounds. The magic of the druids could no longer regrow the forests so logging shrank them by the day. Resources became scarce. Blood was shed on every continent; in war, in grief, and in offering.

"My Lord?" Dorydd the dwarf, one of my servants, knelt by the entrance to the chamber. She was barely a child but served us very well. How long had she been there? "How can I help you?"

She knew. Of course she knew. A wave of rage flashed through me—how dare this dwarf intrude on this most private of time?—but logic told me Dorydd may have been there for a long time; I had been so focused the outside world passed by unnoticed. A human would have revealed themselves during the hours of labour, but dwarves were calm and slow as stone; yet patience that paled in comparison to a dragon's, who could wait for a world to grow and die.

"Thank you," I managed, "but nothing can be done. Prepare the fluid; we will preserve this one as we have the others.

When the Gods return, we shall return our child to life, as we have the others."

Ophiliana did not approve. I could sense it in her breathing, her heartbeat, the faintest shift of her body; no human could have ever sensed this, but I saw it as clearly as a lit torch at midnight.

"As you wish, My Lord," said Dorydd. She dipped her forehead to the stone and left. I watched her go, hearing her retreating footsteps echo as they moved up and toward the upper chambers.

"I should hunt," I said, a lie if ever I had told one. "You will need to regain your strength."

Ophiliana nestled in against me, curling her neck against mine. "Can you not?" she asked, her voice quiet. "Lady Dorydd can bring us some of those dwarven sweet cakes. I do not need meat. I need you."

How I wanted to help her, and how I knew she spoke the truth. What *I* needed, though, was to be alone for a time.

I said nothing and simply waited.

Dorydd returned, towing a cart covered in cushions and pillows. She gathered the coins, careful not to miss a single one. Then she wiped the egg down with a handcloth, cleaning away my mate's golden blood. As Dorydd loaded the egg into the cart she looked as I felt; pained to the core, saddened, drained.

"The alchemical solution is prepared," she said. "I have seen to it." Dorydd folded the cloth and laid it over the dead egg and then, hesitating as though fearful she was speaking out of turn, addressed Ophiliana. "Do not lose hope, My Lady. These things happen. My mother struggled to conceive for years before my older brothers arrived; just as she had considered all to be lost after a decade of trying…twins. Then two more sons. Then I, and I was not the last of her children."

I appreciated her attempt to comfort us but her words grated on me. The struggles of dwarves bored me.

"Thank you," said Ophiliana, dipping her head respectfully. "I am grateful to you for sharing this story with me, Lady Dorydd. I hope, when your own time arrives, you are more fortunate than your mother and I."

Dorydd's features twisted, fighting to suppress some deeply hidden emotion. "Thank you," was all she said, and then she gripped the handles of the cart and began pulling it out of our sleeping chamber.

"I will walk with you," I said. "I want to see the embalming."

Ophiliana touched my side, eyes glinting in the dark. "Must you?"

A simple question difficult to answer. "Our loss is not final," I said. "The Gods will return, and each of these children will live again. They are simply…sleeping."

Once again she nestled in against me; I resisted, pulling my head away. "Death is not to be feared," said Ophiliana. "We live and we die; as will our children, a thousand years hence or tomorrow. It is the fate of all to eventually die." Her voice wavered. "Where is the Contremulus who understood this simple truth? The outside world is a sea of suffering and pain, why must you invite such darkness into your heart as well?"

Lose, grieve, and then turn your eyes to the future. Nostalgia is a craving that can never be satisfied. Wisdom of the Wyrmmaker, patron deity of dragonkind.

My servants did not approve. My mate did not approve.

The teachings of the divine, and the wisdom of dragons passed down through the eons all told me that embalming the failed eggs was an unhealthy practice, and the murmurs of my conscience knew it too.

That voice was mostly a whisper now.

"We could…try reanimation."

If I had suggested she eat her own dung her expression could not be more revolted. "No," she said, her tone mortified. "Contremulus, no. *No.*"

"But we could see them. Talk to them. They would have life, of a sort."

She was silent for a moment. "You are not the only dragon to suggest such things. When my father..." She struggled to say the words, her face tightening. "Died, my mother thought as you did. Eventually a priest dissuaded her. A human. He explained it thusly; the undead are not truly alive. They have the faces of the living and are made from the same flesh, but that is superficial." Her eyes defocused, half closing. "They are whole in the same way a corpse blended up and sculpted into the shape of a man is a man. All the pieces are there but something is fundamentally wrong. That is no way for your children to live."

Every word was true. "I know." Admitting it hurt me.

"Promise me you will never attempt this." Her voice was steel, hard as anything I'd ever heard. *"Promise me."*

"I would promise you the sun and the stars, had I the power."

"Yet you do not. You *can* give me this." She extended a claw, gripping my foreleg. "I want you to say it."

The words were stones in my lungs, struggling to prevent

their escape. "I promise you," I said, the words slipping between my clenched lips. "I promise you this and more."

That seemed to satisfy her. The tension flowed out of her. "Do not go," she said. "Stay here with me."

I wanted to obey but could not. "I will not be long," I promised.

"As you wish," Ophiliana said, kissing my neck. "Know that I love you."

"And I you," I said.

Although I left the chamber with Dorydd I did not go far before an irresistible urge overtook me. Without offering explanation of any sort I turned away from the embalming pools and, instead, made my way towards the twisting, winding cavern that lead toward the surface.

I needed to fly.

* * *

Higher.

The world dropped away below me as my wings beat, carrying me up into the air, up past the trees and the mountains. Up past the lowest clouds that clung to the tips of the highest mountains, up into the ink black night sky. Up into frigid clouds to be buffeted by their winds; to be bruised and tossed, to struggle against nature itself.

Higher. The world was full of such disappointments. Such deep and personal failures. I needed to get away from it all; away from the shame, the anger, the pain.

I had never climbed so high. My wings ached, my breath

came in huge white clouds of mist. The howling chill of the thin air wormed its way between my scales, touching flesh, stealing the heat from my body.

Mountains were flat against the ground. Trees were splotches of green, the towns and cities of the Crown of the World tiny dots of light against the grey snow of the north. Human villages and towns and cities, their feeble lights trying to keep the dark at bay. Night fog rolled in, swallowing Drathari in a blanket of grey.

Dark thoughts swirled in my head. Humans. They had spread across the surface of our world, a rot that slowly corrupted everything they touched. They cut the trees, they mined the hills, they fished the lakes. They took and took and never gave, except when they thought they could gain.

The Wyrmmaker told us all to be kind to those who served us. But he was gone. What did it matter what some dead god told me?

Eventually I could climb no more. My wings beat against nothing; the air was empty, thin, frigid and dry. I had reached the very edge of Drathari, where nobody would see me or hear me.

I roared up into the nothing. Screamed. Painted the night sky with flame. I used my every breath, every ounce of air to vent my rage at the moon, hoping to burn it to cinders. It was my way of dealing with what had happened. The male way.

Females could cry, let their pain ease out like an overstuffed cushion. Their way was to share the load; loss was a wound to be treated with kindness, understanding, compassion.

Males expressed their grief differently but no less powerfully. We took in our pain, made it our fuel, burned it as energy for our journeys. In public we remained strong in the face of pain, suffering, and loss. Males were pillars of strength, giving of their power, but behind the facade of courage our hearts ached as much as any.

In public we wore our masks of stoicism. In private we raged into the dark.

My breath was exhausted, fury played out against the backdrop of the stars and sky. I could fly no longer and folded my aching wings, tumbling towards the ground, a trail of smoke in my wake. It seemed as though nothing below me moved; only tiny patches of cloud drifted apart, imperceptibly slow, as my speed grew and grew.

I plummeted through a blanket of cloud, tail fluttering behind me. Ice broke away from my body, falling as tiny scintillating spears, drifting away from me and finding their own path to the ground.

Perhaps I would follow them to oblivion. Dash my body on the frozen ground of the icy north below and be done with it. The idea nestled into my heart as quickly as it had appeared, and surrounded by a wall of grey nothing it took on a life of its own.

Ophiliana blamed herself for the stillborn eggs. Perhaps it was I that was at fault. Both parents contributed, after all. A stunted seed could not grow in even the most fertile soil.

Sometimes, when she looked at me, I sensed something in her eyes. A longing for another opportunity. I was not the only gold dragon in Drathari; many others, old and strong, would value her as their mate. After a few centuries of grief, she would move on.

She would find another.

She would find happiness.

It would be better if I was gone.

At least I would know what would happen to me. My body would be found, eventually, then carved up and sold to dragonbone collectors. My teeth would become enchanted weapons. My scales, armour for nobles. This was the fate of all our kind who were not preserved.

I burst from below the fog, expecting the shadowy darkness of a frozen land covered in night, but the surface twinkled with torchlight. A fiery river winding its way out of Northaven. Two thousand men or more, marching north, to the very edge of The Crown of the World.

To our lair.

The humans were coming for us.

My death would have to wait. I flared the tips of my wings, the strain pulling on exhausted muscles and tendons. I used my forelegs as brakes, extending them out, the limbs shaking as the frigid air buffed them.

I pulled up, only a few hundred feet from the ground, and I flew toward our home as fast as I could.

* * *

I flew into the wind, my wings aching, and I felt the fire grow in my belly once more; the warmth spread throughout my whole body, melting away the lingering ice.

I cast as I flew, flashes of magic lighting up the night. Arcane power flowed through me, reinforcing my scales, sharpening my claws. Preparations. I was good at them.

As I drew close, it was apparent that the approach of the human armies had not gone unnoticed. All of our servants stood by the cave entrance to our lair, armed and armoured. Even Dorydd had a halfling's sword.

Ophiliana was in human form; long blonde hair tumbled down her shoulders and her back, and she wore a fine suit of plate mail, her hands folded neatly in front of her.

She had no weapons. She needed none.

That told me she wanted to talk to the approaching army. I landed beside her, folded my wings and focused inward; my golden scales melted away and I shrank down, becoming a man.

Humans responded better to their own kind.

"What did you do?" she asked me, her tone curious and not accusatory. Her skin was pale and clammy, the wounds of the birthing unable to be hidden by shapeshifting magic. She should not be here.

"It wasn't me," I said. "The armies have been marching for some time." I lowered my voice to barely a whisper, leaning closer to her. "Are you strong enough to fight?"

"Let us hope it does not come to that," she said, a slight tremor in her voice. She kept her hands folded, eyes on the growling light on the horizon.

The torches of the human army approached, a snake of light worming its way between the frozen hills and mountains of the Crown of the World. We stood in the cold, letting the wind blow against us, waiting.

Horses approached. Four of them, mounted knights, lances glinting in the moonlight. As they rode towards us, Ophiliana clapped her hand over her nose and mouth as though she might be sick.

And then the stench hit me as well; rancid and black, like a rotting beast, half metal and half carrion, infused with dark magic. A dark taint carried on the wind.

Bane weapons, aligned to dragonkind.

These humans were not coming to talk.

I touched Ophiliana on the shoulder. "We should attack now," I said. "These are their leaders. Take the head off a snake and the body will wither."

"We must give them a chance," she said.

"Must we?"

"Always. It is right." Ophiliana stepped forward, her voice magically amplified. "Identify yourselves, men who come with flame and steel to these lands claimed by the Sunscale and the Goldheart."

The horses stopped, the weapons raised in parley, banners fluttering from the tips. The heraldry of Northaven. The City by the River.

My mate could see them as well as I, even in the dim light. This was merely diplomacy.

I had no patience for silly games.

The leader trotted his horse forward, hooves kicking up puffs of snow. "I am High Priest Praxis," said the man as he removed his helm, revealing pale skin. He had a lance in one hand, shield in the other, and an oversized two-handed sword strapped to his back. "Of the church of Tyranus. We ride from Northaven."

Tyranus. God of contracts and papers. Also one of sacrifices and binding. Long dead, like all the others. No friend to the Wyrmmaker, but hardly our enemies.

"State your purpose," said Ophiliana. "We have no quarrel with the Tyrantian church." A half-truth to placate those who had come to harm us. "We mean no harm to you."

"We have come for your heart."

At least they were honest about their intentions.

Ophiliana grimaced, her fingers intertwining. "Long have dragonkind been your allies," she said. "And protectors." She stressed it, rolling the word on her tongue. "If you turn on us, Wasp-Men may venture north and decide that you are easy pickings. Raiders will come across the sea. The elves—"

Praxis curled back his upper lip. "Your fearmongering does not scare me, worm in human's skin. The Wasp-Men are busy dealing with their slave rebellion. Raiders will be easily defeated with the gods on our side once more. Elves are flighty cowards, their eyes turned inward, focused on their own problems." The high priest looked at both of us, *through* us, as though we were steak. "Dragonkind have suffered the least in this Age of Betrayal. You have kept your magics, source of your power. It is beyond time you shared it with all of us."

I focused inward, bolstering my voice as well. "We have suffered too," I said, images of our ruined eggs flashing into my mind. "We lost our connections to the divine. Our suffering is shared."

"Spoken as lords to peasants, complaining that a plague's dead spoil the view of their lands. You know nothing of suffering, dragons."

Anger bubbled inside me, stoking the flames that cooked in my belly. "*You* know nothing, fleshling."

A tense silence fell, broken only by the howling wind and the occasional snort of one of the horses.

"Do not do this," said Ophiliana, the tremble returning to her tone. "Please."

Begging. Is that what we were reduced to? I clenched my teeth to keep fury spilling out.

Praxis pulled the reigns of his horse, turning it back towards his army. "It is already done," he said, and then he and his retinue rode away.

So it would be war. I stepped back, casually resting my hand on Dorydd's hand.

"Child," I said, my voice barely a whisper. "Return to the lair."

"My Lord, I would stay with you. I am sworn to your service."

This was no place for a dwarf so young she had to wield a weapon for a halfling. "You misunderstand," I said. "I am assigning you the most important task of all. Someone must protect the eggs."

Dorydd accepted the lie. Reluctance painted all over her face, she turned and left.

Ophiliana smiled her approval, although it was a gesture that concealed great pain. "I did my best," she said. "I did."

"I know."

Ophiliana rubbed her abdomen absently as the wind whipped her hair around. "I hope we do not have to kill too many of them."

"Unfortunately for High Priest Praxis," I said, inhaling through my nostrils, the air stoking the flames inside me. "I do not."

* * *

Arrows washed over me like rain, each wood and steel drop splattering against my scales and breaking. I clapped my wings together. The force of the air blew a group of archers off their feet, scattering their bows into the snow, and then I exhaled.

A cone of flame fell over them. They screamed with the terror of fleshlings exposed to raw fire; their screams faded abruptly as the fire stole the air all around them, seared their flesh to ash, and then they were still.

Another hail of arrows fell on me but these ones stung; their tips glowed a faint blue, magically enchanted. I tipped my left wing, spilling the air from it, arching over and falling toward the ground, avoiding the worst of them.

Anticipating this, the humans sent in the cavalry. A dozen men on horses, lances lowered. They galloped across the snow, shields raised to protect themselves.

Fools. I took wing again, a few feet off the ground, and my flame washed them away. The scent of roasting horseflesh stung my nostrils. From the smoke, a single rider burst through, her clothes aflame, lance lowered and aimed at my chest.

It bounced off and broke in half. It was not dragonbane.

I knocked the shattered shaft away with a foreclaw, snatched the rider off her mount with my tail, and squeezed. Her armour groaned as I crushed it, and with a snap, collapsed. Her body burst like an overripe fruit, gore painting the snow crimson.

A satisfying victory but distracting. I was too close to the ground. I needed to fly again. I beat my wings, dropping the bloody corpse to lighten my load.

A ballista bolt whistled as it flew past me, missing my scales by inches. The tip was forged of black metal; adamantium. Strong enough to pierce even my hide.

Another flew towards me. I could not afford to drop again. I prepared to accept the hit.

Ophiliana snatched it out of the air, her wings casting a shadow over the human army, and broke it in half, tossing both halves away. She bled from a dozen small wounds all over her body—the arrows had been effective, it seemed—but she seemed stronger than ever.

I climbed. A bolt of lightning, wizard's work, struck me in the gut. My muscles jerked and twitched as the energy ran through me and I lost altitude, gliding instead.

Pain.

"Find the wizard!" I roared, focusing inward, drawing upon arcane magic. A white cloud grew from my clawtips, a poisonous gas that floated towards the ground.

It drifted over human footmen. They fell, gasping, clutching at their throats, limbs spasming as their muscles tightened. No pity.

Ophiliana dove toward a group of soldiers, falling into them in a flurry of claws and teeth. She was a golden blur; her roar drowning out the battle cries of the fleshlings as she tore them to pieces, their steel as paper to her rending talons.

I flew over them, bathing the area in flame. It would not harm my mate, of course, but it intensified the misery of the humans whom Praxis seemed happy to send in waves to die. I saw the wizard, a tall elven man surrounded by a protective wall of foot soldiers, and adjusted my aim. He danced as he died.

One less threat to deal with.

Ophiliana took to the air once more. I banked, moving to fly alongside her, ready to attack again.

And then suddenly, agony in my left wing. I faltered, falling out of the sky, crashing heavily into the snow, throwing up a cloud of white powder.

A ballista bolt had broken my wing. Yellow bone protruded from my scales. I knew the limb was useless.

My main advantage was gone.

I yanked out the bolt with my teeth, spitting it on the ground. A line of pikemen ran towards me, dropping into a formation, shields raised. I breathed. The flame washed over them, but their wall of wood protected them. They emerged from the flames, shields alight, weapons thrusting at me.

I shifted back and cast, conjuring a line of acid from the tip of my claw. The pikemen, though, were well trained; they resumed their wall, and the fluid hissed as it met the hungry flames that clung to their shields.

A pike dug into my chest. Another hit my left foreclaw. A third nearly took my eye. I tried to cast again but the spell died on my lips as steel slipped beneath the scales of my throat. I slapped it away before it could kill me.

I was in trouble.

Ophiliana saw and plummeted towards me. She flared, bringing her dive to fifty feet above the ground; she clapped her broad wings together, inhaled, and the air around her rushed inward, heralding another gout of flame that would turn the tide.

A ballista bolt struck her in the back, turning her breath into a pained whimper. She fell out of the sky, limp, crashing to the ground with a thunderous rumble.

The humans exulted; a primal cry of triumph that almost drowned out my voice.

"Ophiliana!" I screamed her name over and over. "Ophiliana! Ophiliana!"

The pikemen dug their steel into me, pinning me to the snow, and heavy chains were thrown over my body; a heavy hammer broke my other wing, and my limbs were bound. I struggled. Thrashed. Tried to melt the iron with my flame; it resisted the heat, white-hot flames bending around the metal. A steel collar was latched around the top of my neck, keeping my head pinned. I couldn't move. The iron was too heavy. My wounds too great.

The humans had prepared.

Ophiliana crawled towards me, sobbing quietly, a golden trail of blood marking her path. The humans descended on her, throwing chain after chain over her body, each held by six men.

"Contremulus!" She shouted. "Teleport to Eastwatch! Save yourself!"

I could, and could not. Would not.

"I am here!" I screamed, fury and fire coming with my words. "With you, beside you, always! We shall endure this together!"

Heavy hammers broke her wings. The cries of her pain reverberated off the mountains.

Praxis dismounted. He walked towards Ophiliana, unstrapping the two-handed blade from his back. The scent of the dragonbane steel intensified and the weapon glowed with a fierce, inner light.

"Stop!" I commanded. "Praxis, stop this at once!"

They didn't. More chains were thrown over Ophiliana. A metal ring clamped her jaw closed. She struggled as I struggled.

Praxis, his face singed, stepped forward. He reverse-gripped the blade and climbed up on top of Ophiliana's blood soaked chest. He probed with the large weapon, ungainly, searching for the gaps in her scales.

"Stop!" I said again, this time unable to keep the panic, the knowledge of what they were about to do out of my voice. "Please!"

Praxis looked at me. Our eyes met. Some kind of communication took place there; mundane, non-magical. I did not want him to do this. In some way, he did not, either. His earlier fierceness, bluster, anger…it faded now that the moment was before him.

Praxis believed he had no choice.

"There are other ways," I said. "Other means. We can still fix this."

The blade's edge moved away and I found Ophiliana's eyes. She was at peace, smiling at me, her bright golden eyes full of quiet joy.

Praxis thrust the tip down into Ophiliana's chest. That light withered, waned, and died.

All things blurred. Became distant.

The humans cut out her five-chambered heart. They broke through her scales with picks, sawed through her bones, and removed it. It was the size of a horse. They laid it out on the blood-soaked ground as an offering to the sky.

Nothing happened.

They tried to burn the heart.

Nothing happened. Dragon's hearts could not burn.

In desperation, as the sun's light crept over the mountain-tops, the heart was cut into pieces and consumed. Dragonflesh could not be eaten by humans; they burst into flames, frenzied bonfires that danced to their deaths, reduced to ash.

Nothing.

Eventually, the humans went home. I barely watched them go. I could only stare at Ophiliana. Her lifeless, cold body frozen, the heat of her flame long since snuffed out.

I shapeshifted, became human. The chains were now far too large to hold me. I staggered, naked and bloodied, to her corpse. I touched her face with a human hand.

Despite it all, she was still smiling.

That was the first time I truly felt the absence of the gods. No divine being could ever allow something like this to happen.

I cried.

A dragon's cries are thunder on the landscape; deep, booming, a roar and a whimper together, deep and mournful and beautiful and terrible. Northaven, the city of the river, would hear my pain; they would know my agony, my loss, my suffering.

Grief and anger were parent and child. Ophiliana's death could not be final. Could not be. I would not accept it.

She had to be preserved.

Our servants—my servants now—crept out of the cave. They saw the devastation. They saw the body.

They knew what I was going to do.

* * *

I half-carried, half-dragged Ophiliana's body into the dark of the cave. The servants offered to help me, but they were far too small. She was my burden to bear.

Down, down into the cave, into Drathari's stone. I turned down the passage that led to the alchemy room, where Dorydd had taken the egg.

She stood there, shortsword in hand, and I offered no explanation for what had happened. My battered body, her butchered corpse, was all Dorydd needed to see.

The preservative fluid, an amber, viscous liquid obtained at vast cost from Valamar, was stored in a giant glass vat in the centre of the chamber. It was surrounded by smaller vats, almost all of them containing an egg. They were frozen and inert, kept from rot and decay, forever sleeping until the gods came to undo their horrible error.

Only the main storage vat would hold Ophiliana. I pried off the lid and, spilling only a little, I lowered my mate into the stuff. The amber enveloped her, wrapping her body in timelessness.

There she would stay until I could raise her.

The symbolism of this worked for me; a mother should live with her children, their father guarding over them.

But for how long? We had waited so long for the divinities to return. A hundred years? A thousand?

I would eventually wither. I would eventually die. I trusted no servant with this; only I could bring Ophiliana back. Bring them all back.

In this Age of Betrayal, I would have to find some way to live forever.

It would require evil. Greater evil than had been visited on me. I accepted this. I would make any sacrifice, pay any price, to see it through. I would give of myself so that Ophiliana would return.

I had to restore her. Her heart was gone and would need to be replaced. This would difficult. Dragon's hearts were not easy to come by. Obtaining one would require pawns; playthings to be thrown on an altar.

Sacrificed so Ophiliana could live. The truth slowly dawned. Sacrifice *was* the key. The humans had the right idea. But they simply were not thinking big enough.

Slowly, loss hardened and forged itself into ambition. Goals. I could cry no longer, and it would serve no good; all of Drathari knowing my pain was not enough.

They must share it.

A WORD FROM DAVID ADAMS

A good chunk of this story was written on a flight to Canberra, 30,000 above the ground encased in the belly of a metal dragon.

I've always been drawn to dragons. Although my primary series is science fiction, I've recently begun dabbling in fantasy. Contremulus is a character in my series, *Ren of Atikala*, and I wanted to show some his history and motivations. What made him the way he is. *Ren of Atikala: The Scars of Northaven* touches on some of this, but in order to really *feel* what he felt, we needed to see the world through his eyes.

I hope you enjoy reading this story as much as I enjoyed writing it. For more of my writing…

My website is here:
http://www.lacunaverse.com

My newsletter, which announces new releases, is here:
http://eepurl.com/toBf9

My Facebook page is here:
http://www.facebook.com/lacunaverse

It's Time to Change
by Terah Edun

VEDARIS SAT UP AND looked at himself, wincing at the blood that coated his chest and the tears, well the new tears, in the second of the only two pairs of pants he owned. He'd been caught counting cards at the tavern in the merchants' arena. It wasn't illegal, but that just meant the moneygrubbers had to sic their personal guards on him rather than the City Watch.

How he'd ended up still alive in this alley with only bruises on his face and torn clothes to show for it was a mystery.

In fact, he rather preferred death.

He rubbed his head as he slowly felt around on his temple for the source of his pain.

"Ah," he said with a wince as his fingers landed on a sensitive knot the size of a chicken's egg on his forehead and pain shot from the egg throughout his brain.

"That'd be it," he muttered as he sighed and dropped his hand.

He wished he could say it was the only ache he had, but he'd just have to add it to the list of bruises and cuts on his flesh.

Vedaris was smart, fast, and a quick study. Those three things were the only reason he was alive. He'd trade every one for the one thing that should have been his from birth. The ability to shape shift.

He was nothing without that and he knew it. As he stared around the alley morosely he wondered what could possibly be left for him to do. There was nowhere for him to go. No one who wanted him home, and as a freak with no powers he was pretty much guaranteed to be gutter trash for the rest of his life.

The sound of more people coming down the alley quickly forced him to stand. He had all the bruises he could handle right now and he didn't know how to heal a single one, let alone have the coin to pay someone else to do it for him.

He stood and limped away down a side alley, hoping to avoid others. Lost in his dreams.

His life hadn't always been like this. Filled with self-loathing and a meager existence of day-by-day.

"No," he whispered to himself, "It used to be different. I used to belong…before the tests. Before I failed."

He remembered one night when he was young like it was yesterday. He had inherited that ability from his mother. The gift to perfectly recall everything that he'd ever done. To recall every instance of rejection and despair. But also to recall the hope and the dreams of his younger days.

This time he remembered tossing and turning all night. His sheets were wrapped around him and his bed was soaked from familiar night terrors.

The laughter and warmth of the day lingered in his dreams. He ran through fields of green vines that twined around sticks in the ground. It was late spring, pruning season for his mother's gardens. Heat exaggerated the vegetable scents that hung heavy in the air. Sunrays shone down with unrelenting force, scattered in an almost grid-like pattern.

He ran through the bursts of sun that danced like spotlights through the irrigation canopy overheard. As any true Sahalian knew, basking in the splashes of sun was the best part of spring and summer.

If felt like heaven to have these rays of heat and warmth on his skin. He'd been told that upon gaining his wings, a long day in the desert sun would be more enticing than any opiate—whatever that was.

As he continued his play, he stumbled closer to his mother. He could see her through the vines, although she was turned away from him. Clad in gardening gloves and an apron, from behind she looked like any human scullery maid.

He saw that his father, strong and lean with ivory skin, was sneaking up on her. With her exceptional hearing, she turned to him first, of course.

Normally, now would be the time for Vedaris to leave. Usually it got super-gross super-fast, what with the kisses and touches and all.

As he turned to do just that, the tension in his mother's and father's stances halted him. He saw that they faced each other silently in the garden clearing. They stood just a few feet apart, but with the unhappiness radiating from his father's stiff shoulders, it might as well have been miles.

"Did you petition the healers for an annulment of our union?" his father asked.

She raised her chin and said, "I did."

"Why…is our family not enough? Was our love not strong?" He kept his voice low, speaking through clenched teeth, mindful of his children sleeping in the house.

"Our love was strong," his mother replied, "but our union was not."

As he had surged up out of the tangled sheets in the dark night, the last thing Vedaris remembered was the stricken look on his father's face.

Even now he shook as the fading glimpses of his past slipped slowly away.

The Decision

He hadn't really known what his mother meant then. Now he did. Now he couldn't escape who he was…or rather what he had never become. He was a Sahalian pariah. As one of the few outcastes among the dragon race, he could neither transform his shape nor control the elements.

It rankled Vedaris as nothing else did. In a society that prided itself on power and magework, he was a freak. Often, he was considered of lower caste ranking than a human.

The caste system was fickle — based on power, race and wealth…in that order, and often in combination.

Usually being born a dragon meant an inheritance of primacy in all three. He was one of the lucky few to be born a dragon with no power, no wealth and shunned from childhood by all those who knew.

He had been orphaned at an early age with the death of his father — a Steel Magecaster.

His father had been *normal*. He had had extraordinary talent and the ability to cast steel weapons, dragon armor and magical objects.

In fact he had been known throughout the medina as the best dragon armorer in centuries — sought out by both the nobility and the merchants.

Vedaris, on the other hand, was sorely lacking in both his father's ability and his race's natural talent to transform and fly. Although he did look like his father, with large brown eyes, skin the color of ivory and hair so black it shone with hints of blue.

If there were another person such as he, someone who lacked all inherent Sahalian abilities, he wouldn't have been surprised if they'd been killed at the age of six. Six being the time when all natural abilities were made manifest, or the children were hidden away by their fathers in fear.

The shame, especially among noblemen, would be immense.

He guessed that being without family had been a blessing in some ways. His father had never known of his failure.

It was a curse, of course, in many other ways. Not having someone to watch his back on the streets being one of them.

It was midmorning now and he had two choices. "I could go to the whore's dock and beg the madams to take me on as some rich nobleman's amusement..."

Taking a deep breath he thought, "Or I could steal aboard a Sahalian merchant ship as a human runner."

The latter was a risk, he'd have to avoid all the merchantmen he'd tried to shaft last night, and make sure anyone who hinted of the dragon race didn't get a glimpse of him.

Sahalians could sense each other when an individual used the magic unique to their race or, unfortunately for him, recognize another dragon by eyesight.

Any Sahalian who could transform, which meant all of them, had golden eyes with flecks of green in them. Their eyes were a warm brown when born, slowly lightening to a golden hue as they grew. The flecks of green, a sign of power, appeared during the first tests of childhood.

His ordinary brown eyes had never made the transition. He remembered his father saying that it would come. In a particularly frustrating instance at four and a half years old he had been trying to lift a freshly baked meatpie off his mother's kitchen countertop *without* her noticing.

His sister, Noor, had been able to do that trick at three. His father, coming in from the steam baths in the garden after a long day's work, had with a wry glance at him magepushed the meatpie over with a cold breeze to cool it down.

He got the feeling his mother had known what his father had done. She probably would have stayed if Vedaris had been the one to do it.

That time in his life was gone. His father was dead and his mother, as much as the human term could be applied, was gone. She had chosen her duties and taken Noor with her.

Since being orphaned his lack of mage abilities had allowed him to masquerade as a human, first in the cloister and now on the streets.

The appearance of humanity was often the only thing that saved him in his hardscrabble life on the streets. Gangs and packs of kids always underestimated the strength that lay in his wiry frame.

With a wry smile he decided to toss fate to the winds, scrambled up and began to limp down the trash-strewn alley toward the shipyard.

The Journey

It only took a good amount of wheedling and a promise to do some work on the ship's rigging to get onboard the massive vessel going across the seas to his new home.

Vedaris had taken the captain's offer with a wink and a smile, and had gotten settled in a bunk before the hour was out.

Now he sat in his little corner of the large and packed crew's deck trying not to get seasick and wondering what the new world would bring.

"Can't be any worse than the old one," he muttered as he turned on his side and tuned out the game of cow's bones going on on the floor next to him.

Instead, he remembered the last time he'd stayed in a new

place that was neither home to family nor friends. It had been the first day he'd stayed in the cloister. Ado had been so excited. It was a small, compact and homely place with the orphans on one floor and the nuns, all sweethearts, on the floor below.

He and Ado, who was four years younger than him, had shared quarters. Ado had been excited that they had gotten to pick out a room that was a triple but that they could keep just for the two of them. It was comfy looking and Ado couldn't wait to get in there.

Vedaris was not so easily taken in. At that point in his life he'd been shuttled between neighbors for months. He was always on a quest to reunite with family. He was wary but accepting.

Ado, who had spent the past two years on the streets, was pacing around with trembling hands and hopeful glances. Caught up on *kat*, the street drug that induced a temporary high, he had yet to hit bottom.

Vedaris still hadn't gotten the full story from him about why he was on the streets. When he asked Ado where his family was, the tousle-headed boy with golden hair would just hunch his shoulders and frown down at the dust.

It hadn't mattered to Vedaris in the least. They had just met a seven-day before. There was a roof over his head that he wasn't in jeopardy of getting kicked out of for looking at someone the wrong way, and he had time to make inquiries about his missing sister and absent mother.

Though he had to admit, the first night in a warm bed with an actual pallet and frame had been very welcome after months on his step-aunt's kitchen floor and sleeping in the sawdust of his third cousin's gryffin stable loft. The same cousin he'd fled after one too many run-ins with both the beasts and bullies. He hadn't liked the loft. Not least because gryffins really didn't like him. Well, they didn't like dragons in general, but they respected those that were stronger than them. Vedaris didn't fall into that category and the gryffins clearly knew that.

His third cousin hadn't. Vedaris was just grateful Mattis had been too self-absorbed to enquire as to why Vedaris didn't challenge the gryffins for dominance in the stable loft.

In truth, the stable lofts had become a refuge later in his life. Running from packs of dragon brats straight into the claws of the gryffins had definitely saved his bum a time or two.

He had known how to evade the attacks of the three gryffins, but his tormenters didn't. What's more, it was illegal to break the dominant trait of a gryffin without the owner's permission first.

If the brats had taken the fight with the gryffins to the next level magically or transformed into their Sahalian form they would have had to face a dominance battle with Mattis, who was no slouch in the ring — owning three battle gryffins ensured that.

Every day of his life with his family, on the streets, in the cloister and now on the ship presented a separate period of maturity. Now he would have to use all of that knowledge as he made his way in the city of Sandrin.

It didn't take long, however, before the ship's feeling of safe haven was turned into one of open peril. Weeks out at sea and Vedaris was beginning to wish he'd never left his home on the streets. At least on the streets he wouldn't drown like a rat in a vat of dirty bath water.

Vedaris was sure his face was as green as a gilly fish but he was determined to get above deck. Stumbling around as the ship rolled and rose with the waves, he crashed into a wooden pole and then into a person who pushed him away roughly with a curse.

Luckily, the harsh shove encouraged him to move in the right direction.

With a moan, Vedaris grabbed onto the stair railing in front of him and hauled himself above the deck. He'd been living in the belly of the ship for at least eighteen days by his last count and if he was going to die, he was going to do it like a proper dragon. Wind in his face and staring at his enemy like a Sahalian. None of this hiding below decks would do for him.

Water was roaring down the steps, making them slippery and dangerous to get a foothold on.

But he made it to the top deck with a triumphant yell and was promptly knocked to his knees with a look of horror on his face as a fearsome wave crossed the deck and Vedaris stared at death itself.

The eye of a hurricane was descending down on his small ship with mighty winds and a gigantic roar.

A New Home

The ship swayed side to side violently in the open ocean. Lightning rolled alongside and above the sails in clouds of dark purple and blue. They sometimes struck frighteningly close to his small vessel. The sailors rushed fore and aft to keep the ship from capsizing in the waves.

After it became clear that he wouldn't die right that second,

Vedaris did his part by hanging onto the smallest of the three masts for dear life, crossing his heart, praying to the dragon gods and staying the frack out of the way of the crew.

From what he'd heard earlier when he was eavesdropping on the captain and the first mate, not snooping mind you, they were rounding the Windswept Isles.

The area around the isles was known, even to a city dweller such as himself, by tales of the horror of wind funnels from the sea and furies who sailed the winds ready to grab greedy pirates off of ship's decks.

Not that a fury could take a dragon in flight. But the nasty bitches did have a tendency to harry, and the combination of their nuisance tactics and a heavy storm could spell death.

As the ship continued to plow through the waves, Vedaris heard an ominous crack. He wasn't sure where it came from, but all of a sudden the entire ship became topsy-turvy. It was already awhirl from the winds and waves but he would swear to his dying day that this time it was airborne.

The last thing he remembered before the darkness hit was a pirate's surprised face as he flew across the deck, a face that strangely enough reminded him of the baker's son — fat and greedy.

When he awoke voices chattered nearby — a man and a woman. They were moving away from him. Slowly he began to get feeling in his arms and his legs. By the gods, he ached.

As he opened his eyes he saw that he was in a room. Not on a ship and certainly not in the midst of a storm.

The healers were still speaking quietly on the other side of the room. He sat up, too quickly as it turned out, and his head spun. The healers rushed over. He struggled to rise. His legs felt weak and his head was spinning, but he had never had a good experience with Sahalian healers.

As a child the state-sponsored healers tsked at his late development in magical abilities. Assigned throughout pregnancy and delivery to expectant Sahalian mothers, each healer took a vested interest in their charges.

The abilities of the child later in life reflected well upon the nourishment and techniques designed by the healer in the pre-natal and post-birth terms. In his healers' eyes he had been a blemish upon their careers until eventually his father had stopped allowing them in the house and they had stopping calling on his family.

On the streets it was more a simple dislike for healers that pushed him and his acquaintances to avoid them. They were body grabbers — the lot of them. Always wanting poor families and street kids for research for the greater good of Sahalia.

The female reached him first. "Calm down! Please, you'll tear your wounds and your head can't feel much better either."

"Where am I?" Vedaris demanded. "Which borough? ...I demand you call my cousin the..." Before he could finish that thought the male healer said, "You're in the Madrassa Healing Center."

"Madrassa...THE Madrassa?" Vedaris spluttered.

"Yes," the female healer smiled.

Vedaris now knew she was an initiate — they both were. "But...but I was on board a ship just past the Windswept isles."

The male healer frowned. "Are you sure?"

The female healer said, "His clothes...they were caked in sea salt. It seems he speaks the truth."

They frowned at each other and then the male healer looked at Vedaris. "We need to consult with our superiors."

"Please wait here, we'll have food brought for you," said the female.

Where the frack am I going to go? Vedaris thought bitterly. *I feel like gutter trash and I'm fifty miles inland from the nearest port. I don't even know how I got here.*

"Don't worry," the female healer said. "We'll get to the bottom of this."

Vedaris looked at her queerly. "I didn't say anything," he said, and then he remembered that human healers were said to have the strangest powers, including mind healing, whatever that was.

If she thought she was going to spy on his thoughts she had another think coming, and with that last thought he promptly slumped over and fell back to sleep.

The Choice

Vedaris was awake again. This time he was alone in the room except for a person two beds down on the opposite side.

Wincing as he pushed himself up in the silent room he looked around, calculating his next move. As he swung his legs over the side of the bed and stood he could smell illness. He frowned. As a Sahalian his sense of smell was generally greater than a human's. But the illness was…wrong. It stank not of death but of malaise.

It was wafting from the immobile form between him and

the door. As he approached the cot he saw that it, *she*, wore breeches and a breast band and had bandages around her middle.

The stink came from the bandages, but they were unstained by blood or any other bodily fluid.

His curiosity getting the better of him he leaned over, not close enough to get whacked on the head, but close enough to more clearly see what was invisible to the naked eye. It was almost as if a haze hovered over her wound. With a quick look at the girl's face, kind of a sweet face actually, he inhaled the smog.

It's what his kind did when they came upon something that was unknown. They tasted it, they sniffed it, and they savored it.

The complex chemistry of the saliva in their mouths allowed Sahalians to identify the unusual and even the toxic, which is why it was impossible to poison a Sahalian...orally anyway.

He didn't know why or how but as soon as it hit his lips it went from malaise to...nothing. Tasteless, clear air...quite the turn-off actually. He had been hoping for something more... dramatic, or to at least figure out what it was.

Sitara felt ill. She floated in a miasma of uncleanness. It surrounded her. Suffocated her. She woke — surging up and smacking straight into Vedaris's face.

"Ow!" Vedaris howled along with a few other choice words. He stumbled back.

Sitara looked around wide-eyed, as if she was ready to spring from the bed.

Vedaris stood a few steps back, a scowl on his face, staring at her. "Who are you?" they both shouted at once.

Sitara frowned and bit her lip, "I asked first," she stated.

"Not really," he snapped back as he thought, *Is she crazy?*

"*Sitara,*" she said.

He frowned "What? What'd you call me?"

"Sitara, my NAME is Sitara," she said.

"Well, where did you come from?" he asked.

"I could ask you the same question," she snapped.

"No," he said, "I meant, how did you get here?"

She raised an eyebrow. They both turned as the door opened. The female healer was back. She walked in frowning at seeing Vedaris standing far from his bed and Sitara sitting up.

"You both should be resting," the healer said. Vedaris rolled his eyes as she stopped in front of him. "How'd I get here?"

With a sharp look at him Sitara muttered, "Looks like you should be able to answer your own question before asking me." Vedaris shot a glare at her and the healer held up a hand to forestall any further argument.

"I've yet to figure that out but will continue to search for an answer with Research colleagues. I'm sure they'll find your case very interesting."

"Yeah, well," Vedaris responded, "Send me a letter when they finally figure it out." The healer threw him a quizzical look "There's no need...of course I'll just find you in your School."

"My school?" Vedaris responded slowly. He was quick on the uptake and saw no need to dissuade the healer of any notion before he found out what she meant.

"Well yes, we haven't had a Sahalian candidate in quite some time," she replied.

No shit, he thought, his people didn't have the highest regard for humans, who were once considered meals and now were undesired allies at best.

"But," she continued, "You will still have to test for School placement alongside your friend here." Vedaris frowned, both at the reference to a 'friend' and at the thought he would once more face and fail a magical exam.

At this point Sitara interjected into the conversation, to his surprise not a denial of the 'friend' comment, "My name is Sitara."

"My apologies for referring to you out of turn," replied the healer. "My name is Roble. I'm sure you and your other friends will do well."

Vedaris stood just looking at the healer. Only his eyes, which had darkened to a murky olive brown, showed how quickly thoughts were flying through his head.

Vedaris didn't scoff, though he barely held that in check.

Releasing his bottom lip from a bite, Vedaris licked the tender flesh and said tentatively, "And you want…my kind in your human school?"

"Your kind?" said Sitara slowly.

Roble said shocked, "Of course. All races are invited to participate in the test, and if they pass, enroll in the famed school. You especially would be welcome."

Vedaris snorted. "And why is that?"

"Your charming personality for one," said Roble dryly.

Vedaris shot her a wry look.

The healer shrugged. "There's something off about your aura…almost like a dark magic."

Vedaris stiffened as he felt anger rise. He may have been an outcast in Sahalia and have to take whatever was thrown at him like a grateful dog, but he *didn't* have to accept the same treatment here.

Roble must have sensed the tension because she raised her hands in a placating manner and said, "Not there's anything wrong with *different*. All the students here are different from the normal population and some are...special."

"Special? Special how?" demanded Vedaris.

"You'll see if you pass," said Roble.

"And what if I don't want to pass your damned entrance exam? What if I don't want to attend?"

"Then why did you come here?" Roble asked snootily.

"Coincidence," shot Vedaris.

"There's no such thing as coincidence in regards to this school," the healer responded in an eerily calm voice. "There's no way you would have gotten past the wards unless it was intended."

Vedaris crossed his arms in irritation. "Well, I'm telling you I didn't *intend* to do anything."

"Maybe you didn't," Roble said easily. "Maybe it was your destiny, dragon."

Then the healer walked away, leaving a frustrated Vedaris and a contemplative young girl in a quiet ward alone with their thoughts and faced with their dreams.

Vedaris didn't really see himself as having a choice. He could take the test, pass, and stay in the school, or he could fail and head to the coastal cities and make a life for himself.

It wasn't a choice because he would be a fool to try.

Cackling to himself as he grabbed a blanket and tucked himself in Vedaris muttered, "Who in the seven empires goes to school voluntarily anyway? I'm out of here at dawn and back on the road to where I should be. The human cities."

It's Time to Change

Vedaris woke bright and early. He wasn't sure if it was nerves or guilt.

"Why would I be nervous?" he said disdainfully. "I'll take their test, fake an effort, and con them into giving me a ride into the city. Might take some of those magical potions with me…I'm sure the value on the streets is pretty good."

"What'd you say?" the girl muttered.

"What? Nothing," snapped Vedaris. "I wasn't talking to you, bleater."

She glared and rubbed her shoulder in irritation. "No cause to be so rude."

"I wasn't talking to you," Vedaris repeated slowly enough with a flash of teeth that she couldn't mistake it for anything but what it was — a threat.

"Fine," she sniffed and turned away.

He snorted and watched out of the corner of his eye as the healers reapplied salve to Sitara's wound, determined that she should rest for at least another hour, and so she sat in a wooden moving chair waiting for a student to push her.

He shook his head. "They sure do treat people soft here. They don't even *know* her. They don't know me. We don't pay no dues here."

"Come with us," a new healer instructed.

Vedaris eyed them and followed behind without a word. The sooner they got this done, the better. They exited the healing facilities together. The young male student pushing Sitara kept up a steady stream of one-sided conversation.

Neither Sitara nor Vedaris contributed much to his ramblings…their thoughts were filled with the past day's events.

Two male youths and one female already waited in the atrium. All three wore what looked like travel clothes, not that Sitara or Vedaris were clothed any better. The two groups looked at each other and then away, as if the marble rolling beneath the wheels of Sitara's chair, checkered white and black, was the most fascinating design in the world.

After a few minutes of awkward silence and sneaky side-glances, a man in robes walked in. He was dressed in enough silk that Vedaris picked him out as an official of some sort fifteen feet away. He walked to the center of the room and gestured for the five young adults to gather around.

"Some of you have met me before. To those who haven't, I am the Headmaster of the Healing Hall. You may address me as Healer Masadi," he began.

"To all of you I say," he continued, "Welcome to the halls of the Madrassa. An academy not just for learning the skills of a practicum, but also a practitioner's academy where those far advanced in their fields come to strengthen their skills, test their magic and further the knowledge of the schools."

"This morning you will face the admissions test for entrance," he said as he looked at each of them.

Vedaris twitched when Masadi caught his eyes, thinking, *Why's he looking at me?*

"I don't have to tell you that hundreds of students of all backgrounds come to these halls hoping for a place among the schools," Masadi said. "We are very fortunate in the aptitude and quality of our students and hope they take the knowledge and responsibility of what they've learned seriously," he said.

His eyes wandered over each of the candidates to emphasize his point.

AGAIN with the looking at me, Vedaris exclaimed in his head. *And what's her problem?*

This time he gave a side-eye towards the other girl who stood ramrod straight in front of Masadi, almost at attention.

Masadi continued, "Should you pass the entrance exam, you'll be inducted today. Should you fail, we'll have an escort take you to the way station and your fare paid to the city of your choice."

Perfect, Vedaris gloated to himself. *I got two free rides. One across the sea and the other to the city, without lifting a finger.*

"Nothing further about the Schools or the Academy will be discussed until you pass your tests," Masadi concluded. "Now please follow me."

They didn't go far before Vedaris was engulfed in darkness.

He was shocked for a moment but he soon reverted to wary readiness. It was smart of them, after all, to catch the potential students off guard and test them then. He just had to figure out how to fail and make it look like he'd tried.

As the darkness disappeared, Vedaris's vision adjusted and he realized that he stood in a fighting dojo.

He frowned as he looked around. Wooden walls encircled a floor spread with training mats and not much else.

Straight ahead of him stood a tall black man of fearsome appearance and simple fighting robes.

With a smirk Vedaris stepped forward. This peacock didn't scare him. He'd faced down drug lords and would-be kings of the city playground.

If it was a test of fighting skills this man wanted then that's what he'd get. Vedaris would just have to make sure he didn't beat him *too* soundly. He had to get out of here after all.

When Vedaris stood five paces in front of the man, without a word his opponent slid back in a fighting stance, raised his palm and gestured for Vedaris to bring it on.

Vedaris needed no further invitation. With the speed of his kind and strength of his ancestors he would wipe the floor with this human in seconds.

He was in for a surprise. The minute he began sparring with the man he could see that he was talented.

Not only did the man seem to know the dancing fighting styles of the Windswept Isles but also the combat play of the knights of Sahalia.

With a frown, Vedaris wondered what he had gotten into.

Panting with exertion he continued to press for position against his opponent but gained no ground.

He thought to do one final trick which often confused his foes on the streets.

Abruptly he turned, ran full tilt at the wall and ran up the wall...one...two...three...four steps...twisted with an almighty push and kicked out straight into the chest of his opponent.

Or at least he tried to. The push went great, the kick went

well. But his opponent grabbed his leg, not at the last minute, but at mid-stride.

Vedaris landed with a heavy thud on the practice mats, out of breath and madder than hell.

"Who the hell are you? What the hell are you?" the pissed Sahalian said. He had already forgotten about his promise to fail. His pride was at stake.

His opponent merely stared down at him, stone faced, and said, "Do you know why you lost?"

"What?" said Vedaris, still dazed from his abrupt and humiliating defeat.

"Do you know why you lost?" his opponent repeated.

With a frown Vedaris snapped, "Because you're faster and stronger than me...which is IMPOSSIBLE! No human can best a great dragon."

"You lost," his opponent answered, ignoring Vedaris' diatribe, "because you're incapable of winning."

"What?" shouted Vedaris from his seat on the ground where he was nursing his leg, "You insignificant worm-eater, I went *easy* on you..."

His opponent held up a hand to forestall further protest and continued, "You're incapable of winning because you haven't harnessed your magic."

That shut Vedaris up. *Magic,* Vedaris thought to himself, shocked.

"What magic?" he demanded aloud. He didn't *have* any magic. He'd just gone along with that crackpot healer's suggestion because he'd wanted a free ticket out of the school walls.

He refused to acknowledge the little ember of hope in his

chest that had just grown a bit brighter with this second individual's confirmation.

He said I have magic, Vedaris thought dumbfounded. He had a right to be confused. Magic for a dragon who couldn't shape shift was unheard of…and as far as he knew, impossible.

"That, I can't yet tell you," the instructor said. "But I can tell you that you have magical talents. It is my job to help you discover them and train you to use them properly."

Vedaris ears had perked up by then. "Train me?"

"Are you going to repeat everything I say?"

Vedaris glared. "Just answer one question."

The man tilted his head and nodded.

"Would I have to stay at the school to get this magic?"

A faint smile appeared on the instructor's face. "Yes."

Vedaris frowned. "Can't you just give me a book and send me on my way?"

"No."

Vedaris swallowed. Here was everything he'd ever wanted. There in the distance was the chance to get to a city without delay.

Vedaris hesitated and then spoke. "I suppose I can spend a day or two here…to learn the ropes."

The man gave Vedaris an unreadable look and then he bowed.

When he rose from the bow, he said, "Welcome to the School of the Unknown."

He continued, "I am an initiate assigned to you. Consider this probation. When you are ready you will meet with the Headmaster for your true test."

"True test?" Vedaris sputtered as the room disappeared and he was back where he'd started. Staring at a Headmaster whose eyes knew far too much.

Vedaris couldn't help it. He snarled. The man annoyed him. The minute he got his magic…he was out of here.

A WORD FROM TERAH EDUN

I hope you've enjoyed "It's Time to Change".

Dragons have always been mysterious creatures. Mythological beasts that haunt our imaginations and fuel our sense of adventure. Are they the famed carnivorous beast slayed by St. George or something more? I enjoyed taking that to a new level and exploring a society entirely built by and run by sentient shape-shifting dragons.

In my world of Algardis, that land is called Sahalia with references to it running throughout all of my high fantasy works. Starting in 2015, Sahalia will become more than a secondary reality. It will be a fully-fledged society with the publication of the new Algardis series.

You can find out more about that series on my website www.terahedun.com. Feel free to drop by on my Facebook page at www.facebook.com/terahedunauthor and say hello on Twitter at www.twitter.com/tedunwrites.

Thank you for supporting independent fantasy fiction.

Dragon Play
by Ted Cross

"DON'T BE A CRYBABY! We're going to be heroes!"

"I'm not crying, Anja," Birgit said, swiping a hand across her eyes, "but this is not fun any more."

Anja looked incredulous. "Nothing we have ever done and nothing we will ever do in our lives will be more fun than what we are going to do. Ask the boys."

Birgit glanced at the other two members of their group. Halfdan was pudgy and dark-haired, and being the shortest of the group he always tried to be the boldest.

Flame-haired Fridrik, at thirteen, was eldest of the four, tall and lithe—the love of Birgit's eleven-year-old life. He was also gentle and kind, which made it that much harder for Birgit that he only had eyes for Anja.

"This is going to be great!" Halfdan said, picking his way up the rocky slope.

Fridrik gave Birgit a reassuring smile. "Anja, when you said we were going to the dragon's lair, we thought you meant playing a game, not *actually* going. You know it's forbidden to go anywhere near this place."

"You'll get us all killed," Birgit murmured.

Anja of the golden hair was the chieftain's daughter, the pride of their clan and the natural leader of their small gang despite having lived a mere ten summers. She ignored their complaints and paused to examine a small parchment. "It's not much farther. Just there, see? Around that shoulder." She pointed at a spot on the mountain where a cliff face dropped down to meet the rocky incline they had been climbing since morning.

"I always thought the entrance was on the other side," Halfdan said.

"It is," Anja said. "It really would be stupid to walk right into the entrance of a dragon's den."

"Then what *are* we doing?" Fridrik said.

Anja pointed again. "Once we get up there, I'll show you."

Birgit scowled and mumbled under her breath. She was used to Anja coming up with ever more daring games, but this one went too far. Far beneath them the foothills of the mountain ended abruptly at the slate-colored sea. Their village was hidden from view behind a crag. "We should turn back," she said and glanced at Fridrik again, hoping to see agreement in his eyes. Whatever she felt about Anja's plan, she wouldn't leave without Fridrik.

He kept climbing, refusing to meet her eyes. "Let's hear what she has to say."

Birgit looked at the sun and decided it was past the lunch

hour. She was tired and had a bloody scrape on her left knee from climbing over rocks all morning.

It took half an hour more before the ground leveled out and they came to a flat spot near the sheer cliff wall. Anja directed the boys to remove scree from a small area near the wall so they could sit down and have lunch. Halfdan laid out a thin blanket. Birgit set her pack down and pulled out two flasks of weak ale, cheese, bread, and several apples. Fridrik used his knife to carve slices of cheese and bread.

Tired from the climb, they ate in silence despite their curiosity to hear Anja's big secret. When Fridrik swallowed down the last of his meal, he took a swig of ale and said, "All right, let's hear it."

Anja put down the apple she was munching and pulled her knees up to her chest. She chewed her lip and examined each of her three companions before speaking. "All our lives we've heard the tales of the dragon."

Birgit nodded. Of course they had; it was the most popular story told around the clan fire pits. Eight centuries ago the great ebony wyrm appeared out of myth and decimated all of the tribes of the region before claiming a local mine as its lair. It hibernated for years on end but came forth every decade or so to satiate its hunger.

"And Kathkalan?" Anja looked pointedly at Halfdan.

Halfdan grinned. "The greatest warrior ever!"

"What's your point?" Fridrik said to Anja.

Anja looked around at all of them again before replying. "When he went in there to slay the dragon, he brought Aivgaifa with him."

"Didn't seem to help much," Birgit grumbled. Aivgaifa

was a talisman of incredible and unsurpassed power, embodied in the form of a silver armband that had been stolen from druids across the sea. The powerful luck magic that suffused their clan as long as they possessed Aivgaifa had made it the strongest clan on the island. The clan elders believed that all of their misfortunes had come from the loss of this artifact. Their once-powerful tribe was now relegated to living in the shadow of the dragon.

"You don't know that it was the band that failed him," Anja said. "Imagine if we could bring Aivgaifa back to our village."

"There's nothing wrong with dreams," Fridrik said, "but it's not heroic to be dead."

Anja held up the scrap of parchment she had been consulting during their climb. "I found this rolled up in a crumbling scroll that had fallen behind a shelf in the shaman's library."

"What were you doing there?" Birgit said. "Bragi doesn't allow—"

"It's a mess. I was cleaning it for him."

Anja's eyes looked shifty to Birgit. "You're crazy to steal from him."

"It's not stealing. I'm going to put it back. But look!" She flattened the parchment on the blanket. "This is a map of the old mines. They were much more extensive than the stories ever told." She drew a finger over dark lines and symbols on the parchment. "There's the main entrance and the great hall. Lots of small passages lead off from it. And here, where we're sitting now, is a back entrance. See?"

Birgit scanned the cliff face. "I don't see anything."

"Because it's hidden," Anja said, rolling her eyes. "We know it's here; we can find it!"

"Let's say you're right, Anja," Fridrik said. "What then? Crawl around in pitch-black passages while a dragon hunts us down? No thanks!"

Birgit nodded in agreement.

"You're not thinking," Anja said. "The dragon is sleeping."

"You don't know that," Birgit said. "The elders have been warning that it is past time for it to wake again."

"When it wakes, we'll know it," Anja said, "but for now it still sleeps. We were all very small when it last attacked our village. Fridrik, you are the only one old enough to have memories of it. I remember what you told me."

"So?"

"You said it was enormous. That it blocked the sun and filled the sky."

"All the more reason not to go in there," Fridrik said.

Anja shook her head at him. "Don't you see? It has grown huge over the centuries. When it cleared out the mines, it was a slender wyrm, but now it can't fit in these smaller passageways. It uses the large entrance doors and remains in the great hall. It's safe to search all the rest."

"You're gambling with our lives," Birgit said. "I've seen rats and mice squeeze through holes so tiny it seems impossible they could fit through. Maybe the dragon can do the same."

"Anja," Fridrik said. "Even if you're right, the echoes of our movement and the torches we must carry would surely wake the beast."

"We have the map," Anja said. "Let's find the entrance, if we can. We should be safe through all of these tiny passages. When we get close, I'll go on alone if I must."

Fridrik looked at Birgit and she saw the doubt etched in

his eyes. She walked to the overlook and tried again to spy their village. Turning to Fridrik, she said, "We're going to be punished terribly. If we leave now we may be able to make it home before full dark."

Fridrik looked at Anja and Halfdan, who were searching the cliff face for signs of the hidden door. He looked at the remains of their meal. "Let us pack this up."

Birgit frowned at his evasion but knelt to help him clean and pack. There was a sudden rumble of stone grinding on stone.

"Ha! I found it!" Halfdan cried.

Birgit spun about to see Anja fling her arms around Halfdan. A small square hole had opened in the cliff face.

"How did you do that?" Fridrik murmured in awe.

"Here," Halfdan said, indicating a knob of stone. "I pressed this in and it moved, then the door opened."

Fridrik's eyes widened. "Who could build such a thing? Our best craftsmen could never..."

"Get the torches!" Anja cried, her smile wider than Birgit had ever seen.

Birgit took two steps toward the dark maw and stared into the void. A faint musty breeze issued from the darkness. "No. We can't go in there. Don't you understand?"

"You go on home, Birgit," Anja said. "Tell my father nothing. Tell him we went off on our own to play."

"Don't do this, Anja. You'll be killed." Birgit turned to Fridrik. "Please don't let her do this."

Fridrik didn't seem to hear her. He was lighting tinder with his flint, a torch at the ready.

"Go on, Birgit," Halfdan said. "This is a venture for the bold. We'll be remembered forever!"

"You'll be dead forever," Birgit hissed. She stood helplessly while the others readied torches, candles, rope, and other supplies from the packs Anja had insisted they prepare yesterday.

Fridrik stood near the entrance and shoved his torch inside. Birgit went to stand with him. "Why, Fridrik? I believed you wiser than this."

Fridrik gave her a strange look. "No one has seen this in centuries. You saw the map. We can explore a bit and be safe. I want to see what's in there. Aren't you curious at all?"

"There's a dragon in there."

He nodded. "I have no intention of going anywhere near the dragon."

"Promise?"

"I swear. Look, let's humor them for a little while. See what we can find in the first rooms. I bet they get scared and want to leave within the hour."

Birgit tried to force a smile but failed. "I don't know if I can go in there. It's like the mouth to Hel."

Fridrik smiled at her. "I'll hold your hand and lead the way. You'll be scared at first, but when it's over you'll see how fun it was."

Anja joined them, followed by Halfdan. "I'm going first." Without waiting for a reply, she shoved her torch in ahead of her and stalked forward. Halfdan didn't hesitate to follow.

Fridrik squeezed Birgit's hand and drew her after him. As she ducked to enter the passageway, Birgit closed her eyes and held them shut for several steps, trusting Fridrik to lead her safely. Already smoke from the torches was filling the small stone passage, making them cough. She tried to remember how far the first line had looked on the map but couldn't.

"How far does it go?" she asked, her voice sounding hollow and shaky.

Fridrik's face was orange in the flickering torchlight. "Judging from the map, I'd say—"

There was a loud click. Behind them the stone door rumbled down, cutting off the sunlight as it slammed shut.

"Gods!" Birgit heard herself shriek.

"It moved under my foot!" The voice was Halfdan's. "I triggered something."

"Step on it again!" Anja cried.

"I'm trying. It's not doing anything now."

"Birgit, you're hurting my hand!" Fridrik whispered.

Birgit tried to lessen her grip. "We're all going to die now," she moaned.

"That's not going to help us," Fridrik said. "There must be a way to open the door again." He squeezed by her in the narrow passage and led her back to the closed door. "Help me! Feel all around. If you find any irregularities in the stone, press them."

Halfdan had returned and held his torch up to provide light. Fridrik handed his torch to Halfdan so he could use both hands to search. Birgit looked back and saw Anja's pale face, grim in the flickering light.

* * *

Fridrik couldn't judge how much time had passed. Still he went on, frantically searching the walls, the floor, even the ceiling. He pressed and shoved at the unrelenting cold stone long after the others had given up. At last he had to admit defeat. He put his back to the wall and slid down onto his haunches. "We must find another way."

He held out a hand to accept a torch back from Halfdan, then looked at Birgit. She sat on the floor and gazed into nothingness. Fridrik felt terrible, knowing it was only because of him that she had entered this prison. *I'm in her debt now,* he thought. *I must find a way to save us.*

Anja was studying her scrap of parchment. Halfdan had joined her. Fridrik squeezed Birgit's shoulder and whispered, "It'll be all right. You'll see. We'll find a way out." He didn't dare watch for a response, so he crawled forward to peer over Halfdan's arm at the map.

"I don't see any other way out except for the main entrance," Anja said.

"The dragon," Halfdan said. Fridrik had never seen the boy look so frightened.

"There's no choice," Anja replied.

"If it sleeps deeply enough, perhaps it won't awaken," Fridrik said. He looked at his torch. "We had better get moving. Don't want to end up trapped in here without light."

Halfdan nodded but looked as if he might be sick.

"I'll fetch Birgit. Go on ahead and we'll catch up," Fridrik said. He watched them take up their packs and scuttle down the passage before heading back toward Birgit.

"Look at me, Birgit," he said and placed a hand on her chin to lift it. Her eyes were unfocused. "We can't stay here."

"I..."

"Come. I'll get us out of here." He took her by the arm and urged her to follow. Her body responded, though her expression remained dazed. Fridrik held the torch out in front of them and edged forward as quickly as he dared. Birgit coughed at the smoke filling the passage. The light of the other torches had vanished ahead.

Fridrik began to sing under his breath, a warrior's song of valor that he'd often heard as his clansmen went off on expeditions in their dragon-prowed boats. He couldn't say how much time passed, but eventually he saw light ahead of them, and soon the passage widened and they entered a small room where the others awaited them.

Anja approached and put an arm about his neck. "It will be easier now. The other passages are bigger. We can walk upright."

"What does the map show now?" Fridrik said.

"That way looks the quickest," she responded, pointing at a corridor to the right.

He held his torch up high and looked about the room. It was disappointing how little there was to see. Wood so crumbled there was no way to tell what it had once been. A moldering pile of cloth. When he reached down to touch it, it puffed away like ash. His imagination had betrayed him. He had thought he'd find ancient relics and treasures, or at least some fantastic souvenirs to show to his father when he returned home. "Lead on," he said, and took Birgit's slack hand again.

No one spoke for what seemed like days as they wandered down a twisting maze of passages and rooms. Once they found a long room where the stone floor was pitted and scored. Halfdan suggested it was the acid from the dragon's breath. Another time they found a rusty, crumbling chainmail hauberk and a scattering of bone shards.

Anja often halted to look at her map, and at long last she stopped them in a room with only one roughhewn passage leading onward. "Here," was all she said.

Fridrik squatted near her and looked at the map. She pointed out their location. "That squiggle?"

She pointed at the rough stone of the onward passage. "It leads to the great hall where the dragon sleeps."

"How far?"

"I can only guess, but I think it's only another two hundred paces or so."

Fridrik looked at his torch, which was burning down to the nub. "When we get close, perhaps we should go on in the dark. There may be sunlight to show the entrance."

"Maybe," Anja said. "I think I'll try a candle. Father always told me dragons sleep deeply."

"I'll...I'll take the lead," Halfdan offered.

Anja nodded at him, and Halfdan stalked forward into the cave. She met Fridrik's eyes. "Will you ever forgive me for this?"

"We'll see," he whispered. "It's Birgit I'm worried about. Go on. I'll get her."

The rough passage twisted and turned. The guttering torchlight sparkled from crystals in the ceiling and walls. Where the way widened, stalagmites thrust upward from the floor and Fridrik could reach up and touch dripping stalactites.

"Halt!" whispered Halfdan.

"What is it?" Anja said.

Fridrik edged forward to join them, leading Birgit behind him. A deep black slash crossed their path, a crevasse dropping down into the depths of the earth. Far below he heard the sound of rushing water.

"We can jump it," Anja said.

"It's not that far," Halfdan agreed.

"I don't think Birgit can make it," Fridrik whispered.

Birgit surprised them by responding for the first time since their entombment. "I can."

Fridrik turned to her and smiled when he saw life in her eyes again. "You sure?"

She nodded. "You've seen me. I'm good at leaping."

"Yes, you are." He turned to Anja and Halfdan. "You two go first. Then Birgit."

Halfdan shrugged out of his pack and handed his torch to Anja. He took a few paces back up the passage, then lunged forward and leaped easily over the chasm. When he reappeared at the far side, he was grinning. "Nothing to it!"

Anja took packs from each of them and flung them across to Halfdan. The torches were trickier, but Fridrik managed to toss two of them across for Halfdan to catch. Anja paced back and, holding a torch in one hand, ran forward and jumped across with a squeal.

"Now you," Fridrik said to Birgit. "See how easy it was?"

She said nothing as she walked back a few steps and prepared herself.

"Take a few deep breaths," Fridrik said.

She nodded and did as he suggested. Then she bounded forward and made the leap. Anja caught her in her arms and they giggled together.

Fridrik wiped sweat from his brow and grinned in relief. He adjusted his grip on the torch and ran forward to jump across the gap.

Anja collected them together in a huddle. "There should be one more larger cavern ahead, then a short passage leading into the lair. We should exchange our torches for candles now."

They did as she suggested, lighting the candles with the torches before dropping the torches into the crevasse.

Halfdan led the way again, sneaking forward. Shortly they came to the final room before the lair. The room was large and dark even with the candles. Water dripped and pooled among the bones of rats and other small animals.

Fridrik paused to examine what looked like a man's ribcage. He caught an odd movement with the corner of his eye, something high up the wall of the cavern. His heart pounded in his chest as he recognized the silhouette—the long, sinuous neck; the terrible, spiky head. *Dragon! How can that be?* Panic surged in his breast. He tried to shout, but his throat betrayed him. No one else seemed to have noticed the beast yet, so focused were they upon the way ahead. *There's a ledge of some sort up there!*

He swallowed and found his voice—"'Ware!" he cried, but it was too late.

The dragon's head plunged downward and its terrible mouth snapped shut over the head of one of his friends below. It jerked upward, carrying the figure into the air, its legs cycling and arms flailing. With an audible crunching sound, the dragon bit through the neck and the heaving body fell to the floor, blood spurting.

* * *

Dragon! Birgit couldn't believe her eyes. It was supposed to be in the great hall beyond. She saw the awful plunge of the dragon's head, the death of one of her friends, and panic flooded through her like a molten river. She dropped the candle and fled.

Her arm struck someone as she ran. She felt fingers dig at her side and heard a shout, distant, as if from down a deep well. Her mind refused to work. All she could think was—*Dragon! Dragon! Run!*

A tiny portion of her mind tickled at her, reminding her that she should feel shame, that she had responsibilities to friends and couldn't desert them. The overriding part of her mind shoved those thoughts aside and forced her to run faster.

There was another shout behind her and she felt that someone was chasing her. Through the fear her mind teased her again with another thought: *I'm forgetting something import—*

Her foot came down on nothingness.

Her throat jerked out a strangled scream as she pitched forward headfirst, arms flailing. The back of her shoulders and head slammed into stone, followed by her buttocks and feet. Her head rang and she felt consciousness slipping away as she plunged through cold air.

* * *

Fridrik couldn't believe what was happening. There couldn't be a dragon here. He'd seen the dragon with his own eyes as a small child. It was much too large to fit inside this cave. Wasn't it? And now one of his friends was dead.

He wasn't sure which one, but he knew it was Birgit who had just slammed into him as she ran back down the passage through which they had come.

He gave chase. His candle went out as he ran and darkness enveloped him. He heard Birgit's footsteps ahead of him, and he wondered how she could manage to flee without being able to see. Ice ran up his spine as he remembered the chasm, and just then he heard Birgit shriek. The sound cut off almost as quickly as it began. Fridrik halted and reached his arms out to feel for the passage walls. *Gods! She's gone!*

With a growing sense of doom, he turned around in the inky blackness. He could see nothing, but there were terrible sounds from the darkness ahead. Gnawing sounds. Chewing sounds. Every instinct inside him told Fridrik to turn back, regardless of there being no other way out. He told himself that one of his friends yet lived, he hoped, frightened and alone in the gloom ahead. Could they somehow sneak by the dragon while it was distracted by its feasting?

He crouched low and snuck forward, trailing the fingers of his right hand against the wall. Dim light appeared ahead. A few steps farther and he saw a guttering candle lying on the stone floor. He slowed some more. Somewhere ahead, over the horrific sound of the dragon making a meal out of one of his lifelong friends, he heard the sound of weeping. *That's Anja! It must be. So the one he'd seen slain by the dragon — it was Halfdan.*

Fridrik reached down to retrieve the candle. When he stood upright again, he saw a vision worse than any nightmare.

At the far edges of the light, he could just make out the black lump of Halfdan's body. The dragon's snout was buried in his friend's belly, rooting and chewing as if it were the first meal it had had in ages.

The sound of weeping came from somewhere ahead and on the right. Wary of attracting the dragon's attention, Fridrik edged forward until he saw a curtain of stone that cascaded from the ceiling, forming a small wall that divided the room. Anja huddled on the floor with her back to the stone screen, her body shaking from the strength of her sobbing.

Fridrik stepped behind the screen of stone and felt relief that the dragon couldn't directly see him. He crouched next to Anja and put a hand on her shoulder. She gave a violent jerk and let out a cry.

"Shhh! Anja, it's me," he whispered.

Anja flung her arms around him, her tears wetting his face.

"Anja, we have to go now. Quietly."

He felt her head shaking. "Can't...can't..."

Fridrik gripped her arms and pulled her upright. "We must," he hissed. "The dragon is...distracted for the moment. We might make it."

"They're dead, and it's all my fault."

"It's our fault. Let's get out of here alive and face up to our debt."

Anja pressed harder against him, but this time he felt her nod.

"Where's your candle?" he said.

"I don't know. Lost it."

Fridrik cupped a hand over his own candle to shield the light from the dragon. "Follow me."

He slipped ahead. The screen of stone ended and he stopped and searched the gloom. He thought he saw a darker spot in the wall and prayed that it was the passage that led to the great hall. He pointed. "Do you see?"

She nodded.

"I have the candle. Crawl forward until you find the passage, then I'll join you."

"I'm scared."

"So am I. Go."

Anja looked in the direction of the feeding dragon, then took a deep breath and crawled toward the dark hole in the wall. Fridrik counted his heartbeats as they thudded in his chest. He expected the dragon to strike at any moment. Or perhaps it would flood the room with its acid breath. Anja made it to the hole and vanished.

Fridrik blew out his breath and checked to ensure his hand covered the fluttering candle flame. He whispered a prayer to the gods, then scurried toward the passage. Moments later he was panting next to Anja.

"We mustn't stop here," she whispered. "It may decide to return to its lair. Let's find the way out."

Fridrik pressed a hand to her back to urge her onward. He shielded the candle with his body, but it provided enough light for them to see the way forward. A mere ten paces on, they felt the air change and the walls fell away to either side.

"The great hall," Anja murmured.

* * *

Birgit plunged into a torrent of icy water. The wind was knocked out of her, but her mind became alert again. She couldn't orient herself. *Which way is up?* She felt the current dragging her along and her shoulder scraped against stone. She tried to get her feet under her or at least to the side where her shoulder had met the stone. She could no longer hold her breath. Her feet met stone and she thrust hard against it. Her head broke free of the water and she gasped for air in the moment before she plunged beneath the water again.

Birgit had long been a fine swimmer. Now that she knew which way was up, she dog paddled until her head again broke the surface. She saw nothing but darkness, and the sound of rushing water was almost deafening. The water plunged over a drop and her heart leapt into her throat. One leg struck something hard and a throbbing pain jagged up to her hipbone. She thrashed her way to the surface again.

This time she could see a little, as some sort of dimly glowing moss grew in patches on the walls. She saw that the rushing stream was about ten paces across here. There were boulders to either side and some in the stream itself. She was lucky not to have struck any of them yet. The patches of glowing moss nearly disappeared. Just before darkness enveloped her, Birgit thought she saw the stream whip around a bend to the left ahead. She swam to the right, hoping she could catch herself on something as the stream turned.

She fetched up hard against the stone bank, and her ribs protested painfully. Her hands scrabbled for purchase. One hand caught on a small boulder, and she lunged for it desperately with her other hand. Her grip held, and she managed to halt her forward momentum. Her legs trailed out ahead in the flood. She pulled hard with her arms to get her feet back underneath her.

For some time she remained where she was, her body weakening with numbness from the cold. *I've got to get out!*

Her arms trembling with fatigue, she pulled as hard as she could. She inched her chest up out of the water, but her strength gave out and she fell back in. She nearly lost her grip on the boulder. She panted several times and willed strength back into her arms. One of her feet found a tiny ledge on the wall under the water, so she latched onto it with both feet and thrust upward as hard as she could.

This time she was successful and managed to get her buttocks up onto the rocky bank. After a few deep breaths, she clawed her way farther onto the ledge, dragging her feet from the water. Her left hand brushed something strange that didn't feel like stone, but she was too exhausted to care. Birgit pulled her shivering body into a fetal position and drifted into unconsciousness.

* * *

To their right Fridrik saw sunlight limning the cracks where the huge entrance doors stood. His eyes adjusted to the gloom in the vast hall, and he gasped at what was revealed.

Lying curled about itself in the center of the hall's floor lay the dragon he remembered from long ago. It was like a dark mountain filling the hall. The candle fell from his nerveless grasp. Narrow beams of sunlight from the doors dimly illuminated the creature's enormous spiky head, and Fridrik kept expecting one of its plate-sized eyes to open.

Anja took a step toward the dragon. "Look," she whispered.

Fridrik had reached out to stop her, but now he saw what she had seen. He strode forward until he could see more clearly. The scales of the dragon's flanks had collapsed inward and in some places were torn away, revealing ribs larger than the beams on the chieftain's ship. "It's dead," he said, and heard the awe in his own voice.

Anja approached the dragon and trailed a hand over the ebon scales. "I didn't know dragons could die of old age."

Fridrik forced himself to approach the dragon's head. Even in death it was frightening, as if at any moment the massive jaws might snap open and strike at him. It took an effort of will to force his trembling hand to caress one of the yellowed teeth, dagger-sharp and as long as his forearm. He stared up at the terrible void where an eye should be and shuddered. "We shouldn't linger," he said. "The other dragon may still return."

"This dragon had young," she said, in awe.

"Or more than one. Let's go."

"Wait. We should search for Kathkalan's remains. We cannot make reparations for what happened to Birgit and Half-dan, but we could return Aivgaifa to our people."

"Are you crazy? If we get ourselves killed by that dragon, no one will ever know what happened to any of us! Let's go home. Your father can decide what to do about the dragon's progeny."

Anja looked like she wanted to go exploring. Fridrik grasped her arm. "I'm going. Leave the talisman for another day." He walked toward the entrance doors. He prayed Anja would have the sense to follow.

He expected the young dragon to attack at any moment, so he breathed a sigh of relief when he reached the doors. He wondered if he would need to find a secret lever or push-stone in order to open them, but when he pressed upon the ancient steel of one of the doors, it swung open easily as if on heavily greased hinges. Light and color flooded inward, and he saw the red ball of the sun nearing the horizon. He gave a start when Anja's hand fell on his shoulder.

"You're right, let's go," she said. "It'll be a long walk through the darkness to get home."

Fridrik closed the door. "I dread facing our parents, but most of all, I fear facing Birgit and Halfdan's."

"There's nothing for it," Anja said. "The blame should be mine."

"I didn't have to go along."

Anja gave Fridrik a long look, then began picking her way through the rubble of the ancient roadway.

* * *

Darkness, chattering teeth, cold stone, and the roar of water were the entirety of the world for Birgit when she woke.

Her body was wracked by shivers. *I'll die of cold long before I starve, that's for sure.*

She pulled her knees up to her chest and wrapped her arms about them. Gravel bit into her side, but she welcomed the pain. It reminded her that she yet lived.

She was surprised to realize that there were shades to the darkness. She thrust herself to a sitting position and stared about. The underground river raged by from her left to her right. It was to the left that she saw the lighter shading to the darkness. She recalled the glowing mosses. She could see none from here, but she suspected that the lighter coloring of the darkness must come from such moss.

A sharp pain in her left leg made her temporarily forget the cold. She slid a hand over the spot from which the pain radiated, hoping it was merely a bruise. Her head and back ached as well from slamming into the wall during the fall, but they didn't feel as bad as her leg.

The shivers took control again and her wet clothing didn't help matters. *Where am I? Buried beneath a mountain! Trapped and lost forever!*

These thoughts did no good, so she decided that moving around might at least warm her a little. She began to feel about with her hands. Cold, slimy rock was all she touched at first. Thick patches of moss covered much of the rock, though sadly not the glowing kind. She reached through the air in the direction away from the rushing waters, but her hands encountered no resistance. She bit her lip against the pain and slid herself forward into the darkness. Her right hand encountered something strange, and she recalled having felt it just before she lost consciousness.

Moaning with pain, she crawled closer to whatever it was she had felt. She reached out with both hands and explored the area in front of her. Her right hand touched something soft. Her left hit something hard, though not stone. She felt confused for a time, unsure what to examine first. She imagined that if she let one go it might vanish. She grasped both objects and pulled. The soft substance in her right hand gave easily, tearing away noiselessly. The object in her left hand was long and thin; it resisted her pull as if something larger was attached to it.

She released the harder object and used both hands to feel the softer. It felt like thick cloth, though it crumbled easily and tore at the barest touch. The cloth was too decayed to be of any use, which was unfortunate considering how cold she felt. She dropped the cloth and turned her attention to the long, hard object. She slid her hands in both directions along its length. Her left hand came to a break, a place where it had snapped like a branch of a tree. Her right hand encountered something cold and hard. She grabbed it, for it was yielding, and she realized what it must be. *Chain mail!* The realization made her shudder for a reason other than the cold. *This is a body. That must have been bone I was touching. If this person could do nothing but die here, what does that mean for me?*

She got to her knees, ignoring the pain that shot through her leg. Stretching out her arms, she patted her hands over the corpse, seeking to understand just how it lay. The body lay with its legs splayed out to Birgit's left, its arms pulled up close to its chest. The skull still had long, brittle strands of hair, and she yanked her hand back in revulsion as soon as she touched it. *Poor fellow! I should feel sympathy for him, not disgust.*

One hand had found something that could only be a sword. She had brushed the hilt first and had tentatively drawn her hand along the length of crumbling leather that was the scabbard. *What good would a sword do me here, even if it were not rusty and useless? I'd be far happier with a nice cloak.*

A wave of hopelessness descended on her. Tears welled up, and she thrust the heels of her palms into her eyes to dry them. *Breathe! You're not dead yet. Perhaps I can be luckier than he was.*

She remembered the snapped leg bone and wondered just what had happened to the man. She felt along the legs again and discovered that both had been broken in several places. *He must have had tremendous strength to be able to pull himself up here.*

Birgit was seized by a fit of shivering again, so she squeezed herself into a tight ball and rubbed her arms briskly. Something hard dug into her arm. She fumbled for it with numb fingers and found a cold metallic hoop. She tried to pull the object closer, but something resisted. With her thumb she felt a tiny chain running from the object. *A necklace?*

She confirmed her suspicion by drawing the fingers of both hands along the length of thin chain. It reached around the neck of the corpse. Birgit didn't relish the idea of touching the skull, which she imagined was grinning at her in the dark. She tried to drag the chain under the skull with both hands, but it caught on something and wouldn't move further. Grimacing, she used one hand to lift the skull and the other to feel for where the chain was caught. It was snagged in the hair on the back of the skull. She yanked the chain hard and it came free.

She examined her new treasure. The chain had torn some

of the hairs free from the skull, so she picked them off. The hoop at the end of the chain was about as wide as her hand, thin and hard. After touching it for a minute, she couldn't tell what it might be, so she slipped the chain over her head and tucked the object into her tunic.

The worst of her shivering had stopped, though it was still cold. She wished she had something to stuff in her ears to drown out the unceasing noise of the torrent. *Time to find out how big this ledge is.*

Carefully, she eased herself over the corpse, her injured leg protesting vehemently. Her reaching hand encountered slick, stone wall almost immediately. She pressed her weight against the wall and used it to help her stand, hoping all the while that she wouldn't crack her head against a low ceiling. Once she was erect, she inched to the left. She came up short against some large boulders. She reversed direction and after a mere four paces came to another dead end. *There's no way out, at least not that I can find without light.* She supposed there could be some sort of opening somewhere, even high up on the wall, but without the use of her eyes she had no chance of finding it. The thought of reentering the freezing torrent was daunting, but staying here with the corpse appealed to her even less. *What else can I do? I sure wish I could get warmer first!*

She knew that was a vain hope. The longer she remained here the more the cold would seep into her bones. She hunched down near the edge of the raging river. Before she could find excuses to linger, she took a deep breath and leapt out from the ledge into the icy torrent.

* * *

A faint noise caused Fridrik to snap awake. *What was that?* He twisted in his blanket to look at Anja, who snored lightly, her back pressed up against him for warmth. Faint light limned the edges of the mountain above them. *Morning at last,* he thought.

Most of the night had been a grueling trek down the crumbling, boulder-strewn road twisting down the mountain in utter darkness. Even when Anja had turned an ankle they had refused to halt for fear that the baby dragon might issue forth from above to hunt them down. When they had finally neared the base of the mountain, exhaustion had caught up with them, and they had wrapped themselves in blankets and cuddled in the hollow of a large boulder near the road.

Now Fridrik heard the sound again. It was clearer this time. A creaking sound. *Something else...hooves!* He leapt up from his blanket and peered into the gloom. He heard a jangle of harness, and saw a mule-drawn wain approaching, two dark shapes on the driving board, one larger than the other.

In the chilly air, Fridrik felt a spike of warmth down his spine. He had been dreading the long walk home, especially with Anja's injured ankle. Wrapping the blanket tightly about his shoulders, he stepped carefully over Anja's sleeping form and went to meet the wain.

The cart was slow, the road little more than a bumpy track. Rays of sun broke over the mountain and Fridrik saw that the forms on the wain were those of an elderly man and boy a few years younger than Fridrik himself. The old man pulled on the reins and called out to the mule, which stumbled to a halt.

Hair prickled on Fridrik's arm. Their clothes. Their faces. These two were from the neighboring clan, one not friendly to their own.

He felt a presence beside him, and looking over he saw Anja, one hand covering a great yawn.

"You two look to have had a rough night," the old man said. He handed the reins over to the boy and clambered down from the cart.

"Sir," Fridrik said, "might we beg a ride? Anja has hurt her—"

"You're fools to be out in the cold like this," the man said, "and so near the dragon mount. Makes me think you must be friends of the other one."

Fridrik felt his breath catch in his throat. As he fumbled to find words, Anja took a step forward and with a hitch in her voice said, "Other one?"

"Come," the man said, and beckoned them toward the bed of the cart. "Nearly frightened us to death, she did. My grandson and I were tending our flock beyond the mount." The man pointed back at the dragon's mountain. "There's a pond below a waterfall where we like to water our sheep."

Fridrik mouthed silent prayers to the gods as they reached the back of the wain. A blanket-wrapped form lay still on the dirty straw in the bed of the cart. Its face was so pale that at first Fridrik's mind refused to recognize Birgit. Then he saw the two moles on her left cheek and he gave a whoop. "It's her, Anja! It's Birgit!" He jumped into the cart and knelt to grasp Birgit by her shoulders. He looked up at the boy on the riding board. "Is she dead?"

The boy scowled and said nothing, but the old man finished helping Anja up into the cart and said, "Nay, not yet, leastwise. Her mind is with the gods. Twice in my life I've seen men in such a state, and only once did one of them wake."

"What happened to her?" Anja murmured.

"Fell right down off the waterfall into the pond," the man said. "Worst scare I've ever had. Sheep scattered to the wind. We'll have the gods' own time rounding them up."

"Oh, Birgit," Anja cried. Fridrik saw tears streaking her cheeks as she knelt and flung her arms around her friend's shoulders.

"Both her legs are broke," the man continued. "Probably some ribs as well. Come, I'll drive you on to your village."

As the old man clambered up next to his grandson, Fridrik settled into the straw and put a hand on Anja's shuddering back as she wept over Birgit's broken body. He glanced up at the man and said, "Why did you decide to help us?"

The man was silent for a few moments. "Not all of us believe there should be conflict between our peoples. If my son got lost and wandered onto your lands, I could only hope you would show the same mercy to me." The man snapped the reins and the mule began to plod forward.

"What's this?" he heard Anja whisper, and from the neckline of Birgit's tunic she drew forth a tarnished silver circlet, strung on a thin chain. She met Fridrik's gaze and he saw wonder shining in her eyes. "The talisman – I recognize it from the shaman's scrolls. This is Aivgaifa! Birgit found it!"

Fridrik pulled his knees up to his chest and hugged them. He knew he should feel shocked, but somehow he didn't. He looked up at the warm sunlight streaming over the mountain, then looked back at the pale face of Birgit. Against all odds they had survived. An enemy tribesman had shown them kindness. Against the backdrop of horrors that was this day, there shone the faint glimmer, in all their lives, of hope.

A WORD FROM TED CROSS

I developed a love for fantasy very early by discovering Conan, first in comics and later in Robert E. Howard's amazing novels, and that led quickly to *The Hobbit* and *The Lord of the Rings* by J.R.R. Tolkien. I was smitten, so it was no surprise that I plunged headfirst into the *Dungeons & Dragons* craze of the early 1980's. I never actually imagined myself as a writer, though, and I stuck mainly to reading over the next couple of decades.

I went to work with the Foreign Service, a life that took me all over the world, living in countries from Russia and China to Hungary, Croatia, and Azerbaijan. But it was a move to Iceland in 2007 that helped dredge up vague ideas of wanting to write my own fantasy stories. There was a faerie-like quality to Iceland—in its people, the language, and especially in the landscape. It felt as if I might spot an elf or a troll around any bend of the mossy volcanic paths I walked each day near my home.

The official *Dungeons & Dragons*-themed books had always disappointed me. To my taste they always felt cartoonish, or made the protagonists into superheroes. What I wanted was a book that lent gravitas to the subject matter, that treated it not as a game but with a level of gritty realism as if George R.R. Martin had written it. Reading Martin's *A Game of Thrones* and living in Iceland were the catalysts for me to write my recently published epic fantasy *The Shard*.

Developing back stories for characters in *The Shard* led me to a fantastic science fiction idea, though I had thought I would only ever write fantasy. I set aside edits to *The Shard* and wrote a cyberpunk thriller called *The Immortality Game*. Hard as it may be to believe, the two books share a couple of characters, something I explain in old posts on my blog http://tedacross. blogspot.com.

While writing novels seemed to come naturally to me, I seriously struggled to write short stories. I was rarely satisfied with my endings. So I'm grateful to join this group of amazing writers that you find in this anthology. The idea for this story came from remembering what it is like as a child to dream of being a hero and imagining the worst possible scenario for trying to live that dream—sneaking into a dragon's lair.

A Diversion in Time
by Nina Croft

THE FORWARD SCREENS showed the end of the tunnel, a gaping hole surrounded by flashes of bright white light, and beyond that Angel could make out a blue-green planet.

Earth.

In the rear screens, the eerie violet of the wormhole snaked out behind them.

All around the bridge of the *Blood Hunter*, the crew were busy doing whatever they did. Everyone had a job. Except him. He was nothing but dead weight, a passenger, and only that because he'd stowed away.

"We're almost there," Rico said from the pilot's seat. "I'm guessing it's going to be a smooth ride, but you might want to strap yourselves in just in case."

Angel backed up until his knees hit the seat behind him, and sank down, his hands fumbling with the harness as he fastened the buckles and pulled it tight. Captain Tannis took the seat next to his and fastened her own harness with zero fumbling. He turned and found her watching him out of those inhuman violet eyes. He knew she couldn't read *his* mind, but all the same, he always felt twitchy under the intense stare.

"You okay, Kid?" she asked.

He gritted his teeth. Of course he was okay. Why shouldn't he be okay? And he wasn't a goddamned kid. He was twenty-three. "I'm fine."

"No need to get snippy. I promised your sister we'd look after you."

And he didn't need looking after. Whatever his sister—the brand new Empress of the goddamned Universe—believed. Candy was a whole five minutes older than him and had never let him forget it.

"I'm—" His words were cut off as the ship pitched violently then picked up speed, the sudden acceleration pressing him back against the seat and shoving the rest of his words down his throat.

"Holy freaking hell, Rico!" Tannis snapped. "Slow the fuck down."

Rico glanced over his shoulder. He grinned, flashing the tip of one sharp white fang. "Sorry, but as of this moment, I am no longer in control. Just hold on tight and hope she doesn't crash."

Angel's fingers tightened on the arms of his chair. The hole filled one screen now, the light almost unbearably bright. His eyes hurt and his chest ached; he'd been holding his breath. Now he gulped down air, but couldn't drag his attention from the screen. At least they were heading dead for the center.

At the last moment, the wormhole lurched sideways as though lashing its tail. The *Blood Hunter* slammed into the wall with a dazzling flare of purple and they were spiraling out of control. The interior lights flashed on then off, finally going out completely, leaving them in the half-light from the screens. The ship spun faster and faster, the scenes on the screens changing too rapidly for him to get any sense of what was in front and what was behind.

For a second, everything went dark.

He blinked, and the lights came back, and they were out into open space. The spinning slowed to a languid rotation giving alternating views of the blue-green planet and the gaping maw of the wormhole twisting across space behind them.

Saffira was on her knees in the center of the bridge, her eyes tight shut. Then she crumpled to the floor. Devlin unstrapped himself and ran across, crouching down beside her. "Saffira, sweetheart, are you okay?"

She blinked. "Fine…I think. Just sooo tired." Her eyes closed again and she relaxed.

"Passed out," Devlin said. "All her vitals seem fine, though." He looked up, his heated violet gaze fixed on Rico. "You did it again. I can't believe you did it again."

"I didn't do anything."

Devlin ignored the comment. "It was supposed to be easy. All you had to do was think of a date. The day before you left earth. Not difficult. But no—you had to let your mind wander."

"My mind *did not* wander. 2050. It was stamped on my brain. "

2050 was the year man had fled to the stars, because supposedly the Earth was dying. Rico had been part of the exodus—the vampire was nearly two thousand years old and had been born on Earth. But no one actually knew what had happened after they left, and Rico wanted to find out. They'd had nothing better to do, so the crew had taken a vote, and here they were. Unfortunately, Saffira wasn't very good at controlling the wormholes yet, though she was getting better.

"Well something diverted us," Tannis said. "And we were so close, almost there."

"It looks like we're not too far out," Rico murmured, tapping into the systems. "2015."

Tannis ran a hand through her short spiky hair. "Thirty-five freaking years from when we're meant to be. And I'm not sticking around."

Angel wasn't sure they had a choice. A glance at the rear view screen showed the wormhole was a distant ripple across space, black on black, and getting further away each second. With Saffira unconscious, they had no way of calling it back.

"We're not going anywhere right now," Rico said. "The guidance system is fucked and the primary thrusters aren't responding. We've also sustained considerable external damage. We're going to have to land and do some repairs. Luckily, the stealth mode is still functioning. Otherwise we'd be a little conspicuous—not too many star cruisers around in 2015."

"Great, just great," Tannis muttered, pacing the length of the bridge.

"Relax. We'll go down to Earth, fix the ship, by that time Saffira will be recovered, she'll call us another wormhole, and this time we'll get it right."

Tannis narrowed her eyes as though she wanted to complain some more, then she nodded. "So where are we?" she asked. "Are we at least *where* we're supposed to be?"

"Wait a sec." Rico tapped his console, and the screen zoomed in to get a close up of the planet below. They were in a partial orbit, circling a small area. "Scotland," he muttered, his eyes narrowing on the screen. "Well, that makes it a definite—even if my mind did wander, I can guarantee it would not wander to Scotland."

"Not good then?"

"It depends if you like men in skirts, eating sheep's stomachs, rain, and cold, and..."

Angel hadn't unstrapped his harness, and decided he might as well stay where he was for now, just in case things went wrong. Again. He stared mesmerized as the Earth grew larger, filling the screens. It was different than he'd expected. He'd thought there would be more people, but the area they were heading for appeared devoid of life. A flat green expanse, dotted by grey lakes of water, and bisected by what was obviously a man-made track—the only sign of any civilized life. Rico finally touched down, the ship bumping once or twice as he fought for control.

Outside, the light was dim and eerie. Off to the west the sky glowed red where the single sun was sinking behind the horizon. Angel's heart was thumping as his blood raced. He was on Earth. Not only on Earth, but Earth a thousand years ago. He was going to visit the birthplace of mankind.

"Rannoch Moor." Rico sounded less than happy. "One of the most godforsaken places on the planet."

Angel thought it looked interesting. He'd been brought up

on the dark side of Trakis Two where nothing was green. He liked the look of the wide open spaces and inside, his wolf woke and whined in agreement. "Can I go explore?"

"No. Don't leave the ship," Tannis ordered. "It might not be safe."

At that moment, the piercing ring of an alarm cut across the bridge and a whole load of red lights started flashing.

Rico swore. "The docking bay. It's been breached. Could be due to damage when we hit the wormhole." His gaze wandered around, finally settled on Angel. "Hey, Puppy, go check on our other stowaway."

I am not a puppy. But he kept his mouth shut and unfastened the harness. At least he had something useful to do for once.

"Docking bay," he murmured as he stepped into the transporter bubble. It carried him down and the doors opened onto the vast expanse of the docking bay. The shuttles had all been moved to one side to make a big space in the center. A big *empty* space.

Where the hell was Kronus?

The alarm light was still flashing crimson, the whine shrill in his ears. He found the control panel, pressed the keypad, and the noise and light cut off abruptly. He spoke into the comm unit on his wrist. "Kronus has gone."

"What do you mean 'gone'?" Tannis asked, her tone irritated.

"As in he's not here."

"Well, someone that large is unlikely to vanish in a puff of smoke."

"No smoke." In fact, the air felt damp and chill. Angel rubbed his arms and stepped out into the docking bay, looked around. "The outer doors are open."

"No shit. Well, I guess that's why he's not there."

"I'll go have a look."

"Don't you dare. I promised your sister—"

Angel switched off the comm unit. He crossed the space and stood at the open doorway and stared out at the landscape of Earth. There was nobody about, the place eerily silent. Nothing moved, until he looked upwards and searched the darkening sky.

As always, his mind filled with wonder when faced with the immensity that was Kronos. Black with iridescent purple lights rippling across his hide, he hovered above the ship, silhouetted against the red sky. Peering down out of huge violet orbs, his gaze fixed on Angel.

"Come."

The word echoed in Angel's mind. Then the dragon gave a flick of his tail and headed off toward the mountains.

Not giving himself any time to think it was a really bad idea, Angel raced back into the docking bay, jumped into a speeder, and was heading after Kronus. As he steered the speeder through the open doors, Rico spoke over the comm unit.

"Go have some fun, Kid, but don't tell the captain I told you to. We're leaving in…" he turned away obviously to consult with Devlin, "…two hours, so be back with our scaly friend by then."

"I'll do my best."

It wasn't as though they would leave him behind and risk

the wrath of his sister. As he passed the second set of doors, Tannis came over the comm. "Angel, get back here, right—" He shut off the link without waiting for her to finish, pressed the button to unlock the comm unit from his wrist, and tossed it back into the docking bay.

Once outside, the speeder hovered just above the ground. Angel stared up into the darkening sky trying to catch a glimpse of where Kronus had gone. A faint shimmering trail showed the flight path, and off in the distance a black speck appeared. *"Come."*

The word held a hint of irritation this time.

Angel steered the speeder above the level of the few trees that dotted the barren landscape and then headed after the black speck. The air was cutting and soon the icy wind was whipping through his hair. As he increased to maximum speed, he threw back his head and laughed. Wow, he was on Earth.

"Is something amusing…kid?"

There was no point in answering. While Kronus could project his thoughts over immeasurable distances, Angel couldn't project his anywhere at all. And that was probably just as well, he wasn't sure he wanted people to know what he was thinking. Sure, he could see the advantages—the Collective had ruled the universe for centuries, and much of their power had come from their ability to communicate telepathically.

It had taken five hundred years for the ships that had left Earth to find a system capable of sustaining life, and there they had also stumbled across the secret of immortality, Meridian. The substance bestowed eternal life, plus a few other—not necessarily beneficial—attributes, including telepathy, inhuman strength, violet eyes, and eventually wings. The latter was apparently the point when they had realized there was more to Meridian than they'd originally suspected.

Even so, none of them had ever guessed what it really was. Not until the *Blood Hunter* had dived through a black hole in search of an alternative source and found—

"*Kid.*" Kronus interrupted his thoughts.

The dragon was on the ground directly in front of him and he slammed on the brakes. The speeder came to an abrupt halt almost hurling him out of the front seat.

"*Perhaps you should watch where you're going.*"

"Where am I going?" He lowered the vehicle to ground level and jumped out. "And what are we doing here?"

The last of the sun's light had vanished and he peered out into the darkness. Kronus crouched on the grass in front of him, wings folded, eyes unblinking. "*You don't need to know. You just need to do as I say.*" The words oozed menace.

Angel snorted. "Yeah, of course I do. Not. Tell me what you're up to or I'm going back to the ship." He turned and headed back to his speeder. Kronus launched himself lightly into the air, over Angel's head, and came down on the vehicle. His gigantic claws closed around the metal and it crunched beneath his colossal strength.

Angel shook his head. "Tannis is going to be so pissed at you."

Kronus ignored the comment. "*Do what I say and I will see that you return safely to the ship. You will not find your way back without me.*"

"Want to bet?" He sniffed the air, filtering out the smells

from this world, identifying the faintly sulfurous after-burn of the speeder. He could follow the trail back to the *Blood Hunter*. He shoved his hands in his pockets and set off. "See you back at the ship."

He held his breath as he walked away, because really, he didn't want to go back. He was just fed up with people—and dragons—thinking he was a soft touch and they could push him around. What he really wanted was to discover what the dragon was after.

A *hiss* sounded behind him, then the *whoosh* of wings close over his head, and Kronus alighted in front of him. He eyed Angel from those vast purple orbs. Staring into them, Angel knew he could get lost in the immensity of time. Kronus was old, so old Angel couldn't begin to imagine the things he had seen and done.

Long ago, dragons had controlled the wormholes that joined the far reaches of time and space. Or at least the females of their race had. They were time-mancers. But playing with time is a dangerous game, and the dragons had come close to annihilating not only their universe, but the whole of creation. Afterwards, they had rid the world of the time-mancers, so they would never again be tempted to play masters of time. Slaughtered all the females of their race, burned them in dragon-fire—one of the few reliable ways to bring their kind to the true-end—and retreated to their home planet.

So, no more female dragons, and no more time-mancers.

Until Saffira had come along. Now the wormholes were open once again.

Kronus sighed, with a *hiss* of sulfurous breath. *"Okay, I'll tell you."*

Angel crossed to a massive bolder close by the dragon, scrambled up so he was almost level with his eyes and didn't have to crane his neck. "So what are we doing here?"

A trickle of flame leaked from his nostrils as Kronus pondered his words. Angel guessed he wasn't used to explaining himself. *"I wish you to get something for me."*

"And you know this…thing is here?"

"I do. I have been here before."

Something occurred to him. "You're the one who twisted the wormhole. Right at the end. You brought us here." He thought a little more. "And that's why you came on the *Blood Hunter* in the first place. Why you helped me stow away. You planned this all along."

Kronus nodded his great head.

"So what's so important? What do you want me to get?"

"An egg."

"I'm guessing not a chicken egg."

"No, a dragon egg. A female dragon egg."

Angel grinned. "Hey, Kronus wants a girlfriend."

The dragon exhaled loudly, filling the air with his hot, smoky breath. *"I want the power we once had."*

"Isn't that dangerous?"

The dragon shrugged, at least Angel guessed it was a shrug, hard to tell. *"I have learned from our mistakes."*

Angel thought it highly unlikely. More probably, Kronus was bored. "Can't you just ask Saffira to go back in time to before you killed them all and get a female?"

"We didn't kill them all. They…sacrificed themselves so the universe would not be torn apart."

"Of course they did." He'd talked to Saffira, who had seen

it in one of her visions. And the truth was that more than a few of the time-mancers had needed a push.

Kronus ignored the comment. He was good at that. *"But no, they cannot come forward past the moment of their true death. They are stuck in the past."*

"Then why not just go back and live in the past with them?"

"Because I don't want to live in the past." Impatience laced his words. *"Immortality is hard enough anyway, and I want to see what happens next."*

Yeah, Angel could sort of understand that. "And you're not content to just let what happens next…happen next." When the dragon said nothing, he sniggered. "Go on admit it—you want a girlfriend. Aw that's sweet."

"Maybe."

"So where exactly is this egg?"

"At the house of a woman. You will find her over there." He gestured with his great head to the east where Angel could make out a faint glow of light. *"In the big building with the picture of a dragon on the sign over the door. She has red hair. You must follow her home, find the egg, and return to me."*

"Sounds easy."

"Do not let the woman see you follow her."

"Why can't you just take me to the house?"

"I cannot go there. Another self is close and I cannot risk us crossing. Or him sensing my presence."

"You mean you're already here? There're two of you?"

"And if we connect…well, it would not be a good thing."

"Okay. I'll try."

"Do not try…do!"

* * *

The walk took longer than he expected. Once or twice he thought about shifting, but he considered the logistics and decided against it. After ten minutes, the moon rose, and at least he could make out a vague path through the vegetation. Finally he hit a proper track, made for land bound vehicles, and after that the going was easier. He glanced back once or twice, but Kronus was soon out of sight.

By the time he reached the cluster of buildings, he was shivering. The material of his jumpsuit deflected water and retained body heat but was not made for temperatures like these. Christ, he hated the cold. The village was nothing more than a huddle of houses, but as Kronus had told him, at the center was a large structure with a sign swaying above the door. The Dragon's Den. The dragon was not black like Kronus, but red, though otherwise they were similar. The old legends of Earth must have come from somewhere, and he was guessing that Kronus and his kind had been seen in these parts before.

He approached the building with caution. Should he wait outside for the woman to leave? But he was cold and intrigued; he wanted to see as much as he could of this time and place. Inside he could hear the rise and fall of many voices.

As he pushed open the door, the conversation stopped abruptly.

There were no men in skirts.

The room was snug and warm after the chill night air, and a fire flickered in a huge open fireplace. As he stepped inside a prickle of unease ran down his spine and inside his wolf growled. He'd spent much of his youth trawling the bars in Pleasure city, the capital of Trakis Two, often hunting for his sister, but he'd never felt himself the center of attention like this before.

Of course, he was dressed differently. They were all in blue pants, thick heavy coats to keep out the cold and damp. He was all in black, a jumpsuit and knee high boots. No doubt, he must look a little odd to these people.

"You're a wee strange one," a man spoke from the right. He was seated at a table with a group of three others, playing some sort of game with little black blocks.

"Not that wee," said another.

Luckily, Angel got his height from his father, not his diminutive mother. Suddenly he had a wave of homesickness. Would he ever see them again? They had stayed behind as part of Thorne and Candy's administration. His mother was the ex-high priestess of the Church of Everlasting Life and she'd offered to try and bring the last of the Church's people back into the mainstream populace. Thorne reckoned the fighting had gone on long enough and it was time to bring an end to the hatred and bitterness that had nearly torn the Trakis system apart. He had offered everyone who truly wanted it—and Thorne was able to discern their innermost thoughts—an amnesty and the chance for a new life.

Angel gave the men a vague smile. They raised their eyebrows but went back to their game. "Bloody tourists," one muttered.

He searched the room. At first he didn't see her as he methodically went through the tables. There were fewer people

than he'd originally thought; the place just seemed crowded because it was so small. Finally, he glanced behind the bar which
ran along the short edge of the room, and there she was.

He recognized her straight away by her fiery red hair. Not
just red, but bright red, like a halo around her head. Her hair
was the biggest thing about her; she was a tiny little thing,
probably coming up to no further than his shoulder. She had
a pointed face, green eyes and a wide mouth, smiling, showing
small white teeth. She radiated happiness and he found himself
drawn toward her.

As he approached, her gaze ran over him, all the way down
then up again, her grin widening. "You want a drink?"

Did he? He glanced around; everyone else was drinking.
He nodded.

"So what would you like?"

A hard question. Alcohol had been banned not long in
the future, way before he was born. What was it Rico drank?
"Whiskey," he said.

"What sort of whiskey?"

Was she making this difficult on purpose? How the hell did
he know what sort of whiskey? Maybe seeing his confusion, she
waved a hand at the shelf behind her. There were bottles. Lots
of bottles. He pointed at one and she raised a brow but reached
up and pulled it down. "This is single malt, twenty years old
and will set you back twenty-five pounds a shot. You okay with
that?"

"Twenty-five pounds?"

"Money. You know what that is?"

He knew what it was in theory, but he'd never actually seen

any. Money was pretty much an alien concept in the Trakis system.

"Hmm." She considered him a moment longer. "Well, I'm not giving away the good stuff," she said with a sigh, replacing the bottle on the shelf, "But because you're pretty, and have really weird taste in clothes, and are obviously not quite right in the head, you can have a drink on the house." She pulled down another bottle and splashed some into a glass, pushed it toward him and watched, her lips tilted with amusement.

He picked up the glass, sniffed, and swallowed the liquid in one go. It was smoother than Rico's, which always felt as though it was stripping the skin from his throat, and straight away the heat rolled in his stomach.

He put the glass down and stared at it longingly.

Her lips twitched, but she poured another shot, then made a show of screwing the top on the bottle and placing it back on the shelf. "Can't give away all the profits." She came back, leaned her arms on the bar, and studied him, her head cocked to one side.

"So," she murmured, "a beautiful stranger walks into a bar and—"

"You think I'm beautiful?" he asked.

She looked him up and down. "You're not telling me no girl has told you you're beautiful before."

"Er...no."

She stepped to the side and waved a hand. The wall was mirrored behind the rows of bottles and he could see himself. He'd never really thought about what he looked like, though most people said he was the image of his father. Which made him, tall, dark haired, with amber eyes. He stared at the reflection —he didn't care about looks, but who would he really like to see when he looked in a mirror? All his life he'd lived in his sister, Candy's, shadow. Now he was as far away from her as it was possible to get, time to stand on his own and decide who and what he wanted to be. Did he want to be fierce like his father, once the most notorious assassin in the universe? Or good like his mother? Did he want to be all powerful like Candy's new husband, Thorne? Or more like Rico who had no interest in power, and just wanted to get as much fun out of life as he could. Or Tannis, fiercely loyal to her crew? Trouble was he had too many role models.

But what did *he* want? Who did he want to be?

"See." The girl's voice interrupted his musings. "Even you're mesmerized."

He'd never had a girlfriend, though he wasn't a virgin. Candy had auctioned off his virginity to her friends on their twenty-first birthday and only told him about it the next day. He'd believed he'd suddenly become irresistible. Candy hadn't even shared the proceeds. But his life in general had been a little… messy and not conducive to relationships. Now he wondered what it would be like to have someone of his own.

"I think you're beautiful as well," he said. Because it was true. He liked the way she looked with her fiery red hair and pale skin. The freckles across her nose. And he liked the way she smelled, like flowers.

She shook her head, but was still smiling. "So where do you come from?"

That was a difficult one. The Trakis System, around about

a thousand years from now, would only cause disbelief, and she already thought he was crazy, but he found he didn't want to lie. Maybe he was curious as to her reaction. "Would you believe another planet?"

"So you're an alien?"

"Er...no."

"And you were just passing?"

He nodded. "I was...going for a walk and I passed this place and thought it looked nice and..."

She reached across and patted his hand where it rested on the bar. "Well, my friend, you tell a great story. But it's time to say good night." Strolling to the far end of the bar, she picked up a bell and rang it. The conversation in the room fell silent.

There was some muttering, but one by one the customers set their empty glasses on the bar and walked out until only Angel was left.

"You too," she said. "It's closing time."

He didn't want to go. She tilted her head and pushed a red curl behind her ear. "If you haven't flown off to your own planet tomorrow, then come back," she said. "Maybe bring some money. You can buy me a drink."

He nodded, though tomorrow he'd be long gone. With a sigh of regret, he headed for the door.

"Hey," she called out behind him. "What's your name?"

Turning back, he smiled. "I'm Angel."

She grinned. "Of course you are. I'm Mara. I'll see you tomorrow, Angel."

He shivered as the door clicked closed behind him. The rest of the customers had disappeared, and he stepped to the side of the building and hid himself in the shadows. A couple of minutes later, the door opened and Mara stepped out. She locked up behind herself and headed down the single street. Angel waited until there was some distance between them before following her. She walked past the buildings, but continued after the houses ran out. Once, she glanced back, as though she sensed his presence, but in his black clothes he merged with the night. Even in this form, he felt more at home in the darkness than he did in the light. His eyes saw far more than a mere human, his nose picked up the scents of all the strangeness.

Finally, she halted beside a small building, low and long, in complete darkness. After fumbling in her bag for something, she opened the door, disappeared inside, and a light flicked on.

When he was sure she was staying, he headed around the back. He slipped the knife out of his boot and slid it down the catch in the window. Silently he opened it and pulled himself inside. He was in what looked like a living space, comfortable chairs around a viewer. The place smelled of Mara and he breathed in deeply. Music drifted across from the front of the house and he silently crossed the room and out into a corridor. The door opposite was open. Mara stood with her back to him, in what he took to be the galley, making food; she would be busy for a while.

He stepped back and returned the way he had come. For a moment, he paused, closing his eyes to focus his attention, and breathing in deeply. He caught a faint exotic whiff, a scent that spoke of strange worlds and the far reaches of space, of wormholes, and flying through fire. He followed the smell and pushed open another door. This led into a sleeping area. The room was small, a big bed and a tall cupboard took up all the space.

Angel crossed straight to the cupboard. As he opened the door, his nostrils filled with the alien scent of dragon overlaid with the flowery scent of Mara. He'd love to burrow himself in her softness, see if she tasted as sweet.

She'd said he was beautiful, asked him to come back. Perhaps the *Blood Hunter* would take longer to repair than they had believed. And Rico was always telling him he needed to get laid. Maybe he could tell him there was a chance if they could just delay a day or two. What was the hurry?

He'd ask. When he got back tonight. And maybe tomorrow he'd return to the Dragon's Den, talk some more.

The bang of a door closing pulled him from his daydreams, and he shook himself. Time to move this on. Crouching down, he rummaged around the clothes which had been flung into the bottom of the cupboard—she was messy, like Candy. His hand found something smooth and warm to the touch. He laid his palm flat against it and heat radiated out. Pushing the clothes away, he revealed the oval egg, luminous white, but with a faint hint of crimson glowing beneath the surface. It was heavy, almost too big to fit in his hands, and as he picked it up, a strange throbbing beat though his palms. The thing was alive. Kronus might very well get his lady friend. But what did that mean? The dragons had once destroyed all the time-mancers to preserve the universe. Was Angel risking total annihilation by doing this?

But change was important and things existed for a reason. Without giving himself time to talk himself out of it—according to Candy, he thought way too much—he wrapped the egg in one of Mara's flower-scented garments and straightened. As he slipped out of the room, her footsteps sounded on the stone floor. He ducked into the living area and then out of the window, pulling it closed behind him.

"See you tomorrow, Mara," he murmured and headed back the way he had come.

He held the egg close against his chest, letting the heat warm him through his clothes. He walked without thinking about the route, just following the trail he had made on the way, and let his mind wander.

Most people fell into what they were by accident rather than design. That had been him for so many years; his choices limited by the need to keep under the Church's radar while searching for a way to free his parents. They'd been taken prisoner by the Church when he was only twelve. That had shaped his life for so long.

Now he could literally go anywhere, be anything he wanted. In some ways he'd decided on a path when he'd chosen to stow away on the *Blood Hunter* instead of staying with his sister and parents and helping to create their brave new civilization. He didn't want civilization. He wanted to see what was beyond the edge of the universe, where the next wormhole led, what the world had been like a thousand years ago, what it would be like a thousand years from now. He wanted to be an explorer. A good person. He wanted to be someone people would look up to like Thorne, who they'd love, like his mother, who was fearless when going after what they wanted like Tannis, who had an amazing capacity for enjoying everything life could offer, like Rico.

The opportunities were as limitless as time, and a zing of excitement speeded up his steps.

As Angel came into sight, Kronus spread his wings and made a little hopping movement—what passed for excitement in dragon body language, he presumed.

"You have it."

It wasn't a question, but Angel nodded anyway, unwrapped his package, and held it out to Kronus. Spurts of flame trickled from his nostrils, red flame that licked over the egg, singeing Angel's fingers so he almost dropped it.

"Watch out," he snapped, stepping back.

The sound in his head was almost a purr.

"Hey, it's only an egg—don't go all soppy on me."

"Thank you, Angel."

"My pleasure." And it was, he'd had fun this evening and he'd met a girl.

A chuckle sounded in his mind. He wasn't sure he'd ever seen the dragon happy before, maybe it was hard to be happy with the weight of all those years.

"Come," Kronus said.

"Come where?"

"The egg is not ready. It needs another…" he leaned a little closer, *"thirty Earth years to mature. We will secure it in a safe place and return when it is time."* He reached out one scaly claw. Angel looked at it for a moment, flutters in in stomach—he'd only flown on the dragon once before, when he and Kronus had helped each other stow away on the *Blood Hunter*. After tuck-

ing the egg under one arm, he jumped onto the outstretched leg. The scales covering the shoulder were big enough to use as hand-holds and he climbed onto the broad back, slung one leg over, and settled just in front of the wings.

With no warning, those enormous wings spread, lifting them effortlessly into the air. His blood raced with a thrill of exhilaration. So much power.

He leaned forward. "Higher."

They rose and rose. Kronus took them to the edges of space, then plunged straight down to hover fifty feet above the ground. Angel recognized the small collection of buildings with the Dragon's Den at the center, Mara's cozy cottage at the outskirts of the village.

Kronus flew them slightly north to where the mountains rose out of the barren ground, alighting on a tiny ledge halfway up the highest peak.

"Place the egg at the back of the cave, and cover it with rocks," Kronus said.

"What cave?"

Then he spotted the narrow opening. He slid down the dragon's shoulder, teetered on the brink of the ledge, but was pulled back by the dragon's claw hooked in the neck of his jumpsuit.

"Careful."

He sidled along the ledge, and scraped though the narrow opening into a large cave, big enough to stand up straight. After re-wrapping the egg in Mara's clothing, he laid it on the ground, and piled up rocks until it was hidden. Not that anyone would chance upon it up here.

When he got back outside, Kronus was still perched on the ledge, exuding a positive sense of self-satisfaction.

"So you plan to get Saffira to bring you back here in thirty years' time?" Angel asked. "Will you tell her why or will you just hijack them again?"

"Will you tell them?"

"Probably."

"Then perhaps I will tell them first."

"Good plan. But I'm going to ask if we can stick around for a while."

"Why?"

He considered whether to tell Kronus, but why not? "I want to see the girl, Mara, again. I liked her."

Kronus swiveled his massive head and stared at him out of inscrutable violet eyes. A shiver ran through him.

"That would be pointless."

"Why?" He wasn't that bad. She'd actually said he was beautiful.

"Because tonight she dies."

Shock had him teetering on the edge again. How could she die? And how did Kronus know? Because he had been here before, of course. "What are you going to do?"

"Nothing. It has already been done. I identified the location of a female egg and I destroyed it—as was my duty."

"And Mara?"

"Was in the house."

"You have to take me back."

"I cannot. The girl dies—I saw her burn. It is already done. If we change that, it will send ripples through the whole of time."

"Oh, and what about the egg burning? You think changing that isn't going to make any fucking ripples?"

"That is a necessity."

"Only to you. Goddamn hypocrite. Take me back."

"No."

Angel gritted his teeth. Time was running out. "Please."

"I cannot."

He stared across the moor, making out the glow of light from the village and off to the side Mara's small home. Was a younger Kronus already approaching? Flying across the night sky, ready to burn her to ashes. Not going to happen.

He'd never make it in time. At least not in human form.

He kicked off his boots, pulled on the fastener of his jumpsuit and quickly stripped to stand naked on the ledge. For a second, he held himself tense, waiting for Kronus to stop him, the intention heavy in the air. Nothing happened and Angel gave a shudder, felt the magic ripple through him, and a moment later he stood on all fours, his senses acute, aware of the world around him.

Throwing back his head, he howled to the sky, then leaped off the ledge and plunged down the almost vertical incline. He'd forgotten how much he loved this—there wasn't much option for shifting on a space ship—now he reveled in the feel of the power of his limbs, the supernatural speed. In only minutes, he was on the level ground of the moors and racing toward Mara's cottage. A sense of urgency pushed him on, he had no clue how long he had, and every second he expected the sky to rain down fire.

At last he skidded to a halt outside the house. How to do this? Should he shift back? But confronted with a naked man, she might just lock herself in. No, he needed the element of surprise. The sky was still clear, but was that the *whoosh* of wings approaching from the south? He padded around the rear of the building to her bedroom. A faint hint of light came from the curtained window, so likely she was still awake.

He closed his eyes and hurled himself through the glass. It crashed around him, but he landed on the center of the bed, a shrill scream ringing in his ears.

Mara sat bolt upright up, hair wild about her shoulders, mouth wide open. He crouched lower, looking as small and innocent as he could, tried a quick wag of his tail. Through the now open window, he could hear the definite sound of approaching wings. Time was nearly out. At least she'd stopped screaming. He moved slowly, took her bare arm in his teeth as gently as he could, and tugged.

She tried to pull free, and he shook his head. Her eyes widened, but she understood, and when he tugged again, she went with him, her expression more curious than alarmed now. He let her go, prodded her to the window. She winced as she tiptoed through the shattered glass. At the broken window, he nudged her, nipped her bottom when she was too slow. She turned and swatted him, but swung her leg over and was out. He followed.

Dragon fire was the hottest thing in the known universe. How far was safe? He just didn't know. He could sense the immense presence hovering slightly to the south, so he pushed her fast to the north, staying in the shadow of the hedgerow that lined the narrow road. Finally, he allowed her to collapse to the ground, her breathing loud and fast.

"What the hell is going on?" she muttered to herself. "Why am I following the biggest goddamn dog I have ever seen? Okay, so I'm in denial. Why am I following the biggest goddamn wolf I have ever seen? Am I dreaming?" she asked hopefully. "I pinch myself and wake up?"

Angel leaned in and nipped her on the leg.

"Ow," she said, rubbing the spot. "I guess not dreaming then. So what—"

The sky lit up with orange fire. Angel hurled himself on top of her as the heat singed the tips of his fur, filling the air with the acrid scent of burned hair. Behind them her house erupted into a ball of flames. He held her down for long minutes as she struggled, protecting her from the worst of the flames. Finally, he sat up and gazed into the sky; saw the flick of a tail as the younger Kronus vanished into the night.

He turned back, sat on his haunches as Mara pulled herself up and stared at the burning building.

"My house," she whispered.

What should he do now? He wished he hadn't left his comm unit because he could have called the *Blood Hunter* and asked them to pick him up. Now they would have to make it on foot. They? Was he taking her with him? Would Tannis let her on board? Would Rico eat her? Or would Kronus intercept them on the way back and burn her to ashes? But he couldn't just leave her here. Well, he could but he didn't want to.

He rose to his feet, and nodded his head in the direction of the *Blood Hunter*. It would be a long walk for her. She stumbled upright, swayed, but quickly steadied herself. Angel gave a yip, then started walking. Glancing over his shoulder, he saw she hadn't moved. He yipped again, and she gave a shrug and followed. Her feet were bare and she wore what she had been sleeping in, which wasn't much. She wrapped her arms around herself and stumbled on.

A shadow swooped down from above and he went still, holding his breath, waiting for the flames. Instead, Kronos landed lightly in front of them, Angel's clothes dangling from one claw. He dropped them in front of Angel.

Angel took one look at the girl beside him and decided only words would explain this. He shifted back into human form. Didn't look at her as he pulled on his clothes. Only when he'd dragged on his boots did he risk a peek at her face. Her mouth was open, she was staring, but not at him. He guessed she hadn't even noticed he was naked. No, she was gaping at Kronus, as if she'd never seen a dragon before.

"Why?" he asked Kronos.

"I promised your sister."

"Crap." Did no one ever just want to save him? Was it only ever because goddamned Candy asked them to?

"She loves you. And she also knows you are the better part of her, the good part. You just have to find out what else you can be."

Ah well, wasn't that what he'd been thinking earlier? "So what now?"

"The ship is repaired. They are ready to leave. I said I would bring you back safely."

"And Mara?"

"There will be repercussions."

But that wasn't a "no" and he'd worry about repercussions later.

At her name, Mara jumped and turned to him. "Angel?" She blinked, her brows drawing together. "What's happening?"

"We're going on a trip. If you want to."

She glanced from him to Kronos who yawned, revealing super sharp incisors and breath like smoke. "With him?"

He nodded. "He's our ride."

"Oh."

"Time running out here," Kronos murmured in his head.

"You have to decide. We need to go." He held out his hand, held his breath as he waited.

She swallowed, glanced from him to Kronus and back, finally slid her hand into his, and he tugged her toward the dragon. Angel clambered onto Kronus's outstretched leg, then drew her up after him. He climbed the rest of the way and she followed quickly, sitting astride in front of him and he looped his arms around her waist.

As they launched into the air, he was filled with that wild exhilaration. Did she feel it too? Her body was rigid in his arms, but slowly relaxed as they flew higher and higher. This time they didn't stop at the edges of space. The air grew thinner, until he struggled to breathe, and he could feel Mara's frantic breaths as she gulped in air.

At last, when his vision was hazy from lack of oxygen, they breached the stealth mode and the *Blood Hunter* appeared, as if from nowhere, directly in front of them. Mara gasped but said nothing.

The docking bay doors opened and Kronus swooped inside, folding his wings as he landed neatly in the center of the cavernous room. Tannis and Rico stood by the transporter bubble.

Rico had an amused grin on his face, Tannis just looked pissed. "What is freaking going on? Where the hell have you been? And who the hell is she?"

Angel ignored the questions and tightened his arms around Mara. He leaned in close and whispered in her ear. "Welcome to the *Blood Hunter*."

And in that moment he realized just what sort of person he wanted to be. The sort who rescued damsels in distress from fire-breathing dragons.

But he still wanted to be an explorer, and he had a feeling that soon they'd be on their way to 2045 and a visit with the dragon's destiny.

He liked the idea.

A WORD FROM NINA CROFT

While I write mainly romance, I write all sorts of romance—contemporary, paranormal, thrillers, science fiction…whatever appeals to me in the moment. I'm very fond of mixing up my genres, and my favourite series to write has been *Dark Desires,* because absolutely anything can happen. It's a combination of science fiction, suspense, paranormal, and romance, and follows the adventures, romantic and otherwise, of the crew of the *Blood Hunter.*

I wrote *Break Out,* book 1 in the series, after watching *Firefly* for the third time. I really wanted to write a space opera and had no intention of including a paranormal element, but when the pilot, Rico, turned out to be a vampire, I didn't fight it. It occurred to me that space is a pretty good place for vampires. Then in later books we had werewolves and aliens and time travel and telepathy… Dragons first appeared in book 4, *Temporal Shift.*

Recently, I've been trying to finish the final book in the series, *Flying Through Fire,* and struggling a little. I've realized I don't want it to end and I don't want everything to be settled. It occurred to me that stories never really end, they are just part of a much bigger story. So when the chance came to write a short story for the *Dragon Chronicles,* I decided to take a look at what happens after the end of *Flying Through Fire.* And that's how I came to write "A Diversion in Time".

About the Author

Nina Croft was born in the north of England but headed south at the age of eighteen. She studied marine biology at London University before training to be a chartered accountant.

Having worked a number of years in London, the urge to head south hit again. This time it took her to Zambia, on the shores of the beautiful Lake Kariba, where she spent four years working as a volunteer. It left her with a love of the sun and a dislike of regular employment. Since then, Nina has a spent a number of years mixing travel, whenever possible, with work, whenever necessary.

After traveling extensively in India, Southeast Asia, and Africa, Nina has now settled down to a life of writing and almond-picking on a remote farm in southern Spain, between the Sierra Nevada Mountains and the Mediterranean Sea. She shares the farm with her husband, three dogs, a horse, two goats, two cats, and a three-legged Vietnamese pot-bellied pig.

You can find out more about Nina and her books at:

www.ninacroft.com

The Book of Safkhet, Chronicler of the Journey, Mistress of the House of Books

by Kim Wells

"I am the Invisible One within the All. It is I who counsel those who are hidden, since I know the All that exists in it. I am numberless beyond everyone. I am immeasurable, ineffable, yet whenever I wish, I shall reveal myself of my own accord. I am the head of the All. I exist before the All, and I am the All, since I exist in everyone."

–Nag Hammadi,
Trimorphic Protennoia.

Revelations

TO BEGIN WITH, THEY weren't even supposed to be diving in that cave, or even going that deep. It was dangerous. Too far from the coral reefs, possibly filled with tiger sharks or moray eels. But that's what made it exciting. Watching your air bubbles disappear into the light above, knowing how far down in the darkness you were.

Anything could happen.

David was the good diver, the one with all the qualifications. But Anna wanted to try it, too, and they were sure, certain, that nothing *bad* would happen. Maybe something exciting, but then, wasn't that what life was all about?

Then Anna spotted a huge turtle, a gorgeous green and black leathery sea turtle. She followed it, past the depths that David had suggested they keep to. She wasn't paying attention to depth meters when there were turtles to follow. When David saw her swim into a previously unseen cave, he followed her, panicking. He knew how you could get trapped in one of those things and never come out. His bubbles raced above him, frantic, small.

The turtle escaped them both, finding some hole too small for the humans to hide in. But what they found in there was even better.

In the center of the cave, nestled between corals and illuminated by the lights of their diving gear, sat a giant sphere of glass, perfectly sealed, enigmatic. It wasn't very heavy, so they lifted it, carried it to the surface. They thought of pirate treasure, or lost artifacts of the Pharaohs. The green bubbled glass glistened in the sunlight as their boat carried it to shore.

There was the faintest suggestion in the glass of the perfect figure of a winged creature of some sort. Probably a Dragon, its wings spread wide in flight. But no one could ever decide. It seemed to be flying around a single star-like circle, the only hint of color in the glass, like a red star.

When they showed it to their professors (they were students on an archeology summer-school course in Egypt, swimming on weekends in the Red Sea coral reefs) the professors were excited. There were some kind of scrolls, some kind of papyrus documents, sealed inside the glass that could be clearly seen, even through the green of ancient glass. They all knew they had to examine those scrolls. It was not lost upon the professors that this area was teeming with both legitimate ancient texts (the Dead Sea Scrolls, for example) and forgeries. Finding out which this was caused an international academic uproar.

And that was the trick, wasn't it? The glass was clearly ancient, but there was no sign of seams, or, aside from the Dragon art, any imperfections. Once the word about the find got out, the community speculated forgery. Some kind of publicity stunt. But they couldn't be sure until they could see the actual texts for themselves.

They spent months figuring out a way to open it safely. They finally decided to pierce the glass with a special diamond-tipped device while it was in a sterile vacuum environment, take a small sample of the papyrus and then reseal the glass. When it was pierced, the oddest smell, the smell of white lotus flower, to be precise, *Nymphaea Lotus*, completely filled the room. At first everyone was terrified, afraid the scent was some kind of chemical weapon, but no one was harmed, and the smell lingered for days.

After resealing the sphere, they scanned everything inside with a new app that used LIDAR to analyze the patterns on the scrolls. The language there was none anyone had ever seen, even though the room was filled with specialists in ancient languages. The mystery was thrilling, and for a time, the atmosphere of the room was like a party, a carnival.

For a while. Over months, no one was found who knew the language on the scrolls. And when no codex, no Rosetta Stone for *this* language showed up, it was mostly forgotten. Years went by before anyone thought of the scrolls again except in passing.

Eventually, for record-keeping purposes at the archives where they were kept, the documents, which carbon dated so far back (more than 200,000 years old) that it was thought there had to be an error because people didn't make paper back then, were scanned. Cataloged. Placed on the Internet. Of course. The words were digitized and the shapes they made approximated by the computers and OCR programs.

One day, many years later, a young woman named Sonya was working on her dissertation in mythological languages attempting to discover the mythological Ur language, the language all humanity spoke before the Tower of Babel, the language Adam and Eve spoke. She uploaded her work to the Internet as part of her course requirements.

Her computer froze.

It stayed frozen for hours. Nothing Sonya did seemed to fix it, even unplugging it and plugging it back on just gained her the same odd frozen screen. In the third hour, a symbol appeared on the screen, like a star on a stick, covered by a weird nipple-shaped hat. Something that looked like:

She was certain she had uploaded a crazy virus, and sadly planned to take her computer to a friend who was an expert on computers. She worried she had lost all of her hard work of that day (but of course, she had everything saved in multiple spots, on the Cloud and in email.)

But then her computer restarted. At least, it seemed to be rebooting. But it stayed a black screen for many moments, and Sonya was afraid this was the end. What she didn't know was that the program that had begun to run on her computer was actually a kind of virus, a previously unknown and remarkably advanced computer language. Her adding her transliteration and interpretation of the Ur language into the mix had triggered a sort of digital Rosetta stone, a viral program loading that was able to combine the ancient language with computer programming binary. And that the accidental confluence of events was changing her computer forever into a kind of universal translator.

A story began to scroll across the screen. Sighing, and thinking that it was still the virus, the student read along, at first with annoyance, then curiosity that turned into shock and amazement.

And the story Sonya read changed the world.

* * *

The Book of Jude

"Beloved, although I was making every effort to write to you about our common salvation, I now feel a need to write to encourage you

to contend for the faith that was once for all handed down to the holy ones."

–Jude 1:3.

Jude stalked long corridors of the Dragon's Hall in a huff. Everything was going wrong already. His parents had woken him rudely just before the seventh hour. After a hurried breakfast, they had dropped him off with warnings to study hard, with exhortations to "hurry to work" and to meet them back at home later, in hour eighteen. Then they continued talking in rapid, argumentative tones.

Something about politics. It was always about politics. His parents were both Judges, the leaders of their community and ultimately the world, elected by the people once every five cycles to make laws and policy. This meant they were always arguing about something, always worried about something else.

Jude didn't care about the arguments of old men and even older women in the Halls of Government. But he couldn't wait to get out to the Halls of the Elder Dragons, where his friend Yalta-ba-oath was waiting to instruct him further in Interstellar Navigational techniques. Especially the telepathic interface that would allow him to pilot the starships that would take them eventually to other planets and solar systems and the stars. He had the feeling he was almost there, more times than not he could now sense the Dragon's empathic voice just at the edges of his consciousness. A tickle, a mental itch he needed to scratch. He could hear entire sentences at time. He was told he was the one who was blocking the link, and that he just had to keep trying.

The Dragons had always been experts on traveling the other worlds, the solar system and beyond. Rumor had it that they came from somewhere far away, but Yalta-ba-oath only smiled and nodded when Jude asked this question. She didn't avoid answering, but she redirected Jude to answer it for himself.

"What do you think, Jude? Where *did* we all come from?"

Her voice was deep and powerful but kind, a little gravelly. He couldn't wait until he could always hear it through the empathic navigational interface. The Dragons could speak to anyone telepathically, and this was the way they navigated their ships, which were also somehow organic. The ships spoke back to the Dragons but none of the humans could speak to the ships without the Dragons helping. And somehow, the ships and Dragons both needed the human intermediary to translate the ship environment to a hospitable place for everyone.

Jude didn't understand it all yet, but he was studying as hard as he could because he wanted to be a navigator, with the Dragons. He himself had not yet heard the voice of any of the ships. He hoped to someday.

Jude thought about the Dragon's question. It took him a while to work through everything, but Yalta-ba-oath patiently let him think at his own pace. He could tell that she felt she had the time for him to figure it out.

He knew that his home planet was not an easy place to live. Its over sixteen hundred volcanoes were beautiful but could be deadly, and the heat of the dayside of the planet could kill if one wasn't careful to bring water and shade on any trips across the cities on the edge of the daylight cycle. The sharp black sand of the beaches south of his home city, beaches that ended in lovely dark green water, that sand could cut your feet with its glassy points if you forgot to wear your sandals to the water's edge. There the sand was softened, eventually, but you must wait 'til you got right to the edge to go barefoot.

Scientists said that The People, that some called the Tribes, had originated in the cooler mountain lands and that they migrated down and across the planet at some point in the past ten thousand years, while the planet was in its coolest phase, furthest in its relatively circular orbit around the sun. In ancient times, they had been nomads, following the edges of the sunlight, called the Aredvi Sura, sticking to the twilight zones between the dark and the day, the Anahita sides. Nowadays, they had climate controlled buildings that darkened the windows during the planet's long day and let in artificial light during the slightly longer night cycle.

Jude had studied all of that in school, but it just didn't mean all that much to him. The scientists said that the next planet from the sun, which they called Earth-eal, also bore life. Shockingly, their days were only 24 hours long with half of it in sun and half in the darkness, and their orbit around the sun was 365 of those 24-hour periods. Jude thought that was unimaginable.

He remembered something about how there were humanoids on the planet, but they were not civilized, living in a much colder world where the snow that touched the highest mountains on this planet covered large expanses of the ground there. The humanoids huddled in caves around primitive fires that could barely support their existence.

Jude thought it sounded horrible and never wanted to travel there. But the stars—that was different.

The Dragons promised to take them to the stars.

Jude wasn't a scholar. Really, he didn't care where they all came from as long as they traveled to other places.

While she waited for Jude to answer, Yalta-ba-oath yawned, her huge mouth filled with the sharpest, longest, whitest teeth Jude had ever seen. It was early, and Jude had awoken her in his impatience to learn more about the Dragons' ships. She opened her wings, stretching them. They were sleek, spanning almost thirty feet across and half that in width. She usually kept them drawn against her body, but Jude knew that, in the right conditions and with the atmosphere and wind speed just so, she could fly.

She was a red Dragon, her face ringed with pointy tips Jude thought of as her beard. He heard, in his head, her amusement at that label. She didn't seem to mind, even though his mother would have been insulted. High pointed ridges, three on each side of her face, gathered in a sort of crown at the top of her triangle-shaped head. Her throat was covered in cream colored scales, some as small as his fingertip, some as large across as a grown man's hand spread wide. The same cream color could be seen under her wings when she chose to spread them, the strong, muscled arms red and the softer wing leather underneath. Her tail was as long as her body and ended in several spikes.

In spite of this fiercely strong appearance, she still seemed gentle to Jude. Perhaps this was because, as his teacher, he could hear her presence in his head and it never seemed cruel, even when he did the dumbest things—like he had yesterday in his training session on navigating Black Holes. A mistake Yalta-ba-oath told him could cost them all their lives if made in the real world and not a simulated dream.

Sleek, black, and large, the ships could travel immense distances. The Dragons were vague on where the ships came from, vague, in fact, on details about themselves in general, but as far back as anyone on Kiel-e-ken, the second planet from the sun, could remember, they had simply been there. The Dragons would travel often, and the launches of the ships were attended with great revelry by the people of Jude's home-city of Halom.

But it was new that the Dragons had offered to take people with them. And Jude was one of the first travelers, one of the first to study the ships and the navigational systems the ships contained.

Jude finally answered:

"Does it matter where the ships come from, where we come from? Isn't it true that what matters is where we go next?"

Yalta-ba-oath chuckled. The emotion was strong in Jude's head, but you could also hear the huffing sound through her mouth and nostrils if you were standing nearby. Dragons only projected their thoughts to those they chose to project to—if they didn't want you to be in on the conversation, it was private. Jude could almost hear her thoughts now. He felt he was just days away from truly hearing her through their connection, and then, the ship would be next.

"I can see I chose well in you, Jude." Jude could hear the smile, even though it was hard to tell when a Dragon smiled from looking at their face. "You ask the important questions, but then you find the answers you need for yourself."

Jude squirmed under the attention, the Dragon probing

his mind always kind of tickled.

"Shall we get to today's astro navigational maps?"

* * *

What was from the beginning,
what we have heard,
what we have seen with our eyes,
what we looked upon
and touched with our hands
concerns the Word of life.

−1 John

The Letters of John

To: The Congress of Elders, the Judges
        Halls of Government
        Aredvi Sura Parallel

Esteemed Elders,

I write to you today to urge immediate action. The beginning of dangerous events is clearly upon us. There is no way that we can continue this dialogue unless both sides agree to discuss the issues at hand. I urge you to include all groups immediately and not negotiate without their explicit attendance at your meetings. Secret meetings of the Government must cease immediately so that the groups in question are not antagonized further.

The "doomsday device" that has been stolen by factions

that disagree with our plan to travel to other planets, who believe that we should preserve our way of life at all costs because of the superstitions of an ancient religion, must be taken seriously by all the Wise and Learned among us. This device, while dismissed by some as a simple bomb, could change the entire nature of this planet.

What you have heard is correct: the device will, if detonated in the right part of the planet's day/night cycle, possibly lead to an escalating Greenhouse effect that could burn off all of our planet's oceans. The winds will become a veritable vortex, rotating on our planet at something like 60 times the speed of our normal rotation. All animal and human life will die in the lightning storms that immediately follow said detonation. The escalating heat caused by the clouds of Carbon Monoxide, Nitrogen, and Sulfuric Acid that will erupt from this device will then make the planet completely uninhabitable for any form of life as we know it.

I also urge you to consider the implications of all I have written here.

Those who say that it's a simple nuclear bomb that will only destroy a radius of eight miles do not understand the science at hand.

I have seen with my own eyes the danger that these people represent when the leader of the Faction killed dozens of his supporters in order to acquire my energy making machine. I know that I have been dismissed as a doomsday prophet, someone who stands aside and predicts scientific disasters that will never come to pass. The government must listen to its scientists if we are to preserve any semblance of life on this planet. Those who say "But they would never dare to use this device" do not know the level of hatred these people have for anyone who disagrees with them. The fact that they stole the technology for the device from our labs does not go unnoticed by me, and I regret the experiments that led to its discovery.

Those who say "But the space travel will save us" do not realize that the Dragons can only carry a fraction of our planet's life with them. And they do not seem to ask the question of where we will go? The only other potentially inhabitable planet in this system, Earth-eal, is in the midst of its Ice Age—a time when human life is barely supported on most of its continental land masses. The primitive state of life on that planet, where there are no man-made structures and very barbaric humanoid creatures that live like animals, is not to be underestimated. Any of our planet's survivors who managed to land on that planet would suffer a horrible fate.

Esteemed Elders: I, John of Tycho, believe that this device could end this planet forever, and the Dragons are not just the saviors of our kind that some would paint them to be. The origin of their species, as well as the nature of their benevolence to us, is unknown. Their minds are of an alien intelligence, and we cannot be certain of their intent.

Please, Esteemed Elders: take this warning seriously. This is about Life as we know it on our planet. We must convince the factions to bring us the doomsday weapon so that it can be disassembled in a safe environment, in a lab. It never should have been built, and I will curse my own curiosity for the rest of my days.

Sincerely,
John Tycho

* * *

Dearest Love:

I have written to the Councils of Elders and Judges. I don't have any faith that they will heed my warnings. You should take our family and travel as quickly as you can to the Halls of the Elder Dragons and throw yourself and our cause on their mercies. In spite of not truly knowing their intent, I believe they may be our only hope for survival. Plan to leave our home forever. Bring as many of your friends as you can convince to come along. I will try to meet you there soon.

I know this sounds crazy, but if the Faction succeeds in its plan to detonate the cursed weapon that I developed in a crazy bid to provide endless energy to our world, we will all be destroyed.

My love, I long to be with you now, but I am traveling today to the Capitol to try to talk sense into the Judges there personally. I hope that I am not too late.

I send you my heart, my soul, and my endless kisses. I hope that I see you and our children soon.

Love,
John

* * *

To the Leaders of the Faction:

I beg of you, return the device that is in your possession back to its rightful owners. I agree that we all need a dialogue about the direction our planet's governmental rulers have chosen with the Dragons. We must discuss the widespread effects of space travel on our world in an intelligent, rational manner.

Your religious beliefs are strong, I understand. You must please hear me: the device you hold in your hands could trigger an unbelievably catastrophic series of events that could destroy life as we know it on this planet.

We have nowhere else to go that has a home for us to live in, and any emigration to other planets at this point is unfeasible. Please allow me to speak to you about a device and a danger that I never intended.

Can we not negotiate like civilized people? The day is long and the night is longer—but the sun will bless those of us who save our world.

You hold our fate in your hands. Please look at your loved ones, your children's faces, and know that it is within your power to change the world for the better, not the worse.

Sincerely, with hope,
John Tycho, inventor of the weapon you hold

* * *

To: The Elder Dragons
      Anahita Region

Esteemed Friends:

I believe the time for negotiation has ended. You in your wisdom have provided us a means to travel the galaxies, indeed, the universe. But there are those on our world who are afraid of the gifts you give. They will destroy us all in their fear. My search for renewable energy has caused me to inadvertently create a device that could destroy us all in the hands of those in the Faction.

You will recall the stories you have told me about what happened to *your* planet, so long ago, before you came to us. How the Evil Ones took over, and caused a catastrophic meltdown of your planet's energy sources. I fear that pattern is happening here, as well. Your interplanetary travel might be all that saves us.

I wish more of our people knew your story, but I understand your reluctance to share your species origins, that you are extra-planetary beings come here to co-exist with us. I wish we were as intelligent a species as your initial findings showed us to be.

I believe you must prepare the ships to transport as many of our planet's people as possible to the Third Planet in our solar system. As you know from your own explorations of our solar system, it is not very hospitable, and there is no civilization to speak of.

The ships must be well-stocked with supplies, both for building and for medical care, to combat the diseases and environmental disasters that will surely befall our people on the barbaric surface of that planet. Not to mention the dangers of super-carnivores which still stalk the Northern hemisphere, and the primitive tribes of barbaric humanoids who live there. They are our distant genetic cousins, yes. But they have nothing in common with our civilized planet.

It has taken 4.6 billion years since the formation of this

solar system and indeed, the universe. And it will take mere seconds for it to turn into a raging pit of acid, ammonia, and clouds. It will be, indeed, like the Hell their religion speaks of.

I am sending my wife and children to you. Please, I beg of you, save as many as you can. You, and your starships, are our only hope for some measure of survival.

John Tycho

* * *

Acts

I was sent forth from the power,
and I have come to those who reflect upon me,
and I have been found among those who seek after me.
Look upon me, you who reflect upon me,
and you hearers, hear me.
You who are waiting for me, take me to yourselves.
And do not banish me from your sight.
And do not make your voice hate me, nor your hearing.
Do not be ignorant of me anywhere or any time.
Be on your guard!
Do not be ignorant of me.
For I am the first and the last.
I am the honored one and the scorned one.

–Nag Hammadi.
The Thunder, Perfect Mind

From the Desk of Joan Lummoch
Official Transcriptionist of the Courts of the Hall of Judges

Five of the Elder Dragons appeared at the Hall of the Council of Judges today. We were in session, discussing the problem of that Faction having gained access to what some are calling an ultimate doomsday device, and that some are dismissing as mere sabre rattling. There was, from the area of the larger doors, an uproar, voices raised in a combination of alarm and joy. This is not the official record, but my own recollection of what happened. So I may miss things in the excitement.

The Elder Dragons are rarely seen outside of their own Halls, and the Dragons that most people get to see are the navigators and younglings, those who mix regularly with our own children and young people.

These were five of the most respected, wisest Dragons, the ones that people in the know believe are the leaders of their community.

The first through the doors was Xiuhcoatl. Some said he is in charge of wars, and that he would be a sort of battlefield general if there ever came a need to fight. He was huge, his skin green and yellow colored. Unlike most Dragons, he didn't have any wings, even vestigial ones, but instead there was a beautiful spiny ridge of red and green spikes coming from his back, from the tip of his tail to the top of his head. His eyes shone a dark jade-green color, and he swung his head back and forth to observe everyone in the room, as though sizing us all up.

The next Dragon was thought to be a female, named Ladon. Apparently some Dragons can be either male or female, depending on their preference for mating. But she generally refers to herself as a female, so everyone waited to hear from her what her preference was before using pronouns. She was a dark blue, with large purple-red wings that spanned, when opened, twice her body length. She was said to be a water Dragon, who would swim regularly in the great pools out behind the Hall of Dragons, and she clearly was not impressed with the lack of moisture in the Hall of Judges. She looked annoyed and uncomfortable, but also resigned to being here. Being a water Dragon, people speculated later that it was because of her intimate knowledge of the environment, and her scientific training in water and chemistry that she had come along, although she preferred solitude and scientific study to public appearances. I thought she was the most beautiful of all of them.

Third stalked in a large male called Nidhug, whose power-element was his strong, towering legs like tree trunks. He was dark grey, with black spikes and wings that, when opened, as they briefly were while he was settling in, almost seemed translucent. His chin was tipped in dark blue beard-spikes, and his eyes were almost white, as though he didn't need a pupil. Those who had seen him before today speculated that he was a deep-dwelling cave or underwater Dragon, and that impression was not undone with his court appearance. While the bright lights didn't seem to cause pain, one got the sense he, like Ladon, would have preferred to not be here.

Fourth was Pythios, who is said to be psychic in addition to a Dragon's regular telepathic abilities. She can see the future, in addition to what you're thinking, and can project that future vision into your mind, should she choose to do so. She was smaller than the others, perhaps younger, and her green-blue scales rippled in the light, almost as if they were illuminated from inside, perhaps bioluminescent. She had no spikes and her four powerful but still delicate legs somehow reminded you of the fact that most Dragons do fly. Their bones must be especially lightweight, unless the flight is caused by some kind of magic and not evolution. Her eyes seemed to pierce into everyone's soul as though she knew all of your secrets, kept them, but knew what would happen to you because of them.

The fifth and final Dragon was Tiamat, also a female. She is rumored to be a fire-Dragon, who could literally breathe fire if she chose. Her coloring was beautiful—orange-red, with creamy scales along her underside, and golden spikes that looked more like soft feathers rippling down her neck. Some said that she was the matriarch of all of the Dragons on the planet, that somewhere in history she had been the first Dragon. Since nobody knew how old Dragons could be or were, and since both Dragons and Tiamat had been here as far back in recorded history as we had records, it certainly seemed possible. The other Dragons deferred to her, and it seemed as though coming last in line was, to the Dragons, the position of greatest authority.

After the initial excitement, the bailiffs of the court were able to clear a section of the Judges' chambers for the Dragons to gather in. They had indicated that they were here to observe, and not to speak.

This seemed true until one of the Judges spoke of the letters of John Tycho, and his warnings about the device that he had invented.

This caused the Dragons to stir, and as though they had agreed upon this beforehand, one of them spoke. I will record their speeches here, as best as I can remember them. For anyone truly wanting to know what happened, they should consult the official transcript, available in the Hall of Records.

Pythios: Learned Counselors, we are here today to speak to you of our species. We do not, as people believe, originate on this planet.

(At this, there was argument among those gathered in the Court Hall which continued until the Dragons, almost as one, turned their eyes towards the people, who immediately quieted under the piercing eyes of Dragonkind.)

Pythios continued: It is true. We once lived on a planet in a solar system far away. You would know this system as being approximately sixteen of your light-years away, in the constellation commonly called Grus but which we named the Winged Dragon. That planet is now governed solely by a group we call, in your language, The Dark Ones. You would not like to meet them. But their history is one that your planet shares—a history of hate, and intolerance. A history of not allowing open debate. And a lack of a desire to explore outside their own comfort zone.

We who came to this planet long before your recorded history desired to connect with other sentient beings. Longed to explore the galaxies. We found this planet second from your solar orbit with your early humanoid ancestors and came here, hoping to co-exist. The other planet in this system, the third from the solar orbit, was not ready for us, too cold, and too inhospitable for our kind then.

Now it seems as though our shared existence on this planet is in danger. Those among you who question the drive to reach for the stars are gathering, and they are dangerous. I believe there is little chance to alter the future I have seen.

Please, join with me and the other Dragon Elders at our compound. We must evacuate as many as we can to the great Starships, and we must lead a colony to the third plant.

At this, the audience erupted again, and even the eyes of the gathered elder Dragons would not silence them. There were many who ran from the Hall and never returned. The Council of Judges ordered a recess to the proceedings and cleared the Hall of the rest of the assembly.

We do not know what the official orders will be concerning evacuation and colonization.

* * *

Exodus

These are the names of the sons of Israel who went to Egypt with Jacob, each with his family... The descendants of Jacob numbered seventy in all.

—Exodus 1

Jude ran from the academic rooms to the staging area. He looked into the sky where the ominous clouds of a seasonal thunderstorm were just beginning to form. From what he had been told, the storm that was coming would be far worse, and last far longer. He didn't know what to think about the immediate future, but he was glad his parents had made a quick decision to leave.

Frantic crowds gathered in front of the ships holding bags filled with whatever they could carry. Entire families, children crying, mothers trying to comfort them. Men trying to look stoic but sometimes failing and crying too.

Jude knew that Yalta-ba-oath was near. He had finally mastered the empathic link between himself and his Dragon guide required to pilot the Starship just last cycle but it was there. Still tentative, but there.

Jude. This way, towards the front of the ship.

Jude pushed through the crowds. There were people gathered among them, trying to calm everyone, trying to advise them on where to load the Starship, how to stow their baggage. The stewards would handle those details. It was time for him to climb into his pilot pod, nestled next to the Dragon's much larger pod, and boot up the system for its initial checklist sequence.

He knew that the ship, a biological cyborg entity that had a symbiotic relationship with its Dragon pilot, had already cycled through much of the real checklist needs. The ship would have made the environment right for the occupants based on their metabolic patterns, which it could sense. It would have already plotted out exactly how much fuel they needed, and mapped the path they needed to take. The ship simply needed a special translator-team of the biological organisms onboard to translate those needs, to remind it to continue running and adjusting life-support and adjusting for any emergencies.

He stowed his own gear in the space beneath his seat

provided for that purpose and climbed into the seat, which was exactly his size, as though built for him. He scanned the checklist: AUXILLIARY FUEL SUPPLIES— OFF. FLIGHT CONTROLS —FREE AND CORRECT. DRAGON EMPATHIC INTERFACE—LOADING. He clicked his tongue on the roof of his mouth, which was the signal for the headset to begin the software that helped the process.

At this, he felt Yalta-ba-oath's calming mind connect with his. The image of water flowing over dark black rocks, which he had been taught as a way of smoothing out any hiccups in the initial upboot, made his anxiety fade away.

He went down the list: instruments and radios — checked and set. Between themselves, Yalta-ba-oath and Jude checked the engine idle status, monitored the still-in-progress passenger loading status. It appeared that almost everyone was on board, and the stewards notified the two pilots, one human, one Dragon, that they were ten minutes from being ready for takeoff.

Jude made a special sweep with his empathic senses, which now engulfed the entire ship's intricate central nervous system, to check for his parents. They were both wedged in the first forward compartments, nervous, sweating. He could read their emotions slightly in the way the empathic link with the Dragon allowed, and knew that they were still not sure they were doing the right thing, and yet afraid that it was absolutely necessary.

The ship could hold approximately seventy passengers. There were ten ships in all, and all of them were completing the intricate frantic dance of passenger loading and Dragon/

Pilot interface. Jude could hear the chatter from the inter-ship radio that confirmed all the other ships were almost ready, too.

The families that were loaded on this Starship included Judges and all the other staff and legal emigrant candidates that had already applied to the program.

Jude pinged the pod with the two Reuben Judges, who were from a southern province near the ocean, to indicate to them that they needed to initiate their takeoff sequencing. They were the only members of the group that did not appear quite ready. They did not have any children yet, although the empathic vibe Jude was getting from the woman suggested the faintest ripple of a mind within her—perhaps a child was coming soon.

The Simeons, two boys and a girl, along with their parents, were loaded in a pod next to Jude's family. Next to them were the Levis, who had protested and strongly believed this was a premature mistake, but who did not want to risk their family's safety in the backlash against this action that would likely follow. Those pods were near the back of the ship. Their child was also loaded with them, too young to know what was going on, getting bored and a little sleepy now that the loading process was done.

Judge Issachar, Judge Zebulun and Judge Benjamin were all unmarried, but they were teachers also, so they had herded a number of the documented groups of people who had applied to the Interstellar program on board, helped them load into the communal class seating near the center of the back section. The Judges Dan and Naphtali, Gad and Asher were also on board, and because of their advanced state of training, had already loaded the cryo-sleep programs and were in the light dozing state that was suggested before take-off.

None of the families had ever launched from the planet's surface before. This was a new experience for everyone, in spite of the months (and for some, years) of training. The Dragons, of course, had been through this all before. They sent calming vibrations through their human pilots, who in turn were able to send those calming thoughts to the other humans.

Pilots were chosen for their ability to interface with the alien mind of the Dragons and the minds of their fellow humans, and Jude had been told he was the best. Jude and Yalta-ba-oath knew the other ships nearby were also finishing up the final stages of pre-flight, but their ship, the Genesis, would be first to go. Yalta-ba-oath had flight seniority.

Jude was proud he had been chosen as Yalta-ba-oath's navigational partner. Even though he was much newer to the program than many of the other ships' navigators, he would be the first to touch the atmosphere. First to reach out a hand to the stars and the nearby planet.

The final items of the pre-flight takeoff checklist were lit on Jude's navigational board, just in front of his seat and to the side. Stewards reported the doors and windows locked. Jude checked, once more, the fuel mixture. It was full rich but would be adjusted once they were above 3,000 feet. The ship's interstellar lights were set and navigational cameras loaded.

The Dragons had agreed to leave the ship's transponders in the "off" position for now, until it was certain whether any of the members of the Faction were receiving transmissions. Nobody wanted to tip off the enemy, who was threatening to unleash their weapon any moment now, that the plans for emigration to the Third Planet some were beginning to call Terra, others Earth, were activated. Jude checked all the engine instruments and signaled to Yalta-ba-oath that the checklist was covered.

It was time to go!

* * *

Genesis

In the beginning God created the heaven and the Earth.
And the earth was without form, and void; and darkness
was upon the face of the deep.
And the Spirit of God moved upon the face of the waters.
And God said, Let there be light: and there was light.
And God saw the light, that it was good: and God divided
the light from the darkness.
And God called the light Day, and the darkness he called
Night. And the evening and the morning were the first day.
And God said, Let there be a firmament in the midst of the
waters, and let it divide the waters from the waters.

–Genesis 1

The ships, ten of them, pierced the atmosphere just above a land mass shaped vaguely like a bare foot without toes. There was a twisting river that the geographers had decided would be the best possible place to land, and the glaciers which touched most of the planet's upper quadrant were far enough away that there should be warm weather and fertile soil.

It had been a bumpy trip. Just as the ships, piloted by the

Dragons (and their capable human navigators), had been guided out of the atmosphere of their home and leveled off into space's quiet vacuum, a great explosion had pierced the planet's sky.

Clouds of yellow-gold, almost beautiful, definitely terrifying, had billowed upward. Those who were still awake watched the aft cameras, some weeping openly as their planet's atmosphere was forever changed. The initial plume of golden cloud grew exponentially, quietly for them but probably eardrum piercing on the planet's surface. The cities could not be seen from this distance, but the flames that could be seen beneath the yellow clouds were undoubtedly destroying everything. The flames reached as high as the clouds for a moment. Near the planet's southern regions, where the oceans reigned, the watchers could see water plumes vaporizing, the intense heat burning off into steam. As they travelled in space and the cameras began to lose the magnification necessary to see anything other than a vague shape, they could see the vapor adding itself to the clouds, and lightning-like flashes of white-hot energy blasting the entire southern region near the volcano plains.

There was no hope that anyone who had been left on the planet had survived. The ten ships with seventy passengers and crew each had barely cleared the danger zone when the Factions had exploded their device. Its inventor, John Tycho, was still on the planet, having tried to negotiate with the Faction's faceless, nameless leaders.

The families on the ships would never know who it was that set off the planet-killing bomb.

Those who had opted to take the interplanetary journey

without the aid of the cryo-sleep chambers eventually rose and gathered in the crew areas, seeking comfort, hugging, crying. It seemed impossible that their home was gone, and they were on the way to an alien planet.

If it hadn't been for the Dragons, some whispered quietly, perhaps this would not have happened. But if it hadn't been for the Dragons, they would not have been saved, either. The whisperers looked at their sleeping children, faces slack with the dreamless sleep of the cryo-chambers, and sighed.

The new planet was impossibly blue, broken here and there by brown land masses. In the quadrant oriented upwards from the ships, there were large white bodies that the Dragons called *glaciers*. They were similar to the peaks of the highest volcanoes on their home planet, but so much larger. The Dragons said that this was a temporary cycle of the planet's position furthest from the Sola, and that it happened at such an infrequent cycle that it wasn't to be worried about forever.

Larger than theirs, and the Dragons reported that its planetary rotation was backwards! That the solar cycle lasted a mere 24 hours, splitting the period between darkness and light into a tiny fraction of time. There was evening, and there was morning. There were nameless animals creeping over the surface of the planet. Plants that would yield unfamiliar fruits. Flowers with unknown scents waited.

The people on the ship, still reeling from the experience of leaving their home and seeing it destroyed, found hope in their hearts.

The people, who would take to calling themselves the Tribes in Exile, watched as the ships landed in the driest area, similar to the plains on their home planet. The Sola was just rising in the Eastern skyline and there were a few small groups of the proto-humanoids that lived on this planet gathering to watch the Ships land. The Dragons would go first.

They were always first.
It was the end of everything.
It was a beginning.

—Safkhet,
Star Date 21·520·205500

* * *

World News Time-Gazette
January 15, 20—

Ancient Rosetta-Stone-Like Text Uncovered! Scientists Stunned!

The International Scientific community is reeling with the publication of a new translation of an ancient text. Readers may remember the story of a strange sphere being discovered years ago. Many thought it was a hoax, but this new discovery has changed that speculation.

This week, news that the ancient story of an extra-terrestrial race of beings had come to the Earth was uncovered by a graduate student. When her computer was taken over by a virus, Sonya Lake found the initial installment of an amazing story. Publishers are fighting over the rights to release the rest of what might prove to be a historic text that will change the way we view our own evolution, as well as this planet's history, and that of the entire solar system. Computer scientists say that what has been done to her computer is impossible. Top history and archeological scientists have given no comment at this time, but an anonymous insider says the story is huge.

The first of several stories have appeared, and are supposedly written by an ancient scribe named Safkhet. Stay tuned here to the *World News Time-Gazette* for more information as the story unfolds!

For wide release
For more information, contact
K. Zimmer @ Time-Gazette.com.

A WORD FROM KIM WELLS

When I was in college, I learned that Venus rotates the opposite of Earth. So, if Shakespeare had been writing *Romeo & Juliet* on Venus, Romeo would have quipped "It is the West, and Juliet is the sun, arise fair sun…" That was quite a revelation for a young English major. I was fascinated with Venus… the greenhouse clouds that enclose it make it impossible to sustain life. But what if that weren't always the case? Could Venus have fit within the "Goldilocks" zone of planets in our solar system? And that *what if* stayed with me.

The Dragons in this story are inspired by the very first sci-fi I ever read. It was a novel by Robert Heinlein called *The Star Beast*, and it featured an empathic alien named Lummox. My star dragons will have a much bigger story, of their journey from their home planet in a star system far, far away, in the future, I hope.

The other spur for the story was another college course—Linguistics. Also as an English major. Studying communication, the way languages work and don't work, was fascinating. I had always enjoyed writing, and studying grammar, and the way it works to create a language, was something new. I even learned then that bees can communicate through dance, and that they can lie. But more importantly, we talked about the Ur language, the mythological pre-tower of Babel way that everyone on the planet could communicate with each other.

And one night, on a long drive home from college, this story was born. The way most of my stories come to me is the first line—and the rest, the structure of the Christian Bible backwards from Revelations to Genesis, followed. The idea of a culture before our culture, that would help shape human history, a pre-Atlantis, perhaps, is something I'd like to develop more. And I want to write a longer novel with this story as its introduction. With any luck, that will be forthcoming sometime this year.

I thank Samuel Peralta for including me in this collection, and Ellen Campbell for her able editing and awesome support. *Sistah from another Mistah*. Thanks to Lesley Smith for her beta read, where she suggested a little more framing information. And my hubs, as usual, for some of the science-wiencey bits. If I got any of that wrong, it's definitely my fault.

For more information on my other books, including my novel *Mariposa* and its companion series *Children of Mariposa*, starting with *Lady in Blue*, please check out my website at http://www.kimwells.net. I'm also on Facebook at https://www.facebook.com/kimwellswrites, on Twitter at www.twitter.com/dandeliondreams and email at kimwellswrites@gmail.com

…Come say hi!

Grey

by Chris Pourteau

"I SEE YOU CAME TODAY after all. I didn't know if you would."

The girl caught up to her shadow as she entered the cave. As always, the dragon's voice greeted her before she could see him. He'd heard her coming, her sandaled feet scraping on the rocks as she ascended the cliffs. He no doubt smelled her scent on the wind, more acute now that she'd flowered into early womanhood.

"When last you visited, you said you weren't sure you'd return," he said.

In all the girl's years of coming here, in all her visits, the dragon's deep, rumbling growl still startled her when she first heard it. His stare always had a way of raising the hair on the back of her neck, the visceral reaction of a human in the presence of an old enemy.

"I know what I said last time, but I had to come." Her tone

was cryptic as she placed a hand on the cool rock of the cave mouth to steady herself. "And I always come at this time on this day of the week, Grey."

She sat down against the cool wall, opposite his sleepy stare. Despite the age and weariness his heavy eyelids carried, the sheer bulk of him—his long talons and massive teeth, though both were chipped and brittle; his powerful legs and tail, though slack with loose scales and dust colored—made her keep her distance without thinking about it. Whenever she heard his booming grumble or felt lured into the languid slyness of his green gaze, her human instinct threatened to overwhelm her, make her run screaming from the cave.

The dragon regarded her with his large, lizard eyes. "Why do you insist on calling me that? It vexes me. Being unique among creatures, I need no name."

The girl shifted her weight on the thin dirt of the rocky floor. She'd been in such a hurry to get here today, she'd forgotten the blanket she usually brought to sit on. The sharp stone bit at her bony frame.

"Because your scales are grey," she said for the thousandth time. The old exercise of sparring over his name salved her human fear, as it always did. With a quip in her voice, she added, "They're your most distinguishing feature."

A long, low exhale. A rumble of airy bellows pockmarked with holes. Stronger once, more powerful. Old now, but still deep and yawning, like the caverns around them reaching far into the earth.

"You are nothing if not a practical girl. If I were blue, I suppose you'd call me Blue?"

The dragon lifted his head and peered sharply at her. The eyes were old, yes, but they could still pierce her with their burning curiosity. His front legs were crossed, relaxed, and his tail wrapped unmoving around his massive body to keep him warm against the winter cold.

The girl smiled as they settled into their familiar greeting game. "Of course! Thank goodness you're not fuchsia." Each time she visited, they teased one another in this way, and each time she reminded Grey just how much worse her nickname for him could be.

The dragon's mouth broadened into a massive smile. Though once full of shining, sharp teeth, only lonely sentries, yellowed and worn down in their twos and threes, now stood guard over their domain.

"Perhaps I should call you Red instead of Amanda." One scaly eyebrow rose slowly as he said, "Your hair is *your* most distinguishing feature."

She closed one eye and replied with a barbed tongue, "But it's not my name."

Low laughter from Grey. "Fuchsia—that was a good one this time," he said. "I'm glad you were able to come. I needed a smile." The dragon's expression grew serious as he said, "Few are left to defend the border, you said. And your village is picking up stakes."

"The Bane are still gathering along the frontier," she answered, nodding her head toward the cave mouth. "Scores of them, maybe hundreds. My father refuses to move until they cross it. We still have time, he says."

A thrumming whisper, the sound of air wheezing. The

dragon's way of sighing, she knew. "Your father will be surprised by Death itself when it comes, I think."

"Well, that wasn't a very nice thing to say. Death could come across the frontier tomorrow. For us all."

Air releasing again, a bored sound. Like the dragon had played this scene many times before and was growing tired of the repeat performance.

"No, I suppose it wasn't. And what of the king?"

Now, it was the girl's turn to blow out a breath. "He sits on his throne. He'll sit safely in his mountain keep and let The Bane burn all his lands, rape all his women, and enslave all his men. Only when they threaten him directly will he come down and fight."

Grey blinked slowly and lowered his head back to the floor, relaxing again into his usual repose. But he never took his eyes from the girl. "Some things never change. There are always more cowardly kings than courageous ones."

The girl shifted her weight. The rock was digging into her rump again, no matter how she moved. And Grey's declaration, rendered with malice, irritated her. Especially now, when her people could use a brave leader. "Perhaps there would be more courageous kings if you dragons hadn't killed them all."

His eyes narrowed at her. Less sleepy now, more fiery.

"Well, Amanda, given that only I remain while many of your kings yet populate the land, I would say we dragons fared the worst."

Now more than her butt was uncomfortable. She often had a way of speaking before thinking, especially when anger fueled her words. But in truth, she hadn't meant to hurt his feelings.

Despite their sometimes gruff exchanges, she'd considered Grey a friend since she'd stumbled into his cave as a little girl looking for a refuge from the cold.

"Shall I light the fire for you?" she asked.

The airy bellows again. The throaty sigh. "I suppose if I'm to be warm tonight, you'll have to. Thank you."

It was difficult, almost impossible, for Grey to produce fire now, a surrender to his advanced age. So whenever she came, Amanda always offered to light one for him to warm his home. She moved past him, not quite on tiptoe, to the open crevice that formed a natural chimney. That nagging horror of prey for hunter tickled her neck as she turned her back on Grey to gather the wood. The self-same dread that had inspired humans to exterminate the dragons. All save one.

But she pushed it aside in her mind—replacing it with the trust she'd formed for the old dragon over years of talking until sunrise, snuggled against the cold—and that soothed her heart. "I wish we were stronger," Amanda said, arranging the kindling in the circle of blackened, thick stones in the wall. "I wish we could fight The Bane. I wish we didn't have to move."

"Conquering others is a way of life for some. Being conquered is the lot of the weak."

The dragon's voice, as always, filled the cave even when whispering. When bitterness salted his speech, as it did now, the dull anger in his tone was unmistakable. In the silence that followed, Amanda planted the stick into the small hole in a rock and began rubbing it between her hands.

"I can't stay long today," she said, ignoring the challenge in his voice. Rubbing faster, at last she achieved a wisp of smoke.

"But I'd like to be happy while I'm here. It might be my last visit. Really, this time. Can we *not* talk about what the humans did to the dragons?"

Grey breathed, a gravely sound. "Of course, my dear. Old wounds can open without us even knowing it. I don't wish to spoil your time here. Or my mood during your visit."

The fire caught on the dry sticks, and Amanda arranged the logs within the stones so they'd catch quicker. "Tell me again, then."

"Again?"

"Yes."

Grey's lips opened once more into a smile. "You wish me to speak of birth, not death? You're a clever girl, Red."

Amanda finished arranging the stones and took off her vest, placing it on the floor against the cave wall. She resumed her seat opposite him, her rump much happier now.

"It's *Amanda*. And the birth of the dragons is my favorite story. And you tell it very well."

One massive eye winked slowly. "I have to agree. I'm the best dragon teller of dragon stories there is." Then the wink became a wince. "There I go again. All right, I'll be good."

"I don't have much time today," she said again.

"Very well," said Grey, lifting his head from its resting place as he always did when he told her stories. "Sit and be warm and I'll tell you again how dragons came into the world."

* * *

My dragon ancestors came from deep inside the earth. At

first, they merely crawled out of caves like this one. When the sunlight met their scales, they drank it in like nectar. Having known only the cold, wet dark of the Underearth, coming into the sunshine mesmerized them. The warmth lulled them. They lived lazy lives of leisure, eating that which was easy to reach: plants, small animals. This was their existence for eons.

When the world changed, when the earth heaved and split and vomited fire, many of the dragons died. Those who could, mainly the young, climbed above the boiling earth to find safety in cliffs of stone, high above the stinking black rock skin that now covered the earth. They learned to hunt for food in the higher reaches. No longer could they merely slap at low-hanging fruit with their tails or lay in wait for a small animal to wander into their lair. As each generation of dragons was born, lived, and died—as the earth itself shuffled off the black shell of rebirth—the lazy lizards who first looked upon the sun with reverence became crafty predators. Hunting required them to become wily and sly. And fast.

Dragon broods, once closely knit, were split. Not just by the upheaval of the earth when so many perished, but by the nature of their new homes. Like this cave, they were small and close. Tight holes of stone nestled along cliffsides, high above the black crust below. Over thousands of years, we grew wings to help us hunt from our caves, which became storehouses for hard times. We guarded everything in our caves, and fiercely. Our wings let us soar over the earth, ranging far from our homes to seek food across blackened lands, but they also made it possible for us to rely less on one another. Whenever one dragon saw another, it wasn't in kinship he greeted him, but as a rival for his hoard. Thousands of years of living alone and away from others had bred distrust in our kind, even for each other.

Dragons became solitary creatures who rarely sought the company of others—or their own kind, except to mate. By the time the world's skin began to grow green again and creatures of all kinds—including humans—made homes below, dragons had become the solitary, isolated hunters of the skies you've only ever known them to be.

When the lands below grew green again, dragonkind rejoiced. Food was more plentiful and easier to find. Flight became not merely necessary for survival, but joyous, a way of engaging with the world again. The sky felt more like home than the cliffside caves we'd learned to tolerate to avoid extinction. Ancestral memory began to recall that time of leisure when we'd first crawled into the world.

And then the humans came. At first, one left the other alone. Dragons kept themselves apart, living in their aeries, coming to earth only when necessary to hunt what they couldn't find in the mountains. Humans kept to themselves as well, fearful of the massive flying creatures that looked so much like snakes with wings. They had little affinity with, or need for, one another.

But over time, each race increased in number. As each new patch of green grew from the ashen earth, humans settled and farmed it. Dragons too, with more food and more freedom, mated more frequently and had more young. Inevitably, the two races clashed. One, small but numerous and clumped into tribes, always looking for new lands to conquer and settle. The other, large and powerful but independent, preferring to live alone and apart from its own kin.

Skirmishes escalated to wars. Wars became vendettas. Dragons learned to hate entire lines of human kings. And kings killed dragons for sport. Soon, whole generations of one race had nothing but loathing for the other—

* * *

"Stop!"

The dragon closed his mouth. "Do you have to go?"

"I thought you were going to tell the story of how dragons were born."

Grey blinked his lazy, heavy-lidded eyes. "And so I did."

"Why did you have to tell the rest?"

The dragon hesitated before answering. "You're right. You asked for a pleasant story. It's hard for me to separate the birth of the dragons from the story of their death. I apologize."

"Why must you always remember the bad parts?"

"The bad parts?"

"The parts of the story that make me sad. And make you mad. And you know I might not be back again."

"So you said the last time you came. And you asked me for the story. Never ask for something you do not truly want."

Amanda stared hard at him. The fire had finally caught, and she could see his scales reacting to it. Bristling, but in a good way, as if stretching out to feel the heat. It reminded her of Grey's description of the first dragons, when they climbed from their holes in the earth and became drunk on sunlight.

"Do you want me to leave?" she asked, beginning to rise.

"Not especially," he said. His voice was cautious but prideful. She knew this instinct in him. To push her away until she threatened to go. Then he'd retreat, drawing her back to him. This particular game she didn't like, so she stood and gathered her vest from the cave floor, brushing it off.

"Amanda, wait."

The girl turned and looked at him, her expression fierce. "I might not return! Ever! And this is how you wish to end our friendship?"

The dragon turned his head. "I don't wish to end our friendship at all."

"That's not how it seems," she said, thrusting her arms into her vest.

"Maybe..." Grey was thinking. She could see it. The way he sometimes did when he wanted to take his time and say something exactly right. "Maybe it's important for me to remember. As the last of my kind. Perhaps if I forget, then I'm afraid I'll be forgotten too."

"What do you mean?" Grey had never spoken of being afraid before. It was a strange turn for him to speak of feeling that way. Usually, it was she who had to control her fear in coming here. "People will always remember dragons. How could we forget?"

Grey curled his lip over his broken teeth. "Your people will only remember human stories of dragonkind. Tales of fire-breathing serpents raining death upon villages of women and children. Roasting them alive. Chivalric chronicles of kings on quests, heroically slaying flying monsters." He puffed out a thick sound that smelled of sulfur. "Lies."

"They're not lies!" The words sortied from her mouth before Amanda could stop them. "The dragons destroyed whole villages, scouring them like cooking pots that need cleaning. Men, women, children... it didn't matter—"

"We defended ourselves!"

Grey's voice embraced the stony walls around them, filled the cave up. The rock shook with ancient anger. And yet under that power, beneath its rolling beat of war drums, a strident sound. A desperation Amanda had never heard in Grey, like the fear before. She opened her mouth to respond, thought better of it, and pursed her lips closed.

"History is merely a collection of stories we tell ourselves to understand how we came to be where we are now," continued Grey, more calmly. Yet, the tremor beneath his words remained. "And soon, there will be no dragons left to tell our side of things. The choir of history will lose our voice forever."

"I have to go," Amanda said, suddenly uncomfortable. Sadness and anger roiled within her. And inside her, Grey's own rage had reawakened the old terror that skin feels for scales. "I shouldn't have come here today. There is much to do before we abandon our village." Her words were laced with bitterness. She turned and walked toward the cave's entrance.

"Amanda," said Grey. When she didn't stop, his voice filled the cave again. *"Amanda."* More the desperation, less the anger.

She stopped, her whole body tingling with fear and loathing. She had trouble controlling that natural human reaction upon hearing a dragon's voice, bred by millennia of dying in the thousands, roasted alive. She hated how it consumed her in that moment, how it made her afraid of Grey without the shield of their friendship to protect her from herself. Her need for him, especially now, terrified her more than any dragon ever could.

More softly, he continued, "Why *did* you come here? I sense a desire in you to say something but not the will to say it."

Without looking back, Amanda placed her hand on the sweating stone. Brushed by the fresh wind beyond the cave's mouth, it felt like her hand might freeze there. She let the cold bite at her face. The pain felt good. It gave her something other than her anger and fear to focus on.

"Amanda?"

Grey's voice echoed on the stone, but quietly, with the patience of the old.

"I wanted to ask you something," she said without turning. "But now, I realize it's foolish."

Grey turned his head again, ever curious. "No question is foolish, girl. And I don't want our last meeting to end like this. We both have our peoples' legacies to contend with, the wrongs we've done one another. But you and I, we have no quarrel. Only friendship. What did you wish to ask?"

Amanda turned slowly. She thought of the friendship between them Grey spoke of. Remembering all the times she'd come here, the time they'd shared together, helped her to focus. She remembered how, that first time as a little girl, she'd gone exploring alone and wandered into the cave. Stumbling upon Grey, his snores peppering the walls, had terrified her. And when he'd stirred in the darkness, his tail uncoiling like a snake, she'd shrieked, frozen to the cave floor. But he'd met her screams with a warm smile, and as a child who yet knew nothing of dragons and their shared history of hatred with humans, she'd quickly wrapped herself in the comforting depth of his reassuring voice. Amanda remembered how she'd curled against him, and he'd wrapped his tail around her to protect her from the cutting cold on a night much like this one. This was how their friendship had begun.

"Will you help us?" she whispered. Between the frigid wind and the crackle of the fire, she wasn't sure he'd heard her. If he had, she expected a roaring response of anger. Or perhaps, and worse, a pitying laugh roiling up from his enormous belly. But what she hoped for was agreement, the generous gesture of one friend coming to the aid of another. "I said—"

"I heard you."

Amanda turned around and moved a few feet closer to him, away from the wind and toward the glow of the budding fire. She wanted to touch him one more time. Feel his tail stroke the red hair on her head as she fell asleep, like that first night she'd found sanctuary here so long ago.

"No," said Grey. His voice was quiet but firm.

The ice in his answer chased away Amanda's warm memories, a wolf scattering sheep from a quiet meadow.

"No?"

Grey cleared the bellows of his long neck with a grunt. "No."

Now it was Amanda's turn to be angry. "Why? The Bane will kill us!"

Despite his earlier fury, Grey seemed entirely calm now. "Not if you leave. Give them the land and survive."

"That's your solution? We should run?"

"It was yours too, until a moment ago. And why should I

help you? I am old. The Bane are many. What help could one old dragon be, in the end? I have no wish to end my race. Or my own life."

"You are nothing if not a practical dragon," she sniped back. "Yes, The Bane are many. They'll find us, wherever we go. My people are simple farmers and herdsmen. There will always be someone wanting to kill us and take our land."

"All the more reason to move on, if such is your fate. Delay Death as long as possible, as I have done." Grey laid his head down again, but as always, his eyes stared into Amanda. "Caves make good homes. Climb into the mountains. Don't come down from them. Be smarter than we were."

Amanda's eyes began to well. Not simply because Grey had refused her request, but because his coarse tone, his coldness toward her now seemed to wash away years of cuddling on cold nights and sharing stories until dawn. All banished by this moment of feeling utterly betrayed.

Perhaps she'd only been a distraction to him, she thought in that instant. A human toy he could play with once a week. A mantel to place his trophy of guilt upon for past wrongs. Her anger at feeling so used rose from her gut like venom.

"You speak of lies," she spit at him, her voice breaking. "All of *this* was a lie! Your friendship was a lie! All these years I've come to you and all that we've shared... not friendship, just pretense from the forked tongue of a dragon!"

Even as she screamed it, Amanda didn't truly believe it. But she was furious with him. Grey wouldn't save her village. He wouldn't make it possible for her to come back here again, week after week, and curl up with him when it was cold and talk until the sun rose. He was old and he would die and leave her one day, or his refusal would force her to leave him and flee The Bane today. Her helplessness to stop the fall of any of these fated footsteps fired Amanda's belly with rage.

Grey had jerked his head up at the old insult. "Believe what you will, human. Speak your platitudes about dragon serpents and their forked tongues." His tone was dismissive, but his words sounded thin to Amanda, as if he were speaking lines from a play. "I won't stop humans killing humans. I won't betray the memory of my race by helping those who destroyed it."

"I'll die!"

The dragon regarded her sadly. "As must we all."

Tears burned her cheeks with cold trails. Crying them made her angry, furious with herself because now Grey could see how much she was hurting. How much he'd hurt her.

"I hate you! And all dragons! Best you die soon and rid the world of your false friendship that never was!"

Before Grey could answer, Amanda rounded and fled the cave, head set hard against the wind.

All that remained was the crackle of the fire and the old dragon's breathing, the sound of air pushing through worn-out, leathery lungs.

"I am old," he said to the fire. "What could I do? And why would I ever help a human do a single, solitary thing?"

Grey regarded the flames as they grew in the hearth, set to warm him by the girl who'd been his friend for nearly ten winters. He felt a pang in his chest as he realized they no longer shared that bond. He blinked once and for the first time in a long time, a tear soaked the thinning scales beneath one eye.

* * *

"There's no more time," she heard her father say to another village elder. "We must move at dawn or be overrun."

Amanda lay in her bed of hide-covered straw, her little brother next to her. It'd been nearly a week since she'd last visited Grey. He'd merely sat, alone and unmoving, in his cave. As if he waited there for Death to finally take him, a task no human warrior had ever accomplished. And now Death came on thundering hooves for her as well. For all of them.

"The wagons are loaded," she heard the elder say. "We have but to mount them and move west."

A horn sounded. One long blast, followed by three short ones. The border guard. The Bane.

"What? So soon?" the elder's voice slapped against the icy gale. "The king sent word that—"

"Go, now!" her father barked. "I must look to my family."

Shuffling sounds as her father opened the door to their home and yelled, "Ameris! Get the children up. It's time. I'll hitch up the horses."

The door opened and closed again as her mother sprang from bed and stumbled sleepily across the small room.

"Children!"

"I heard, Momma. I'll wake Markh and grab our winter clothes."

"We don't have much time, Amanda."

The girl could hear the terror in her mother's voice. Not fear for her own safety, Amanda knew, but the dread of seeing her children slaughtered in front of her.

"I know, Momma. Grab the jerky and flatbread." Her

mother was looking at her, unmoving, eyes wide with fright. Amanda touched her arm. "Momma! We'll be all right. But we must go *now*."

Ameris nodded and moved away to gather the family's foodstuffs.

Another long blow of the border guard's horn. One long, then two short blasts.

They're closer than we knew, Amanda thought. They'll be here any moment.

Outside, other families were stirring. Pulling together the preparations they'd made for the long flight west along the Trader's Road. Some were screaming. They too had heard the horn as it was cut off.

Amanda gathered up her little brother, who protested his sleepiness, and both their bundles of winter clothing. Ameris, a heavy pack of food on her back, opened the door and put her head down against a driving gust of snow. The dogs of the village barked relentlessly, another alarm of the approaching horde, as yet unsilenced.

Her father was desperately trying to hook their two gaunt horses up to the wagon. She could see his hands were clumsy from cold and fright. Her mother slung their food in the back and moved to help him. Markh complained of the cold and a need for sleep as his sister pushed him to climb into the wagon.

Amanda stared east. Villagers from the far end of the settlement, the end facing the border, were running in their direction. Like animals fleeing a forest fire burning all in its path. She watched her parents' fingers fumble with leather straps and iron buckles.

They weren't going to make it. They should've left yesterday. Or any other day before today.

Damn Grey, Amanda thought as she watched her friends and neighbors run past, their faces stricken with terror. *Damn all dragons!*

The dogs were yelping now, not braying – crying out as they attempted and failed to protect their masters.

She could see The Bane charging into the village from the south, cutting down everything in their path. First one, then ten, than dozens.

Massive warriors on huge, shaggy horses. Horned towering helms, topped by animal heads fastened upon them to make their bearers appear larger and more frightening. Half covered in black furs, half exposed muscles, heedless of the freezing cold, swinging weapons of iron and wood. One warrior leaned over as he galloped by and swung his warhammer so hard, the head of the village blacksmith left his shoulders and bumped along the ground. He was so large, Amanda guessed that the fearsome giant on horseback must be The Bane's leader.

"Father! Mother! Grab the food and clothing, we have to go!"

Amanda leapt into the wagon and gathered up Markh in her arms again. *No way we'll get out. No way*, she thought, counting the carnage in her head as if keeping score in a game.

The Bane were simply galloping through from one end of the village to the other, murdering indiscriminately. They seemed content to pick the slaves from the survivors later.

The terrifying warrior with the stag's antlers atop his helm saw the family struggling with the supplies on their wagon and wheeled his horse around. Amanda released her brother and found the axe they used for chopping wood in the bottom of the cart. She picked it up and stood her ground as her parents screamed at her to retreat with them to their hut. Seeing her, the warrior smiled and kicked his heels into his horse's flanks, raising his gigantic warhammer, a promise that her fate was sealed.

Amanda heard the whump of his wings before she saw Grey. She thought it merely a gust of wind playing a trick on her ears.

When she looked back for the source of the sound, she could hardly see the dragon—a dusty blur of wings and claws against the white sky of winter. His roar seemed to command everything to stop its movement, as if time itself were surprised to hear the boom of a dragon's voice again after so long an absence, an assumption of extinction.

Grey drew his wings in and plummeted through the air, then expanded them again to sweep fast and low over the tops of the huts and heads of startled villagers. Even they halted their mad flight westward to watch in awe as he glided gracefully by.

The mounts of The Bane fought their human masters, instinct making them thrust their hooves out in front of them and shy away from the shrieking dragon. Even the monstrous warrior with the warhammer diverted. He jerked his mount left and away from the girl with the axe standing boldly and alone in the wagon.

Amanda watched, unbelieving, as Grey swept by overhead. She thought she saw him blink or wink, but in the haste of his flight, she couldn't be sure. But she smiled. For her people and for Grey's. She smiled for friendship.

The fire was weak when it came. But Grey's wings pumped,

working the bellows of his belly and neck to vomit flame upon his enemies. A screaming cry of roasting horses and men wrapped in blazing furs rode the arctic wind. It coursed the length of the village like a banshee's wail of suffering.

The Bane's leader turned his horse back to his warriors and shouted something, gesturing at the dragon, now turning to make a second pass. Bows lifted in unison from fifty different directions and loosed their arrows. Many bounced off the dragon's thinning hide, but some did not.

Grey thundered his pain and rage and unleashed another, lesser stream of fire at the ground. Amanda watched him pass again and saw blood from a score of wounds streaking red the dragon's grey hide. Still, his fire set as many of The Bane aflame as arrows he carried.

Her father rushed past her. As she watched him running toward the invaders, pitchfork in hand, she saw another villager hurry by her, then another. They were fighting back.

The mountain with the warhammer dismounted and stood in the middle of the settlement as his warriors engaged the villagers. He raised his weapon high and shouted at the dragon as it banked against the wind.

He looks weak, thought Amanda. She could see Grey struggling to turn. A maneuver that would've been easy for him before—when he was younger, with tougher skin, and unhurt—now appeared difficult to execute.

The Bane's leader swept his arm forward and another brace of arrows arced through the air. There were fewer than before but these tracked more sure. Many of them found their marks, tearing rents in the thin membrane of the old dragon's wings.

Amanda watched him fight to stay aloft. He was aiming

his next attack at the leader, she could see. But when he passed over the massive man's head, Grey could only roar, and weakly. There was no fire.

The mountain with the warhammer shouted in triumph as the dragon passed over him. His exhortations made clear that The Bane had won. The beast was wounded and heading down.

Amanda's eyes followed Grey as he angled toward the ground. The holes in his wings and drooping rudder of a tail made his landing rough and awkward. The earth threw up snow and dust at the impact, and then all was still.

Ignoring the fighting around him, the leader of The Bane walked toward Grey, savoring the moment.

She shouted the dragon's name against the howling gust, but he made no response or movement. She shouted again, this time at the enemy's leader, but he ignored her as he strode toward his fallen foe. Raising her axe, she shouted a third time, a warrior's cry, and leapt from the wagon.

Grey lifted one eyelid. He saw the man in the black furs— arms bare and bulging, warhammer in hand—stalking toward him with purpose. He lifted one lip in a feral smile.

The giant of a man reached him and stared down at the one eye open looking up at him. Saying something in a language Grey didn't understand, The Bane's leader removed his horned helm and threw it aside. He raised his warhammer in triumph, the gesture making it clear to all who saw that he'd be wearing a new helm made of dragonhide soon enough.

Amanda, screaming. Grey heard it before he saw it. The girl running at the warrior. The warrior turning to meet the new threat.

Grey roared. Again no fire came, but he pushed himself

from the frozen ground with cracked claws. His tail whipped around, sweeping The Bane's champion from his feet. The air whooshed out of the huge warrior when he hit the ground. Grey placed one weathered foot over the savage king's head and used the bulk of his body to hold him down. Amanda reached them and stood over the writhing leader, who beat uselessly at the dragon's claw.

"Do what must be done," said Grey.

His voice was dry and wheezing, full of pain compounded by age. Desperate to be done with all of this.

She looked at the creature that had caused Grey's suffering. That had led The Bane on their quest to rape and murder her family and all the people in her village. She watched him struggle under the dragon's great weight.

"Do it now, Amanda." Barely a whisper.

She summoned the courage of their friendship from deep inside her, channeled it through her arms, raised the axe, and split the chest of the struggling champion. Then she pried the axe from his breastbone and brought it down again. And then again.

Grey's tail at last came between her stroke and the rapidly cooling corpse on the ground. "It is done," he breathed. "Are they running yet?"

Amanda came back to herself and, with some effort, pulled her eyes from the gaping chest of the mutilated man in front of her. What remained of The Bane was scattering. Villagers were finishing off those too wounded to run.

"Yes," she said, mostly to herself. Turning to Grey, she fell down beside him and wrapped her arms around his head. "Yes! They're running!"

A grunt of acknowledgment from the dragon. "Kill their strongest, the weaker run. It's old knowledge, but good knowledge." Despite the pain of his wounds, he smiled at her.

"I'll get the healer," she said. "He'll help you—"

"No," said Grey. As final and willful as when he'd refused her pleas for help in his cave. "No, he wouldn't. And there's no need."

"But Grey!"

"You should know, Amanda," he said, his breaths coming shorter. "I didn't do this for them. Not for the humans of your village. I did this for you. For the friendship we forged together."

"Grey, please—"

"Make a home in the cliffs, Amanda. And don't come down," he said. He laid his head down and winked sluggishly at her to show that, in his humor at least, fire remained. "It's old knowledge, but good knowledge. Don't forget."

Then, when Grey closed his eyes, the last of the dragons passed from the world of men.

* * *

The sun of twilight was descending below the mountains in the west, and he was lost. That much the boy knew. Lost and alone, and soon the temperature would be freezing. And tomorrow his parents would be furious with him. But at the moment, he was concerned only with one thing—surviving the night.

He climbed higher, hoping to find shelter. With wood and flint stone in it, if he were lucky. Something, anything, that would burn until morning. This was the last time he'd take a dare to climb Grey's Peak. *The absolute last time,* he swore again to the household gods, asking them to bring him home safe, if only so he could worship them and thank them for doing so.

The boy found the cave as the last of the sunlight descended into the west. It would be cold, dark, and many hours until dawn. But at least he'd found shelter.

The cave felt warm as he entered.

But how can that be? he wondered.

"And who are you?"

The boy nearly slipped on the floor of the cave's entrance, slick with melted snow. Heat wafted to him from within. He wanted to run and hug it like a mother, but the old voice had startled him. Fear of the unknown crept up his spine.

"Well, boy?"

"My name's Markh!" he called, trying to be heard over the wind. Strange that the voice coming from within needed merely to speak to be heard. Perhaps the warm air made it easier for him to hear somehow, the boy thought.

"I had a brother by that name," said the voice, sounding ancient but still young in its wistfulness. "He died many years ago." Less musing, more melancholy.

"I'm sorry your brother died," said Markh, shivering. He didn't know what else to say and so offered another silent prayer to the household gods. One thing he knew for sure—he really wanted to embrace that fire.

"No need. He lived a long life. Will you stand out there to become a frozen statue as a warning to others? Or would you like to share my fire?"

Markh leapt into the cave. When he saw her, his eyes grew big as saucers.

"Sit down before you fall down," she said.

"You're the Matron of Grey's Keep! You guard the dragon's hoard!"

"I've heard I'm called that," she said, folding her auburn hair, streaked with grey, away from her face. "And you can call me Red. But there is no hoard of gold here."

The boy's face fell as he moved deeper into the cave and nearer the fire. He was disappointed by the old woman's news, but his eyes glowed hungrily as they focused on the fire.

"Come! Use that blanket there to pad your rump," she said, gesturing to the wall opposite where she sat. "Sit and be warm. I'll tell you how this mountain came to be named. And how dragons came into the world."

A WORD FROM
CHRIS POURTEAU

I'm a fantasy geek from years back. I'm one of the folks who thought Tolkien was cool long before Peter Jackson came along. My early '80s lunch table in high school was like the round table in Camelot—the launching pad for many a quest courtesy of Dungeons & Dragons (first edition!). And I bought the first mass-market paperback copies of Margaret Weis and Tracy Hickman's *Dragonlance* series to roll off the presses. After that it was Terry Brooks and David Gemmell, *Warhammer: Fantasy* (I painted an entire army of Dwarfs, which is how Games Workshop spelled their name)—my list of "fantasy loves," like Bilbo Baggins's road, goes ever on and on.

So, when Samuel Peralta asked me to write a story for *The Dragon Chronicles*, my geek meter immediately spiked to 11. I was excited about joining my story with those of so many authors I admire, but I was also terrified. I was about to contribute to a canon I've revered for as long as I could read. No pressure.

At first, I only had the title. Approaching 50, I find I'm a little more attuned to issues of age, and so I knew I wanted my dragon to be old and rather decrepit but—as I hope for myself—not quite ready for retirement yet. I love exploring relationships in my stories, and so I gave Grey a friendly foil in Amanda to create the crux of my story. One of the themes I explore is the idea that, if we can just get to know one another as individuals—without bringing all the baggage of prejudice and preconceived ideas to the table—we might find friendship faster. While instinctively frightened of dragons (and all reptiles really) when she first meets Grey, Amanda is quickly won over by his kindness. As a little girl, she hasn't yet been indoctrinated by human propaganda to hate all dragons, so instead, she comes to know him as a friend first. Grey's ultimate answer to Amanda's request for help is his way of overcoming his own prejudice, long ingrained in his race. Ultimately, Amanda returns the kindness by becoming the oracle of dragon history—as they, were they still around, would tell it themselves. I hope you enjoyed reading the story as much as I enjoyed writing it.

Before I let you go, I need to thank a few folks. Samuel Peralta has done a wonderfully generous thing by inviting independent writers to participate in his *Future Chronicles* series, and I'm personally very grateful to him for asking me to contribute to this collection: thank you, Sam. My wife, Alison, is my alpha reader and always offers wonderful advice and support throughout the writing process; thanks, sweetie, as always, for being a friendly but honest first reader. Hank Garner, David Gatewood, Dawn Herring, Debby Stapleton, and Catherine Violando provided awesome feedback as beta-readers and helped me to improve the story for you.

If you want to find out more about me and my writing, please visit me at http://chrispourteau.thirdscribe.com or email me at c.pourteau.author@gmail.com and say howdy.

The Storymaster
by Vincent Trigili

"PAPA, IT'S TIME TO get up," came the ever-cheerful voice of my eldest granddaughter.

It most definitely couldn't be time to get up yet. "Go away, Myrill," I groaned and pulled the thick wool blanket tighter in a vain attempt to ward her off. I was sure she was shorting my late afternoon nap more and more each day.

"Now, Papa, the children are waiting to hear from the Storymaster," she said.

"So go find one, and let me sleep," I grumbled.

"I did, and he's in here shirking his duties," she chided.

I think she thoroughly enjoyed putting me through this every day at this time. Maybe it was payback for all those times I'd had to wake her up for something when she was a small child. Or maybe she just had a sadistic side. Probably both.

I knew there was no escaping it; I'd have to get up. It was just that it was so warm under the blankets, and the thick feather mattress was very comfortable. It would grow cold once I got up and I'd have to warm it up all over again.

I slowly rolled back over and tried to untangle myself from the blanket. "You better have some tea on if you expect me to travel all that way in the bitter cold."

"Papa, they're just in the next room over, and we have a good fire going," she said.

"Still, there'd better be tea, or I'm coming right back here! Now, where did you hide my cane this time?" I asked as I finally got my legs free.

"It's right here, exactly where you left it, of course." She picked up my old bamboo cane. It was worn smooth at the grip, and the base was rough from use. It was a good solid cane, one I'd had for many years now. I could walk without it, but my old bones much appreciated the help.

She handed it to me and I slowly made my way out to the room where my great-grandchildren were playing. Seeing their energy and vitality just made my advanced age feel even older. I wondered how many of them would remember me after I was gone and they started having their own children.

I knew that Myrill was right. I needed to get out of the bed and move around. I really did enjoy the children, but moving was getting harder with each passing day. The long cold winter nights didn't help either.

As I lowered myself into my rocker by the fire, Myrill tucked a wool blanket around me. She had made it for me earlier this winter, and despite my complaining, I really did appreciate all the attention she paid to my comfort.

After checking to be sure I also had pillows, she said, "I'll be back shortly with your tea."

The children all ran up to my chair and called out, "Story-master! Tell us a story!"

"What story should I tell you?" I asked them. Their excitement was a bit contagious and I drew strength from it. A million stories came to my mind, and a thousand heroes leapt for attention.

They all called out different stories at the same time and I honestly couldn't understand any of it. "'David's Last Ride' it is, then!" I decided to go with one of my favorites instead of fighting through the cacophony of noise that only a gaggle of children can produce.

There were some cheers and some "Awwws," but everyone settled down to hear it. It was one of the more exciting stories, and the little ones especially liked hearing it. Or so I told myself. David held a special place in my heart for many reasons, so I loved to tell about him.

"David was the last of the truly great dragonmasters. A few lived on after him, but none could match his skill and cunning. His dragon, Lyrroth, was a sleek and wise black dragon. They had many adventures together before and after the war. As you recall, the war almost completely wiped out the dragons, but they still held on for a time. There were perhaps a half dozen or so of them left when David made his last ride. It was a warm morning, sometime in the spring…" I started and then allowed myself to fully slip into the character of David, and for a short while I left my aching body behind…

* * *

This would be the last generation of dragons, as there were no breeding pairs left. I couldn't even think of a single living female dragon. In a few generations we'd just be a legend, and probably a few more after that people would start to doubt that they ever really existed.

"Good morning, David," came the deep rumbling voice of the mighty Lyrroth.

"Morning, old friend," I said and stretched out. The sun felt good on my obsidian skin as I walked out of our cave. I found Lyrroth lying in the sun. He was a massive beast; twelve grown men could easily lay down head to foot from the tip of his tail to the tip of his snout. His scales were an iridescent black and had a colorful sheen in the morning light. His maw was filled with fangs that could rend an armored man in half with a single bite, and smoke rose from his nostrils as he relaxed in the sun.

"Did the supply ships come in?" I asked.

"No, and now they are two days late. I think we'd better go look for them," he said. There was a great weariness in his voice.

It was hard to greet each morning and each new adventure with joy like we used to. We had lost so many friends and family members to the war, and the few dragons that were left were slowing dying off.

"Yeah, I guess we'd better," I said. It was a bad sign that the supply convoy was late. The towns below us badly needed building materials and other supplies. The island base was practically impregnable, but during the war the farmland was torched, as was much of the forest. It would be years before the humans could support themselves again. Until then, they depended on supplies from the mainland.

"Where are the others?" I asked.

"Rhenvaar and Barioth are lounging by their caves. The rest have flown off on other errands."

Rhenvaar and Barioth were inseparable twin red dragons. They did everything together, and often that entailed creating havoc. Their riders were also twins, and they went out of their way to dress and act exactly alike. This caused all kinds of confusion, and they enjoyed every minute of it.

Red dragons were by far the most common of the species, and by far the largest. They were larger and stronger than black dragons like Lyrroth, but they were also slower and less maneuverable in the air. Red dragons had been the bulk of the fighting force at one time, but now only these two remained.

Before the war, I would have flown this reconnaissance mission alone or with two other black dragons, but there were no other black dragons left. Lyrroth was the last, and no one dared fly alone anymore.

"Wake them, and let's get in the air. Hopefully we'll find the ships sailing peacefully along, but we'd better be ready just in case," I said.

He rose to his full height, and I could see the many scars on his hide. We were both old and had both taken many wounds. We'd cheated death more times than I could count, but Father Time was as relentless as he was patient.

Lyrroth leaped off the cliff and extended his wings for a

gentle glide down to where the brothers lay talking. I walked over to watch him fly down and was impressed at the grace he could still show given his age.

I was sure that it would be dark before we returned and it wouldn't do to pass out from hunger while in the air, so breakfast was the next order of business. We had hunted recently, and there was still plenty of meat hanging to drain. It made for a fine breakfast roasted over our cooking fire.

As I finished my meal, Lyrroth returned, landing near me with a gentleness that seemed impossible. Had I been human and not a dragonmaster, the heat that he radiated from his internal furnace would have been at the very least uncomfortable, and likely would have turned my skin red from exposure.

Dragon fire came from a mixture of iron, oxygen, and aluminum that was ignited by magnesium in their internal furnace before breathing. A dragon had to keep the furnace hot, which meant his blood was constantly carrying heat away from the furnace to his scales. His scales then radiated the heat off to prevent the dragon from burning himself up.

For me, the heat he radiated was welcoming. It was what friendship felt like.

Rhenvaar and Barioth were circling overhead with their dragonmasters, obviously itching to get going. They missed the constant action of the war, and were probably hoping we would find trouble out there.

"They're ready," said Lyrroth.

"Then let's get airborne," I said.

I climbed onto Lyrroth, strapped myself down and focused my mind into his. When dragonmaster and dragon bind, individuality ceases. Each personality, each set of abilities, memories, and everything that makes an individual an individual blends to make one new creature. Mentally, I fell into Lyrroth and we became one. It was only when bound together like this that each of us was complete.

I, as Lyrroth-David, stretched my wings and leapt into the air, flying between the circling Rhenvaar and Barioth. They roared their greetings as I passed between them. Three dragons and three masters, perfectly blended together.

"Follow me!" I roared.

Our den was in a mountain valley, so we had to climb high through the cloud layer to clear the mountains, and then dive fast towards the ocean. I quickly outpaced my slower companions, and the rush of the wind in my face and the sight of the ground racing towards me were exhilarating. No matter how old I got, I never got over the thrill of raw speed. I let myself go. Behind me Rhenvaar and Barioth pushed hard to keep up, but continued to fall behind. I wondered if they enjoyed these high-speed dives as much as I did, but decided they were too slow to understand the joy of raw speed.

Pulling up at the last moment, just barely clearing the tree-tops, I roared past the tiny fishing village and over the open sea. Villagers waved their arms and children jumped up and down. I knew they'd be cheering too, but their tiny lungs could never hope to produce enough sound to reach me.

It was one of the many tiny towns that dotted our domain, and they always enjoyed seeing us in the air. I also enjoyed seeing them, as they reminded me of why we still get up every morning. Villages like the one below counted on us to protect them.

With the others so far behind, I figured I had a little time for a show. I inhaled deeply and breathed fire while executing a loop that created a massive ring of fire in the sky. I continued looping smaller and smaller loops, forming a spiral of super hot plasma until I had finally exhausted my breath, and then with a wave of my wings headed back on course at a slower speed.

Rhenvaar and Barioth decided to join in the show as my fiery spiral dissipated. They came in low and pulled up hard, breathing fire as they twisted around each other, making a great column of fire in the sky. Below us in the village the townsfolk jumped and waved the flag of our nation, obviously enjoying the impromptu show.

Rhenvaar and Barioth dove down from where they had completed their pillar of flame and came racing up behind me. We headed towards the main shipping route, hoping to find good news about the supply convoy. The rocks made the seaport treacherous, but long ago a channel was cleared with the help of a team of green dragons. If the supply ships were close, they would be in that channel. If they had wrecked, the most likely place would be near the channel on either side.

I allowed some more of my speed to bleed off, and the two red dragons pulled alongside me. "We should start by following the channel out to the open water," I called out.

They roared their agreement, and we flew out low over the water. I wanted to be low enough to spot debris if they had run aground, but there was no sign of them.

* * *

Myrill came with my tea right then and I stopped to take a drink. The tea soothed my throat and warded off the coughing fit that I knew would follow without it. I supposed I'd spent too many seasons sitting by the fire, breathing in the smoke while telling stories.

The youngest of my great-grandchildren, Silverleaf, took advantage of the break to ask, "Storymaster, why didn't the dragons just carry the supplies?"

I smiled. He was one of the most inquisitive people I had met. I guess it was his age. I wondered what it was like to be so young and full of hope. It was too far behind me to remember. I guessed I might have been a lot like him at his age. It took an exceptionally inquisitive mind to be a storymaster.

"They did at one point, but by this time there were too few of them, and they had to stay and help protect the island," I said.

I took another swallow of the honey and licorice tea that Myrill always made for me. She said it was good for the throat, but I didn't really know much about that. What I did know was that it was real easy going down on these cold winter nights.

"Now, where was I?" I asked. I, of course, knew exactly where I'd left off. My body was failing, but my mind was as sharp as ever. It was just a fun way to see which children were actually listening. Besides, it added to the old and helpless image I had to keep up if I wanted to keep my supply of tea coming.

"Lyrroth, Rhenvaar and Barioth were flying out over the channel looking for the supply ships," piped up young Tamerale.

"Ah yes," I said and continued the story from where I'd left off.

* * *

We flew the entire route of the channel and found no sign of the ships. I hadn't expected any. Had they run into trouble this close, surely someone would have been able to make it ashore and get word to us.

"Let's head higher and spread out. Fly towards the mainland port they came from!" I called out over the noise of the air rushing by.

They roared and I pulled up, leading them into the sky. They spread out so that we formed a great triangle in the sky and covered a much wider area than any single dragon could have.

The great raptors that patrolled the sea looking for fish gave us wide berth, silently acknowledging that we were kings of the domain of the air.

The ocean was rough, but nothing the big ships that carried our supplies couldn't handle. They were well acquainted with these waters and should have had no problems navigating the conditions.

We flew for about an hour when Rhenvaar roared that he'd found something. Barioth and I turned to follow him. He had found the supply ships all right, and they were beset with pirates!

A dozen pirate ships had encircled the supply ships and were pounding them with broadside after broadside. The ironwood sides of the supply ships were starting to splinter under the beating, but lived up to to their name. I doubted they could hold out much longer, but they wouldn't have to.

"Attack!" I called out and dove towards the farthest ship

with the sun at my back. They wouldn't see or hear me until it was too late for them. As I closed in on the ship I took a deep breath, fanning my internal fires. These pirates would never again bother supply caravans, that was for certain.

As I closed in I opened my great maw and breathed white scorching hot flames and saturated the ship with fire. The dry wood of the deck and the cloth of the sails caught flame easily. The fire became a hungry beast with a mind of its own racing throughout the vessel as the men started abandoning ship in panic. Soon the flames reached their kegs of black powder and the explosions ripped through the hull, sending deck hands diving for cover as shrapnel ripped through the air around them. The sloop had taken the full force of my breath, and was nothing more than a brilliant bonfire.

Rhenvaar swung wide and low and went at two more of the pirate ships at once. Using the advantage of surprise and speed he breathed his flames into the hulls of the ships above the water line and right across the cannon ports. Men screamed as the ship burned and more black powder ignited, sending a rain of debris and body parts everywhere.

He didn't even pause in his breathing as he finished his pass on the first ship and began his pass over the second. Fire leapt across the bow of the ship and began its deadly dance through the wooden planks that made up the deck.

Barioth was the more cautious of the twins and stayed high as he dove through another group of pirates, but that didn't lessen the fiery fury that he breathed across them.

In that first pass we left five of the pirate ships in roaring flames. I banked hard and came back for another pass when one of the pirates launched a counter attack. Massive nets flew into the air towards me, attempting to entangle me and send me crashing into the sea, but I'd seen this move many times before and was ready for it.

I deftly turned my wings up and began beating against my flight path, causing me to stall in place. The nets flew harmlessly past, on a perfect trajectory to where I would have been had I kept flying.

With a great roar I flipped over and resumed my attack run. The pirates didn't have enough time to prepare a second set of nets, and they never would, because I unleashed my scorching breath across the mainsail, setting the boom and stern aflame. The pirates dove into the sea, abandoning their ship as the hull became engulfed in flames. Kegs of black powder erupted, throwing debris everywhere.

Black smoke filled the sky above me as I banked hard to avoid crashing into the ship and headed towards my next target. I needed a few more moments to let my internal furnace get hot enough to produce more fire, but I didn't let an opportunity pass to take down another target.

These pirate ships were of the sloop style and weighed almost double my own weight, but that wouldn't save them. I beat my wings hard and aimed for the broadside of one of the undamaged ships. At the last moment before impact I changed my flight path and smashed my tail into the bow, knocking a large chunk of the ship off, and sending great cracks through the hull. The unforgiving sea rushed into the breach and the ship began to sink.

The slam forced me to beat my wings hard to regain altitude, and for a brief moment, if the pirates had been the quick sort, I was vulnerable to counter attack. I wasn't concerned that the pathetic pirates could take advantage of that weakness. They were too busy trying to keep their footing as the ship lurched under the force of the blow, and I climbed safely back into the sky.

Seven of the thirteen pirate ships were out of the fight, and their crews were swimming for the remaining ships. The supply ships turned away from the fight and were making good time tacking towards safety.

As I watched, the twins made another pass, deftly avoiding the nets sent their way, and destroyed three more of the pirate ships. With only three ships left, the pirates seemed more intent on fleeing than fighting. Large bonfires marked this battlefield for now, but before long the sea would claim what was left of the ships and there would be no indication the fight ever happened.

"Let the rest go," I called out as we regrouped.

"Why?" asked Rhenvaar.

"So that they'll tell others about what happens when you attack supply ships destined for this harbor," I said.

"I doubt they have the sense to stay away. We should finish them off," said Barioth.

It would almost be a kinder fate to kill them all, I mused to myself. The three sloops would take on what was left of the crews of the nine lost ships. It would be crowded and miserable. Pirates weren't known for getting along in the best of times, and this wouldn't be the best of times, for sure. But honor demanded we let fleeing combatants flee.

* * *

"Wait," said Silverleaf. His little brow furled as he tried to reason out his question. "If it was more merciful to kill them, why would honor dictate they be miserable?"

I was impressed with this little one's reasoning. He showed wisdom beyond his seasons.

"That's just the rule, and rules are rules," said Tamerale.

I smiled. Tamerale wasn't quite old enough to grasp that there are times when things are not so black and white, but in the end his answer was right.

"Silverleaf, the rules of honor were intended to bring some civility to combat, and in most cases they did just that, but no rule can be perfect all of the time. It's up to the honorable warrior to figure out how best to apply them in any given engagement," I said.

"But then he should have killed them," reasoned Silverleaf.

"Perhaps, and the twins sure would have been happy to, but Lyrroth was in charge and he decided to let them go," I said.

Myrill's husband Nasir said, "Keep in mind, by letting them go he was giving them a chance to improve their life and learn from their mistakes. Perhaps one day they would learn to use their knowledge of the sea to help others, or they might have had children at home waiting for them. If he had killed them, then all the possible futures go away."

Nasir's display of insight let me know my time as storymaster was almost up. Indeed, my time left in this world was nearly complete. I would have to speak with Nasir after story time.

"So, then, it really was more merciful for him to let them go?" asked Silverleaf.

"It could have been, but we don't know what happened to them after that," I said. In reality, I figured they probably didn't learn anything from it and went on to cause more trouble. "But, that wasn't the end of Lyrroth's troubles that day..."

* * *

We circled above the supply ships while they got back in formation and set sail for the harbor. The three undamaged pirate ships picked up what was left of the other crews and made haste to get out of the area. Everything seemed calm, but I was on edge. Something wasn't right.

"Keep alert and—" I started, but before I could finish there was a loud roar, and something large and green slammed into the back of Rhenvaar.

As they tumbled out of the air, I saw what had hit him. "Feral dragon!" I roared. That wasn't good. When a dragon lost his dragonmaster, it was like they lost all sense of reason and became pure predators. They destroyed anything in their path until they were either put down, or they finally succumbed to hunger. All they did was destroy, rarely, if ever, stopping to eat.

Barioth and I were powerless to help as they twisted and turned, falling from the sky. They raked each other with great claws and it was impossible to tell who was winning. The pair of them crashed into the sea among the still-flaming boats, spraying water in every direction, but they fought on.

The violent tumbling and fighting in the water created massive waves that threatened to capsize the already damaged pirate ships. If there were any crew left in the water, there was no way they could survive the maelstrom being created as the two dragons wrestled.

Hot dragon blood spilled into the ocean in great quantities and created massive clouds of steam, further obscuring the battle. There was far too much blood being spilled, and it wasn't looking good for Rhenvaar.

I wanted to dive in and help, but there was no way to get in without risking attacking Rhenvaar. Barioth and I circled, watching for an opening, but none presented itself. I watched helplessly as the battling dragons roared in frustration. The green dragon had gotten the jump on Rhenvaar, and they were in the water; that meant he had all the advantages.

My fears were soon realized as the green dragon burst from the water and Rhenvaar and his master slowly sank into the darkness. Inseparable in life, and inseparable in death. Before I could react, Barioth roared and dove straight at the green beast, breathing fire as he went.

Dragon skin isn't vulnerable to fire, but a face full of fire would temporally blind, and Barioth used that to cover a fast course change to come around behind the green dragon.

The green dragon was no youngling and was ready for the move, and at the last moment he rolled over and raked with his claws.

Barioth was ready for the counter and rolled with him, slashing at his side.

The beast howled with anger and twisted violently, sending his tail slamming into the side of Barioth's face, knocking him back.

I saw an opening and dove with the speed that only a black

dragon can reach, raking my claws across its back as I went by. I twisted into a tight spiral to come around for another pass, but Barioth was already on him.

The green dragon spun into Barioth's attack, biting hard into his neck as Barioth tried to pull back. I watched in horror as Barioth's move caused the green dragon's mouth to rip away a chunk of Barioth's neck. Red-hot dragon blood flowed freely, and Barioth fell from the sky into the sea.

The green dragon turned and came for me next, but I was faster and more nimble. I dove under his attack, raking at his belly as he went by. Hot blood flowed freely from the wounds, but they were not deep enough to slow him down. He tried to turn back on me, but he was too large and slow for that maneuver. I followed him through and came around for another strike.

He dove into the ocean to avoid me, and I pulled up just before hitting the water. As a black dragon, I was faster and more nimble in the air than a green dragon, but if I followed him into the water his superior size and strength would easily carry the day. I pulled back into the air, putting distance between myself and the ocean. I knew he would burst out without warning and I wanted sufficient space to react.

My anger at his attack and the death of my friends boiled inside of me, but I forced myself to wait for him to come out. The feral dragon was insane; half of his identity had been lost when he lost his dragonmaster. That insanity would force him out of the water and back into the sky to get me. I just had to wait.

I didn't have to wait long. With a great roar he shot out of the water straight towards me. I waited for him in the air as he rushed at me, and then I took off, baiting him higher and higher. I had to move the fight away from the supply ships.

Once I broke through the cloud layer I doubled back, and as he came through the clouds I was there with my claws extended. He tried to turn back, just as I expected, and that exposed his chest. I ripped and tore through the thick scales there.

He wasn't through yet. Now that I had closed the distance, he kicked hard with his back legs, sending me tumbling back through the clouds and towards the sea again.

I bent and twisted until my body was reoriented correctly to stretch out my wings. I quickly changed directions and came back around. The green dragon tried to match my speed and turn, but swung wide, allowing me to get behind and above him.

I knew I could just outfly him and get away, but that would leave the supply convoy at his mercy, and he would surely kill again. No, I had to put him down now while I still could.

He was bleeding from a dozen or more wounds now, but it didn't seem to slow him down one bit. For my part, I was feeling the toll the fight was taking on my well-aged bones.

Again I dove for him with all the speed I could muster, and this time I caught him unawares. All four of my clawed feet hit his back and I raked hard as I leapt off his back into the air, leaving deep gouges in his back.

He roared in pain, but didn't yield. He turned back towards me and tried to get inside my turn to cut me off, but I changed direction and came around behind him again.

I had to hit something vital and put an end to this fight

before he got a lucky blow in like he had with Barioth. I dove again at his back and again raked through, digging for his spine or a vital organ of some kind, but he twisted away, preventing me from landing a solid blow.

I pulled away from him and watched as he struggled to right himself in the air and regain some speed. I had won, and any sane dragon would have beat a hasty retreat. But this one was feral. It didn't know to retreat; it only knew to destroy.

He found enough strength for another charge and came at me with all the speed he could muster, but I was above him. I had superior position and speed. I dove towards him, right into his charge. At the last possible moment, I broke to the left, slashing at his throat as I went by. This time I scored a vital hit and ripped open his jugular.

I swung away as he tumbled into the sea, the blood from his many wounds boiling the water around him. I watched to make sure he was done. I wondered what had happened to his rider. With so few dragons, and so many dragonmasters, it was even more shameful to see one go down. He should have been matched to a new rider long before he succumbed to the madness.

With deep sadness at his plight, I flew off to check on my friends, but neither of them had made it. Two dragonmasters and three dragons, lost forever. It was yet another dark day for dragonkind.

The end of the age of dragons was at hand, and there was nothing anyone could do to stop it.

* * *

I sighed and held back the tears that this story always brought on. I wished I'd been alive to see the dragons. They must have been something to see up close.

"But what happens next?" asked Silverleaf.

"No one knows for sure," I answered. It wasn't the truth, but there were secrets that these children didn't need to be burdened with. "David and Lyrroth flew off that day and weren't seen again anywhere in the kingdoms. The other dragons eventually died off, and now all that remain are the stories."

"And the unfortunate dragonmasters," said Tamerale.

"Yes," I said. "Dragonmasters were still born to every generation, but without dragons to be bound to, they also go feral eventually. Just like the green dragon in the story. Most times they retreat into the wilds and are never seen again, but a few lose control in a populated area, and that always results in a violent end to their short lives."

"Is there really no hope for them?" asked Silverleaf.

"None has been found yet," I said.

"It's not fair. I'll find a way to make it right," said Silverleaf.

The boy had a determination in his voice that was way beyond his years. I almost believed it could happen. He certainly at that moment thought it was true. I wanted to believe, but knew I would be long gone before he was old enough to work on that dream.

Tamerale started to say something, but Nasir placed a hand on his shoulder to silence him. That was for the best, as it was probably some barb, and I didn't want to see Silverleaf's dream crushed by childish teasing.

"I believe you could if you set your mind to it," said Nasir.

"I will, you'll see!" said Silverleaf.

Myrill called the children to her, and they went off to play and eat dessert, leaving me alone with Nasir. It was time to take care of business.

Nasir was about to leave to help her, but I stopped him and said, "Come with me."

With my joints warmed some by the fire it was slightly easier to walk, and I led him back to my room. Once inside I barred the door and sat in one of my chairs. Nasir found a second chair and sat across from me. I was worn out from the exertion, but there was more to do yet.

"The story doesn't really end there," I said.

"What do you mean?" he asked.

"David truly was the last of the greats, the last real hero this world has seen. In his final years, he wanted to make sure the world never forgot the dragons and how we destroyed that noble race. David didn't disappear. In fact, he became the first storymaster," I said.

"Really?" he said with surprise.

"Yes, he wrote everything he knew on the scrolls, and we storymasters have kept and copied them throughout the generations, passing them down with great care so that nothing would be lost."

"Why are you telling me this?" he asked.

"Because you will succeed me as storymaster and you need to know the secrets," I said.

A look of shock passed over his face. He tried to stammer out words, but was speechless. He was so young to be a father, not even a third of my own age, but he was humble and sharp.

He was a good man, and one I was proud to have in the family.

"Don't look so surprised. You've memorized most of the stories already, and you have the gift of insight," I said.

"But I'm not one of your descendants," he said. "Don't I have to be born into the family?"

"Bah, as far as I'm concerned you're my grandson, and as the oldest living storymaster I get to make the rules. I say that you'll succeed me, and that is final," I said.

"I… I'm greatly honored," he said.

"Now, what you must know is that dragon blood runs strong through our family. It's practically certain that some of those children running around out there will be dragonmasters," I said.

"Yes, Myrill warned me," he said.

"What she didn't warn you, because she doesn't know, is that I'm a descendant of David, making your children part of his bloodline," I said.

"By the gods!" he gasped.

"Yes, you married into royalty, but that's not the real secret. We call that story 'David's Last Ride' and tell everyone that David flew off, never to be seen again in order to protect a great secret. David left a set of scrolls that no one has opened since his death. He left instructions that one day one of his descendants who is also a dragonmaster should open it, but only one who doesn't go feral. So far, no one like that has risen up. The storymasters have kept these scrolls secret so that no one violates that order. They have kept a close watch on all of our kinfolk, hoping that each generation would be the generation that it would happen, but so far, nothing. These scrolls will pass from me to you, and you must guard them with your life," I said.

"But do we have any idea what they say?" he asked.

"No," I said. I paused and decided I'd better elaborate. "Oh, well, some think they tell of a second age of dragons, but I think that's just wishful thinking. I don't blame them. I often dream of what it would be like to fly with the dragons, but alas, that can't happen this side of the grave."

I did more than not blame them; I wished they were right with all my heart, but I knew it was impossible. Dragons couldn't just reappear out of nowhere. You needed mature dragons to make dragon babies.

"I'll keep them safe," he said.

There was a reverence in his voice that told me volumes. I had definitely chosen the best man to replace me.

"You will find all my scrolls in a hidden chamber under my bed. Study them often, make copies of the oldest ones to preserve them, and find the other storymasters to cross-check for errors. They're our stories and must live on, no matter what may come."

He nodded. "I will."

"Good. Now please call my granddaughter, as my time is nearly done. I'd like to say goodbye properly while I still can," I said.

Concern passed over his face and he rushed out to get her. I slowly climbed into my bed. I'd had a good life, and I was ready for my eternal rest. I'd spent each day living the stories for the clan and had grown to really love some of the heroes of old. Soon I would join them on the other side, and it would be like meeting old friends.

Many storymasters had gone before me, and I couldn't wait to meet them. No one ever told *their* stories and I wondered what they were like, what they struggled with and, most especially, which stories were their favorites.

My granddaughter came flying into the room with tears already in her eyes. "Papa?"

"My dear, don't weep for me. I may have a season, perhaps even two more, and then I'm going to a better place, a place where the stories live. But now is the time to set things in order, while I still have my wits."

"We'll miss you," she said.

"Only for a little while, and then we'll meet again. Perhaps by then I'll have learned how to ride a dragon. Look, my days are nearly spent and I want you to witness that I'm naming Nasir as my successor, and you both as heir to all that I have left."

She gasped. "But, Papa…" her reply trailed off.

By naming her husband as my successor, I'd done more than just ensure the stories were carried on. I'd made sure she was provided for. Nasir's appointment guaranteed him an income for as long as he lived. She cared for me in life, and now I would care for her as I passed.

I just smiled. "Now, please allow me to rest, and when the news spreads please keep everyone at bay. I'd like to spend the last of my days teaching Nasir what I can."

A WORD FROM VINCENT TRIGILI

I am very fortunate that this is my second time writing for the *Future Chronicles*. I appeared first in *The Telepath Chronicles*, in which I wrote a standalone short called *The Null*. *The Null* was deliberately outside of my wheelhouse (which until then was primarily space opera). I had wanted to try something different and wrote a superhero tale. It was well received, which has created the problem that some have contacted me and requested I write more in that world. Perhaps someday I will. The Null was a fun character to ride with, and I would not mind riding along with him on more missions some day.

When the opportunity to write for *The Dragon Chronicles* came up, I jumped on it. I had no idea what I would write, I had no story in mind, but they had me at the word "dragon." What greater beast has roamed legends? What other beast is so majestic that isolated cultures around the globe all speak of it? What if, long ago, great fire breathing lizards truly were the masters of this planet? What if the feathered dragons of the American continents once demanded the worship of the puny earthbound bipeds? What if the tales of knights slaying dragons had some truth to them?

There is obviously something common in the history of our race that dragons represent. Some think it was dinosaurs, and I suppose that is possible. Whatever it is, the majestic creatures have captured the minds of writers from the beginning of history till this very day.

The Storymaster is about a man who tells their story: the story of a species long since gone but never forgotten. A man who knows that he himself will soon be forgotten, but the stories he leaves will live on for eternity.

Human culture has always recognized the power of the story. It is through our shared stories that we as a people can keep the past alive and the adventure going. It is how we fight back the darkest nights and celebrate the brightest days.

Imagine a world in which the bald eagle never again flew, or the tiger never again hunted. Would we not tell their story? Would we not long for their presence? Would we not use their likenesses in our art? Think about it for a moment; if the tiger were lost, then all the stories of hunting and seeing the tiger would become legends and then, perhaps in some far future day, *The Tiger Chronicles* might be released.

That is the world the storymaster lives in.

The Storymaster is a prequel to a longer work that will follow the life of young Silverleaf. You can find out more about Silverleaf by following this link: *The Silverleaf Chronicles*. For more information on my other novels, please stop by my main website: http://losttalesofpower.com

Judgment
by Monica Enderle Pierce

IT WAS NEAR CLOSING TIME and McKay's Saloon was full of chasers and herdsmen talking, laughing, and caterwauling when Peregrine Long staggered past and stumbled up the wooden stairs to the Sheriff's office.

At Peregrine's insistent banging, Sheriff Wolfberg unlocked and opened the door.

"You better have a darn good reason for waking me at this hour," the sheriff muttered. Yellow light spilled from the doorway and, mid-yawn, he spied Peregrine's bloodied face and sooty clothes. "Long? What in Sam Hill happened to you?"

Peregrine rasped, "Get me a stiff drink, and I'll tell you." He scuffed across the wood floor, dragged a chair back from the deputy's table, and groaned as he sat.

Wolfberg poured a double shot of Dragonfire whiskey and

clunked the bottle down beside Peregrine's hand. "You need a doctor. Your story can wait."

Peregrine grabbed the man's brown vest and pulled him forward until their faces almost touched. "No, sir, it can't. We've got less than one day."

"Or what?"

Peregrine released him and tossed down the whiskey. He wiped his lips with the back of his hand, leaving a grimy smear. "Or the Judge will be here looking for payment."

Sheriff Wolfberg planted his palms on the scarred, wooden table and leaned over Peregrine. "You'd better explain that, son. You better explain very clearly what you've done to bring that hellish beast down on Bonesteel."

* * *

EARLIER…

The leather saddle creaked as Peregrine swung down from his blue roan's back. With a practiced hand he hitched his new pony beside Deputy Isabeau Hightower's buckskin gelding as he squinted at the blue March sky with his good eye. It was midmorning. He sucked in the cool mountain air.

It was a fine day to be alive.

Peregrine patted his horse, Tohcta, then swung around and headed for McKay's Saloon. Like a swamp reed, his lanky frame had an unmistakable bend when he moved. Spurs jangling and boot heels thudding he crossed the wooden walkway and pushed through the saloon's doors into a dim room.

The air was warm and thick with the stench of ale and sweat. Cigarette smoke hovered around the lights, twisting into ghostly patterns as Peregrine passed through it.

"So I says, 'Why'd you go and kick a big ole snapping turtle like that for?'" Bobby Mack, a mouthy troll chaser from Shao San's Circle S Ranch, was repeating his favorite story to everyone within earshot. Bobby loved big stories, especially when he was telling them.

"Whatcha doing in here, Long?" Jack McKay asked from behind the scarred, mahogany bar as Peregrine bellied up.

"Buying a drink." He surveyed the one-room saloon for Isabeau but spied her sister, Simone, beside Bobby. She musta been riding the deputy's horse. Peregrine fought a snarl. His like for Isabeau was countered by his dislike of Simone. She was dirty, in more ways than one.

None of the riders acknowledged him. Bonesteel was a company town, controlled by Pico Connelly. People lived and died working Pico's Double L sheep herds. The man had built Bonesteel from nothing to wealthy. And Peregrine was a one-eyed outsider.

McKay swiped a beer-stained rag across the bar. "You don't drink."

Bobby sneered at Peregrine, and then continued his tale. "So he says, 'I thought it was a rock.' Can you believe that? A rock!" He hooted and swigged his beer. "Dumb as a duck, that boy."

Simone glowered at Peregrine as he leaned on the bar and answered McKay.

"Today I do. Dragonfire."

The red-haired bartender shrugged and poured a shot of amber whiskey. He jerked his chin toward the saloon's wavy glass windows. "That a new pony for Pico's string?"

The shot burned all the way down and put fire in Peregrine's gut. He cleared his throat. "She's mine."

McKay's ruddy brows rose.

Bobby and Simone squinted through the window. "Where'd *you* get the money for a fine pony like that?" Bobby asked.

Peregrine clunked his glass down. "Saved it."

For eight years Peregrine had worked the Double L's pony lines. But his odd eyes—one brown, the other gray—made men uncomfortable. The color of steel, the left one didn't focus and made the world blurry. He was born that way and often wore a black patch over the eye. But it didn't keep Peregrine from being a fine and fast shot with a revolver or from doing his job well.

Which had turned out to be a problem, because every year he'd pushed to be promoted to troll chaser. But Pico'd always passed him over, saying good linemen were too hard to find. Peregrine figured it was because of his eye. So he'd scrimped and saved, and he'd just bought Tohcta, his own troll pony. Granted, her muzzle was more gray than blue, but she suited Peregrine; he was going gray at the temples, too.

Simone Hightower tapped her shot glass on the bar and McKay refilled it. "Isn't that one of Darla Sanchez's prize roans?" she said.

Peregrine tossed a copper coin on the bar and stepped back. "Was." He tugged his black, wide-brimmed hat down and faced Simone. "Mine now."

Her eyes narrowed.

Judgment be damned, Peregrine thought as he headed for the door.

Outside, he pulled Tohcta's reins from the hitching post and climbed onto her saddle. The pony's ears twitched as Peregrine turned her away from Bonesteel. She'd grown too old for mountain troll work. But there'd been problems down on the plains, incursions from the Shadowns. He'd make a good living in Cyanide chasing prairie trolls away from the buffalo herds. With a nudge of Peregrine's heels, the blue roan strode out and they soon passed under Bonesteel's gray stone arches.

Peregrine sank into the creaking old saddle, tugged down his hat, and took in the view below.

Bonesteel Butte stood over a vast, golden plain, its sloped base covered with thick evergreens up to a clear line where its sides became sheer cliffs. The butte's pancake top—home to the small town of Bonesteel—covered six square miles and ended in the Judge's Spire, a great stone pillar as tall as the butte was wide.

Peregrine squinted at the top of the spire where a wisp of black smoke curled from an angry gash that led into that deadly trap. When the winds blew west the town gained a fine coat of greasy soot and the stench of charred carcasses made the residents gag. No trees clung to the sheer stone. And no one passed through the Judge's Hollow at the pillar's base. Not voluntarily anyway.

Peregrine looked away. He'd be glad to put some distance between himself and judgment, even if it meant leaving Isabeau.

The trail from Bonesteel was worn and sloped sharply downward, cutting in switchbacks along the butte's rocky sides. It afforded travelers an expansive view of the Shadowns' barren canyons, the green plains with roaming buffalo herds stretching forever, and the distant tree-covered Black Hills.

The trip down the butte took a good two hours, plus another hour to pass through the shadowy forest that ringed the butte's base, so it was after midday when Peregrine and Tohcta emerged from the trees. Peregrine straightened in the saddle. He retrieved a cigarillo from his brown duster's inner pocket and lit a match off his boot heel. A long drag warmed his lungs.

When he reached Cyanide, he'd head for Stetson Zmiejko's Black Bar Ranch. Stetson'd promised him a place on his crew as a troll chaser if Peregrine got a pony, and Stetson was a man of his word.

Peregrine glanced over his right shoulder at the thudding of hooves. Six riders were coming up fast. He moved Tohcta off the path to let them pass. But the group reined in their mounts and surrounded him.

Simone Hightower was among them. "We want a word with you, Long."

"What about?" Peregrine took in her companions: tow-headed Bobby Mack and his stocky brother Beauregard, Matikai with her intense, dark gray stare, Mitchell Fishman whose dark fists were hard and fast, and his former boss, Pico Connolly. All but Pico were troll chasers from the Circle S or Darla Sanchez's rancho.

Pico spurred his blood bay gelding forward. "You got a bill of sale for that little roan?"

Peregrine's eyebrows rose. "'Course I do." He reached into his duster. Six pairs of eyes watched his movements; six hands edged toward holstered guns. "What's the trouble, Pico?" he asked as he proffered the folded paper.

Pico took the certificate, studied it, and frowned. He passed the paper to Matikai, who was Darla Sanchez's foreman. She glanced at the bill of sale then crumpled it and threw it at Peregrine. "That ain't a legitimate bill of sale, Pico."

"Damn." Pico shoved up his hat brim and looked at Peregrine from beneath his shaggy, gray brows, a slow, steady gaze that brooked no argument. "The trouble, Peregrine, is that you didn't buy that pony from Darla." As he said it, he slid his revolver from its holster, cocked it, and pointed the gun at Peregrine. The other riders mirrored him. "This pony's stolen and Darla's dead."

Peregrine took another long drag on his cigarillo and squinted at the man. "You calling me a thief and a murderer?"

Beauregard hawked and spat then said, "We sure are. You can't afford a Sanchez roan, and everyone knows how much you've been wanting a pony."

Peregrine ignored the halfwit. "Eight years I worked your lines, Pico. You ever known me to steal, cheat, or hurt anyone who didn't deserve what I gave 'em and more?"

Pico shook his head. "The evidence is clear. You've got the pony, the forged bill of sale, and the motive."

"Then I was set up. I bought this pony from Dom Hightower."

Simone leveled her gun at Peregrine's chest, and her voice and hand shook as she said, "You saying my brother killed his boss and framed you, Long? You saying he murdered the woman who took my kin and me in when we had nowhere else and no one else?"

Pico held up his hand. "Calm down, Simone."

Peregrine wouldn't put it past her to shoot him. "I'm saying I bought this pony from one of Darla's representatives."

"Well, Dom ain't here to defend hisself," Mitchell lisped.

Peregrine replied, "Then let's go back to the butte and Simone can get him. He'll prove that I bought the pony from him."

"Impossible," Pico said.

"Why?"

Simone bared her teeth. "Because he's dead, too, and you know it!"

Matikai grabbed Simone's shaking hand. "Let the Judge decide if Long's lying. Let her punish him."

"The Judge?" Simone looked at Matikai. "Sure." Her snarl twisted into a vicious grin. "That'd be more than fair."

Pico bowed his head then nodded, his silver hair flashing in the early spring sun. "All right." He gestured at Peregrine's revolver. "Don't do anything foolish, like reaching for your gun. You just put your hands up."

Beauregard and Bobby cocked their revolvers as Bobby said, "You may be one of the best shots in Bonesteel, but there's six of us, Long."

Beauregard added, "And Simone would welcome an excuse to kill you."

"You're punishing an innocent man, Pico," Peregrine growled. "There's nothing fair about the Judge, and you know it." He itched to draw his gun, but Bobby was right—six against one was no winnable fight. He'd have to stay calm, keep his wits. Maybe he could talk some sense into Pico. "You know me better than this."

Pico took Peregrine's Colt from its holster and met his gaze with a steady eye. "I know you've been grousing for years about not getting a fair chance. And I know you don't earn enough to buy one of Darla's ponies."

"I'm an honest man. You know I've been saving my money."

"I don't know anything about how you spend your money, Peregrine. I only know what I pay you."

As Mitchell tied Peregrine's hands to the saddle horn and Matikai took Tohcta's reins, Beauregard said, "Ain't nobody ever trusted you, Long. Nobody."

They pulled Tohcta around and headed southeast toward Judge's Hollow at a fast lope.

Peregrine clutched the horn and tried to work his hands free. Facing the Judge was certain death; he'd rather be shot in the back trying to escape than meet her head-on. But though he worked at it, Mitchell'd been a lineman once and knew his knots. By the time they topped the Hollow's blackened rim, Peregrine's wrists were raw and bleeding but still firmly tied.

"Simone." Peregrine looked at the sister of the woman he desired. They looked so alike—small-boned, dark-haired, and hardened by a hard childhood. "Did you ask Isabeau if she thinks I'd do a thing like this?"

Simone turned cold brown eyes on him. "Isabeau's mourning our brother. I ain't gonna tell her Dom died at her *friend's* hands. She's gonna believe that you left her to chase trolls and a fat wallet, Peregrine. She's better off without you sniffing around her skirts."

Beneath him, Tohcta shifted and pawed the ashy trail, and the other horses snorted and pranced. Facing a troll was one thing, but a hungry purple dragon was quite another.

Mitchell loosened Peregrine from the horn and yanked him from the saddle. He hit the ground and curled into a ball as the chasers kicked and pummeled him while Pico held the horses and watched.

Finally Pico called, "Enough. String him up and let's get out of here before the Judge takes notice."

Bloodied and squinting through a swollen eye, Peregrine was shoved down the trail to the shadowy, bone-riddled bottom of Judge's Hollow. The stench of soot, burned tallow, and decaying flesh made him gag. He doubled and vomited while his assailants laughed, their faces covered by bandanas to cut the smell.

Peregrine struggled as they dragged him toward the stand, a charred stump set beneath an equally charred oak tree. He dug his heels in and strained to escape their hold, but Mitchell and Bobby kept a tight grip on his arms. A rope was tossed over a thick branch and a noose tied around his neck as he was made to stand upon the stump. The noose was pulled up until Peregrine stood upon his toes to keep from choking.

"Should we kick the stump, Pico?" Simone's voice was low and thick. Peregrine squinted at her. Did she have regrets?

"Couse we should," Beauregard said and the stump rocked beneath Peregrine. "Thieves are presented swinging."

Peregrine gagged and snuffled, desperate to keep his perch, desperate for air. The stump held. His good eye watered. He wanted to speak, but couldn't.

"Murderers ain't." Pico replied. "Darla and Dom were shot in the back. Let Peregrine see death coming. Leave the stump and summon the Judge, Matikai."

There was a metal chuck wagon triangle hanging from the oak, someone's idea of humor. Its sharp, metallic clanging pulsed in Peregrine's ears.

One knell.

Two knells.

Three knells.

The snort of the ponies. The clatter of hooves.

Soon only the wind groaned through the hollow to join the sounds of Peregrine's wheezing lungs and the creak of the rope.

And then, from beneath his cramping feet, came a thud. It traveled up his spine and through his bones.

And then another. And Peregrine's stomach twisted. He gasped a bubbling breath.

The thuds came faster. Harder. Shaking the ground. A heartbeat beneath the butte. A heartbeat that expanded and contracted the mountain itself.

The triangle jangled. The oak creaked.

Thud.

Dust and ash rose.

Thud.

Rocks skittered down the sides of the hollow.

And then there was nothing but the wind and small rock-slides clattering, Peregrine's wheezing.

Now there was scraping, like granite being dragged over ice.

The Hollow's cool air turned balmy.

Sweat beaded Peregrine's forehead and lip. It trickled down his back and stung his eyes. He tried to kick the stump away. He closed his good eye and lifted his feet, but the pain, the stretching, the burning made him put his toes back down.

"Damnation." Peregrine cursed fate and himself. He wanted to live. He wasn't a thief. He wasn't a murderer.

"*Welcome.*"

Peregrine opened his eye to see two great silver eyes in a deep purple, horned face and a mouth full of jagged teeth, each as long as his arm.

The Judge hadn't uttered the word aloud; rather it pulsed inside Peregrine's head.

He stared and swallowed.

"*You're strung up like a murderer, Peregrine Long. Are you one?*"

He opened his mouth to answer, but couldn't get a breath past the tightening noose.

With a curved, black claw long enough to run him through, the Judge slashed the rope, and Peregrine hit the ground.

He lay in a pile of bones and soot, sucking in air and coughing out blood.

"*Well?*"

He sat up. How did she know his name? How did she get inside his head? Why hadn't she eaten him? He slowly, gingerly shook his head. "No, ma'am," he rasped. "I ain't a murderer or a thief. I've been accused of a crime I didn't commit."

"*Really?*" The Judge straightened into a sitting position, her long neck curving high above the oak tree. She cocked her massive skull. "*I've heard that from every murderer and thief I've ever judged. What makes your story different?*"

"Story?" Peregrine started working on the knots binding his wrists. "I ain't telling you a story, ma'am. That's the truth."

"Hmmm. Peregrine Long, I have only three things that interest me: Solitude, my stomach, and the occasional interesting story. Since you've broken my solitude, you'd better tell me a good story, or I'll put you in my stomach."

"What happened to judgment?" Peregrine looked over the enormous beast. In the eight years he'd been in Bonesteel, he'd seen the Judge only once as she'd taken flight, circled high overhead, and then set the hills south of the Bonesteel Butte afire.

But close up, she was far larger than he'd perceived; her head alone encompassed the length of three ponies standing end to end. Her iridescent scales were a purple so deep they looked almost black, but showed every hue as she moved, much like the wings of butterflies. She bore three black horns from nose to forehead, and a jagged ruff encircled her neck, rising and lowering as her moods changed. She was magnificent and terrifying. But Peregrine never expected to find intelligence within the silvery depths of the Judge's eyes.

"Judgment comes after your story," her voice whispered in his mind. *"A true story, Peregrine. I'll know if you're lying."*

"I ain't a storyteller, Judge. I'm a lineman who just lost his hard-earned chance to become a troll chaser. I bought that pony, fair and legal—had the papers to prove it. And I didn't murder anyone. I've got one friend in the world, but she'll hear the lie that I'm the monster who killed her older brother, and I'll have lost her, too." Peregrine considered the dragon as she lowered her head to take him in. "Honestly, you oughta just end my existence, Judge. No one's gonna care if I'm dead now."

The dragon shook her head, kicking up a whorl that raised

ash and dust all around Peregrine. *"You were doing so well until that last sentence. That one was a lie."*

He finally slipped the ropes free and flexed his bleeding wrists. "I ain't a liar. I told you the truth."

"No. You'd care if you died."

The Judge had emerged from a jagged opening at the base of the stone pillar, though half of her remained within her lair. Peregrine stiffened as the dragon now pulled her entire body free of the cavern. She was as long and powerful as a locomotive pulling four passenger cars.

"You could've kicked that stump and snapped your neck, but you didn't."

Bones and gravel crunched as she encircled the hollow, and him, her wings furled tight against her body and her movements sleek, powerful, and serpentine.

"You wanted to live. And you still do."

The Judge stopped and raised her furled wings high above her back. *"You're not much of a storyteller, that's true. But, though short, your story was truthful. I will strike a bargain with you, Peregrine Long."*

"A deal with the devil?"

She filled his head with amusement, and Peregrine almost smiled.

"Perhaps. You are, as you claim, an innocent man. But I have an agreement with Bonesteel. My solitude is disturbed only to pass judgment, and then I am due payment. If I'm to be denied my supper now, you must bring me a replacement."

"I need to bring someone for you to judge?"

"Yes. That's how it's done in Bonesteel. Judgment is swift and

payment swifter. Bring me the real murderer, and I will judge him." Quick as a wink, her head snapped around, and she pinned him with her silver eyes. *"If you don't honor this bargain, I'll fulfill it myself."* She cocked her head to the side and added, *"Maybe with that woman you covet."* Her muzzle came forward until she was so close, Peregrine could have touched her glistening scales. *"And then I'll come for you."*

His fists clenched. "How'm I supposed to find a murderer? I'm not a lawman."

The Judge's enormous muzzle filled Peregrine's view.

"Simple. They're all guilty until they prove their innocence." She exhaled a putrid, steamy breath then turned away. She snapped her wings down to her side. Then the Judge slithered back into her cavern and out of Peregrine's mind.

But she left him with a parting message: *"You have one day, Peregrine Long."*

* * *

Peregrine downed another shot of whisky as Sheriff Wolfberg poured himself a drink. The sheriff opened his mouth to respond to Peregrine's tale, but was interrupted by Isabeau's appearance at the door.

"Peregrine?" she said. "What happened? You look like you fell off the butte and landed on your face."

Peregrine smiled and tried to open his gray eye, but it was too painful. It wasn't like it was useful anyway.

Isabeau crossed the room and shoved the Sheriff aside. "Where're you hurt?"

"Bruises mostly, broke a tooth." He gestured toward his face. "This eye's doing better already." It was a lie. The bad eye was worse than ever.

"He shouldn't be sitting here, Wolf." She pulled back Peregrine's duster before he could stop her hands. Her eyes widened as she spied the rope burns around his neck. "What the hell?"

"What the goddamned hell is right."

Peregrine didn't need turn to know who'd spoken. Simone's husky voice was a match for Isabeau's.

"That man is a murderer and a thief." The office door banged shut behind her as Simone entered the room. She jabbed her finger at Peregrine. "I don't know how you escaped the Judge, Long, but you shouldn't've come back to Bonesteel. Sheriff, you need to arrest him and take him back to Judge's Hollow."

Sheriff Wolfberg straightened, pulled off his hat, and gestured with it. "Now hold on, Simone. I'm not going to condemn a man on your word alone. There's something called due process. And there's more to this story than what you're saying."

Isabeau was staring at her sister. "What *are* you saying, Manny?"

"I'm saying he killed Dom. I'm sorry. I didn't want you to hear about it. I thought I could keep it quiet. But he's got some nerve coming back here." She kicked a chair and it careened across the floor and into a table. "I knew I shoulda shot you when I had the chance, Long. You son of a bitch!"

Isabeau stared at her sister then put her hands on her hips and said, "Damn your hot head, Simone. Peregrine had nothing to do with Dom's death."

Sheriff Wolfberg said, "Can you prove that, Isabeau?" He looked at Simone and added, "And can you prove that he *did*?"

"I can." Simone stuck her hand in her jacket pocket, pulled out a piece of crumpled paper, and handed it to the Sheriff. "This is the bill of sale that Peregrine presented as proof that he *bought* a little blue roan from Darla Sanchez yesterday."

The Sheriff nodded. "I can read. This looks legitimate."

"Matikai says that ain't Darla's mark. The certificate is a fake."

Peregrine shook his head. "I told you and your vigilantes down on the trail, I didn't buy the pony from Darla. Dom sold her to me. That's your brother's mark as Darla's representative."

Sheriff Wolfberg scratched his beard. "Well, until I can pull Darla's records and compare this mark to others that Dom may have made, I can't say with certainty that you're not a suspect in Darla's and Dom's murders, Peregrine." He looked at Isabeau again and added, "Unless you have some evidence to support his claim?"

She shook her head. "I just know he wouldn't do that, Wolf."

Peregrine downed another shot of Dragonfire. His aches were easing with each small glass. "What about the Judge? She exonerated me. That dragon crawled into my mind, read my thoughts, and let me go as an innocent man."

"I don't know much about that beast, and I'd sure like to keep it that way." Wolfberg turned back to Peregrine. "I'm no fan of vigilante justice, but in this case, it seems to have given credit to your claims, since you faced the Judge and she let you go. Which is why I'm not locking you in a jail cell tonight. But I'm a lawman, and the law states that I need hard evidence to clear you, Peregrine. A dragon in your head isn't evidence. But this is." He folded the bill of sale and slipped it into his pocket.

"Provided this mark matches Dom's signature in Darla's files, you'll remain free." He nodded at Isabeau. "You gonna help him with those injuries, Deputy?"

"I am, Sheriff."

Simone began to protest, but Sheriff Wolfberg cut her off. "Drop it, Simone. You had your chance and you best look to your own affairs. You and your accomplices could face attempted murder charges if Peregrine's claim of innocence stands."

Simone cursed and stomped from the Sheriff's office. Pausing at the door, she snarled, "I don't know how you escaped the Judge, Long, but you won't escape justice for good. I promise you that." The door banged behind her.

The Sheriff stood and looked down at Peregrine. "Son, you best go heal and keep out of my way while I investigate this matter. I don't want to hear about more folks being served up to a hungry dragon." He pulled a small, leather-bound notebook from his pocket and a pencil. "Give me the names of your assailants." He jotted something in the book and added, "I already got Simone down."

Peregrine wanted to curse. The Judge wanted a body and she didn't care whose. He wouldn't be safe until he brought a villain to Judge's Hollow. And he was a dead man walking in Bonesteel—there were half a dozen suspects who'd rather see him strung up for the Judge than end up in that Hollow themselves. And the townsfolk would look the other way if sacrificing Peregrine meant keeping their own hides from catching fire.

Peregrine downed another shot then said, "Matikai, Bobby and Beauregard Mack, Mitchell Fishman, and Pico Connelly."

The Sheriff looked up, his eyes sharp. "Pico?"

"Yes, sir."

"Fine." The Sheriff settled his hat on his head. "You stay away from these six, you hear me?"

"I don't want revenge, I want justice, Sheriff. Are you gonna give me that and spare Bonesteel?"

Sheriff Wolfberg straightened. "Is that some kind of threat?"

"No," Peregrine rasped. "But the Judge will have her payment. She dismissed the case against me, but she wants the real murderer instead. If I don't produce one, she'll be back. And, in her eyes, we're all guilty."

Wolfberg rubbed the back of his neck and surveyed his shadowy office. "One day, you say?"

"That's right. Probably less since it took me half the day to climb up here."

The Sheriff sat and leaned close, lowering his voice. "All right. Since you say you want to serve justice and spare this community a dragon's wrath, I'll trust you. I'm already tied up with these murders; don't have the time or the men to chase after your attackers. If you're willing to take the oath, I'm willing to deputize you, Peregrine." He held up the little notebook. "But your sole task is to find the men on this list and put them in my jail. I want them alive. You understand?"

Peregrine sat back in his chair. A lawman? He'd never considered the job. But this was a chance to bring a killer to justice. Among the group that accused him was a murderer or someone who knew one and was covering for him. Or her. He glanced at Isabeau. Her expression was unreadable, but then she met his gaze and gave the smallest nod.

"Agreed, Sheriff."

"Good. Go see Doctor Ross then come back to my office and I'll get you set up. No time to waste."

* * *

The sky was rosy-gold with the rising sun when Peregrine and Isabeau emerged from the Sheriff's office. He wore a scratched and dented tin star on his chest and a new patch over his left eye. He hadn't lost his sight, yet, but his vision in that eye had tunneled and grown dark.

"Deputy Long. That don't sound too bad," Isabeau said as she struck a match off her chaps and lit a cigarillo. "You want one?" She offered her open mother-of-pearl case, but he shook his head and studied her.

She was all opposites and upside down. Not exactly refined with her blue jeans and dusty chaps. And not exactly pretty with a crooked nose and hazel eyes that stuck out a bit. She'd kept a firm hold on her grief over Dom's death, hadn't shown a lick of it, though they'd been very close. Isabeau would never let her emotions get in the way of her job.

She took a long drag, and then pinched a little tobacco off the tip of her tongue and spat. "What you staring at me for?"

Peregrine tucked a stray lock of her chestnut-colored hair behind her left ear. "Cause I'm thinking about making you a dishonest woman."

Deputy Hightower exhaled smoke into his face and barked a laugh. "You're gonna have to make me honest first."

Peregrine smiled though it hurt his jaw. Then he sobered. "And stop a dragon."

"Yep, that too." She hooked her arm through his and swung him toward the little house she sometimes shared with Simone and Dom. "Listen, about Simone."

"You don't need to speak for her."

"She's scared of you."

He snorted. "That makes no sense."

"Sure it does. She can't figure you out. You don't react to her the way the other fellas do and, well, she's afraid I'll go off with you."

Peregrine shrugged. "Then she doesn't know you too well, huh?"

Isabeau shrugged, too, and said, "Maybe I've changed."

Instead of answering, Peregrine stopped. Beauregard Mack had come out of the Horseshoe Inn across the dusty street and was gawking at him and Isabeau. The fair-haired dolt rubbed his eyes as if he'd seen a ghost, blinked, and then turned beet red.

"You best stay clear of this," Peregrine said to Isabeau as he stepped off the wooden walkway and headed across the wide dirt lane.

"Don't go thinking that I can't handle an idiot like Beauregard," she replied as she followed him.

Peregrine announced, "You're under arrest, Beauregard Mack."

"Why ain't you dead?" the chaser asked.

As if in answer there was a thunderous rumble beneath the butte and puffs of red dust rose from the ground. Horses started, whinnied, and snorted. A large flock of speckled starlings took to the sky and dogs started barking.

Beauregard's eyes widened. "You cheated the Judge?"

"I was acquitted of all charges. Now Sheriff Wolfberg wants to see you about a murder and an attempted lynching."

Beauregard's gaze darted from Peregrine's face, to the tin star, to his revolver. He licked his lips. "You should be dead. We had the evidence. I didn't kill no one."

"You tried to kill me." Peregrine's hand dropped toward his hip. "Don't pull your gun, Beau. I need you alive." Being one-eyed didn't stop Peregrine from being a sharpshooter. He had to be; trolls loved the taste of pony and lineman.

But Beauregard's hand dropped. He got the revolver out of its holster but not cocked before Peregrine's bullets knocked him off his feet.

The dying man writhed and groaned on the ground, a red bloom spreading across his chest.

Isabeau tried to stop the man's bleeding, but it was over in minutes. With one last shallow breath, Beauregard Mack's life ended. She closed his dull, staring eyes as the Sheriff reached the scene.

Wolfberg muttered, "Damned fool. He knew he couldn't beat you."

Peregrine nodded. "Yep. Didn't want to face the Judge."

Isabeau straightened. "You think he was the murderer?"

"Don't know. Never will." Peregrine turned to the Sheriff. "I need to borrow a horse. Gonna ride out to the Circle S and pick up Bobby Mack."

"All right. But be careful. Word may have spread about your return. You've got a target on your back, Deputy Long."

Isabeau said, "I'll go with him."

"No, ma'am. I'll go with Long to the Circle S, and then

we'll ride out to Pico's. You get over to Darla's, pick up any records that can prove Dom's signature, and arrest Matikai. She's at the top of my list of suspects; she'd've known Dom's mark."

"What about Mitchell Fishman?" Peregrine asked.

"We'll pick him up at Pico's." The Sheriff turned to Isabeau. "I expect that your sister will turn herself in. But if she doesn't, I'll make the arrest. You don't need to be involved in that."

Isabeau nodded and looked away. "I appreciate it, Wolf."

Peregrine squinted at the sun as it neared zenith. "Time's getting short."

* * *

Pico's Double L Ranch sat at the base of the Judge's Spire. He raised the finest silken wool mountain sheep west of the Sklaa River and was one of the few breeders to produce Silver Sheens season after season. Their wool commanded top prices on the open market and had made Pico the richest man in his industry. It was a wealth he'd shared with Bonesteel, offering loans to his competitors and funding town projects with generous repayment terms.

The approach to the Double L took riders through a long, shallow valley and offered an impressive view of the looming spire. A view that, as Peregrine and Sheriff Wolfberg approached, became all the more imposing as another thunderous rumble shook the ground beneath their horses. There was a tremendous whoosh and cracks in the spire glowed orange as a great flare of dragon fire erupted from the top. Both horses snorted and shied, trying to bolt.

Sheriff Wolfberg was cursing beneath his breath. They'd just come from the Circle S where they'd learned that Bobby had met up with Matikai and headed out that morning. "If they aren't here with Pico, we'll have a chase on our hands."

"Yep." Peregrine tightened his hold on the reins. "Whoa. Easy, girl."

"Even after we have your lynch mob in custody, we need solid evidence or a confession from the murderer. I'm not keen on feeding an innocent man to that dragon, Long."

"Agreed, Sheriff. If need be, I'll negotiate with the Judge for more time."

The Sheriff nodded toward the buildings as the rancho spread out before them. "Sure hate to see Pico caught up in all this."

"You and me both."

Gunfire split the air.

The Sheriff ducked in his saddle and grabbed his thigh.

With a curse, Peregrine leaned low over his horse's neck, caught Wolfberg's reins, and spurred the ponies off the trail as more shots were fired. Bullets ricocheted and hit the trees around him.

Burning pain flashed across Peregrine's left shoulder as they reached a stand of pines. A bullet had grazed him. He pulled the Sheriff from the saddle as he slipped off his own horse. He released the ponies, and they galloped back toward the safety of town.

The Sheriff groaned. His right trouser leg was dark with blood. Peregrine pulled off his belt and fashioned a tourniquet.

Another tremor shook the ground and the trees. It kept

shaking them and built to a roar. Peregrine rocked back on his heels and grabbed a tree trunk. He risked a glance at the spire.

The Judge erupted from the upper cavern in a blaze of smoke and fire. Embers trailed her as she took wing, soared over the butte, and then banked to come up the valley.

She roared, a screaming tornado that made Peregrine clap his hands over his ears and raised the hairs on his arms. And then she shot straight up the length of the Judge's Spire and came to rest upon the top, her tail and body twining about the stone. She spouted a great gush of fire then glared down upon the Double L and Peregrine.

Was she looking at him?

As if reading his mind from afar, the Judge's voice slithered into Peregrine's head: *"Tick-tock, Peregrine Long. I'm hungry."*

"I'm busy being shot at right now, Judge," Peregrine muttered.

"Oh? If they hit their target, our agreement will be fulfilled."

"Already grazed my shoulder. You want a taste?"

Her amusement lightened his mood, and he chuckled.

"Who're you talking to?" The Sheriff was staring at Peregrine, his voice sharpened by pain as he worked the tourniquet around his shattered thigh.

Peregrine jerked his head toward the spire. "The Judge. She's watching us."

The Sheriff squinted. "Sam Hill take me, I forgot how big she is."

Another shot and wood splintered off a tree beside Peregrine.

Wolfberg asked, "Who's shooting?"

"Can't tell." Peregrine risked peering around the trunk. He was rewarded with a volley of gunfire and a glimpse of movement near a wall of straw bales between the barracks and the bright blue shearing shed. "Best I can tell it's coming from the hay by the shed."

Peregrine surveyed their spot. "I think there's enough cover from the trees to get me from here to those boulders." He jerked his chin toward a rocky outcropping that jutted up among trees closer to the main house. "From there I can draw a bead on the shooter."

"I'll do what I can to cover you, but you'd best move fast. Not sure how long I can stay upright."

"I move fast when properly motivated, Sheriff."

There was the clack of two guns being cocked. "How's this for motivation, Long?"

Peregrine turned slowly, his hands up.

Pico had gotten the jump on them.

With one revolver pointing at Peregrine and the other trained on the Sheriff, Peregrine's former boss said, "Shame that everyone's gonna hear how you double-crossed the Wolf and tried to pin it on me, you one-eyed bastard."

Wolfberg growled, "Pico, put your guns down. No one's gonna believe that cock-and-bull story."

"Sure they will when there's no one around to dispute it."

Peregrine watched Pico's eyes and said, "Isabeau already has."

Pico snorted. "And Simone's disputed her. That leaves my word, and I'm the most upstanding citizen in Bonesteel."

Sheriff Wolfberg pulled his gun.

Peregrine lunged to the side.

Pico fired.

The Sheriff pitched backward, a gaping hole in his chest.

Pico turned toward Peregrine, both guns aimed at him. His gaze strayed past Peregrine for a moment. "'Bout time you showed up."

The snap of twigs announced another person coming up behind Peregrine. Then a shotgun barrel appeared over his bleeding shoulder, but it was trained on Pico.

The rancher froze.

"Hands up, Pico, and drop those guns." Simone nudged Peregrine with her elbow, but her gaze was locked on the armed man. "Move your keister, Long."

Simone stood behind Peregrine but was siding with him. It was the first time ever that Peregrine had been happy to see her.

Pico raised his hands and snarled, "What the devil are you doing, Simone? He murdered Dom!"

Peregrine took Pico's revolvers, and Simone replied, "Like you just murdered Sheriff Wolfberg? That was cold-blooded and too easy for you, Pico. And now I've doubts about Peregrine's guilt."

"Time's up," the Judge whispered.

Peregrine looked up.

With another thunderous roar, the dragon launched from her spire. Simone jerked around and aimed her gun at the beast as the Judge folded her wings and plummeted down the length of the stone column. She flattened out her dive at the last moment and streaked up the valley with great sweeps of her iridescent wings.

The wind from her passage knocked them off their feet. Branches were sheared from the treetops and crashed down around them.

Peregrine tasted blood and dirt as he hit the ground. His eye patch was dislodged. He blinked and stared around him, squinting his left eye in the sudden sunlight. What the devil had happened to his vision? He shook his head, disoriented. He could see perfectly with the left eye. How was that possible?

Pico scrambled to his feet and charged toward the shearing shed. Peregrine and Simone gave chase. The rancher reached the door but was brought to a standstill as the Judge set his rambling house ablaze.

The dragon circled the ranch, spouting flames. The straw bales blazed. The chasers' empty barracks went up in a blast of hellfire.

"Where's my payment?"

Sheep stampeded across a field, bleating their terror, as the Judge landed in their midst and roared. *"Shall I start with these?"*

"Simone! Peregrine!"

They turned at the shout. Isabeau, fighting her half-crazed pony, rode to their sides. She dismounted and released the terrified animal to run for his life. Eyes rolling and tail streaking out behind him, the horse charged back the way he'd come.

The Judge's head whipped around and she locked her gaze on the Hightower sisters. *"Or will it be two for the price of one, Peregrine?"*

"Run!" Peregrine shoved Isabeau and Simone toward the boulders.

The Judge lunged at him, but he stood his ground as the

women reached cover. Black, choking smoke curled around him as the dragon stopped inches from his body. She opened her jaws and exhaled a gout of blistering, fetid heat. But she didn't burn Peregrine though the acrid stench of his own singed hair stung his nose.

"Where's the murderer you promised me?"

Peregrine shook his head. "I have suspects, but I need more time to prove guilt. I won't condemn any man or woman for a crime they didn't commit."

Simone shouted, "Give her Pico! He murdered the Sheriff."

Peregrine looked over his shoulder and his voice was strong as he said, "Not without a fair trial, Simone Hightower. I'm not gonna do to anyone what was done to me."

"He's behind the murders, Peregrine," Isabeau shouted. "Mitchell confessed his part and turned state's evidence against Pico, Bobby, and Matikai."

The Judge hissed. *"Bring this man to me. I will try him."*

Peregrine shook his head. "We need a complete investigation. Then you can have him."

The Judge's head pulled back and up as she reared high above him. *"Bring me the man, now, or I'll destroy Bonesteel and turn the woman you love into a pile of ash and bones."*

He really had made a deal with the devil. Peregrine's shoulders hunched. He had little love for Bonesteel, but there were innocent people among its citizens. He couldn't condemn them for a man he knew to be a cold-blooded killer. And he'd never let the beast have Isabeau.

"No." Peregrine gazed steadily at death's face. "I believe in the law. We had a bargain it's true. But Pico Connelly is due a trial by his peers, not you, Judge. So take my life now, and our score will be settled. If you're meant to have others, they'll come to you by a court of law."

The Judge stared at him, black smoke curling from her nostrils.

Peregrine held his breath.

A wooden door banged somewhere on the ranch.

Sheep bleated.

"Fine." The Judge reached out a clawed forefoot, her dagger talons poised to strike. But instead of tearing Peregrine to pieces, she ripped the roof from the shearing shed and threw it into the trees.

Peregrine stumbled toward the safety of the boulders as wood and debris clattered all around him.

Pico screamed and kicked open the sagging shed door. He tried to dodge her, but the Judge's foot came down once more and pinned the man to the ground.

"No! Please! I'm innocent! It was Bobby and Matikai! I'm begging you!"

"What's your story, Pico Connelly? Be truthful. I will know if you lie."

Pico stiffened and stared at the dragon. Tears dampened his face. A stain spread across his trousers as he pissed himself. "I'm innocent," he sobbed. "I've been set up. Matikai and Bobby Mack are the killers. And Peregrine stole that pony. That's all I know. I swear it. I *swear.*" But there was another story snaking through Pico's head, one of betrayal and greed, one that showed his hand manipulating the course.

Isabeau and Simone clung to each other and shrank back from the scene. "What's happening, Peregrine?" Isabeau asked.

He blinked. They couldn't hear the Judge. Was it strange that he could? "She's asking to hear his story. She knows if you're lying. She gets inside your head and reads your thoughts."

"Merciful gods," Simone muttered.

The Judge lifted her foot off Pico. *"Rise to face my judgment."*

Pico blinked, a weak smile on his face. He stood on shaking legs. "You see? You see my innocence, Judge?"

The dragon's snout came down until it was right in front of Pico. He coughed, and then reached out as if to touch her. But just before his fingers reached her shimmering scales she arched her head up and over him so that she was gazing straight down her snout at him.

"No. I find you guilty."

Pico screamed as the Judge exhaled a plume of fire and set the man ablaze.

Peregrine's guts twisted. "Don't watch," he said as the sisters shrieked.

Pico staggered forward, his arms flailing.

The Judge's snout shot downward and she snapped her front teeth around his flaming skull. She jerked her head up and back, tossing his headless body in the air like a cat toying with a mouse. Then the Judge caught Pico's corpse in her jaws and swallowed him.

A rumbling purr vibrated the ground, and the Judge said, *"Very satisfying."* She eyed Peregrine and added, *"Our agreement is complete. Justice has been served. But there are others, Peregrine Long. The woman named Matikai and the man called Bobby Mack. They took two lives."*

He nodded. "So I heard."

The dragon cocked her head. *"Did you?"*

"Yep. Every word."

She lowered her head to take him in. *"How unusual. And did you see his thoughts? The truth behind his lies?"*

Peregrine's jaw dropped. He nodded again, slowly, and whispered, "I did, Judge." He glanced at Isabeau and Simone then turned back to the great purple dragon. "What does that mean?"

"You are a dragonsage."

"I am?"

"Yes. I have gone many decades without one."

Simone touched Peregrine's shoulder. Her hair had come loose of its braids and her face was tear-stained. "I want to face judgment, Peregrine."

Isabeau grabbed her sister's arm. "What? No!"

But Simone shook her off and stepped toward the Judge. "I done Peregrine wrong, Judge. I was one of the group who strung him up in your hollow." She crossed one arm over her chest and added, "Truthfully, I was the most insistent on his guilt."

Once again, the Judge's snout came down until it nearly touched Simone's body, and the woman stiffened and stared. *"Indeed, you are guilty. But you speak honestly, Simone Hightower."*

Isabeau trembled as she clutched Peregrine's arm. She opened her mouth, but remained silent when he shook his head.

"I'll accept your punishment, Judge," Simone said.

The dragon nodded. *"Turn away."*

Simone faced away from death. She chewed her lower lip,

but kept her head high, accepting her fate.

The Judge slashed two curving talons across Simone's back, and the woman shrieked and fell to her knees. Her duster and shirt were bloody tatters. Great gashes revealed muscle and bone, diagonal wounds from shoulder to hip that would heal but leave terrible scars.

"You will wear your guilt upon your body until the day you die, Simone Hightower." The Judge studied the fallen woman and Isabeau, who'd gone to her sister's aid. *"But you have been spared by your honesty."* The dragon crouched and considered Peregrine for a long moment. *"Dragonsage, you will find the others who wronged you and committed these crimes. Bring them to me, so that they may be judged."*

"Why do you care about the feuds of my kind, Judge?"

"Because unchecked feuds become war, and war feeds the Shadowns' beast. Five dragons exist—five powers—and only we hold back the monster that seethes and plots against your kind and mine." She tipped her snout toward Simone and added, *"You will take Simone Hightower when she is well enough to travel. She will assist you in your search."* Then the Judge coiled her muscles, unfurled her wings, and sprang into the air.

Isabeau and Peregrine covered Simone as dust and debris engulfed them with each powerful down-stroke of the Judge's pinions. The dragon cleared the tree line and swooped over the terrorized herd of sheep. She seized one in each claw, and then winged up to her promontory, snapped her wings tight to her body, and plunged into the darkness of her lair.

"I'll hitch a team," Isabeau said and ran to the only standing building on the property, the carriage house.

Simone gasped as Peregrine lifted her into his arms.

"I think I still hate you, Long," she said through gritted teeth.

"You'd better get over that, Hightower. The Judge has tasked you and me with bringing Matikai and Bobby to face judgment."

Simone groaned. "Where's a chair when I need to kick one?"

Peregrine took in the obliterated rancho. "Not even a stool for as far as my eyes can see."

He returned Simone's weak smile as Isabeau led a team of black draft horses from the stable, hitched to a cart.

Peregrine gazed up at the blue sky. The sun was well past zenith, and soon he'd be leaving Bonesteel. Again. He moved toward the approaching cart.

It was a fine day to be alive.

A WORD FROM MONICA ENDERLE PIERCE

The first dragon book I read was Anne McCaffrey's *Dragonflight*. Gawd, that woman was a genius. It was both fantasy (telepathic dragons!) and science fiction (killer Thread from space!). McCaffrey seamlessly mixed genres in a way that made her books unique and exciting and, man, did I want to write like her. But I was eleven, impatient, and fickle. So I daydreamed about being a dragonrider (and a Jedi, and an elf, and a…), and I grew up. I moved on to American and English classics, Shakespeare, Brontë, Milton, and non-fiction. Then, after graduating from UCLA with an English degree, I joined the workforce, and I stopped reading—for more than a decade.

But when I was thirty-nine and mother to a toddler, the writing urge kicked into gear. I remembered the power and appeal of McCaffrey's mixed genres, so I tried my hand at combining post-apocalyptic fiction and space opera and produced my first self-published novel, *Girl Under Glass*. Wanting to try something different, I then wrote and published my second book, *Famine*, a blend of dark fantasy and historical fantasy about the Four Horsemen of the Apocalypse.

But I hadn't returned to dragons…until I was offered the chance to contribute to *The Dragon Chronicles*. I dipped my hand into the genre pool and gave it a good swirl, hoping for an idea that would challenge me. Immediately the notion of a spaghetti western with dragons bubbled out of my brain. Ohhh, yeahhh.

But why mix cowboys and dragons? Because looking at North America's jagged saw tooth mountains, the eerie stone buttes, and the broad prairie expanses, it's easy to imagine something wild, magical, and more than a little dangerous soaring above the cowboys and their herds. Maybe it's just me, but cowboys and dragons don't seem that far-fetched a combination; both are iconic symbols of strength, freedom, and determination. Yet they're rarely depicted together. I wanted to change that.

"Judgment", and the rest of *The Bonesteel Saga*, is an intimate story in a setting that's both familiar and strange, just like Sergio Leone would've done. It features iconic characters—Peregrine, my hat-tip to Clint Eastwood's Man With No Name, and the Judge, an archetype often seen in westerns but, in this case, embodied in a massive telepathic dragon.

Yep, give me a genre and I'll mix it with another to give you something unique and unexpected. Want to see what I mean? Come crawl inside my mind and experience the magical, wild, and dangerous ideas lurking in its shadowy corners. You'll find a list of my work at www.stalkingfiction.com, and I invite you to sign up for my mailing list at www.eepurl.com/SUYon

A NOTE TO READERS

Thank you so much for reading *The Dragon Chronicles*. If you enjoyed these stories, please keep an eye out for other titles in the *Future Chronicles* collection, a series of short story anthologies in speculative fiction. Currently available titles in the Chronicles include:

The Dragon Chronicles
The A.I. Chronicles
The Alien Chronicles
The Telepath Chronicles
The Robot Chronicles

Available later this year will be *The Z Chronicles*, *The Immortality Chronicles*, and *The Time Travel Chronicles*.

And, before you go, we'd like to ask you a very small favor, if you please: *Would you write a short review at the site where you purchased this book?*

Reviews are make-or-break for authors. A book with no reviews is, simply put, a book with no future sales. This is because a review is more than just a message to other potential buyers: it's also a key factor driving the book's visibility in the first place.

More reviews (and more positive reviews) make a book more

likely to be featured in bookseller lists (such as Amazon's *also-viewed* and *also-bought lists*) and more likely to be featured in bookseller promotions. Reviews don't need to be long or eloquent; a single sentence is all it takes. In today's publishing world, the success (or failure) of a book is truly in the reader's hands.

So please, write a review.

Then tell a friend. Share a link to us on Facebook, or maybe even a Tweet—link to our books at *http://smarturl.it/future-chronicles*. You'd be doing us a great service.

Thank you.

Samuel Peralta
www.amazon.com/author/samuelperalta

———————

Subscribe to *The Future Chronicles* newsletter for news of upcoming titles, and to be eligible for draws for paperbacks, e-books and more – *http://smarturl.it/chronicles-news*